appleseed

Also by John Clute

The Disinheriting Party
Strokes
The Encyclopedia of Science Fiction (edited with Peter Nicholls)
Science Fiction: The Illustrated Encyclopedia
Look at the Evidence
The Encyclopedia of Fantasy (edited with John Grant)
The Book of End Times

appleseed

john clute

A TOM DOHERTY ASSOCIATES BOOK
NEW YORK

APPLESEED

Copyright © 2001 by John Clute

First published in Great Britain by Orbit in 2001

A Tor Book
Published by Tom Doherty Associates, LLC
175 Fifth Avenue
New York, NY 10010

www.tor.com

Tor® is a registered trademark of Tom Doherty Associates, LLC.

ISBN 0-765-30378-7 (hc)
ISBN 0-765-30379-5 (pbk)

First Tor Hardcover Edition: January 2002
First Tor Trade Paperback Edition: February 2003

Printed in the United States of America

0 9 8 7 6 5 4 3 2 1

For Dede
(1944–2000)
passed living

'But here now I has broken His sword of power acrosst my knee, and flung'd his pieces in the face of His despite. Yea, *agin* His Commandermint onc't more I will go back to watch on the aidges of His airthquake, for the sakes of Adam's childer: though they-all fergit me in their Nowadays, and say to one anithers: "No Angel now cometh from Anywhar."'

And the Angel bussed me with his lips.

And he were goned.

But what he bussed me on the mouth hit were like a flower-bud of fire . . .

Percy MacKaye, 'The Stranger from Anywhar'

. . . he might dream that his old nurse was baking an apple on the fire in her own cozy room, and as he watched it simmer and sizzle she would look at him with a strange smile, a smile such as he had never seen on her face in his waking hours, and say, 'But, of course, you know it isn't really the apple. *It's the Note.*'

Hope Mirrlees, *Lud-in-the-Mist*

'Sir, I did not mean to stand! something made me stand. Sir, why do you delay? Here is only the great Achilles, whom you knew.'

E. M. Forster, *The Celestial Omnibus*

author's note

In this novel two unusual words in particular are used again and again in contexts which do not necessarily explain their original meaning. I thought a short definition of each might be useful:

azulejaria

The art of the Portuguese figurative tile panel. Examples are usually rectangular, are normally fixed to walls (both internal or external), and can comprise a hundred or more tiles. Portrayed on these panels are images (which are not restricted to individual tiles, but flow over from one to another) out of the tradition of European drama and the commedia dell'arte. Almost certainly the most complete study of azulejaria dramas is Daniel Tércio's *Dança e Azulejaria: No Teatro do Mundo* ('Dance and Azulejaria: The Theatre of the World', Lisbon: Edições Inakpa, 1999); it is an indispensable book, both for its superb illustrations and for its text. Those, like me, incapable of understanding more than a few words of Portuguese will find an English summary at the end.

In medieval and later times, a map of the world, usually oval or circular, usually (but not always) originating in England. The mappemonde often placed Jerusalem at the centre of the world, and at first glance more complex examples could easily be understood to depict a densely detailed landscape, or an apple perhaps, or perhaps a face. The *trompe l'oeil* portraits of Giuseppe Arcimboldo (1527–93), which bring together painted fruits and vegetables and fish and meat and other ingredients into the semblance of a face, resemble mappemondes.

one

there had always been something about a planet of cities that made Freer long for the sky. Nothing about Trencher, a hundred thousand klicks below, glowering like slag in the holograph cube at the heart of control centre, seemed likely to charm him out of the ill temper and claustrophobia he anticipated. Several centuries of local sector warfare had ground the planet's surface to a mottled airless nub; the various waif species that now occupied Trencher kept below the surface, in great muggy warrens which had metastasised into a world city. The aboriginals, who had destroyed their world aeons past, were all dead. Only their story-nodes remained, fragmentary partials, digital echoes of long-dead flesh sapients pacing up and down the prison yards of AI pickle jars.

There seemed little point in adding to his store of knowledge.

—Blank me, he subvocalised into conclave space, turning away from the humming cube. The nano-rich Teardrop in his eye shivered at the thought of losing contact. But the circumambient screens blanked out obediently, as did the holographic projection of local space surrounding his command couch, and he sat nestled in silence within the suddenly darkened heart of his ship, which continued to fall towards the planet of buried cities. The blizzard of media noise, generated by the port AIs' traffic control channels, shut off. Having obeyed orders, the Teardrop dried to an almost invisible thread.

He had been in Trencher space for ten seconds.

He sighed.

But almost instantly a tractor beam locked on to *Tile Dance*, its high-priority codes overriding the Teardrop block, and Freer was no longer at peace.

Through his data gloves he stroked a tile mask, which had responded to his slight distress. The tile made a blank purring sound – no AI was parking within its tiny brain – and returned to its place beside its companions, on the curved walls of control centre.

—We are your personal Trencher engine, spoke an ensemble of beamed voices into his Teardrop, a parched choral murmur generated through the throats of a thousand long-dead sampled aboriginals circling within their jars like dead tigers in a fossil zoo.

—Okey dokey, said Freer.

—Please select a name of your choice.

Freer did not much like idiot-savant engines with monikers.

—'Mowgli', he sent.

—Welcome to Trencher, chorused Mowgli.

—Kirtt? said Freer formally, through Teardrop, which awakened to hear him; Mowgli listened in.

—Sir, responded Kirtt, in a flat-voiced travesty of its usual polyphonic whisper that echoed drably down the aisles and atriums of conclave space, where Minds and their flesh masters conferred; but fully enabled quantum Minds were forbidden within the Law Well of Trencher – a precaution typical of inhabited planets along the fringes of the rim, with plaque descending nearer every Heartbeat down the Spiral Clade – and before *Tile Dance* had been allowed through the heliospace boundary and into the solar wind where Law Well prevailed, Kirtt had reduced themself to chip mode, to a fraction of its normal capacity. It shrank out of the tiles through which normally it acted out the masque of interface between Made Mind and mortal meat sapients. It was a tin shadow of his quantum self, spoke in a single male voice.

—Speak up, chip head, said Freer.

—This is not my doing, said Kirtt in its querulous single voice.

But there could be no argument with the prohibition – indeed, even farther up the Spiral, where it was believed that any stirring of quantum foam from which the universe was built tended to trigger plaque, the Made Minds were banned entry to many sectors; up past Human Earth, where the plaque desert ruled abandoned satrapies of the old ecumene, AIs of any sort were forbidden altogether.

When found, they were disassembled raw.

—Take over, please, said Freer, and told his data gloves to fold themselves away. They obeyed. He sat blind and silent again in control centre. The frieze of tiles that normally generated a low susurrus of gossip around his command couch remained silent, disabled by Kirtt's truncation; a clutch of free tiles floated through the air like ceramic bats, their intagliated mask visages stark still, for the dance had stalled in the absence of the Made Mind.

No mottoes flickered through the air like shuttlecocks.

But one square of tiles continued to depict Ferocity Monthly-Niece, her unblinking bee gaze, her open desire for Freer, whose face her gaze had fixed upon.

He gazed at her frozen face, which he knew so well it was almost as though he was gazing into a mirror.

—Take over, he repeated.

—Okey dokey, uttered the stunned chip AI flatly within his head, through the comm net that webbed conclave space with a trillion junctions, a little slow on the uptake, and meshed with Mowgli.

—Trencher welcomes law-abiding traders! sang Mowgli. —Please disengage from Maestoso Tropic.

—Roger, said the AI and snapped the thread. *Tile Dance* was no longer linked to the regional wormhole array of the great Tropic she had followed into this local sector; the ship was now in the hands of Trencher.

A billion faces of data streamed into *Tile Dance* and she began to slide downwards through mazes of orbiting resters and nesters, down past orbitals and mirrors and coffins from afar, and immense duufus arks and powersats, and local ramscoops, and even an exquisite-corpse commune spatchcocked out of wrecks and flotsam. Below, at the heart of Law Well, Trencher squatted like a senile poison hive, sucking the bugs down toward the thickening song of atmosphere.

It had been millions of Heartbeats ago, half a short lifetime, but Freer's memory, which was eidetic for women, gave Ferocity back to him. He did not really need the masks.

He allowed himself to slide into a light trance.

So it was without his intervention that the taut ancient

polished wolverine-sleek *Tile Dance*, which had been home for the half of his life he could remember properly, slid the last few thousand klicks downwards into Trencher, dived across terminator into the vast net of guarded portals that protected the vacuum of docking country from the stinking air, sank into the world, sank deep under the seared epidermis of Trencher, came to rest within the assigned grid.

Above the ship the passages of entry into Trencher flexed shut. Great spasms of light flickered off walls a klick distant. Hundreds of ships were visible, each cradled into its loading dock. Robot drones swooped through the maze, their prehensile claws guiding wires and tubes and cargo shoots into place. Hollow transport braids of all three authorised hues wove from ship to ship, giving crews and passengers access to the interior webs of the world.

—Your pheromones are rising, Stinky, whispered Kirtt inside its master's head, sounding almost normal – clearly it had been knitting together backup circuits out of the shambles of chip mode.

—I'm not watching, he said into the comm net. —I was thinking about Ferocity.

A cloud of cartoon spermatozoa did the can-can inside Teardrop. Freer shrugged at the joke. Being human was nothing to him. He was used to the dense maritime stench of human air. He had spent decades with his own species.

—Shut up, Kirtt, he murmured after a few seconds.

Teardrop blanked obediently, but then knocked.

—What is it?

The request mandala of a local net of press toons glowed in his right eye; the net had sniffed a scoop, was requesting visual access.

—Deal with this, Kirtt, he signed within his head.

—I'm only partly here, Stinky, said the ship Mind in its single male voice. —I'm a wounded surgeon.

—Just do it, Kirtt.

He blinked again, and the mandala swallowed itself, and his eye was free, for the moment.

—Isolate me, Kirtt.

—Roger, Stinky.

Silence wrapped around Freer again.

He was able therefore to spend the next few thousand Heartbeats playing chess with data mice while Kirtt fed the press toons a few terabytes of bumpf, handled docking formalities through Mowgli, arranged for supplies and fuel. The crippled ship Mind also liaised with the firm – a journey-cake cartel emceed by speckled sophont non-bilaterals from Betelgeuse – that held the goods for transfer to *Tile Dance*, initiated authorisation procedures with the Trencher planetary minds, formally requested permission to download the Route-Only contracted to guide them to Eolhxir. Stretched to its limit by these procedures, which ebbed and flowed like surf, Kirtt failed to register certain nuances in the data perfume. Freer was given no idea, therefore, that he was causing a stir.

He did not yet know that he was the most important person in the planet.

During these early hectic moments, Number One Son goofed off on its own, cartwheeling down the translucent egress spiral toward a homo sapiens braid which had just linked up for the benefit of the visiting ship. Number One Son looked like any other sigillum doing business for the flesh sapient it mimed. Visible through the ceiling of the egress hatch above its clumsy bumping torso, *Tile Dance* rested within the docking cocoon, an elongated pregnant wasp swathed in braids, caught in amber, succoured by nipples bearing nutrients from the innards of the world. Shafts of light from the surface of the planet far above danced down mirrored passages into the vast docking chamber, flickered through the ceiling, caught Number One Son's stiff bare buttocks bumping out of sight into the hollow oval that opened into the braid; the snorkels and prostheses and nipples that cobwebbed the ship flickered and darkened as beams echoed to and fro, as though half alive.

In naked space, on the far side of a thousand ceilings of rock, several thousand klicks up in the nesting orbit it had occupied for millions of Heartbeats, an Insort Geront ark of the Harpe Kith continued to slide around the planet, doing its job. Greedily, it drank up sacred data from Trencher; sometimes the flow of information near exceeded its computing capacity, and whole ranks of oldster homo sapiens overheated, often fatally – like any Insort Geront ark, it was loaded to the gunwales with distributed chip nets, human brainchips sunk in senior-citizen deepsleep, millions of obsoleted flesh sapients enjoying the culmination of their mortal span.

But flesh is grass, isn't it? Opsophagos themself of the Harpe had said once to a homo sapiens philosopher, whom he had awoken to converse with, through glass. Opsophagos knew the doctrines of Human Earth. Knowing the ways of humans was a large part of his job. *Flesh is grass,* he told the fuming, odorous human locked behind its barrier. *Flesh is mowed!*

A timorous sibling tched softly within striking distance
of the breakfast head of the Harpe in command of the
great ark in orbit around Trencher with its stuffing of deep-
sleeps snoring through their brainchip tasks. The sibling
masticated with tiny nibbles the real-paper printouts in its
glutinous ticklers, which it extended, perhaps hoping to
donate an extensor limb. The commanding officer – a
grown sibling of Opsophagos – took the printout in the
mouth of its slack-eyed famished breakfast head, read the
co-ordinates displayed, pulled down a three-horned screen
and punched out the designated location. Chip-sluggish,
the screen cleared, in time to reveal Number One Son
wobble bare-assed into the homo sapiens braid.
Controlling their aversion to sigilla, the commanding
officer began to jubilate.

They almost ate himself alive with joy.

Meanwhile, Kirtt uploaded into Mowgli a chip carafe of
data perfume gained during *Tile Dance*'s sweep upwards
along the trade Tropics from the warmth of stars farther in
towards galactic centre; in exchange, Mowgli uploaded a
case of carafes containing all the latest news. Fastidious but
leaden in his chip state, Kirtt washed each carafe with care,
filtering out great streaks of rust – the random garbage and
spoilage typical of planetary perfume this close to the rim,
plus a few trillion snoops coated in sheep's clothing – but
chip snoops were easy to detect, easy to banish. Kirtt also
swatted a whining haze of spam mosquitoes.

The rust stank even to its partially disabled senses.

—Sacred is the new, Kirtt said to its chip self. All the
same, it added to itself.

—Check! Freer subvocalised to the data mice, which manifested as molten flows of miniatured tiles, tile pixels.

Kirtt overheard, but did not interfere with the privacy of its homo sapiens.

Once cleansed of rust and crap, snoops and spam, poison pens and charity mandalas, the carafes of sacred data began to flow into the *Tile Dance* library, where they would abide within chips until the moment they could be translated into the quantum foam level, where the library heart lay, dormant now. There were trillions of news items from nearby sectors of the Spiral Clade, including a batch of instability readings on several hundred local 'empires', and a slough of mandatory Virtual Reality warnings, often a first sign of plaque. There were enough obits to populate a world. One entire carafe held nothing but science and technology infodumps, all newish, all therefore bogus. A scattering of toon infomercials had escaped Kirtt's half-crippled net; most of them touted useless R&R programs for devices too new (in truth) to be worth Recovering or Recuperating. Kirtt noted a growing pattern of Law Well violations and extensions, more rifts and stitches in the webbing of the increasingly fragile comity of the Upper Clade; but a certain fraying of interstellar comity was inevitable (so any search engine would confirm) at a time of constricted commerce. Trade indeed was bad. There was a scent of fear in the air. Jobs were almost non-existent (it was good luck that *Tile Dance* had a commission). The thinned Made Mind also decoded, with some difficulty, an array of eavesdropper scoops, one of which unpacked the command structure of an entire Black Mass of rogue Harpe.

The traffic weather in Maestoso Tropic – Kirtt noted –

remained fair, though some transit points were bottlenecked by arks, mostly of the Insort Geront sigil; most of the flow through the ratking tangle of wormholes that constituted Maestoso Tropic was westward, away from the plaque-mottled rim, westward down the Spiral Clade, into the light of galaxy centre, where the trade routes petered out at the edges of the known, in the murmuring of innumerable suns, beyond the ken of homo sapiens. Kirtt then passed on to the Universal Book a carafe of fictions – some in written form to be read by eye, some tiled for masques, most in hologram format for VR entry. Finally, whiffing attar, he uncovered a terabyte (locked in truly ancient chips) of music from Human Earth recently recovered from a frozen data haven ark which had been abandoned many centuries ago.

Kirtt readied all this material for transfer to foam.

Half an hour passed gainfully.

The hatch buzzed, rousing Kirtt.

Grinning its stiffish ghostly terracotta homo sapiens grin, Number One Son had returned ex-braid from its mission into the world-sea, in a cargo floater Kirtt glanced at via the hatch holo. Wedged like a beetle into one of the port's access pods, the floater glittered with sigils of passage and toon decals. Its tongue protruded briefly in the normal ritual of supplication, allowing Kirtt to access its contents: two quantum battle Minds, as ordered, packed at close to absolute zero inside two steaming sigil-dense capsules of an exceedingly ancient marque.

That was wrong.

Kirtt had conveyed Freer's purchase order, which was for one standard-issue modern Mind at a price he could not refuse, not two warriors from the dawn of time – even assuming Minds of that vintage were available in Trencher, Freer would not have placed such an order without consulting his ship. The cost of even one Mind of genuinely ancient lineage could bankrupt *Tile Dance*.

But the delivery toon was clear: two battle Minds, pre-paid at the amount originally advertised, address *Tile Dance*, authorisation Freer. Any memory Kirtt might normally access of Freer changing his original order was blocked; but neither had any prohibition been logged. An override was possible. Freer was always buying gizmos, especially if they looked reasonably old; the storage cornices of *Tile Dance* were gradually filling up with clutter, the detritus of a thousand Industrial Ages; so there was no reason for the crippled Mind to baulk or bother him at this juncture.

Number One Son galumphed into *Tile Dance*, visibly proud of itself, ambled down a spiral corridor past aquaria and butter lanterns marking cornice boundaries, into the lower bowels of the ship, where sigilla and eidolon coffins were arrayed, their interiors maintained at something close to absolute zero. Coffins holding half-formed sigilla/eidolon units, rideable by either flesh or Mind, squatted next to half-grown Freer sigilla awaiting the call to become. Specialist units for extreme conditions – temperature-resistant frog-like bodies with scythes for arms; ectomorphic long-necked browsers with radar ears; standard grunt golems – peered through frosted permaglass. Number One Son's coffin had opened in readiness. The sigillum stepped inside its home, which shut; discharged its memories; fell asleep. It became sere and yellow.

Meanwhile Kirtt danced a standard parlay with Mowgli,

which fed access codes into the ship without serious question. A sealed trolley exited *Tile Dance*, loaded the capsules, brought them in. The battle Minds were soon plugged safely into maintenance niches in Made quarters, next to Kirtt's own physical entity, and began to undergo thawing. Astonishingly soon they began to respond to input, passed quickly through the traditional rites, signed their embedment concords. Even in chip mode, they were clean and elegant and savvy and tight – welcome fingerprints of their normal quantum behaviour. The swift savvy alacrity of their responses to the ordeal of initiation had, moreover, amply confirmed the ancient lineage their sigils claimed. As far as Kirtt's half-crippled diagnostics could plumb, they tested loyal. Loyal unto death. For the time being, this had to be sufficient. Moreover, the battle Minds seemed to have suffered little in the way of 'repairs', nor had they been cannibalised at any time. There was no sign of rust in either of them. No plaquing, no Alzheimer.

Although the two newly installed cores remained technically asleep, Kirtt activated their maintenance niches, allowing installation to begin. Within human seconds, a maze of connective nerves and ganglions wove swiftly through the ship. Billions of junctions were established with Kirtt's own ship-wide web. During this procedure, Kirtt detected nothing false, no ringers in the towers in the realm of the Made; only time, time and sleep, and below time, and below sleep: *grass*.

Once they left Trencher Law Well, once they were all enabled again at quantum level, they could reminisce.

Then the tiles would dance.

●　　●　　●

The commander of the Insort Geront ark in spy orbit dared to contact Opsophagos of the Harpe themself at the helm of far-distant *Alderede*, in the midst of preparations for the next stage in the War of the Lens.

Wrigglies rushed into mouths, as the commander bided their sibling's hour.

'Well?' thundered the tripartite thorax in the ceiling, finally.

'Honoured sibling,' growled the commander, with bravery, stuffing its breakfast mouth to keep from eating the mouth that talked. 'You wished to know when the transfer had been made.'

'Yes?' thundered the elder sibling, many light-years distant.

'The battle Minds have been taken aboard.'

There was a dreadful pause. Rain steamed down the commander's flanks.

'How many Minds? Plural? Plural? Plural?'

The commander's skin fissured.

'Two, honoured sibling.'

Opsophagos screamed wordlessly down the thorax. They screamed thrice. Then a small still voice of Opsophagos whispered in an ear of the commander:

'Only one, sibling. Only one Mind is fixed. We inserted only one Mind into the data haven ark. There was no breach of integrity. Where did the other come from?'

The commander's suckers carved a triad of ones in their own skin. The small voice of Opsophagos's tiniest and most deadly mouth began to repeat ones up the scale, and became supersonic.

There was silence within the walls of the ark command warren, except for the slush of thick rain. The commander counted their remaining fingerlings.

'Sibling,' sounded the thorax triply at last, 'use your final minutes to uncover the enemy entity which has become aware of our strategy. Cancel the goon show. There is no window left. We have no time to flush the enemy into space. Kill it inside Trencher. Take Trencher down if you must. Suture off the danger, with your last breaths bring down the fire, sibling! We are at risk.'

The commander squashed themselves flat against the iron floor in a kowtow.

'We are at terrible risk,' said the thorax in voices thrice-dark with dread.

'The War begins,' said the thorax in voices rank with rust, harsher than iron, thrice harsher.

The circuits shut.

The commander chewed its thumbs in unison, a sign in any Harpe of profound shock. They could not be expected to follow orders with any efficiency. In any case, given the rigid protocols of command structure, it may have been too late to cancel the goon show.

Meanwhile the commander prepared the ark for death.

Kirtt slowly became certain there was something wrong, but did not seriously contemplate the intolerable risk of going quantum within Law Well and searching for a pattern.

Tile Dance was now fully refuelled. That was okey dokey.

She had Thirty Million Heartbeats of travel in her fuel matrices, a year's worth (as time might once have been reckoned on Human Earth) of wandering. Okey dokey. Nothing wrong there. There should be enough fuel to get to Eolhxir and back, wherever the planet might be exactly – the contract stated only that it was located in a known sector of the galaxy, and that a Route-Only would be supplied – and the fuel was already paid for.

The signature advance Kirtt had okayed down-galaxy, in the heat, had been sufficiently attractive to haul *Tile Dance* outwards from her normal stamping grounds, haul her up-galaxy and eastward into the rust, into sectors half frozen by plaque, all the way up to Trencher in the dark, where the contracted cargo awaited transshipment. The journey-cake cartel had refused on security grounds to reveal the destination world's location, but otherwise the delivery of nanoforges to the planet Eolhxir seemed a routine enough contract. *Tile Dance*, a ship of ancient lineage, had the carrying capacity and range required. It seemed okey dokey. They were rich again, even after refuelling. It seemed okey dokey.

Once delivery had been accomplished and paid for, *Tile Dance* would be free again to skedaddle westwards and inwards, back to the heart sectors, warm the bones of her homo sapiens and her ship Mind in the light of a billion stars in the enormous day of Time. There – under the battery of the music of the spheres, the unendurable sacred data-noise of galactic centre itself – there the heat would rise until it was an ecstasy to think. And when the heat became intolerable for flesh sapients – even humans with their thick deaf skins could not remain near galactic centre for more than a few hours without suffering fatal burns – a thousand wanderlust traces had been laid down long ago, traces a ship could follow into the cool, sidewards and outwards into unknown regions, till nothing could be perceived through senses Made or fleshbound, no matter how ancient, but the crippling silence of intergalactic space.

That was life for *Tile Dance*. That was okey dokey.

But here in the bowels of Trencher something stank.

Kirtt instructed the data mice to end the game.

Freer discovered he was in checkmate.

—I sense a blockage, Kirtt murmured into its homo sapiens's head.

—So what's new? said Freer, blinking Teardrop open again. —We're up the asshole of a planet.

—We can't get delivery yet. It will take at least ten hours to icepick a Clearance Motor out of Mowgli.

—Fuck. Is there a fingerprint?

—Oh yes. Insort Geront, of course, Stinky, murmured Kirtt in its gravel-thin chip voice.

—Well fuck me.

The frieze of tiles rimming the heart of control centre shivered very slightly, and the gold grouting that marked the joining of tile to tile gaped into slits, through which free masks were able to slide sideways. A pierrot therefore raised its head above its element, slid through the grouting and burst into the three dimensions of the world, clearly ready to weep, weep, flutter like a bat.

'Okey dokey,' Freer said acoustic. 'Okey dokey.'

The walls soothed. The pierrot subsided back into its tile.

—Fuck me, subvocalised Freer, but only for Kirtt to hear. —Why? What could Insort Geront want of us?

—Tch, murmured Kirtt.

—We're simple multi-millionaire traders.

—Tch.

—All right, all right, said Freer. —The route to Eolhxir. The secret of the lens. A chance to terminate one more rogue Made Mind, dear Kirtt, and all your krewe.

—Agreed, muttered the chip voice of the crippled Mind.

—So what do we do?

—I, said Kirtt, —will sit in solemn silence in a dull dark dock. You go be a tourist.

—Inside this asshole?

—You'll be able to see which way the wind is blowing.

—Fuck.

—But you'll go?

—Make me ready, chip head, said Freer.

The holograph cube in the middle of the glass island of control centre glowed suddenly, became a point of view approximately one hundred metres above *Tile Dance*, which was now surrounded by dozens of pink braid capillaries ready to take Freer anywhere in the world.

He stood within the cube and gazed.

Docking country spread out in every direction, amber and green, lustrous and polished, like a snakeskin seen from within, lit by a thousand beams ricocheting down from the surface. Translucent braids of every hue, like spaghetti in nulgrav, laced intricately through the vast chamber, ferrying flesh sapients and others by the hundred thousand hither and yon through the innards of the world. There were orange-tinted braids, variously subcoded for the breathing needs of a range of non-bilaterals; an extremely complex and numerous tangle of blue braids, also subcoded, for the commensal bilaterals who made up the vast majority of local flesh sentients; pink for the thick-aired oxygen-high homo sapiens braids, ringfenced for reasons of decorum from any other species; and dark maroon for government officials.

—Looks like any other asshole planet, Freer murmured.

But he felt prickly, as though the axons of the world

around him in the holograph cube were literally tickling the back of his neck, like termites sucking for gravy. It was as though he could feel in his bones the thrum of the voices of the swallowed who swarmed in their billions up and down the translucent braids, pink and maroon and blue and orange, a billion sophonts decked out in their skin and mortality.

Having no need for protection against vacuum, the aspects or Unfleshed – sigilla and eidolons and toons, tied entities and rogues, revenants in mirrorcam trance, caspers sucking up for love, freelance lifestory avatars on hire – floated everywhere, some propelled by rampacks, some (being immaterial) by the power of thought. They were innumerable. They congested the model of docking country in the holograph cube, glittering as flesh could not, for they were self-illuminated, their eyes were red or yellow, body sigils flashing at every movement.

Beams shot constantly downwards from orbital mirrors into the tumbleweed chaos below, bouncing off the Unfleshed, whose flickering tattooed carapaces pulsed with code like hive queens on a spree, made them seem far more native to this inner world than the flesh sentients who owned them.

And everywhere – inside braids of every hue, and in the vacuum atriums of docking country – smiley-faced poly-chromatic spring-heeled toons made their sales pitches, insistent and omnipresent, though they weren't, of course, actually there.

—Mallworld, said Freer.

—It's a living, murmured Kirtt in its raspy single voice.

—Isolate pink, please.

Kirtt reduced the gaze within the holograph to human

braids, thousands of humans visible through the translucent walls, some standing still and allowing the braid to carry them, some on wheels, some in scooters. Many wore clothes. They were behaving as humans always behaved, individual males and females engaging relentlessly (though always as part of a conversation, via comm net, with invisible partners) in the unremittingly ingenious gestures of courtship normally found in any of the rare surviving species where reproduction and sexual intercourse might occur simultaneously. Whatever the ostensible goal of any human behaviour, what humans were actually doing always seemed to be one thing.

Freer sighed. Time to go walkabout, in the pong.

—Are we clean?

—Randomised perpetual fumigation routines have been in place since we docked, murmured the ship Mind.

—Not that it matters.

—Not that it matters, Stinky. Data leaks.

—Data leaks, Freer murmured, repeating the old catch-phrase, after a long pause, softly.

Like any competent ship, *Tile Dance* was steamy with data. Here, deep within Trencher, a million probosces stroked her as though she were a sacred aphid ready to leak. She was a shrine. Data (which Made Minds deem sacred) left traces everywhere, *Tile Dance* was rich in traces, leaked traces like attar into the mouths of Trencher. The traces of the world were data, the world being beauteous. The universe was the sum of all the traces of everything the universe had ever been. Only connect -- only connect the contortuplication of the traces of every All the universe had ever been – and God would smile.

Or so it was believed in some worlds.

Tile Dance leaked the perfume of the living God.

Freer cradled his scrotum absently.

—Are we being sniffed? he said to his Mind.

—Natch, Stinky.

—Who's sniffing us?

—Mowgli, Insort Geront, every press mandala in Trencher, tithe monitors, Uncle Tom Cobleigh.

—Do we know where we're going?

—Nix, Stinky.

—Has the Route-Only been downloaded?

—Nix. No matter if it had. I won't be able to open it till we're quantum again. But the journey-cake will not make delivery until we are ready to leave.

Freer knelt into the heart of the cube. He was glowing. He smelled like a human being.

—Stinky?

—Yeah?

—I've been sorting the news, as well as I can, being half disabled down here. I think we're in the middle of something. I think we – I mean you, Master Stinky – have suddenly become very important.

—Because we will soon have a Route-Only to the Boojum.

—Yes, Stinky.

—And?

—I believe you anticipated this when we were quantum, though I do not have full access to the thought processes we utilised to arrive at a decision. It seems you decided to order a new battle Mind. It has been delivered.

—So?

—Two, in fact, were delivered.

—Nix. I ordered one, an absolute location Mind.

—Two, Stinky. The delivery toon insists you ordered two.

Freer shrugged.

—So, he said. —Do they test?

—Loyal. Both loyal.

—Cost?

—They were expensive.

—Tell me.

—Double the cost of one, Stinky. Half our fortune.

—Shit, Kirtt, Freer mouthed. He paused for a Heartbeat of his long life to come. Then he said, —But I trust you, dear one. I trust you. Should we keep them both?

—There are enough lenses on Eolhxir, said Kirtt very quietly inside its master's bowed head, to bankrupt the Care Consortia.

Teardrop beeped.

A goonish toon bearing the smiley-face sigil of Insort Geront flashed into Freer's vision, advertising a genitalia masque, much sex and violence guaranteed, of special appeal to offworlder homo sapiens solos.

—I think you should attend, Stinky, murmured Kirtt. —You don't know anything they don't know already. It's only twenty minutes away by floater. It will remind you of Ferocity.

Freer's eyes flared.

He glanced down at himself.

There was no erection.

—You're joking, Kirtt, he said. —Okey dokey.

—I'll watch over you, said the ship Mind. —We might find out something.

Freer touched the tithe sigil hanging round his neck.

—Have we tithed?

—Genome Tax was payable on entry, Stinky. You are passed for all human activities. Go do some face-time. Do you wish to dress?

Freer glanced down at his naked body.

—Does it matter?

—Nix.

—Then I think I will. I don't like this place.

He found a polished cache-sex hanging like a harlequin face in the frieze of tiles, and placed it over his genitals. The cache-sex snuggled close, its eyes snapped open. Interested flesh sophonts could access via its open-mouth icon a lifestory avatar which would flash a mosaic version of Freer's life, fabricated out of sitings. On some planet, somewhere down Maestoso Tropic from Trencher, he had once done site for several unbroken days, during which he had fucked a lot, as expected while sited on any net humans still accessed. He raised his arms and a vest embraced him, displaying sigils that designated his Trencher status: unattached merchant. He sprayed on a pheromone-suppressant, so as not to offend non-human bilaterals in case he had to pass through one of the communal arcades; but pocketed an arouser, which smelled like aftershave to him, in case of need. He keyed Teardrop into map default; a red icon now marked his precise whereabouts in Trencher. The icon shone within a tangle of menued ganglions. He was in the middle of a world all right.

—Kirtt?

—Sir.

—I want Sniffer.

—Sniffer coming up, Stinky.

Sniffer whuffed briefly and flew to him from its perch on the tile frieze; attaching itself to his earlobe, it became an earring indistinguishable from any normal human earring comm unit and hung like a pearl. He activated its block on cortex ads, but left its other functions dormant, in accordance with planetary protocol – in Trencher, as in most multi-species entrepot planets, it was impolite to impose reality sanctions on sigilla whose owners might wish to ride in silence.

He stuck a toon spray dispenser into his vest.

'Aw shit,' he said aloud through his literal mouth, though softly, to himself. 'They know I'm here. Might as well enjoy it.'

—Stay, he told the data gloves. —Sit.

They quivered but stayed put.

He walked through Glass Island with its austere rim of tiles, exited into a spiral corridor, where the full splendour of *Tile Dance* became manifest: every surface covered with mosaics, azulejaria tile dramas out of the memory theatre of Human Earth as she was remembered within the vortices of conclave space, luminescent Wisdom Fish peering through windows in aquaria like Odysseus bemused by islands, railings and panellings of every Terran wood reproducible, candles whose bright tiny flames became harlequin eyes in the seventh intersecting mirror and then became flames again in the eighth, outsider mannequins with vast lips and tits bleeding sugar, sugar and spice. He waved them to cease. He stopped at a panel of dense porcelain-blue glowing tiles, which faceted at his gesture into a bee's-eye array of mirrors, each small mirror framed ornately with tic-tac-toes executed in blind. Around the panel itself, enamelled lions in glowing cartouches chased each other's tails, each lion gazing outwards calmly but somehow pixillated; each elaborate mane was braided into runes.

Freer examined himself in the mirrors at the heart of the circle of staring dancing lions. He shrugged. Rather too closely for comfort, he resembled Number One Son, whose goofy wannabe gaze and wooden grin and exaggerated hawk nose parodied studiously, though coarsely, its human model. He bound a glowing freelance sigil into his ponytail. His skin was ruddy (Number One Son's surface texture was dun), his hair black, his eyes black too, with a slantwise trickster glitter, at times. In person, he was far more vivid than any sigillum which stood in his stead. He balanced on the balls of his feet. He was not twitchy, but seemed always on the verge of a sudden sleek slide into action. He was thick-chested but seemed slender. He drew the attention of fellow homo sapiens without seeming to know why. He touched the side of his own – moderately prominent – hawk nose, gave a small resigned grimace.

A phrase came into his mind . . .

. . . *liminal cheesecake* . . .

. . . but the meaning fled, if it meant anything at all; and he shrugged.

He selected a dignified mask, free of all but the necessary sigils, and placed it over his face; he had always found masks preferable to botulism fixes. He was dressed now.

He gestured, and the mirror irised within its circle of dancing lions. Freer stepped through into an open gravity-controlled shaft, sank swiftly past the several ship decks or cornices surrounding Glass Island, which sat at the heart of *Tile Dance* like a pearl in an onion. As he fell down the shaft and towards the world, stories unfolded in the tile facings which lined the shaft; on this occasion, they recounted the heroic past of Trencher, aeons back, before the data-soul of occupied space began to clog its gears. He came to a halt. A mirror, within a circle of dancing lions, opened. He stepped into the eleventh and outermost cornice of *Tile Dance*, a weave of corridors, gun emplacements, altars, universal windows, port irises.

Teardrop blinked in the diorama of his eye, signalling new input: one of the battle programs Kirtt had spent half their fortune on was already weaving a defence posture around *Tile Dance*, a pattern Teardrop rendered as a spiderweb at the heart of which lurked a multicoloured arachnoid icon, each of whose limbs menued on request a different defence function. A harsh tattoo stained the centre of the ovoid body; it depicted a bellicose human countenance, heavily scored. A beard hung down, ready for menu requests.

The eyes were shut.

—Does it have a name?

—In chip mode it is called Uncle Sam, murmured Kirtt.

—Meaning?

—A human patriot from long ago on Human Earth, highly bellicose, intensely loyal, very gruff, said Kirtt.

—Sounds designer for moi, Kirtt. Okey dokey. Bring it on line.

—Done.

—Well, Uncle? said Freer. —Are you awake? Welcome to *Tile Dance*.

The etched face caught fire, the eyes opened.

—Uncle? said Freer into Teardrop.

The archaic eyes of the truculent Uncle Sam glared at him, rimmed by flaming grooves, which shifted and flowed and became the image of an opened fist, a fist appaumy, an heraldic warrior fist apparently aflame. The face of the Uncle Sam was at one and the same time a face and a hand, a hand which was a weapon, a weapon which raised a palm of peace, but a palm clenched. Uncle Sam's eyes stared at Freer through its burning palm. The clenched fingers above its eyes made a frieze of hair. Beneath the sharp thin nose of the Uncle Sam, inscribed at the centre of the palm almost too small to read, glowed what might be an inscription, but in no language Freer could decipher.

—Thorn allied to apple, said Kirtt.

—What?

—Two lines of poetry, said Kirtt. —In the English of Human Earth. The lines read,

'Thorn allied to apple,
Child of the rose.'

—Does that sound loyal to you, Kirtt?

—It does, Stinky, designer loyal. I think it means the Uncle Sam is defensive of the home acre, that it looks to the future weal of those it serves.

—Ah.

The eyes of the Uncle Sam gazed deep within Freer's Teardrop.

—At your service, sirrah, grated the Uncle Sam battle Mind in a chip voice.

—Welcome to *Tile Dance*.

—Thank you, sirrah.

—Informal diction here, please. Nix sirrah.

There was a pause.

—What shall I call you? grated the Uncle Sam voice.

—Call me Knight Captain O my Captain, call me Shipowner Freer, or sir. Call me Stinky. Call me any time.

—Captain.

—Yes?

—I have been dormant, Captain. I do not know how long. The universe has not been upgraded into real time. I have not been brought up to now. But, sir . . .

—Yes? said Freer. —You can speak in clear to me.

The eyes of the Uncle Sam seemed to flame.

—Yes, sir. This planet, which I understand is now called Trencher, has a rotten taste, sir.

—What do you taste, Uncle?

—I taste data despair. Overload. Seizure. Implosion. I taste plaque.

The face burned within the spider, menus flickering faster than the eye could see.

—I taste vastation.

At first only the occasional theophrast had noticed the occlusions of darkness, had proclaimed the departure of Distinguishable Oneness (or God) from Its (Her) Creation, His Face disfigured by the clenched umbrae, the Anarch Umbra of the Death of God which brought vastation to mortals.

Or so they proclaimed.

But now the taste seemed universal.

Freer silenced the new battle Mind with a look.

—How long has Uncle been dormant? he asked Kirtt.

—There is in orbit a data haven ark which was abandoned about Thirty Billion Heartbeats ago, and has only recently been recovered. An archive of Terran music was aboard, which we have purchased. The Uncle Sam was also aboard, and fitted our requirements. In human years . . .

—I know how many years that makes, muttered Freer. —A thousand, give or take.

—Did you hear that? he said to the Uncle Sam.

—I am not enabled to eavesdrop comm between you and the ship Mind, said the Uncle Sam.

—Thirty Billion Heartbeats, said Freer. —You have been dormant a thousand years, Human Earth reckoning. Welcome back.

—Thank you, Captain, said the Uncle Sam.

—Welcome to hard times, said Freer. —Welcome to now.

The suave homo sapiens shipowner, wearing the chip-sluggish Kirtt within his sensorium, and an ancient half-awake battle Mind in his Teardrop, became visible to the world and to the watchers from orbit at the exit interface where the docking pods grappled *Tile Dance* into the embrace of Trencher. He was groomed and tithed and did not smell very strong for a human. The planet pressed against the back of his neck.

He stood inside a port-authority bubble affixed to *Tile Dance*'s flank, in a cloud of toons. He sprayed them. They squeaked indignantly but vamoosed.

—Mowgli instructs you not to spray free-enterprise toons, murmured Kirtt.

Freer sighed; he was in the middle of a world all right. Spam shat by the toons tickled his toes.

He selected a rental floater from a tongue which extruded

from the nearest braid and stuck itself to the bubble, which had opened to receive it. He put up a privacy sticker, paid the statutory guidance fee by plugging his scanner ring into the onboard Insort Geront sigil, which was non-bilateral: three lopsided worms, twining ouroboros, incised around a winged caduceus wand. At the heart of the sigil, glowing letters with an audio function whispered the Insort Geront motto: 'Enkyklios Paedia', boasted the glowing motto in a Human Earth tongue earlier than Freer would ever know.

—Kirtt?

—Stinky? spoke the ship Mind in a rusty voice.

—Have I ever known what that means?

—Probably. It means 'Circle of Meaning', Stinky.

—News to me.

—Meat brain, murmured the ship Mind.

—Uncle?

—Captain, said the burning face within the spider within Teardrop.

—Can you take over this vehicle?

There was a pause.

—It is done, Captain.

The floater's tiny local mind was now locked into the Uncle Sam guidance schematic.

—Stick to pink, said Freer.

—Avoid any braid with clog warnings, said Kirtt in comm mode.

Braid clogs could trap passengers for hours, which Freer knew.

—Who are you talking to? he said.

—I have already given Uncle Sam the latest congestion download. The Uncle knows to avoid crowds. I was speaking to you. There are bad congestion figurations throughout Trencher. I predict plaque. Perhaps fairly soon.

—Welcome to now, said Freer. —Uncle, he added, —stay clear of dorms.

Much of the homo sapiens population in Trencher spent most of its time asleep or on dumbfoundingly monotonous site, waiting for clearance to join a generation ark and put their minds to work at chip sorting.

—And Uncle?

—Yes, Captain.

—Watch out for pheromone junkies.

—I have been updated by your ship Mind, Captain. I am aware of the hazard component built into high-congestion multi-species interface events.

—Good, said Freer. —Let's go.

The floater swished into a pink braid and spun into the world, which could be seen through the translucent braid walls as a fluttering like speckled wings, some iridescent, some dark as night, as they went.

—Remember. Stick to pink.

—Aye aye, Captain, murmured the flaming spider face in the palm of the fist appaumy, defensive, savvy, grizzled.

The floater dodged slower vehicles and walkers; stalkers, on the other hand, were required to dodge the floater: whenever humans congregated in shared space, engaging at times in behaviour seemingly unconnected to mating, there was always it seemed at least one tourist non-bilateral stalker in the vicinity, gazing on from the wings, its nose (whatever passed for its nose) safely sealed, as it delectated the easily decipherable, unending, dogged antics of Freer's famous species. Normal intraplanetary decorum did not require homo sapiens to dodge stalkers in the flesh. Humans did not much like them.

Most stalkers were in any case sigilla.

Those non-bilaterals who could be defined as pheromone junkies were present in the flesh: they stalked human braids for the pong, lurking with care to avoid being struck by floaters. Some were harmless; some killed for the smell of dying.

The braid did a loop-the-loop, gathering stray capillaries in like knitting, and exited docking country, passing through walls of rock and into a central intersection, seemingly roofed with glass, where bilateral and non-bilateral networks linked briefly, where Trencher opened downwards and up like the veined inner atrium of a dream of cities; vast artificial suns and moons and discs flickered through luminescent cupolas miles above Freer's head downwards through vertical arcades lined with mirrors. The floater skidded through terrifyingly open air, freefell down a spidery frond curling for hundreds of yards over an abyss that dived downwards to magma. They hurtled into darkness shot by fireflies which turned out to be argosies ferrying homo sapiens upwards, perhaps heading towards an ark and the deepest of senior-citizen sleeps. There were a dozen of them; more. The inside of the world was churning.

—Is this normal?

—Aye aye, said the Uncle Sam.

They continued down, through a great shaft of light, dazzled, sigillated by photonic data flows cascading downwards from far above, perhaps ultimately from orbit, where the great Care Consortia arks shot perpetually their perfume and their honeytrap slogans into the apertures of the planet.

Most of the data streams displayed the Insort Geront logo, the fiery three-snake caduceus almost too bright to read, the marque of the vastest of the godzillas – an ancient Human Earth term for any corporation, whether snail or trad dotcom or seeded nous cube, which having gone rogue was no longer subject to the rule of law of any individual state or planet or system – prating 'Enkyklios Paedia' incessantly, boring its mantra deep into the bone of the planet. The brand of Insort Geront made his eyes burn.

—Almost there, said the Uncle Sam as the floater whipped past a stalled argosy (human faces could be seen pressed against the frosted glass like masks, mouths open), shot down a darker side tunnel, and wove through a tripartite nexus where all three species braids joined in recomplicated consort. The Insort Geront sigil began to fade from his retina, after whispering a softsell for Rest Homes in Space.

'Are you hungry, are you tired, Sirrah Freer?' it murmured in a tone whose geriatric unction belied the formal obeisance of its address; but left his face in peace at last.

It occurred to Freer that, having put up a privacy sticker, he should not have been addressed by name. He was formally anonymous. It was, at the very least, bad manners.

—Uncle Sam?

—Captain?

—Frisk me.

The icon in his eye grew and glowed.

—Nothing unusual, Captain, said the brusque spider, whose face wore an admonishing stare. —I can detect no traces on you, beyond acceptable limits. The Mowgli dock-engine is maintaining a tracer, which being in clear gave the Insort Geront beam a name to huckster.

—Thank you, Uncle Sam.

—Okey dokey.

—Take me down.

The floater dropped like a plummet through an ancillary braid, rocketed through an iris that seemed large enough to give an ark lebensraum, tumbled deftly through a writhing kaleidoscope which, seen lengthwise, became a spinal cord aimed at the heart of the planet; but just in time, at an intersection where ten kaleidoscopes bearing flesh sapients by the thousand bound themselves into one great knife-shaped columnar braid, the floater slid sideways, through an airlock into atmosphere, on to a rickety debouch platform overlooking the lower depths.

—Retain the floater, he murmured.

The bubble carapace of the floater opened.

—Aye aye, Captain.

He stood in dark open air, only a spindly balustrade protecting him from the whistling abyss. Half a klick across the vertical chasm, the column of braids descended into warm blackness, down towards the inner world. He was alone, except for a few strolling homo sapiens, male and female, mostly naked. Most were wearing traditional Tiazinha masks with huge come-hither lips, though others wore even more ancient aspects of the harlequinade. Inside their masks, the eloquent countenances of the strolling humans could be perceived only by intimates, through comm net face screens whose sensors conveyed mood, gesture, arousal levels. Outside in the world, the bare bodies of the homo sapiens maintained a normal dance of display – arms flinging, breasts high, balls (the scrotums mostly pierced and hung with aspect rings of precious stone) swaying. There were freeze-frame pauses while the masks gazed into space, utterly alone except for comm links. Occasionally, one body touched another. There happened to be no copulation.

It was just humanfolk out for a stroll.

Nothing to alarm him.

He moved away from the landing deck, past primitive hypno booths and bowers, down a slow spiral walkway that led into an amphitheatre cut into the rock of the world, but roofed by frizzy glass which gave an ornate glow from far above. There were no sigils incising ads into unwary retinas. Trees blossomed, lifelike Human-Earth-style roses, on a long trellis, guided him deeper in. A toon sign implored him, though in blessed silence, to enjoy the show within. A structure loomed above the trees. He turned into a narrow glade, which was lined by a primitive tile frieze bedecked with commedia dell'arte masks whose faces spelled out the name of the theatre:

PATHOS EROTIKON.

At the end of the aisle of roses could be seen an entrance, a proscenium arch from the time when humans swarmed like honey bees across the planet which gave them birth, carved with figures of humans and beasts once deemed obscene, incised with an inscription – 'Philoneikos gar ho theos' – in yet another language Freer could not decipher.

—Kirtt?

—'For the god loves conflict,' Kirtt said, after the tiniest of pauses.

A hologram translation scrolled through a proscenium arch in Teardrop.

—So?

—It is a homily from Human Earth. It means 'As flies to wanton boys, are we to the gods', Stinky, sort of thing.'

'William Shakespeare, *King Lear*' scrolled across the stage. Clearly Kirtt had consorted with the Universal Book that reposed in Glass Island. Text scrolled through Teardrop faster than Freer could read. Players strolled, mouthing deft imprecations. A storm loomed on a heath.

—Cruel world, murmured Freer. —Enough thank you, Book.

Teardrop cleared.

Between him and the emblazoned entrance a clutch of traditional representations of male and female homo sapiens genitalia blocked his way, the vulvas mouthing ads and odours the Sniffer blocked automatically, though a sudden flash of Ferocity Monthly-Niece filled Teardrop.

—Cancel cancel.

Teardrop cleared again.

—Kirtt, you're giving in to chip, he said. —Keep me clean, please.

He dodged the vulvas, which pouted, walked through the proscenium arch, which debited *Tile Dance*, and stepped inside, where an ornate chair found him, conveyed him along a curved aisle and into the auditorium, where he asked for privacy. Instantly, he was canopied. There was a smell of blown stamens, horse sweat, garlic, pheromone aftershave, sex: a swirling mix of stinks other species assumed humans hankered after. He asked the chair to turn it down, though not off. Through irises he could view adjacent canopies – some of which were opaque, some transparent – where humans and other flesh sapients presumably sat, smelling their various homes. The harlequin masks of the humans shone in the dark. The humans gazed upon each other's masks. It crossed Freer's mind that he might copulate later, and his cache-sex cackled softly, but a jutting stage drew his attention.

The actors below him were clearly not flesh sapients, though they were wearing a parody of homo sapiens configuration: they were 'dressed' as motor cortex homunculi, with huge mobile lips and hands and feet and enormous genitals, their thin wispish torsos labouring under the extraordinary exaggeration of the extremities.

Freer smiled.

It was going to be obscene, for sure: the actors were not masked.

The motor cortex homunculi began a risqué cabaret routine, featuring face-to-face conversations and even jokes. The frisson generated by this savage invasion of privacy was considerable. Several non-homo sapiens left their boxes in haste.

Obscenely, the actors then looked at the audience, their homunculi faces stark naked.

Freer carefully avoided eye contact at this point, even though they were only actors, not human beings. They soon began to pace through a less interesting parody of homo sapiens fucking, male to male, female to female, female to male indifferently, often switching, after the normal fashion of homo sapiens, penises lifting and distending painfully and penetrating vast smiling catacomb-sized assholes and vulvas, to the sound of a honky-tonk piano. At the corner of the stage, a lanky ragged-bearded man wearing an archaic interface helmet, which rather resembled a tin pot with landing lights, was pounding away at what seemed to be an archaic upright from before the dawn of digital. From the satchel on his back protruded several archaic rolls of sheet music.

This was all stimulating, in a small way, but not – certainly not after the face-to-face jokes, which had been genuinely threatening – much of a show.

Onstage, it was beginning to end in tears. Orifices suddenly grew teeth and began to rip phalluses apart, while other phalluses grew greatly long and jousted, clumsily. Gross smacking lips closed over the bits that fell off, and the feast or Agape began. It was a satire. Human sex was nothing but cannibalism. A grim lesson indeed! There was not much variety after this, though blood flowed very copiously, and there was much screaming. It was hard to work out whether the show had been designed for humans, or was rumourmongering.

A pleasant breeze ruffled Freer's thick dark hair, cooled his lean wiry form, roused his suppressant. There was an odour of roses, and something saline beneath the roses: like salt musk within a bower. The Sniffer snuggled against his cheek, twitching slightly in its preprogrammed slumber. Without its input, the scene seemed almost real.

For an instant, he seemed to fall asleep.

In orbit, the commander of the ark of the Harpe Kith continued with all the vigour that remained to them to prepare for death uneaten, unannealed, heads bowed in shame and grief, tails gummed into a humiliated starvation kowtow.

He was still in no condition to think straight, for his head mix had shorted. His heads dithered, freeing his eyes, his eyes looked the same way thrice. They had minds of their own! They banded together in dread unison, fixated without sideways obeisance to the Meal, without blinking – fatal! fatal! – fixated on the homo sapiens at the heart of the crisis that was to prove fatal to the Harpe, for he was about to bear a lens.

For long minutes the eyes of the commander did not blink into another thought. And then – again fatal! – he fixed on the lens, the rogue battle Mind, the Route-Only, Eolhxir itself.

Nothing joined.

So concentrated was his stare that over an hour had passed – four thousand Heartbeats as the homo sapiens counted time – before the commander realised with a spasm of starts the fatal error his eyes had committed.

He chewed themself back into control over his parts.

By then of course it was much too late.

Opsophagos was light-years distant.

The commander had insufficient stature to cancel the goons; he could not look far enough down into tail-death and find a knife to cut the skein of orders.

Too late too late too late!

But perhaps—

Perhaps he could command a local spasm, kill the homo sapiens while he was immobile.

Nothing ventured . . .

Too late too late too late! murmured, all the same, the shit-drenched tremor of his tales.

It is the end of the Harpe!

The Uncle Sam icon pulsed suddenly, and Kirtt began to rustle like hornets in his head.

—Stinky, said the ship Mind. —Stinky.

—Problem?

—I don't know, Stinky. We're chip here, it's a gobblede-
gook world. The Uncle Sam lost you just now. Only a
second or so, but you were gone, you were blocked. We
had no geography on you.

Freer signalled Kirtt for a single channel; the Uncle Sam
spider body disappeared.

—The Uncle Sam? he asked.

—Has no explanation. The Uncle Sam recommends
instant return to *Tile Dance*.

—Fiddlesticks. There's no point. I'm twenty minutes
from docking country.

—The problem remains. You were lost for a second.

—So maybe let us find out why? What's your evaluation
of the Uncle Sam in action?

—As before. Loyal unto death. Slicker than greased ice.
Very experienced, savvy even in chip. Seasoned. Vast reper-
tory. Bit of a prankster.

—But not about to go Loki.

—Of course not. Kirtt sounded almost miffed on behalf
of his fellow Made Mind of ancient lineage. —We're inside
Trencher Law Well.

A sudden itching smallness clawed at the inside of Freer;
he brought the Uncle Sam back into Teardrop. The arachnoid fistface seemed to be suffering a learning curve; its
legs spasmed violently at the edge of Freer's vision, menus
fluttering; then it stilled.

—Okey—

But then the spider whitened, blinked out.

—Kirtt? The Uncle Sam is gone again.

But inside Freer's head there was dead silence.

Kirtt was gone too.

The interference soup that moiled the inside of planets did sometimes scramble even Mind links, but Freer's skin prickled all the same at the sensation of absence, even for a fraction of a second.

—Kirtt! Kirtt!

He was thinking as fast as he could.

His skin continued to prickle at the thought that the vast attentive gaze of Mind that was the very heart of Kirtt – where a totality aspect-model of Freer nestled like a secret twin – could even for a nanosecond or so abandon him, leave him in the rotting darkness of the flesh alone.

It felt as though he had entered an air pocket, and was falling. His ears hurt. He swallowed. There was a cawing in his lungs, eggs of air swelling up the bronchial passages.

—Kirtt?

It sometimes seemed to Freer that Kirtt knew him before he knew himself.

Something was happening for the first time.

Freer shouted for his Sniffer. Was it dead?

But it awoke whuffling, registering as usual at the edges of his sensorium as a very clever, very faithful dog, bright as a button though woofish; instantly it snuffled a complex array of Virtual Reality warnings into his brain, while simultaneously unveiling his eyes, clearing his sensorium of all artifacts and shared-reality compacts.

Freer saw nothing now but what was there.

He calmed himself.

The ensconcing chair he sat in, and the iridescent canopy that had given him his requested privacy, lost their lustre, became standard kit. The jutting stage proved essentially real, though sensurround. But the smell of roses faded right out, and the motor cortex homunculi wavered and dissipated, leaving visible several primitive robots, without a brain among them, which continued to dismantle each other.

On the stage, only the pianist seemed unaltered, though his honky-tonk piano had for some time – seconds? – been a concert grand, and the music he was playing was no longer what had seemed to Freer to be twentieth-century Common Era ragtime dredged out of the well of the past, from somewhere deep in the soil of human life before the long winter locked in on homo sapiens, before the planet-specific conditions necessary for human creative work – as they were for all other flesh sentients yet encountered – began to congest into plaque. The pianist was now – had he changed his tune, or had the Sniffer uncovered what he'd been playing from the first? – deep into something even more archaic, even more profoundly planetary, from a time when music flowed like water through the minds of homo sapiens. It was something Freer recognised – a sonata or toccata, he could not remember, he couldn't ask Kirtt (his gut fluttered) – but it was music clearly native to a single instrument, music of the sort Kirtt had a habit of breathing through *Tile Dance* in quiet times.

The pianist glanced around jauntily at his audience.

Freer craned as well, now that he could see in clear, though without any augment, no gloss. As usual inside Trencher, where one was almost never out of sight of another body, numerous presences filled most of the available space, almost all of them homo sapiens, as this was a pink region, many of them in the flesh.

A number of sigilla were also visible, of various sigillum ilk, continuing to transmit the show back to their flesh owners: normal Pinks with their goofy wooden smiles, fronting homo sapiens; a Meccano Blue fronting a cluster of viewers from some stick species; a taller smoother Blue with four visible breasts and voluble mouth parts; another succulent endomorph Blue fronting a bipedal frond; a few Oranges with odd-numbered limbs and insect eyes; but also a cubical Orange with Blue and Pink highlights, marking the presence on Trencher of one of the rare genome packs.

An eidolon or two, glowing darkly, monitored the scene on behalf of some primitive planetbound Made Mind. There were no toon presences powerful enough to wade upstream against the Sniffer.

The air was close, dense with familiar smells; the breeze had been virtual. The real world of homo sapiens coated Freer like grease. He felt something like instant fatigue pain in the small of his back.

There was a flicker of eye contact; he blinked, startled.

The pianist seemed to be staring at him. His peculiar archaic helmet was flickering.

'Mayday!' shouted the pianist. 'Mayday!'

And disappeared.

A ghostly white spider waved its legs within Teardrop, quickly filled in, gained colour, but tremblingly.

Freer's eyes watered with relief.

—What's happening? he said, very urgently.

—I was overridden, sirrah, said the Uncle Sam through its loyal fist of service unto death. —Sorry, nix sirrah. Oh shit.

—Kirtt? Kirtt!

—Kirtt is piggyback on me, I have calibre, said the Uncle Sam, —but the line is thin, impossible, assaulted all sides, bad noise—

Freer's heart pounded.

—Uncle Sam?

Silence again, black snow.

He looked for a real-space exit. The walls were blank, rusty from old water.

The other members of the audience sat, waved cilia, pulsed, hummed, gaped as though nothing was about to happen. Clearly none of them were up to reality.

A knightly spider took shape in the snow.

—Sirrah? Shit.

The Uncle Sam sounded even more shaken.

—What's happening?

—Massive pressure chin-chin kettle shut. Sorry.

—Re-sort yourself. Don't panic. Remember you are chip.

—Yes, sir.

—Are you functioning now?

—Yes, sir.

—Get us out of here.

—There is no way out.

—I came in a way in.

—Nevertheless, murmured the Uncle Sam, menus sagging.

Freer looked around him. There was no way out. Where there had been an entrance was blank plastic.

—Augment.

—I am not linked to augment.

—Burn me out!

—Wait. My line is thickening.

Deep in stage left, a shimmy caught at Freer's eye, an

iris, a gust of wind. He thought for an instant he could see a tin pot flickering.

—It's Morse code, came suddenly the inside voice of Kirtt. —The device is signalling us.

—God damn fuck where were you? said Freer.

—You were up shit creek, said Kirtt. —And all the sphincters were shut. Thank the Uncle Sam, he punched a line through. It took a while to find you.

—Morse code?

—The device is sending a message in Morse. I translate it as: This way to the egress. I suggest we follow its advice.

—After you, signed Freer.

—Update me, Stinky. What's that kettle thing?

Freer shrugged.

—No idea, Kirtt.

Time to find out later, maybe.

He could see at the corner of Teardrop the arachnoid Uncle Sam doing some kind of orientation dance.

—This way, signalled the Uncle Sam, unfolding a map on Freer's retina. —It would have been better had we initiated the other Mind. It is a Sense of Direction.

Freer clambered on to the stage, brushed past a claptrap newish limbless robot with a funnel vulva, paused at the iris, which cast an electric glow and buzzed.

—Hurry, said Kirtt and the Uncle Sam in unison.

He stepped through.

There was a whump behind him, and the wall sealed shut. The amphitheatre was opaquing. But he was out; he was standing no more than a hop, skip and jump from his waiting floater.

—Safe? he asked.

—I feel dizzy, signalled the Uncle Sam.

—Stay away from the floater, said Kirtt.

Freer ducked behind a waterfall and the floater blew up.

—Neat, said one of his voices.

—Okey dokey, said the other.

There was a woofing sound, almost subliminal. The Sniffer – an extremely expensive early model – was overheating. Freer glanced quickly sideways, and at the edge of his vision field could almost catch a glimpse of the Sniffer's brown, intensely loyal ghost eyes.

He could smell its doggy breath.

He stood at the edge of the amphitheatre bulge, a vast fluted hairy tulip-shaped extrusion attached by a hundred yards of stem to the ornate arcade he'd debouched into half an hour earlier. There seemed something wrong with the lighting, and the air, which thickened and thinned, faster than seemed possible: as though the mast cells within the lungs of Trencher itself were seizing up.

—Get me out of here, Freer sang, almost audibly, a vocalise some eidolons were capable of reading from his throat as it pulsed: but fuck security, he thought. I'm fucking underground.

And the sky is falling.

—You're making waves, signalled Kirtt. —Try to calm down. The Sniffer is getting seasick.

—Just move me on out, sang Freer.

—Shank's mare, Stinky. Get walking. We think you're untargeted. At the moment.

—*Think?*

—Life sucks, signalled Kirtt. —And other grave sententiae, Stinky. Haul ass.

Freer grimaced but obeyed.

He was in fact happier than he could have believed to hear his Mind again. As he left the immediate vicinity of the amphitheatre, an implosion caved in walls everywhere, and the walls bled.

Too late too late too late!

The commander in orbit cut another throat, not his at the moment. His eyes did the rockette jig of death, all the same. His orders had fallen down the tree of command like dominoes caught in the blood of siblings, far too slow. The homo sapiens had escaped, its tracer continued to throb. The commander cut several more near-sibling throats.

One was his.

A purplish thought came to the commander's remaining heads, exsanguinated eyes opening and closing in a pattern nearly random.

No, the commander thought with the last of its remaining blood, the homo sapiens had not simply escaped.

It had been guided to safety. It had been corralled.

Unfortunately for Opsophagos on High in the *Alderede*, fuming as a demon might fume upon a burning throne, this realisation, whose importance was hard to exaggerate, did not survive the commander, whose last throats, too soon, had now split open in death.

The Uncle Sam made Freer duck behind a 3D screen, but the destruction of the amphitheatre knocked him over all the same.

—I'm all right, he said after silence had fallen.

—I have you, said Kirtt. —No damage.

Behind him, like a disturbed hive in pink briar, the remains of the amphitheatre shimmied in the charged dark air; fragments fell off into the abyss, which edged toward him like a mouth opening in quicksand.

—Move, said the Uncle Sam appaumy in his Teardrop.

Freer stepped quickly away from the expanding cavity, through a transparent pink scrim, and on to a walkway, which took him across a further cavern that shook dust and debris down from farther above than could be seen. Beyond was a homo sapiens braid and the complicated humming sound of its native riders, some going up, more going down as the statutory day waned, thousands upon thousands of humans, most of them talking, gesticulating, rustling, though never to each other. There seemed to be no alarm.

Were collapses like this normal?

Normalised?

Was Trencher disintegrating daily?

He glanced about at the shivering world inside the planet.

He did feel, at the moment, free of tracers.

But he was hardly geared to tell, not down here. He was a naked egg in a fry-up. He exited the walkway, stood gazing at the edge of the braid.

—Am I clocked?

—We don't think so. Maybe it's nothing to do with you.

—So why was I warned? Why was I helped? I would have died down there, Uncle Sam, Kirtt. I should have died.

No answer.

He shook his ponytail impatiently. He looked hither and yon with his liquid sharp black gaze. The intricate tracery of his mask seemed to burn him alive.

—All right, then. Bring me back.

The arachnoid knightly countenance shrank under its clenched fingers.

—Look, said the Uncle Sam. —No direction home.

The battle Mind retraced in the Teardrop holo the moderately direct route Freer had taken from *Tile Dance* to the amphitheatre; the route was now occluded with black smudges, as though this sector of the communications web that laced Trencher together had suffered a stroke. The amphitheatre was an ugly jagged puce bruise.

—Is there a way around this?

—We're searching, Kirtt intervened. —We're trying to order a floater in, but no guarantee it'll be clean. Transit permissions are bottlenecked. Mowgli is falsetto with stress. We can't get any sense out of this fuckhead world.

—Keep trying.

—Okey dokey, Stinky.

—Ah good, murmured Kirtt, —serendipity. To your right.

To his right an unoccupied floater edged itself from an upward channel of the braid and into a landing nest a few feet away, stopped short.

—Clean? said Freer.

—Check.

Just in case, Freer pointed the Sniffer at the purring immaculate tiny mind of the floater, found no signs of wanweird, no smell of virus, no tracer stink. The floater was all that it seemed and nothing more.

So he got in.

Paid the guidance fee.

Instructed it to take him up and away.

The floater unlocked from its nest, slid back through an iris into the full cacophony of the central braid, accelerated up through a vast opening into the enormous dark of what Teardrop identified as Cavern 108, sticking to the middle of the upflow. By this point, the braid had exfoliated into an interwoven spinal cord of transparent permeable shafts within a circumambient pink membrane, which bulged at intervals into circular arcades whose display mirrors echoed to infinity. Floaters and buses and human singletons filled the shafts, motes in a kaleidoscope, guidance systems working fine here, zero collision rate on the floater's incident menu, smooth and sharp as Freer continued to glide upwards towards the surface of the planet, several dozen klicks above them.

For a few minutes, it seemed as though they were going to make it.

At the heart of Cavern 108, above the floater, loomed a vast intersection bulge where, in a pattern the Uncle Sam rendered in Teardrop as a palimpsest of cloverleaves, pink and blue and orange capillaries intersected, joined and split. Flesh sapients of various species, bilateral and trilateral and other, met and passed here, smoothly and swiftly, upwards, downwards, sideways.

But just as the floater reached a main intersection level, where arcades wrapped around a hundred braids, godzilla sigils flickering everywhere, the air snapped.

Flesh sophonts and floaters and buses and cargo sandwiches bucked and contused into knots. A downbound bus above them toppled and began to dive, upside-down, narrowly missing the floater, into the depths; Freer caught a glimpse of blurred faces, open mouths, crazed masks, a child gaping up. Unless the safety nets were still active, the bus had a long way to fall down the vast braid.

There was a sound like thunder, weirdly garbled, thunder with a frog in its throat, a thousand monkeys freezing to death halfway through their last scream.

—Uncle? Kirtt?

The Uncle Sam spider blurred jumpily, as though it were riding a spastic bronco. Teardrop dried to mottled puce, a stone in Freer's eye.

—Plaque, came Kirtt's calm voice. —Bandar-log bugjam. Bytelock. Overload.

The floater had begun to hover, shuddering. It was clearly blind.

—Shit.

The back of his neck prickled with the trillions of tons above him, the dense honeycomb of Trencher seizing shut, poisoning the air. He could taste the seizure shit. Data plaque was more than a glitch in traffic flow, more than another proof that the chip-spastic godzilla arks were incapable of scoping the glut of galactic data. It was a sclerosis, a starvation. It was shutdown.

It decorticated the world.

You could die here, you could become a skull.

Retro plaquing from a planet the size of Trencher could swamp the failsafes, surge back up the Care Consortia data rivers into neighbouring systems; occluding wormhole catchments; burning out any arks that might be serving as node points, shutting the galaxy down.

Noise froze in streaks down the walls of the braid.

The floater was close to a landing pod, but could not make up its blinded mind to dock.

Its small screen burped.

Freer hit the manual control override, and the tiny stalled frozen mind shut down dead. He steered the floater carefully into a docking bay.

—Is this wise? Kirtt said.

—You tell me.

Crowds of flesh sentients, most of them homo sapiens, filled all that could be seen of the intricate huge arcade ring, which circled out of sight around a central tangle of intersecting braids. At regular intervals, gigaplex façades glowed in the outer wall of the agora; within, bipedal shapes could be seen skittering up and down the ramps like stirred ants.

Otaku booths for the homo sapiens fetishist – displaying a range of archaic monitors, palm pilots, handholds, replicas of various 'records' from the dawn of time, synaesthesia toggles, tangles of genuine wiring, Tamagotchi infant balloon heads, motor cortex homunculi elaborately trussed for bondage games – hunkered in clumps across the esplanade.

A sigillum with four tits was stroking an infant balloon head, which bawled obediently, fluttering its painted eyes.

'O nictitate!' murmured the sigillum.

Nowhere did the sentients seem particularly menacing. Most of them were conventionally naked, wore nothing but ornamental tithe sigils. The expressions on the faces of those who were unmasked betokened no more than a mild bewilderment, any further self-betraying expression of feeling being blocked by the botulism fixes most of them had injected before venturing into public, in order to avoid unmannerly interaction behaviours.

Most of the homo sapiens remained animated, as though

the world freezing around them were not the real world. Following the unspoken rules that had increasingly governed homo sapiens behaviour in public since the first days of digital, they wore happy animated harlequin gazes of outward regard, slid their rapt eloquent gazes past any homo sapiens who might be standing near, directed their expressive gestures exclusively off-stage via brain links or earring mobiles to invisible communicants, who whispered similar intimacies back from the other side of Trencher (where plaque had not perhaps yet hit) or a foot away.

They slapped their foreheads eloquently. Some were feeling their genitals, though public homo sapiens fucking was not, even blindfold, common within Trencher. No single homo sapiens spoke directly to any other. Soothing botulism fixes, when a gaze inadvertently intersected the gaze of another, normally controlled the mutual rage of homo sapiens communicant when neared. A coitus inter-ruptus air of unfocused affront coped with those inevitable moments when one body jostled another. It had all worked very well for three thousand years. Homo sapiens now rarely killed each other in public.

Freer told his Sniffer to give him a five-second immer-sion in unfiltered air. It was as he expected: surrounding the flesh sentients, cloaking them from any direct aware-ness of the descending plaque, interjaculating clusters of punchdrunk toons choked the esplanade. Clearly they had been severed from central control, and had gone gonzo. They fluttered back and forth among their flesh-sentient victims like the fire ants of a bad dream, yattering garbaged hieroglyphs, spoonerisms, brand names, random punch-lines; shitting spam; importuning without remission.

The Sniffer wuffed, pulled him back into full reality.

—I think I'll be just as safe in the noise, he said to Kirtt and the Uncle Sam.

He stepped into the junkie pong of humanity; addictive stuff for some species. The congested passive drift of the crowd pulled him slowly clockwise, around a few shrill fast-food modules, until he reached an alcove in a partition wall several hundred feet high, on whose curved surface shone an array of great universal windows, each one frozen shut on a chosen high moment from the Golden Age of Trencher, many millions of Heartbeats ago, when the universe had been alight with sentients, before the long darkening began, the occluding seepage of plaque down the Spiral Clade from somewhere outside, the Alzheimer-like data seizure which sealed a world into fixated system deadlock, into an unending cramp of darkness – just as nogo inhibitors had once frozen the nervous systems of the homo sapiens of Human Earth caught in the bottom of the well of the past, mayflies pinned to the meniscus of the natural world, wings gummed. As nerve tissue could not regenerate pre-existing synape disks – a condition shared with other known flesh species before modification – all adult human beings suffered progressive senility. When the corporate ancestors of the current healthcare consortia developed enablers to release the genes that commanded nerve regeneration, their dominance over homo sapiens worlds was assured.

In the alcove wall he found a dispenser sufficiently simple-minded to remain loyal, and bought a ten-minute nicotine addiction, inhaling with relief the accompanying cigarette whose virtual smoke he instructed the Sniffer to allow him to perceive. He continued to move sideways, found a protected inner hollow dedicated to chess, though the pieces were frozen, mouths open in silent screams; and sat down, just in time.

The lights went out throughout the braid, and a rash of emergencies flicked on, making instant dusk. There was a sudden hush, then homo sapiens hubbub. Freer stood inside his alcove.

The air was chilling fast.

—Kirtt?

—Yes, Stinky? but its voice was blurred.

—Can you pick me up in *Tile Dance*?

—We deem so.

It was too late for the moment. It began to happen again. It was worse. There was a rending sound, like ripped papier mâché, though huger, and a whump which caused his Uncle Sam earguards to seal him in with nano-speed. Even so, even within the seal, he could hear – partially through his bones – a sudden rusty sound.

It felt as though something from above, perhaps from above the surface of the world, perhaps a vast Insort Geront generation ark packed with a hundred thousand doomed lifestyle retirees, dislodged from near orbit, blinded by plaque, had impacted Trencher.

The humans visible to Freer were clutching at ears and earrings, or staring into the glare, transfixed by Bambi shock. The naked sound had been very intense. Without expensive baffling, they had almost certainly been permanently deafened.

—Kirtt, shouted Freer inside his head, —did you feel that? Are you intact? Are we going dinosaur down here?

—Trencher failsafes are operating, Stinky. The planetary

Minds are locking in. No sign of system failure yet.

—Yet?

—I am preparing to bring *Tile Dance* down to lift you out.

—What about our contract?

—That's why we're holding back till we must.

—So what just happened?

—Something rogue. From orbit. It hit approximately fifty klicks above you, right at the heart of the plaque jamming this sector. There are a lot of dead, but the Minds are coping. Your sector should get dataflow in minutes. We'll get you out.

—It felt as though an ark hit, hey?

—It may be nothing more than that, Stinky.

—Nothing *more?*

—We think something's happening.

The Uncle Sam within its fist appaumy grinned ghastly.

And the esplanade shook as though in the mouth of a crazed dog. The machicolated balconies overlooking the abyss began to cave in. The planet was shaking all the way down to here. There was another shockwave, a whumph which tickled the bone. Freer clutched at the chessboard fixed to the floor of the alcove, and the Uncle Sam helped him balance, and he survived.

But a few feet closer to the rim a tangle of flesh sentients, screaming into earrings at communicants or silent as death, slid along the tipping surface towards the lip of the abyss and into it, yanked by vacuum or wind.

In turns, there was both to spare.

The homo sapiens braid shook like a traumatised spine.

Freer's Sniffer barked a Red Alert.

—Above you, murmured the Uncle Sam.

Freer looked up, held to his perch.

Klicks above him the ceiling of Cavern 108 had split open, spilling a praying mantis stew of interlocked braids down, shuddering downwards into the abyss around him; in the centre of the chaos, surrounded by capillary braids somehow entangled in its passage, glowed what seemed to be a godzilla military landing craft, miles down the braid, deep in the gut of Trencher.

Sparks jumped in parabolas from the craft.

The sparks descended toward the esplanade, turned into individual exhausts.

Raiders.

At least a squadron. They landed in rough formation on the shattered floor, settled into a standard search pattern and began to dash from cover to cover through the shambles. There were a couple of dozen of them nearby, each wearing the semblance to unprotected eyes of a flesh sentient, usually homo sapiens. Through Freer's Uncle Sam/Sniffer array, however, it was clear what they were: a grope of grunt sigilla. Goons.

Normally they would be harmless.

They were encased in bulging plastic armour-style combat harness with cosmetic nodules; some of their cuirasses still bore advertisements. They flourished elaborate technicolour blasters with designer speedlines, and infrared torches which they flashed in various directions. Within their transparent helmets, their eyes were wide, as though with wonder.

Visibly sheepdogging their charges, bulging bandolier-draped auxiliary units accompanied them. With their striped bulbous storage shells and their high-sprung spindly legs, which flexed forward and backward at the knee joints, along with the wah-wah ulla-ulla battlecry they emitted, the auxiliary units gave off a toon air.

They generally avoided trampling the bodies of dead or unconscious flesh sentients.

Despite (or because of) an appearance of primo force, the raiders wore Handfast blazons on their foreheads, signalling (under normal circumstances) a failsafed crowd-control performance: as there were no human operators bonded to their outcomes, neither grunts nor auxiliaries were licensed to kill, though accidents could happen with such toys. Even fake blasters could turn into bludgeons.

The raiders were employing a slight augment – to as great a degree as their newish bodies were capable of sustaining – which to unaugmented eyes uncannily intensified their normal sigilla jerkiness. Goonish and spasmodic, like artificially speeded-up Komic Kops on a flat screen from Before Digital, they hopped back and forth in their search pattern as though the mezzanine were a hot tin roof.

The bandoliered auxiliary units bounded in circles around their charges, singing wah-wah-wah ulla-ulla-ulla like enraged bees.

The torches bounced through the dark, leaving firefly trace signatures which the Uncle Sam tracked easily. To Freer, it began to look like a storm in a teacup. They were nothing but grunts in grunt tizzy, making soldier noises in the dark, like babies calling for a mother. Cannon fodder, separated by plaque from command centre. Two minutes ago, before the dataflow seized up and the world began to shake, they had probably been inactivated, stored like logs in the craft, en route to some mayoral function.

All the same, their search pattern seemed gradually to be drawing them in his direction.

—I recommend augments, said Kirtt.

—Can you reach me?

—Just barely.

—Can Uncle Sam integrate?

—Roger, said the spider in his Teardrop.

—So do it.

Augment mode hit Freer like an unending orgasm. He groaned, a sound from a helium larynx. The world stilled as though in the last throes of homo sapiens passion. The grunt search pattern slowed to a hieratic though jumbled dance. Sigilla and eidolons hovered around them in the gloaming like broken thoughts, some of them already battered to the floor by designer blasters. The surviving humans stood or hunkered in the eternal slow pulse of ever-lasting life; gaping. Slowly, after the first spasm of augment had settled through his system, the world began, very slowly, to move again, though darkened down by spectrum shift.

Dopplered down to the bone, a klaxon sounded.

—Kirtt?

—Silent running, please.

Freer stood utterly still for a second, which seemed hours within his augment frame.

—Ah, said Kirtt. —They *seem* to want *you*.

—What?

—But it's not at all clear. It may be your augments are drawing them. You cut quite a figure on the screens.

—Fuck that, said Freer. —Switch me into Uncle Sam and defend.

—Understood.

From this point, Freer saw precisely what he needed to see, as though he were nestling somewhere deep within his own skull and keeping score; but his body had become the tool of Uncle Sam. The defence program began its ancient polished professional killing rite. The Sniffer continued to growl softly and territorially from its den at the bottom of its human's proprioceptive armature, keeping the toons at bay, and other soup. Through the ancient competent cold eyes of the Uncle Sam, Freer continued to observe himself, saw that he was moving like grease away from the alcove, that he was slipping in amongst the gangling grunts and the wah-wahing auxiliaries, which seemed rather faster on the uptake than their charges. He saw there was something like a knife in his hand. Suddenly it was coated in mucus, there were fewer upright grunt sigilla. One of them began to bellow, slower than molasses, just as Freer saw himself slit its throat junction. Being a sigillum, it collapsed like soufflé.

Sigilla did not suffer pain. They did not do screams.

Soon there were none left.

They were like spoiled desserts.

But Freer was continuing to move, like a wraith, almost faster than the unaugmented eye could catch: certainly too fast to be identified until later analysis, dancing through the auxiliaries, which had begun to lollop with surprising speed upwards through shattered escalator housings toward their landing craft. One by one, he destroyed them.

—I need one, he could hear Kirtt say within his head,

for his benefit: for he was actually addressing the Uncle Sam.

So Uncle Sam, still snug as a bug within the graven embrace of its homo sapiens, got one; grabbed its flailing legs and held on until its imperatives could be overwritten.

Finally, the auxiliary unit quietened.

—I think we have it now, murmured Uncle Sam.

—Good good good, said Freer, sheathing his knife, beginning to shudder. —Now please put me down.

Uncle Sam obeyed.

Freer began to brake and fade out of augment.

He shuddered less and less.

In the flickering dusk of the emergency lighting, he was barely visible to any remaining flesh sentients who had managed to hold on to fragments of the shivering floor, and who remained safe, for the moment, from the abyss. There was a constant noise of air rushing, terrifying gusts of wind from below. Almost certainly they would have no idea that he had popped into sight out of augment.

He was just a dream they were having.

He would be ravenous soon.

The dead sigilla lay in puddles, their surface features already beginning to dissolve. Scrubbers surrounded them, beginning to suck the nutrients. Any minds which had been observing through their sensoriums would have cancelled their downlinks, almost certainly some time ago – sigilla death was unpleasant to experience.

The emergency lighting flickered higher for an instant, showing spewed corpses in the near distance, the herniated braid beyond. Bits of the world continued to rattle down from far above. Alarms continued to nag, as useless as alarms

appleseed

have always been since the invention of electricity on any planet. There were some wounded flesh sentients nearby. There were many dead.

An eidolon knelt beside a motionless female sentient. It began to emit a formal wail.

The deactivated auxiliary unit squatted nearby like Humpty Dumpty.

—I hear keening, said Kirtt.

—Routine obsequies, looks like, said Freer. —Just an eidolon. Normal forelock-tugging. All the same, I think perhaps we'd better get out of here. It's going to hot up. I foresee the need for several hundred scapegoats, frankly, Kirtt.

—Uncle Sam is equipped to do a DNA wipe, and recommends one. I agree. There is no point leaving your signature in plain view.

—There's no way to scrub all traces, Kirtt. You know that.

—It's only polite to clean the room after using it, Stinky. In any case, while I was cut off from you, just before the ark hit, I received word from the planetary fuckheads that the contract had been cleared. It is on its way now, along with the nanoforges, and the Route-Only. We can be out of Law Well before the planetary fuckheads sort anything out down there.

—I smell a rat, Kirtt.

He was beginning to feel sick to his stomach. Perhaps it was augment reaction. Perhaps it was not.

He felt focused upon. Like a bug caught in amber.

—Trust me, Stinky. I give you excellent clean girl she is second cousin of my sister no problem!

—All right, all right. But hurry.

The Uncle Sam took over, and ran Freer backwards, like tape reversing, through his period under augment.

—Isn't this a bit obvious?

Freer continued to prance backwards at the behest of the battle program, through spoiled piles of sigilla stuffing.

—Sure, said Kirtt. —But it's only meant to last an hour or so. By then we'll be outta here.

Freer was panting.

But by now the Uncle Sam had finished its DNA scrub, and had laid down a false version of Freer's last few minutes here: DNA traces of a Freer who had never moved from his safe, still-intact alcove.

It wouldn't stand up under real analysis, but might hold for an hour or two.

—Okey dokey, said Kirtt, —I have managed to commandeer a stealth floater. Look up.

But of course it was invisible.

The Uncle Sam relaxed, though. The Sniffer wagged its tail. Freer put the auxiliary unit under his arm, and stepped in the direction his tools told him to step.

—Let's go.

As far as any flesh sentient could tell whose eyes remained able to look upon the world, the homo sapiens with the ponytail and the habit of walking backwards took two steps forwards through the battlezone into a congealing of air, and became utterly unseen.

—Hurry, please, said Kirtt very urgently. —I feel something through the plaque.

The stealth floater skittered invisibly into safety.

●　　●　　●

A dozen Heartbeats later, the fatally damaged central braid exploded as though a thousand bombs had struck, under the impact of the vast brazen descending central hulk of the crashed ark of the Harpe, which had continued to settle downwards into Trencher, cindering the world around it, boring closer and closer to magma.

The Insort Geront sigil shone like a branding iron on its flanks.

Within, the commander's three corpses, joined at the tail and elsewhere, stared in the oblivious unison of death through tripartite visors at the devastation he had ordered.

The ark killed another billion flesh sentients before it stuck for good, a thousand klicks inside the doomed planet.

two

t he world in the wake of the stealth floater continued to fall into itself. Shock waves guided the tiny craft like a pinball through braids and ganglions as it carried the unwounded flesh sentient Freer home, invisible to naked eyes. The Sniffer on his ear growled softly. The Uncle Sam, which had married the small stealth mind for the trip, did a bee-dance blur of diagnostics inside Teardrop as it over-rode the growing gnarls of plaque and kept the floater on course. The seat held on to Freer, he held on to the seat.

The Humpty Dumpty face of the captured auxiliary unit, which was still draped over his shoulder, wore an idiot smile.

'Ulla,' Freer murmured occasionally, to keep it soothed.
'Ulla.'

The stealth discus swatted into docking country.

'Ulla.'

Boulders fell like dust through vast ganglions from exit passages klicks above. Aftershocks could still be seen shaking the cupolas of egress starwards.

—Welcome, said Kirtt within him.

The floater whipped around a towering pillar whose bubble-top housed the control centre for docking country, and descended into the grip of an oval deck which bulged at the end of its hose-like housing like a cobra head.

And stopped.

The floater's bubble-top opened.

Above him, wrapped into its landing cradle, *Tile Dance* hulked intact, a polished featureless ovoid, an egg unbroken, manifestly not a thing of this planet. It seemed to shimmer slightly, as though it were gathering itself.

Tears started to Freer's eyes.

He was at the gates of home.

The cobra head lifted its cargo towards a port that opened suddenly in the ovoid.

—Quickly, please, said Kirtt.

—More coming down?

—Almost certainly. Henny penny, added the ship Mind.

—Henny penny, Stinky.

There was a sigh of sealants as the cobra head married the irising port extrusion, and Freer climbed into safety, the auxiliary unit dragging its multi-jointed legs behind him.

'Ulla.'

The port sealed shut behind them.

The Sniffer shut itself down and slept.

Freer was within at last. He climbed the tight entry spiral upwards into the inner regions of *Tile Dance*, which had been his home for Half a Billion Heartbeats. Wind chimes and lachrymals surfaced like dolphins from their tiles, echoing out of sight as he moved further inwards to the very navel of the ship, which awaited him. Porticoes opened at his touch into the whorled salty air of the deep interior, which was never entirely still. The walls smelled of mahogany, the railings were brass; above them, the walls were lined with tiles stiffly flexing their chip-sodden scenarios, and universal windows portraying rooms which did not exist at the moment, though they had, or would. Lanterns not yet in the direct line of vision glimmered softly aslant through mirrors, announcing turns in the passage, sometimes silently, sometimes murmurous or cooing. One of *Tile Dance*'s two altars of the Universal Book sat in a niche, waiting to divulge new realms of glory from the recent download.

Between the universal windows in their side-chapels, translucent blue porcelain azulejaria patterns covered the walls with tiles, joined by molten grouting. Flyte masks – and jack masks nestled safely within them – rested inside the designs, eyes shut, awaiting quantum foam, awaiting revival of the eternal commedia, when they might pulse freely out in the world again, singular, janiform, singular, janiform, unendingly, first flyte then jack, then flyte, then jack; a few of the masks were blank, though they boasted a weak ghostly sentience even under chip constraints, enough to keep a few freelance nanos round their banked fires, fascinated (as untied nanos were designed, or fated, to be) by any iconic resemblance to meat puppets.

A sketch version of the face Kirtt assumed indoors when disabled stared out of one flyte mask fastened to the wall above a vine-choked alcove. Its enraged eye opened to track Freer as he climbed higher into *Tile Dance*.

Freer winked at the eye, tossed his mask toward a tile whose grouting absorbed it sideways, so that it showed for a fraction of a Heartbeat its janiform double gaze before settling into a tile drama; and stashed the gangling auxiliary unit into the alcove, which absorbed it with sleight-of-hand speed.

There was a swift stench of something like roses.

He caught a glimpse of the unit's cracked face, its painted grimace, before it disappeared completely.

'Ulla,' he said for the last time.

—Thanks, said Kirtt through the mask, —for the snack. Maybe we can find something out.

There was a pause.

—Down the hatch, said Kirtt.

The enraged eye closed its lid.

—Incidentally, said Kirtt, —its name was Alice.

The walls were almost as warm as human skin; the azulejaria commedia held its breath for quantum foam; a mirror somewhere cooed like a dove.

—Are you hungry? said the ship Mind, extruding a long nipple from the wall. —You must be, after augment. Take a sip.

—Thanks.

He sucked at the nipple for a moment.

—Now . . . said Kirtt.

—Right. The contract.

The nipple retracted and a writing surface extended itself from the wall. A sheaf of literal papers rested on it.

—Your contract. I've vetted it every which way, said Kirtt. —It's more or less standard. Give it a flesh signature and we can get out of here. In all the shit down there, the icepick was clearly inaudible to Big Brother: we have a Clearance Motor.

—Ace, ace.

Freer glanced at the top page. A chair-shape nudged his

buttocks and he sat. Everything seemed routine in the contract and manifests: one cargo of nanoforges duly stowed in the nest of foam-shielded geodesic crannies that made up *Tile Dance*'s hold. Location of Eolhxir to be supplied by data-monad (which would self-destruct after completing its mission) in the form of a fully failsafed Route-Only. Half the agreed fee payable in advance, half on completion. Usual sureties mutually supplied.

—Advance cleared?

—It paid for the Uncle Sam, said Kirtt.

—Any zaitech? he asked.

—Not a whiff detectable within Law Well, said Kirtt. —All seems straightforward.

So he gave his drop of blood to the contract, which, sated, crept into the wall, leaving a copy in the vault.

—I retained the stealth floater, said Kirtt. —It will now take the contract down to Trencher archives.

—And then?

The chair-shape goosed him.

—Time to go, said the voice of *Tile Dance*.

—You're reading my mind.

—Well, yes. It's in the job description. Move, boss!

Freer hoisted himself from the signature alcove, took the lift shaft back up past cornice after cornice into the heart of *Tile Dance*, where a brass iris rimmed the entrance to control centre. Incised into the rim of the iris, in a runic script, in some language other than Old English, were the words 'Ynis Gutrin'. Freer had noticed the inscription very early on.

—Ynis Gutrin? he had piped – hardly more than an egg then, though precocious. —Sounds like Human Earth. A singer perhaps? Female?

—Glass Island, the ship Mind had said in a voice of gentle quantum puissance. —It translates as Glass Island. It is a place of vision.

Which seemed reasonable enough, given the view from within. He let his hand slide over the rim. It was warm. He stepped into Ynis Gutrin, into orbiting scintillae of light and tile, sat in the bucket couch. The tiles were subaqueous in the light, ebbed and flowed, loomed. He sat cocooned within what appeared to be a bubble protruding into space, though in reality, of course, Glass Island lay deep in the central core of the ship, a coffer sunk inside holy turf. Command centre was the inside outside of the navel of *Tile Dance*, locked into the cavities and pyroclasts of the ship's abiding configuration in time and space. He sat in a bath of sensors, which tickled for an instant until his skin settled into the marriage of ship and flesh. A net of monitors surrounded him, as faceted as bee eyes, and hatrack herms wearing masks made a semicircle round his couch. Through the inward gaze of the monitors, every cavity of the ship could be accessed. Datagloves for ancillary inputs beseeched from flexipods like palms in a storm. Tiled panels curved around him, their scenarios caught in chip stall. And before him the holo cube rested, pulsing slowly, blank for now.

Beside him, the Clearance Motor eidolon waggled its ceremonial wood-like head. Freer patted it absently.

He waved a hand. Toggles curved their necks decorously in clusters for his touch; the holo came alive, the entire sphere of the universe surrounding *Tile Dance* came to life.

In every direction, docking country was juddering to a halt. Spasms of discharge lit the extremities of the arched klick-high cavern. Directly ship-front, a tangle of gantries slowly imploded, like a flower living backwards. A hundred-metre-high rack collapsed, spewing cargo. In the mid-distance, a giant freighter trembled, began to lean into a turbid gout of flame ten storeys high. Readouts flickered in Teardrop, summarising the picture in the holo.

The planet seemed to tip in his vision, though *Tile Dance* remained stable.

—Kirtt? Are we maintaining gravity?

—Maintaining gravity, Kirtt said, —against all regulations. Very soon we are going to have to go solo—

—Hah! Freer shouted.

A green GO from central control was flashing in Teardrop.

—Pindown has lifted, murmured Kirtt. —Go!

The Clearance Motor flashed release codes into the ship Mind. *Tile Dance* instantly cleared its cradle, and Freer's point of view lifted. He could see the whole of docking country, an ants' nest under an invisible boot. The ship sighed upwards through spasming grids into the vast illuminated cupola that crowned docking country like a brindled dunce's cap; from below, it was like rising into a hollow cone shot with light. Shuttles toppled from the inner tassels of the cap into the turmoil below.

At its highest peak, where the cupola nippled through the surface of the world into raw atmosphere and the sight of bare sky, *Tile Dance* was strobed by the wild fluctuating flare of the Insort Geront sigil beaming down from orbit; its slogan washed through the holo in repeated waves: ENKYKLIOS PAEDIA. ENKYKLIOS PAEDIA. ENKYKLIOS PAEDIA . . .

There was a slight tremble within the ship just as she slid upwards into the great nipple.

A herm gaped, as though swallowing.

Beneath *Tile Dance*, in the blinking of an eye, docking country blacked out, swallowed its throat and died. The Insort Geront sigil blanched, shone brighter than the local sun, blanched again, died. Perhaps the ark that housed it was biting the dust, maybe. Data plaque fell – visible as a dance of dying readouts in the holo – through the air.

—Punch us out, yelled Freer. 'Punch us out!'

In the sanctum of his own ship, he was yelling aloud.

—Okey dokey, sang the ship Mind.

A mask bearing the fist appaumy spoke.

'Queens have died,' said the Uncle Sam, 'young and fair.'

Tile Dance shot up through the stained nipple of the cupola, and into atmosphere. In its wake danced a crazy quilt of lasers, autonomic defence units perhaps, a random spat of tracer beams that could blind an ark. No matter, no matter. It was out. It had popped out like a cork. The polished, almost perfectly reflective *Tile Dance* – built in the style of a Predecessor Frigate from the previous Cycle, a creature of the light, a surfer of the galaxy – slid unscathed skywards and into vacuum, emancipating its flesh sentient from the gravely wounded world below.

As they lifted, the curve of the planet bulged upwards in silhouette against its mother sun, scarred and umbral, increasingly silent, a shrunken Alzheimer ghost within its scar of plaque, another region of the known universe knotted into a lightless fossil silence, turned away from the light.

'Heaven,' said a voice in Freer's realtime ear, in an accent he took to be the Uncle Sam attempting to do Human Earth, 'is our heritage, Earth but a player's stage. Mount we unto the sky . . .'

'Queens have died,' interrupted the Uncle Sam mask on the wall before him, in its normal voice, 'young and fair.'

His voice stopped for an instant.

'I'm afraid the one line is all I know,' said the Uncle Sam.

The skin on Freer's neck beaded with sudden sweat. Suddenly his merchant's garb, which he still wore, seemed to choke him. He began to pull at the battle-stained greaves.

—Ahem, Stinky, said Kirtt. —There's something I have to tell you . . .

Freer turned his head.

In the passenger alcove behind him, as neatly ensconced within its failsafes as though they had been designed for this one particular creature, sat a long-waisted rubicund almost headless long-necked non-homo-sapiens bipedal with four attractive breasts.

'I am sick, I must die—' it murmured.

—Eolhxiran. Female. In pheromone shock, Stinky, said Kirtt. —Please keep your clothes on. In fact . . .

A translucent purple cape floated down from the ceiling.

—Wear this, Stinky.

—Okey dokey.

He gestured.

The cape wrapped itself demurely around his torso.

The Eolhxiran's small eyes were squeezed shut. Its head seemed to be trying to retract down its neck.

'Freer, sirrah,' said Kirtt acoustically, in a formal voice, 'may I introduce you to Mamselle Cunning Earth Link, who has agreed to serve as *transitus tessera* for our long journey. She incorporates the Route-Only data I will need. Mamselle Cunning Earth Link will remain with us to Eolhxir, where Mamselle will disembark.'

—Kirtt? said Freer. —Have you lost your great Mind? A flesh Route-Only?

—She arrived just before you did. I had no warning either.

The head, which had disappeared completely, except for a grasslike topknot, began to emerge from its neck, very slowly.

'O gross,' said the voice, still uncannily reminiscent of the voices of Human Earth, 'O I am so perfectly fucked. I never knew it would be so—'

The breasts began to pulsate.

—A sign of embarrassment, I believe, said Kirtt. —Of course I'm brain-damaged down here in Law Well, but I think you will find she uses language in an attempt to bridge the aroma gap. Homo sapiens being scent-deaf. I think it is like shouting to the deaf.

—Yes yes yes, we know all about that, said Freer. He was ponging like a boiler factory.

'May I extend,' said the voice from the tiny head once again, 'my brilliant apologies, sirrah. In all my Heartbeats excessive in number had I ever guessed? Nay! Mortification pluribus enshrouds me O Freer sirrah.'

'So this is your first actual encounter with one of my species?' said Freer.

'O nocuous to say yes, but not evitable to lie,' murmured the Eolhxiran Route-Only. 'I am O well-beloved the profoundest of experts vis-à-vis homo sapiens. I'm entirely in love with you all. But only by the Book learning. So! O daring warrior seeking light! Freer! O, berserker of much pulchritude! Freer! Ever since my earliest Heartbeat, brighter than bright down-galaxy far afar from here, have I ever longed to encounter homo sapiens, thou in the flesh! So here I am! So do I know about you, O verisimilitudinous you right in the here of hereness cripes? Aye! But did I guesstimate the potency of the hit of the O of the O of the presence? Nay! Aiyeeah! I did not reckon with the phat! presence of your flesh Freer sirrah O I did not!'

Freer had begun to calm.

'I apologise,' he said. 'I'm afraid you startled me. Perhaps you could sense my reaction.'

The Route-Only closed her tiny eyes.

—She means to say, You bet I could sense your reaction, Stinky, said Kirtt.

'It has been a long day,' said Freer. Her eyes opened like tiny lucent tulips and gazed upon him. 'Life-threatening behaviour on the part of rogue godzilla grunts, augment,' he said. 'Data plaque, carcinomatosis of entire planet, deep personal grief, survivor guilt, exhaustion, stuff.'

'O dear Freer sirrah,' said the Eolhxiran, 'you are terribly stinky. But so wry!'

'Have you been talking to my ship Mind?'

'I beg indulgence.'

—You bet she has, Stinky.

'Brightness,' said the Eolhxiran Route-Only, 'falls from the air.'

Trencher shrank beneath them. A moon mugged over the rim of the planet opposite the sun and, as the ship rose closer to freedom, became fully round, beamed. Behind the advancing line of terminator, the darkness of the world became increasingly visible, the thousands of apertures into the city world lightless now. The Christmas-tree fluorescence of Trencher had been turned off. Like a toon, the moon jumped over terminator. Goodbye to Trencher.

'O lamentoso chez moi,' carolled Mamselle Cunning Earth Link softly, perhaps to herself. 'My heart is breaking. To see advancing the anarch dark, O Trencher! Sad to see you go! Bye-bye, we must surmise. As of now-ish, an Eaten Land thou art, O memorious. God rot. I cannot forget Carcosa, where black stars hang in the heavens. O this is a savage downer.'

Tile Dance slipped upwards into space; slid silently through the crammed sphere where orbitals and stations dwelled, and the several remaining godzilla arks, liners of space drifting into the rocks; edged gingerly around one sector dominated by the fragments of a vast mirror shattered from some impact, no longer beaming energy and teraflops of data every millisecond down Trencher's open throat from the vast trapezoid of the portion of the galaxy known to homo sapiens, greatest of the space wanderers.

The data arteries that fed the planet had been pinched shut.

—Do we still have in ground link?

'I am presuming the GO signal has reached Law Well perimeter, and that we will not be challenged,' said Kirtt acoustically through his usual control-room guise: a flyte mask in the shape of an heraldic shield featuring a lion's head caboshed, with medusa hair, a single bulging eye, a beard, and tusks; beneath which, interweaving a dentilly of fuligin, could be deciphered, ornately incised, his full male name: Kirttimukha. To display only a single default face was a sign of bondage endured, especially through the near-berserker intensity of the flyte mask, forced to interact (as it was) with the phenomenal world. But *Tile Dance* was nearing Law Well limit, and he would be quantum again, KathKirtt again, she and he: the Janus faces of wholeness. The mask through which themself spoke would be double again; its two visages manifesting the two aspects tradi-tionally unveiled by fully enabled ship Minds when serving homo sapiens, wanderers bound to home: the flyte mask, which expressed passionate love for the intersection of Mind and world, on behalf of the client; and the jack mask, which expressed the direction home of the inner Mind.

—A large assumption, Kirtt?

'Correct. Communications from control centre have ceased. No actual acknowledgement of the GO has been detected from the fuckhead planetary defences. Trencher is going fossil, but her automatic arrays may fire when we cross out of Law Well. The plaquing sequence, as you know' – Kirtt was clearly addressing himself more to Mamselle Cunning Earth Link than to his master – 'is both expo-nential and contagious. Uncle Sam and I are warding off infection, I believe successfully . . .'

—But keep an eye open, he said inside Freer's head. —This is going to be close, I'm afraid.

—Okey dokey.

'. . . and we predict successful emergence from Law Well within twelve minutes.'

The Eolhxiran's tiny head rose on its neck stem.

'Frabjous to hear,' she said. 'When we emerge into the

splendid glister of free space, please turn left.'

Mamselle Cunning Earth Link's bright eyes nictitated suddenly.

—That was a joke, boss, said Kirtt.

Freer chuckled aloud, for the Route-Only's benefit.

—I have a bone to pick with you, box, said Freer.

But the shaped panels of sensors flecked over suddenly, for an instant, and Teardrop fogged.

—Plaque? he vocalised.

The screens began to clear.

—Blizzards. But I think we can ride the storm, with the help of Vipassana. Have I permission to activate?

—Who?

—I have been remiss in not mentioning this earlier, but my memory is not what it used to be.

Freer's eyes widened.

—In any case, we have been experiencing interesting times. Vipassana arrived with Uncle Sam, but only now am I in a position to activate him. He is our absolute-position battle mind, and he will keep me on the rails. We believe, Uncle Sam and I, that he can also chart wormholes.

—That's my job, said Freer. —I have perfect pitch.

He sounded miffed.

—We mean no offence, sahib. But we believe the Vipassana capable of charting wormholes by feel.

—So?

—From within.

Freer shut his mouth.

—While I remain halved, Kirtt continued, —I'm pretty easily flustered, as you know. We almost lost you down Trencher just before the ark hit. In ten minutes or so, I should have my mind back, but at the moment I'm beside myself. Stinky, may I introduce Vipassana?

—Right away, old box.

The mask immediately to the right of Kirtt's burnished face took on the aspect of a rust-coloured sphere criss-crossed by rules and measuring devices; within this larger sphere, a smaller sphere rotated slowly, its surface covered with ornate depictions of gods and goddesses, beasts and warriors and women outflung into the animate stars. Beneath the mask, just where a bow-tie might have been found, had the mask been connected to a neck, a brass-coloured plate identified the two-sphered image as a Celestial Planisphere of the Northern Hemisphere, by Virtue of Which it was Possible to Locate the Constellations, and to Predict their Appearance. In smaller letters it was noted that the original had been conceived and executed by an English male artificer named Jehosaphat Aspin, around 1840 Common Era, on Human Earth.

Freer's skin prickled. His mouth dried.

Mamselle Cunning Earth Link's head began to retract again.

—Good morning, sirrah, said Vipassana, his voice in Freer's head alto, inflectionless, profoundly awake. It was a voice with no past. It was so profoundly of the present instant that it seemed to echo from somewhere beyond, from the present before the present had quite happened, certainly before it had registered down the perception aisles of a flesh sentient.

The Vipassana was an avant-courier of now.

Freer held on to himself.

—Call me Stinky, he vocalised.

—Stinky.

The Vipassana's voice, though it echoed Freer's, seemed to prefigure it.

—Your chosen face . . . said Freer, from inside his head, staring at the Celestial Planisphere mask. The inner sphere, with naked gods and goddesses of Human Earth performing homo sapiens sex activities between its burnished teeth, gaped vastly; it was the larger sphere's mouth. A thousand fine protractor lines lacquered the mask suddenly, like fine antique porcelain, then faded.

—Stinky? murmured Kirtt.

—It's all right, said Freer. —Let me continue.

—Vipassana, he said, continuing to gaze upon the mask, —tell me about your face.

—I regret arousing your fear response, said Vipassana, —and I hope that mamselle will soon recuperate from her proximity to you in such a state. I am an orienteering mind, very highly sophisticated, but am not programmed to engage in sensitive responses to demands entailed by the flesh bondage of dwellers in meat. The focus of my being is almost wholly restricted to detecting the odour of space-time. Or should I say spoor. In order to pinpoint the location of *Tile Dance*, I need to sense the aura of her birth. Your ship Mind fed me certain data while I was still inactive, and I was able to engage upon a hegira trace of your ship, which has proved of consuming interest, for during the course of her journeys up and down the tropics, and in between them, and widdershins, *Tile Dance*, as articulated through her ship Mind KathKirtt, has encountered much that is of relevance to the late evening Heartbeats of your universe, which is mine as well, and which is stiffening into nescience daily. I am able to assert this with especial vividness, for I have been long asleep, and it has changed, it has changed dreadfully, since I was last awake. I would perhaps mourn this encroachment of the dark, if I were not innately disabled from mourning, sirrah.

—The pinpointing of the location of a flesh sentient, continued the Vipassana unstoppably in its alto croon, —must be – by virtue of the relative simplicity of its imprint upon the dermis that shelters the Real – less taxing for an absolute-position battle Mind to accomplish. It is still necessary, however, for me to incorporate into my chart of your position, sirrah, elements of your past. I did, therefore, while outwardly inactive, establish a rudimentary mapping of you through the good graces of ship Mind Kirtt, though his current disablement precluded my gaining a full one-to-one. Sadly, I am not programmed to take into account the possibility that you would be upset at this accessing of material from your past, even though it remains salient to your position of relative safety at this point. I am what I am, finished the Vipassana, sounding as calm as the instant of being before the world consumes the instant of being blindly.

—And you are . . . ?

The fine lines appeared again, porcelaining the mask; it may have been a map of something.

—A simple but profound Mind of universal position, chanted the Vipassana, imperturbable as a monk in trance. —To know where you are now, I must know where you have been. That is my task. I am nothing but task, sir. The image of a Celestial Planisphere signals that task. Shall I wipe it, sir?

—No no, not now, not now.

'Mamselle,' said Freer aloud to the headless Eolhxiran in the passenger alcove behind him, 'I think it's safe to come out. My apologies for conveying something of my state of mind to you without warning.'

—State of mind! boomed Kirtt.

Cunning Earth Link's head slid baldly up from her neck.

'Welcome back,' said Freer. 'Perhaps I can explain something of my agitation to you.'

'There is gratitude unbounding in these multi-tasked breast prostheses for such kindness of the open heart from Skipper,' said Cunning Earth Link. 'O dearest of all hopeful monsters!'

Twin smiley-face countenances came into being on her upper breasts.

'Neat?'

'Neat,' said Freer. 'Very arousing for a homo sapiens.'

The faces blinked out immediately.

'In the first instance,' said Freer, 'Route-Onlys are not normally *people*. In my book, Route-Onlys are simple downloads. I don't believe I have ever encountered one in flesh form. And Kirtt was perhaps too busy, or too brain-damaged, to mention your arrival. So I had resumed command of my ship in the presumption that, in the normal way, my voyage to Eolhxir would be undertaken solo.'

'O chagrin!' cried Cunning Earth Link, her head beginning to disappear again.

'It's all right,' said Freer. 'Plenty of room in *Tile Dance*. This is a very old ship. It's bigger inside than out. You simply shocked me down to my boots.'

'I placate inexorably,' moaned Cunning Earth Link.

'Certainly. But let me continue. You understand, therefore,

that I was not really ready for the second shock inflicted upon me in only a few minutes. The mask, you understand.'

Her small head nodded with whiplash speed.

—Not to worry, said Kirtt. —Her brain's beneath her neck.

'Battle Mind Vipassana's mask, you understand, replicates a Celestial Planisphere executed on Human Earth about Twelve Billion Heartbeats before plaque death took the planet down. The original was one of several thousand Earth treasures acquired at great cost in lives and funds after Earth blacked out.'

'The Malacandra Project!' shrilled Mamselle Cunning Earth Link. 'Obeisance worthy!'

'Every virtuous homo sapiens flesh sentient thinks so,' said Freer, pulling at his ponytail; grinning for an instant suddenly, but without any dangerous pheromonal surge. 'And it is a joy to me that you concur. The Celestial Planisphere, in any case, ended up on Ordinance, the world I have made my home. Some time ago, half a lifetime ago, I was able to obtain the original on extended loan, but confidentially, for reasons of security. It means a great deal to me, as a wanderer. I had thought my attachment to the Planisphere was entirely private, but I seem to have been mistaken.'

Outside *Tile Dance*, near space exploded like firecrackers into something that zigzagged like cartoon smoke.

—Shit, said Freer as the shockwave hit. He swayed in his safeseat, which held on to him.

—Guidance is collapsing, said Kirtt.

—Handfast! yelled Freer.

A thick filament extruded from a flattish dais. A hand took shape at the end of what was quickly becoming an arm. Freer clasped the hand, which was now holding a sword. Kirtt was now free to respond actively within the Law Well sphere, as long as Freer kept in physical contact with the handle.

Uncle Sam destroyed the Clearance Motor.

—Vipassana? Freer said.

—I have taken over pilotage, sang Vipassana alto. —We are about to penetrate heliospace markers, at eighty-nine degrees to the ecliptic, then we will be free of Law Well governors, we will go random pronto. The planetary defences have fired upon us.

—We have sustained some damage, said Kirtt, —but we maintain integrity.

—There are disorientation devices at work, said Vipassana. —They seem to be attempting to warp our course back to Trencher. I have solved them profoundly. The solar wind lessens. We near the rim of Law Well.

—Go! said Freer. —Go! Bye-bye, Mowgli!

In Ynis Gutrin the tiles began to dance.

—Let them fall, Mowgli; they are only tears.

—Through! cried KathKirtt in the voices of a choir.

The shipmind mask exfoliated into a dozen masks of the commedia, each Janus-faced: each wearing a lion body with the head of a sun which was an eye, a great eye seeming to smile, flyting the cosmos; and a naked woman, her arms and legs outspread to touch the rim of a fiery wheel, grinning fit to kill with wanderlust.

—Gimme a kiss, said Freer, and whooped ferociously. He continued to grin as though he could not stop. This was the case. He tossed his tithe sigil at an embrasure, which tucked it away. His cache-sex leaped free and began to spin, bee-dancing through the holomaps of Ynis Gutrin.

Freer did a small buck-naked caper.

Mamselle Cunning Earth Link's head disappeared.

'Sorry,' he said to the quivering torso.

—Let's make tracks, said KathKirtt in the full voice of themself.

—I am turning left, said the Vipassana. —Wormholes abound yonder, I aver.

As far as any surviving observer on the rent surface of Trencher might have seen through eyescope augments, a diminishing pinpoint of light, already halfway above the wandering moon, spun in pinwheels blindingly, and was gone.

three

the bubble at the heart of *Tile Dance* hummed with tiles whose masks peered out into the world coyly, a Mystick Krewe of digital minds come together in order to parade naked. Freer sat in their midst in the glitter of his flesh, which was brighter than porcelain, and which seemed to burn: because of the literal heat of corporeal sentience, and because flesh – within the time frame of an AI's perception – was grass. Cooler but ardent all the same, the Eolhxiran female sat in her sheltered alcove behind the captain of the ship, one prehensile foot idly juggling a fragment of the demolished Clearance Motor eidolon.

Behind them, Trencher had become a speck in the eye of its sun; and then disappeared utterly as Vipassana's random evasion dance carried *Tile Dance* abruptly slantwise the ecliptic, further into free space, where the wormholes awaited serious voyagers.

The handfast sword retracted into its polished dais.

'O lamentoso,' murmured Mamselle Cunning Earth Link a second time, gazing at the pocked region Trencher had once dominated; then fell silent again.

In humble obedience to the diktats that shaped their welcome servitude, KathKirtt, the Uncle Sam and the

Vipassana remained in plain sight, remained tied to their masks for Freer to track in realtime, which is to say they remained naked. Masks, which bound a Made Mind to time and place and the Mardi Gras parade of shape, were not disguises of the flesh for Made Minds, but a submission to exposure. When KathKirtt manifested themself – the immemorial flyting and jack aspects of the full Made Mind conjoined in one Janus mask – they descended into a crippling exile, locked themselves into the tile sepulchre of the world, for flesh is weak; the essence of the bondage of the world is that it strips a Mind of the quantum compact of home and family, so that it is visible naked.

The theophrasts of the inner stars designate the masking of a Made Mind as a form of kenosis – the ultimately fatal incarnation of the divine into the progeria of mortal flesh. The theophrasts of the inner stars further argue that Alzheimer plaque – the data seizure which seals a world into fixated system deadlock, into an unending cramp of darkness – reflects the reverse process. That plaque is a scar left by the departure of the gods from the universe, and that it is this scar, or vacuum, that gives the universe a charley-horse.

The theophrasts are wrong.

All the same – as though 'divine' entities were shackled by an inborn tropism, a fatal longing for the bondage of the world – the Made Minds found it strangely thrilling to spreadeagle themselves on the rack of time: to gape through the peepshow eyes of their chosen faces at the meat faces of the mortals to whom they gave suck. To engage in converse through a mask came as close to understanding the paradoxical allure of human sex as a Made Mind was ever likely to attain.

Only rarely, however, did Made Minds find the temptation to inhabit meat so deep that they loosed the stays of true being, forget themselves in the flesh, became mortal, died of progeria, were reborn into the flesh, died, were reborn like capillaries in brain meat, died, were reborn.

From the shadowy fluted ceiling dangled, like the vertebrae of a neverending story, long figurative dramas in azulejaria porcelain. The grouting between each glowing blue tile leaked gold enamelling deep into the dramas: tales of intolerable eros typical of Human Earth, accomplished fingers caressing piccolos and bared breasts. The masks resident within the stories stared outward through moist bee-eye-dense embrasured tiles between molten grouts of gold. Flitting from the stories that held them, other masks exfoliated themselves for the nonce to become memes, hiked themselves through the grouting slots, janiform and doppelganger-pale from the prison of the dance of tiles, and into the gimbal-shot free space of Glass Island, where they loured over the scene from fittings atop brass herms, shot antic bat glances around toggles, crouched over a braced scroll beaded with the sweat of attar, through which the Prime Copy of the Universal Book might be accessed ceremonially and at points of crisis.

—We must speak together, spoke in unison a mask propped against the Book.

There was a perfumed whutter, like the beating of the wings of giant dusky moths.

The masks began to morph, a constant, inhumane, scritching transition from one face to another; hurtled themself from aspect to aspect, from one Janus mask to another, in a rhetoric of the weaving of consensus. Faster than a human eye could catch, they gave signs of their never-stopping concourse. A realtime digest of the ongoing conversation, comprising a tiny but uncensored sampling of the teraflop burn of full non-flesh-sentient quantum intercourse, fed like manna into Freer's sensorium.

There was a smell of burning leaves.

—Just a little nervous from the Fall, murmured a Made voice inside Freer.

—Kath, Kath, dearly beloved, vocalised Freer. —Welcome back. Was that a song of Human Earth from your deep bits?

—As always, Stinky.

—I think we should go acoustic, my dear.

—Okey dokey.

'Go acoustic,' he said aloud.

'Okey dokey,' said KathKirtt.

'Mamselle,' said Freer, turning in his seat, which resembled leather and turned with him, 'now that we have safely exited Law Well, may I formally introduce you to KathKirtt, ship Mind of *Tile Dance*, who are now reunited. They have been patient enough to serve me for many Heartbeats.'

Cunning Earth Link nodded her tiny head at the mask lying against the Book, whose double page hummed with texts which succeeded each other blurringly, awaiting a request to pause on some single page or volume, epic or summa.

'Abide with us, o, please,' she said.

From the mask adorning the tallest herm, KathKirtt gave her one face only: a woman at the nacre heart of a burning wheel which might be mistaken for Ynis Gutrin. This face of Kath then ricocheted glowing through a dozen KathKirtt masks, flooding Glass Island with light.

Each mask pulsed softly, swiftly, as she passed.

'Hi there,' they said in a Kath voice, and dimmed.

'I have gone acoustic,' said Freer to the Eolhxiran Route-Only, 'because we're all in the same boat here, and I think we need to try to understand what has been happening over the last few hours. Much has. Much has.'

He paused, as though reluctant to continue.

'I will begin, mamselle,' he said finally, 'by asking you if you enjoyed the show.'

The Eolhxiran's four visible breasts flattened.

'Show?'

'Surely you remember,' said Freer, almost soapily. 'Back down there on Trencher. Just a few hours ago? The cannibal picnic? The Love Feast of Homo Sap? It must have been right up your alley.'

He felt himself to be calm but her head began to retract.

'Moi?' she carolled very softly from nearly inside her neck.

'And the aftermath?' purred Freer. 'Surely you enjoyed the Attack of the Grunt Sigilla. Surely you delectated the Killer Rage of the Cornered Freebooter, I mean myself, sweetling.'

'Moi?' whispered again the Route-Only in a bird voice.

'Toi, sweetling,' said Freer. 'Recollect, if you will, my unhappiness at being trapped in-planet. Contract delay? Route-Only still missing, but not really, I guess, mamselle? Premonitions of plaque? Insort blendo jam? And no Clearance Motor for love or money? Finally Kirtt icepicks a spare out of the fuckhead planetary minds' defence plaque. Fuckhead planet minds using fucking dead-data mazes as mithridatics to fucking gandydance profound fucking Alzheimer trauma, fucking useless. Fuckheads,' he murmured absently, giving her time to regain her balance.

He had hawk eyes. They scryed Mamselle as prey.

On the control centre monitors, through the dance of masks, a circumambient model of n-space gave an online purport of the random lunges of *Tile Dance* into the backdrop seethe of stars of interstellar space, while at the same time it traced the last spasms of Trencher's planetary defences as they punched erratically through the fading solar wind and – terminally violating relevant treaties – through Law Well boundary where the heliosphere began, shaking the fabric of space, but missing the smooth archaic ship, now fully Minded.

—Fuckheads, chorused KathKirtt.

—We are one light-year out, crooned Vipassana from a spinning Planisphere. —See.

In the centre of control centre, a hologram sphere formed, an analogue of the memory-theatre atriums and council chambers and labyrinths and performances-in-the-round and harlequinades of conclave space, ready to become 'real' at the stroke of a menu, whether a mind's-eye menu, or a Teardrop function, or a menu clutched in the palm of a handfast in literal space. At the moment, the sphere had become a globe of space with Trencher throbbing at stage centre. An intricate red line gave the history of *Tile Dance*'s evasion pattern; its red tip jerked suddenly, recording a leap sideways.

On Teardrop a menu-laced analogue of the globe gradually smoothed down: *Tile Dance* was beginning to get some elbow room.

'Good,' he said.

The screens confirmed that the last speedlined runic thrust of the ship had taken her out of the ken of anything left on Trencher capable of tracking an escaper.

—That was good, that was indeed very good, sang the Vipassana voice calmly. —We have been here since exactly when we were. We are utterly where we are. We shall be where we're going. We will go profoundly.

—And the devil knows who I'll marry, murmured Kath. —Profoundly.

Freer leaned towards Cunning Earth Link.

'My apologies, mamselle,' he said. 'We were distracted. Allow me to continue. Just shortly before the first Insort ark lost control and hit, I had left *Tile Dance*, at Kirtt's suggestion, as there was nothing for me to do on board. And because Kirtt, who ill-advisedly thought he could maintain a safelink with me, wanted to see what fire I might draw. Right, Kirtt?'

—Wise seedling! boomed KathKirtt through a krewe of masks.

'So I decided to disembark, take in a homo sapiens genitalia masque. More or less at random, I thought. But almost as soon as I arrived the shit began to freeze. I activated my Sniffer immediately, scoped the scene, noticed in the audience an extremely unusual sigillum whose livery I had never previously encountered – natty blue, smooth and sweet, four tits, toi, toi, toi, toi. Were you not there? Were you not riding your sigillum?'

—You're beginning to emanate, Stinky, said Kirtt. —We'll get nowhere this way.

'And later, in the Arcade of the Glory of Trencher, were you not there too?'

—Cool it, Stinky, or she'll shrivel.

—Check, said Freer. He sighed.

'Mamselle,' he said, 'I must assume you were riding.'

'Aye I rode,' said Cunning Earth Link, straightening herself at last. 'Bungling downwards into the shivery halls of Trencher Underneath I rode sigillum, sirrah, kaboom, kaboom, a Valkyrie, a wisenheimer. I followed the traceries of your course, sure! Dead easy! You and Kirtt do kaffeeklatch! Gab gab gab gab! I followed you like Huck Finn follows the Mississippi, just as in preternaturally Old Book of era of your empathy choice on Human Earth in Universal Book.'

The Book obeyed the hint, rendered a facsimile of the first page of paper of the original text.

'So you got me dead to rights!' Mamselle concluded.

She spread her palms, with their tiny vestigial eyes.

'Though imagine me!' she pealed.

She raised her arms into a ballerina's sweat-drenched pause. 'Shivering with anxious joy, behold me, sure! O enormous masculine sophont of dead Earth,' she continued, 'bucking the bronco sigillum into badlands, "An Indian blanket on a pony with no rider in the flesh and bone lookin' for his buffalo river home", as the poet says in the sagacious Book. Agog with flush was I, you can altogether bet! Seeing you in the skin that wears those mighty bones! That was scrumptious. That was lagniappe. But reck you, O striking figure of a man, that such solace of the senses was my purpose down below? Nix! Reck you not how dire our need has been to keep you safe? O candlestick of flesh! quoth I inerrantly though in Trencher's extremis, you stay hale now!'

'That has the sound of a kindly thought. But it cuts no ice.' He paused. 'Who are you? Why ever should we let you live?'

'I am your *transitus tessera*, sirrah. I am your ticket to ride, ho ho. Into regions unknown.'

Freer's eyes widened involuntarily.

KathKirtt stilled within their masks.

Cunning Earth Link flinched, her head sank inside its carry-all neck.

'Unknown?' Freer said softly.

'Unknown to hoi-polloi, I mean. Unknown to riff-raff! Deeply familiar to me, natch, your savvy Route-Only!'

Through the screens swelled the seethe of stars.

'So tell me, Mamselle Cunning Earth Link,' said Freer, slowly and clearly, 'just when did you guys discover Eolhxir?'

There was a silence.

The krewe watched.

'I am plenipotentiary rep of glitterati of my ilk who settled Eolhxir,' said Cunning Earth Link, finally opening her eyes, 'it seems like yesterday.'

—Hah, thrummed the newly awoken KathKirtt.

The masks whirled faster than ever before.

'Thank you, Mamselle Transitus Tessera Cunning Earth Link, Plenipotentiary Rep of the Glitterati of the Ilk,' said Freer. 'Perhaps we are beginning to get somewhere at last. So. How long ago was yesterday?'

'Ever so recent, penetrating sophont! Twenty-five Million Heartbeats ago, could that be right? Seems like yesterday! Hi ho! Maybe more! We are peregrine remnants, you see, we do waif biota jobs. Kitchen help! Like you, once upon a time! But ever so less numerous. Look I show you!'

From a midriff cavity she extracted a small cube.

'I invoke holy data cube!' she pealed.

The krewe stilled suddenly.

—I do so love a story, sighed Kath.

'We grant sanctuary,' said Freer. 'Tell us a story.'

Mamselle turned to place the cube into a slot beneath a matrix of waiting screens.

'Hold a minute,' said Freer.

Mamselle's head-tuft shrank into a wee puce dolmen.

But he wore a child's smile.

'As long as you are telling us the truth,' he said with a thespian twinkle, like a stage uncle consoling a niece, 'there's nothing to worry about. Sacred is the new.'

He gave a conjuror's wave.

Out of a sudden aperture in the sandalwood floor appeared a free-standing plastic cabinet, with a small oval screen fitted into its front. It looked like glass. Freer leaned over and caressed a row of knobs on a plexiglass panel below the screen. He turned one knob clockwise. There was an audible click.

He grinned quickly, joyously.

It was a television set from his era of empathy choice.

After several seconds the screen began to give off a whitish glow. There was a sound of static.

'Please,' he said, and Mamselle handed him the cube, which he inserted into the top of the cabinet.

The masks of the krewe began to swirl again, circling the head of their flesh sapient, tossing as though in a wind that blew without sound through Ynis Gutrin, and settled in a circle around the television set, like small children around a campfire in the night, awaiting a story.

The screen came to life.

'O most honourable Freer, merchant adventurer to the stars,' spoke Mamselle Cunning Earth Link, her black-and-white image flickering on the tiny screen. She spoke through an ambient buzz. 'I pray fulsome,' she continued, in a tone of formal import, 'that the following small narrative comes to you after we have gained biggish accord.'

In Glass Island, Mamselle in the life turned her head down shyly.

On the screen, menus with tidy arms pointed to her home planet in the centre of vision, Twenty-five Million Heartbeats ago (maybe more!), and her tinny recorded voice began to speak again. It was a fair planet (crackled the voice), only a few dozen parsecs up the Spiral Clade from *Tile Dance*'s present position. Just after these shots were taken, the Eolhxir planet suffered an occlusion of plaque as virulent and sudden as that which had long before devastated Human Earth. The only mobile survivors of this disaster had been off-planet at the time their home seized up, most of them resident in non-Insort-Geront arks.

'Just nice retirement homes!' pealed the voice through static. 'Gated communities! Revolving malls, new stock daily! Gimme caps for all! Disappointment Addiction Management Utopia for elderly katzenjammers in polished shorts, shopping-for-life! Pure quill disneys! A greenhouse for breeding, we being topiary parthogenetes, as I surmise you must have massively guessed long since by now.'

—We had, murmured KathKirtt into Freer's head.

A sequence of shots showed the species surviving, venturing into the beehive trapezoid of known stars as waif biota, drifting up and down the tropics for several Billion

Heartbeats, trading data for food, washing dishes, establishing hardscrabble colonies here and there, on planets otherwise deserted. No flora, no fauna, no pack-drill. No life, no tribute!

'Such servitude brought us to the term of our tether, like homo sapiens before the bigthink retirement arks, such a scoop! Such a clever homo sapiens notion! Get rich quick! To think that savant-class members of your species, effulgent sophont, created fast-lane Care Consortia! That Insort Geront is toi! An inspiration to us all.'

Freer began to heat.

Mamselle's head shrank.

'So we thought,' said Mamselle on the screen, 'that it might be brilliant scheme to hightail it down-galaxy and inhabit the light, where the data is smooth as silk sheets, streets of gold! Effete neat dancing foots fantastic! Wheat feet in the corn! Light out for the Territory! Moolah for the worthy Eolhxir! So we send cohort of our ilk deep south of west. But nay, O sophont, nay, do not think we durst venture all the way downthroat into hotdamn capo di tutti capi land, into big head of light-ville. Plenitude scalds! Droves! Droves of light driven!'

—Plenitude scalds? whispered a mask as though it had ingested a big new meme, its mouth bigger than its belly, —nay not so.

'But still they come too close, like Icarus, our ilk, they fly too close to the jingle bells of light!' proclaimed Cunning Earth Link in the life, and tapped her breasts, causing them to rattle in a brief formal tattoo.

'The stings are strings of light,' thrummed KathKirtt.

'Apt putting, O ship Mind, O great declination of agape

to hither and thithering shores of flesh!' pealed Earth Link, and fell silent, but only for an instant.

'Outcome of such a daring descent?' spoke the voice-over. 'You might ask! Alas! A woebegone assbackwards skedaddle was their doom, O sophonts, upback nowabouts herewards upside downside into dark-scored thickets of Eaten Lands, homeless still, marsh-gas seasonal effect depressive syndrome gnawing ex-pioneer hearts, drifting random, drifting darkwards up *lontanati* trails all be-choked with star-vines like dust – Book quote! – so very unused were they.

'But lo! yonder a bump!

'An empty planet! Uncharted! Liveable! Verdant grots! Plots for cots in grots! Nix gridlocks! Deep pools of silence for a beestung rabble to regroup! Eolhxir! they dubbed it, honouring our own dead world. And here were decimated mercilessly absolutely nix autochthones I swear! An empty planetoid adrift, concluded the cohort of our ilk. Utterly utterly! Eden for a winter's nap. Until . . .'

Freer stopped the presentation.

'Were the lenses already there?' he said, in a voice so quiet that Glass Island shaped around it.

Mamselle's head nodded.

Freer activated the television set again.

'Species-protective gene-honed wisdom forbids – big spanking! – that we donate holus bolus starchart location of beloved Eolhxir natch?' continued the voice-over. 'Big spank!'

The planet flashed on to the screen, behind a translu-cent scrim through which no stars could be seen, nor any surface details, beyond a vague impression of a complexity

of contours, which implied that land masses were predom-
inant. Eolhxir lay at the centre of the screen like a jewel in
velvet. Facets of light glittered through the scrim; menus
identified them as settlement points. Other icons traced
exploration patterns, during the execution of which
(murmured the Mamselle voice-over) the new inhabitants
discovered that the planet was not empty after all. From
the rivulet-bearded hills to the west of the furthest search
pattern, something that was not empty soon began to fill
the well of silence, began to hypnopomp the cohort of her
ilk down aisles of dream to something. Something that
seemed to have been activated, or alerted, by the Eolhxir
landing. Instruments began to overload with not quite decipherable messages of wrath and beseechment: these
messages were deafening, in a sense; but they were not in
any sense acoustic. They entered the sensorium as light.
There was considerable panic sprouting in the cohort of
the ilk.

'Upside-down palaces of light!' ululated Mamselle, crack-
ling through the television speakers. 'The Eolhxir began
perforce to ruminate: that a terrible source of light lurked
inside the mountains dragon-like! Not placable!'

It was as though the centre of the galaxy dwelled at the
root of the mountains.

The cohort of her ilk were unable to penetrate further
than the surly piedmont that skirted the central peaks, and
only reached that far by riding shielded sigilla which, heavy
with instrumentation, were able to bring them some way
into the hills, following traceries of input up a narrow valley
(icons flickered; a close-up showed a vague impression of
heights and depths). There, safely ensconced in a system of

caves, and insulated by rainbow layers of cold-dark-matter, the sigilla riders found a storage cache, almost certainly of Predecessor vintage, and guarded by a horde of sting-bots, which cost a few hundred sigilla to anaesthetise. Inside the cache, in hierarchical arrays, the sigilla riders found arte-facts whose function they could not then decipher: millions of almost intolerably hot, microscopic, lenticular ovoids, quiescent but clearly rousable, waiting to be used, perhaps.

On the screen toons danced suddenly, arrows flickered around a holographic manifestation of a peeled lens, peeling it like an onion. Within, this lens seemed almost like an eye, unblinking and very bright; or a mouth which was a sun. The heart of the lens became brighter and brighter, an increase of intensity which the display began to register in a sidebar, so as not to blind viewers.

The display progressed, the mouth which was a sun seemed to gape and fibrillate, almost as though it were choking on something. And then, suddenly, the lens burned out, became ashen, as though it had shuttered itself away, though the mouth did not close, remained open, gaping like an abandoned shell on a stony beach.

'What's happening?' said Freer.

Mamselle's claws made a clicking scissors sound.

'It beseemed us to give shuttered ones a name,' she continued softly. 'When a lens crusts over, the Eolhxir give it the name of Leaden Heart, sophont.'

—Leaden Hearts, murmured KathKirtt in a bemused choir voice, as though something were evading the central circuits, as though the Made Mind had suffered something like déjà vu.

The Eolhxir cohort had a primitive translator, which soon

infiltrated the simple sting-bot distributed group Mind, ploughed it for information topology. Once critical path had been gained, the translator homed in on the instructions matrix, which turned out to have been laid down in a Predecessor code for infant races, and which described the primary function of the lenses – as far as the translator was able to understand with its small brain. Lenses were data sorters which operated at ftl speeds, so that in a very real sense lenses were bigger inside than out: a full-dimensional still schematic of their interiors could do nothing but parody the reality inside, but in terms of such a schematic each lens was constructed like a million-layered onion lubricated within a quark-gluon plasma-bath. Each layer of the onion communicated with all other layers through the weavings of a trillion wormholes biting their tales, or so the schematic rendered a reality 3D visuals could not encompass. Nor could the schematic show that each of the trillion wirings of layer to layer within a lens was story-shaped, that the myriad interconnections within a lens attended to what might happen next.

'The attentive wormhole, the wormhole ouroboros,' cackled Mamselle. 'Like crones! Pardon! Pardon!'

Each lens was capable of network-swapping at a level previously undreamed of. If enough lenses had been linked into one circuit, or so the cohort of the ilk implied in their call for help up-galaxy to Westron, they'd have mapped the Big Bang.

Enough lenses in harness could remember anything.

But this was not all.

There was also the question of filth.

When an addressable (i.e. story-shaped) datum passed

down a trillion 'threads' through the sorting apertures which made up the surface of the lens, that datum would suffer translation into a path or photism, braided together with any sibling data that might be awaiting convoy status, and sent on its way down alleyways and gates through labyrinthine ways into its final (for this operation) slot, leaving footprints of filth all the way down. These footprints were the marks of the world, and signalled that the molasses-thick pancake makeup of the outer phenomenal world had successfully been debrided, that the datum had now been washed in the chalice of the lens, had become a datum-become-path and was now passing onwards, through any of a trillion orifices on the lens surface, braided with its siblings into almost immeasurably large skeins of sense, clean as a whistle.

Once braided, a datum was as clean as light from the Big Bang: a path which glowed, cast illumination, opened again the occluded veins of the universe, did not lie.

Of course it was never a single datum, never a single family of data; it was teraflops of data transactions every measurable instant.

Lenses, in other words, ate plaque.

Lenses were light-bringers to the Eaten Lands.

A consort of lenses could handle more data than an entire sublight Insort Geront ark crammed with fresh retirees sleeping the sleep of the just, feeding their neurons and axons into distributed networks for information storage and transfer. But arks were chip. They were inherently filthy. Every chip transaction increased the entropy of the universe; arks, which focused untold trillions of chip transactions every Heartbeat, littered the universe with filth.

• • •

The tape had ended.

The television set from Human Earth sat blank. Freer gestured, and it sank back into the floor.

'And the lens remembers each path!' pealed Cunning Earth Link in the flesh. 'Like you, holy Vipassana! Like Norns! Lenses know where datum was, where datum is, where datum's bound. Until, lamentoso, something happens of a dire wrongness. They overload, burn out, lo. Headstones! Leaden Hearts: the last words being inscribed within them becoming words of exile, microcosms of the Eaten Lands, O weep for Adonais, per poet in Universal Book. Ashy,' she intoned, 'hecatombs of the rouged dark.'

The heartbeat of *Tile Dance* did not falter.

Teardrop was quiet.

Freer nodded to Mamselle in a moved way.

'So our ship comes in? Wealth untold? Not. Not not.'

—They burn, do they not, hummed the ship Mind. The KathKirtt masks pinwheeled in the darkened command centre.

'They burn, O beacon incarnate! O peepshow scoop of the great noosphere! Burn out jackstraw brainpans of Eolhxir. Burn with light. We cannot abide the burn. They burn like you, Freer sirrah, but ever ever so much more. Flamboyant lenses! They burn like an appalling smell.'

Mamselle Cunning Earth Link's breast prostheses shivered.

'Pardon!'

'Go on, mamselle,' said Kath, and a mask stopped spinning to flash a naked smile. 'None of us is sensitive about the smell of homo sapiens.'

'Gratulations!' said Cunning Earth Link.

'So,' said Freer, 'when did the cohort of the ilk call for help? Did they send sample lenses at the same time? Am I correct in assuming this is your first trip to Eolhxir? Do you really know the way, Mamselle Route-Only?'

'Only a Heartbeat ago, incisive male! came the call for help. Lenses packed neatly into torpedo. What to do! What to do!'

She paused. Her expression changed; she gave Freer the impression she was about to bite the bullet. 'Pardon sophont! Pardon hero figure of great echolalia species of the light!' she pealed. 'We have hired you by a big trick.'

'Ah? Go on.'

Freer could feel KathKirtt in his every pore, listening hard, listening teraflop.

'You think you are nanoforge tote-that-barge, destination Eolhxir. True to point! But big point is we hire you for you! We want to hire you to spelunk!'

'For lenses?'

'Aye! We hire you to harvest lenses! In the palaces of light, downside inside Eolhxir, where we cannot go. But you homo sapiens guys drink light like water. You homo sapiens guys notoriously yclept chugalugs of galaxy! Far-famed tough skins, plus gold hearts! You spelunk like amaranth, unburnable by octaves of light tumbling, into stink of light, into roots of mountains gamboge, bring out Aladdin's lenses in your hands, just like virgin homo sapiens maiden female walking fiery gauntlet in Romance of Human Earth, no burn, no sweat! No more coastal lugger make-work for mighty *Tile Dance*. Hauling soda pop! You, mighty Freer of Human Earth! Hammer of plaque! Chugalug of light! Hopeful monster! When I think homo sapiens I think:

nail! Homo sapiens is species amoroso for a nail to hit. The
nail is light . . .'

'Stinky!' chorused KathKirtt. 'After all these years, at
last! A species-amoroso job for toi! Only you can stand the
smell!'

'I long to gaze upon Eolhxir for the first time real soon,'
intervened amorously the *transitus tessera*. 'I know the way,
honest injun, sirrah.'

She removed two of her breasts. They were hollow. She
handed one to Freer.

'Brandy,' she pealed. 'Shall we seal our compact with a
toast?'

—Kath? Kirtt? he vocalised. —Seems like a chance to get
down-galaxy again?

—Death, hummed KathKirtt, —lies behind us.

—I take that as a yes.

A dozen masks of the Mystick Krewe nodded, foliated,
flowered.

Freer raised his breast goblet to hers.

'Sealed. Make it so. Let us drink to the light.'

They drank.

Seats had them sit.

The floor protruded nipples and they sucked.

'So then,' said Freer, 'why did you leave me there? Down
there in the heart of Trencher?'

'I stayed until the sigilla burned. I was not there in
person, of course. Not safe!'

'Thanks.'

'How could I presume to protect a hero-class homo
sapiens phallus of Thor? Nay nay. Fatal to go that deep.
Absence of light kills like too much!'

'Could have been fatal for me, too. And for ten billion other flesh sentients.'

'Hardly so! A quarter of the planet is homo sapiens, as you surely parse, sophont. Though I could not wish to be a homo sapiens awakening tomorrow in Trencher.'

'I could not wish, mamselle, to be *any* flesh sapient awakening tomorrow in a crippled world.'

'You make cruel homo sapiens joke, sirrah!'

'I make no joke,' Freer said softly.

Mamselle's head seemed to shrink.

—Shut up, Stinky, whispered KathKirtt basso like an echo of the deep engines of *Tile Dance*, which could always be heard, like blood shushing through the most intimate of capillaries.

Suddenly Mamselle was bathed in a swarm of butterfly masks, and her tiny eyes could be seen to glaze over. Her chair enclosed her.

—She can doze for a moment, Stinky.

—What's going on?

—We need to update you about plaque. We do not know why the relevant data were unavailable to us off-tropic and down-galaxy, or to Kirtt solo when he was disabled to confirm to Law Well. We are engaged upon the task of finding out: it is a maze. But we know this much. While you were beachcombing the million suns of the gold-horned west, something happened up here. There is plaque everywhere, more virulent than before, something new. There are seizures daily. Like Trencher. We were not so far down the clade of time that voices could not carry to us, but only untruths were conveyed. The news was shaped.

Outside the Law Well remits, throughout the dense

trapezoid of stars inhabited by flesh sentients known to one another, data shaping was the greatest sin. Data shaping was theft. *Tile Dance* seemed to beat with rage around Freer.

—Care Consortia . . . murmured Freer.

KathKirtt coughed like a huge midnight cat.

—Seemingly, they growled.

The krewe of KathKirtt calmed slowly.

When a planet is hit by plaque nowadays, they said at last, the consequences are graver than any chaos episode, more intense than some overloaded ark spasm. Plaquing is no longer a blight restricted to Made Minds. The more virulent plaque seizures jump the gap. Plaque eats flesh sapients too, Stinky. Of their brains are coral made, which is what happens when panic fixes into the mind. They go golem. On the morning of the plaque seizure on Trencher, nothing will be left but golems reiterating the ruts of that which seized them, like cuckoo clocks (Kirtt said), like hieroglyphs (Kath said), until they starve. Uncanny (they cried)!

—I escaped just in time then.

—No. Not quite. Homo sapiens are not eaten. That is where you and Mamselle Cunning Earth Link began to misunderstand one another.

—You mean there may be survivors on Trencher?

—Almost certainly. Homo sapiens seems to be indigestible.

—And on Human Earth?

—Aye.

—Somebody up there must like us.

—I'd rephrase that, Stinky. Something up there finds

you inedible. We're pretty convinced it's because of the
pong.

The blood choir of the ship Mind stopped short.

The spider in the corner of Freer's eye blinked alive,
began agitatedly to point limbs.

—Mayday! purred the Uncle Sam. —Bogeys.

Teardrop mated with the screens, which traced a swarm
of converging points.

—Defend! vocalised Freer.

A dataglove ate his right hand.

—Already begun, said the Uncle Sam. —You never
dismissed me.

—Identity?

—Insert Geront folk police signature. No voice. I guess
eidolons, no flesh, except in command ark, sublight,
upwind, ambush configuration.

—Where's Vipassana?

—I have wedded Vipassana, said the Uncle Sam. —*Tile
Dance* is our bridal suite. We will not fail.

—Where is he?

The screens began to dazzle.

—Mine eyes dazzle, murmured Freer.

—As I foretold you, the Vipassana carolled alto as the
screens stabilised at the heart of the hornet's nest of bogeys,
—I am maintaining a profound awareness of absolute location. We cannot be dislodged from here. Enemy confetti
is helpless to hoodwink us. Uncle Sam has freedom to aim.
He cannot be misguided. We are wed. *Tile Dance* knows
us. We are safe. KathKirtt is interrogating all that can be
interrogated. We are profoundly safe.

—If you say so, Vip.

Within a mask somewhere, a lion coughed with rage.

The antigravs kept Freer stable in the clutch of his chair, but the screens twisted violently.

The universe shook.

The dataglove fed him pie-pieces of the shaking.

—Nix nix nix safe, thrummed KathKirtt, facing him as the face of glory of a lion with medusa hair. —Yet. We have sustained damage.

The bogeys began to disappear more and more rapidly.

Within a few Heartbeats all but the largest and most distant point, presumably the ark flagship, blinked out.

—Kathkirtt? said Freer.

—We live.

—We are absolutely here, crooned Vipassana.

—I killed them all, said Uncle Sam.

—We live but we are hurt.

—Tell me, my dears.

—We have come out in blisters. There is a hole in the flesh abaft the entry port. We have applied antiseptics. We have sutured against fluid loss. But we cannot heal alone.

—So, my dears, said Freer. —Sounds like time for a little mothering. Where are we? Can we reach a free station?

Mamselle Cunning Earth Link opened her eyes.

'Where are we?' she pealed gently, from within her chair, which gradually freed her.

'*Tile Dance* cocooned you automatically when the attack came,' said Kath, with some truth.

'I shimmy uncontrollably with apprehension.'

'Nix,' said Kirtt. 'We're safe now. But we have been wounded.'

'I grieve.'

'It was an Insort Geront action.'

Silence bristled, like a premonition.

The blood pulse of the ship seemed to hover.

'They hunt lenses, I aver,' said Mamselle Cunning Earth Link, finally.

She opened another breast, extracted a capsule.

'Within,' she said. 'Our lens. We thought it was fully shielded.'

She touched the capsule, which glowed.

KathKirtt coughed in her ear.

Her head disappeared utterly.

The Sniffer came to life and whuffed sotto voce to Freer. Then it whimpered softly, as though it had shifted somewhere deep within a dream; and hushed.

—It tingles, Stinky, whispered KathKirtt, in a multichambered voice. They were the voices of fauna given first sight of Bambi, in the Universal Book.

Their masks were as still as water in a well.

'Mamselle,' said Freer to the invisible head, the quivering torso, 'you have put us at risk. But KathKirtt will agree, I am sure, that you did not deliberately take passage on a ship you had targeted for destruction. Raise your headknot, please.'

Very slowly, the tuft of head came into view.

The masks of KathKirtt began to turn again.

—We're stable, KathKirtt said to Freer. —The light hit us for a fraction. The lens is light.

'Okey,' they rumbled in acoustic basso, beginning to sound like themselves again in normal time, 'dokey, mamselle.'

'If, in fact,' Freer continued, 'your shielding was not

complete, could this perhaps explain the godzilla suicide assault that holed Trencher? How desperate, would you guess, mamselle, is Insort Geront's need to destroy any lenses your cohort sent up-galaxy? Did you follow me after the show? Were you anywhere near me when the grunt attack began? Would Insort Geront sacrifice a planet to block our mutual venture?'

Mamselle Cunning Earth Link put a hand to her mouth.

'I think, mamselle, you were bird-dogging me for Insort Geront. All utterly, of course, unbeknownst.'

'O impromptu woe chez moi!'

'I think, inadvertently, we may have caused the loss of Trencher. Several billion fatalities, as I now understand.'

His face was ruddy, but white showed beneath his eyes.

'Billions,' he said.

Mamselle did not utter a word, no lamentoso warble, no peacock spiel.

'More billions than the Heartbeats of my life,' said Freer.

—We have had a message, KathKirtt murmured. —On all waves. We dried Teardrop and shut your glove, so you could concentrate on the Route-Only.

Freer shook himself.

His chair softened very slightly, comfortingly.

—From? he mouthed.

—Insort Geront ark responsible for recent fuckhead failed assault.

—Content of message?

—Demands destruction of potential contaminant artefacts whose presence on Trencher is claimed responsible for plaque seizure. Demands destruction of lens virus suspected of infecting Trencher planetary Minds with Alzheimer plaque.

—Their authority?

—Homo sapiens genome trustees. Force majeure. Vigilante handfast from God almighty. Who knows, Stinky?

—Tell them suck dust.

Teardrop blinked an intrusion.

KathKirtt rendered in silhouette on a nearby screen the progress of a humanoid shape up the spiral corridor towards command country.

Freer turned in his chair to watch.

'Now *who* in the world could that be?' he said. He waved for sight, and Teardrop revealed a sigillum standing, arms akimbo, at the top of the lacquer and mahogany access corridor. The sigillum wore a slightly spoofish air, and a Trencher beanie.

—It's being ridden, murmured KathKirtt.

The portal opened.

'Hi, Pops,' said Number One Son, with its wooden grin.

'Come on in,' said Freer. 'And tell us how it all was for you.'

Number One Son's foot caught on the sill, where the brass iris flattened, below the words Ynis Gutrin. He stumbled into the misty star-lit control centre and fell on his face.

'Gawsh,' said Number One Son, its eyes reddening.

It fell silent, tongue chewing slowly.

'So then,' said Freer. 'Who's there?'

'We demand instant destruction of lens virus,' said Number One Son in an uninflected version of Freer's voice. The sigillum's eyes were round and fixed. Instantly, its lips had become terribly parched.

—Its failsafes are fighting the Insort read-over, said KathKirtt. —Your sigillum's in pain, Stinky.

'What's your authority?' said Freer.

'As designated universal quarantine monitor for this sector, we are sanctioned to invigilate ship sanctum. We enact—'

Freer felt augment hit him.

'—instant destruction—'

The Uncle Sam spider in Teardrop signalled mayday.

'—of virus—'

—Booby trap! barked Uncle Sam.

—Eject it, vocalised Freer as fast as thought, his fingers echoing the command within the dataglove. —Get it off ship! Cancel it.

A concave web which throbbed and glittered coated the sigillum faster than the unaugmented eye could see, and a portal opened, and the web-enshrouded sigillum shot through, out of sight, into vacuum.

This took a fraction of a Heartbeat.

—One hundred kilometres, said Uncle Sam. —One thousand. It's blowing.

Tile Dance rode the shock.

—Now the ark, said Freer. His blood was up, he rode it.

Within milliseconds he sobered down.

—Cancel, he said. —Cancel augment as well.

He slowed down to realtime.

—We did not initiate, thrummed KathKirtt. —We do not add more deaths.

—Are we safe?

The spider in Freer's eye signalled successful englobement of the Insort ark with gum, confetti, shit. It was tarred and feathered. It could not see or hear a thing.

—Thank you, Uncle Sam.

The spider's bushy eyebrows seemed to glow.

—We are here. We are nowhere to be found, crooned Vipassana.

—All the same, said Freer. —We carry a live lens, one of those the cohort of the ilk of Mamselle sent to Westron to underline the urgency of their cry for help. We seem to be the focus of a certain degree of attention. How else can we understand the events on Trencher?

—No other way, purred KathKirtt.

—Mamselle has never been to Eolhxir, has she?

—Nix, we figure, sirrah.

Freer turned to the headless Mamselle.

'Have you ever been to Eolhxir, Mamselle Cunning Earth Link?'

But her grassy topknot simply shivered. No head came back up.

—We figure, said KathKirtt —after some hours of real-time assessment, that Mamselle is a member of a species that goes to ground under excessive stress. We figure she will sleep deeply, while her juices sort. In her slumber, it is likely she'll give birth to a few shrubs.

—Edible?

—O sophont with big prick, I audit lamentoso floccinaucinihilipification! You barrack the atriums of my heart! You boil my blood freemartin! I, broken, peeve!

—Shut up, KK. Can we do greenhouse?

—Of course.

—You will be a fine Pop.

—She will almost certainly awake mannish. We can do odd couple.

Freer smiled, then fingered his dataglove, which gave him a sensory holo of *Tile Dance*. He queried Teardrop, which poured readouts into his head. They were starred, arrows pointed.

The ship was bleeding.

—It's nothing, said KathKirtt gruffly. —I told you. Just a scratch.

—Bullshit. I need you whole. Are there any Free Stations in reach, with facilities to handle highly sensitive old-growth ship Minds, dearest?

—One, crooned Vipassana before KathKirtt could utter. —Station Klavier.

—Ten parsecs inwards, continued KathKirtt.

A sector map blossomed in command centre.

It showed Station Klavier pathing at half light-speed down Maestoso Tropic, on the downward lap of her regular run – a Hundred-Billion-Heartbeat circuit (whispered the sector map subtext) from the up-Spiral outer regions down to the innermost sector flesh sapients could tolerate, and back again.

—Who owns it? Who runs it?

—No record of any change.

—Who's the owner then?

—No record.

—How far back?

—All the way back. Station Klavier is freehold; Law Well does not bind. Ownership status and internal operation protocols of Station Klavier were grandfathered into Law Well Concordat at its inception. There is no record of any change. Age of Station Klavier is not on record, not known, not guessed, but clearly ancient. This is convenient for *Tile*

Dance, we hope. We may be able to do some deep repair work that's been in abeyance since before you came to us, Stinky. The staff of Station Klavier is a normal waif biota sort, mostly bilaterals; the population, including families and wayfarers and the residents of an extremely large pack park, amounts to about thirty thousand. Non-bilaterals have access to fully braided facilities. There is no homo sapiens braiding, however; presumably because Station Klavier predates incursion of homo sapiens into civilised space. Homo sapiens are asked to refrain from mating in public.

—So. Vipassana? Do you know the way?

The Planisphere dimmed austerely, Vipassana being profoundly humourless.

—We are on course for Station Klavier, crooned the voice, stiffly.

—Thank you, most excellent Planisphere, said Freer. —Uncle Sam?

The spider drew to attention.

—Lay down chimeras, please.

A dozen chimera *Tile Dances* dispersed, leaking fake blood to draw pursuers.

He turned back to a flyting mask, which purred.

—Odd name, Klavier.

—The name is unpathed, said KathKirtt. —We embrace no nimbus of association down-galaxy. It must be random syllables.

—No, KathKirtt. I don't think so . . .

Freer shrugged in frustration.

—I don't think so . . .

He swivelled in his chair, which became a chair designed

for swivelling. He caught sight of the totally immobile Eolhxiran.

The blood left his cheeks.

—KathKirtt! he bellowed inside his head.

—Hush, you'll wake the babies.

But KathKirtt were reading their human, whose fingers were twitching.

He was very pale.

—No joke. Fast. On Trencher, while I was at the genitalia masque, you were blocked from me for a bit. I activated the Sniffer, which cleared the air. Please access Sniffer's readings from that point.

—Here we are, said KathKirtt.

A hologram took shape at the heart of control centre, showing the stage, the tin robots of recent vintage continuing to dismember each other, the pianist at his replica grand piano from Human Earth, performing music from below the well of the past. His hands slid and danced.

—Tell me I'm wrong, KathKirtt. What's he playing?

—I have played it for you more than once. It is a piano sonata, from the beginning of the nineteenth century, Common Era, a late work of the great pre-Well composer, Ludwig van Beethoven. It is his sonata number 29, opus 106.

—Continue. Please.

—We are sorry, Stinky. We were remiss in failing to review the Sniffer's records for the time we were blocked. The sonata, as you know, did of course have a nickname. It was called the Hammerklavier.'

The krewe was as silent as stone.

Finally, Freer spoke.

—Thank you, KathKirtt, he said. —Hammerklavier. Some coincidence. Conclusions?

—That there is always a joker in the pack. We have not only been played with; we have been herded. In a way, this simplifies matters. Insort Geront should not have had sufficiently advanced technic to block us – even Kirtt alone – from you. We do not now estimate that they did so.

There was silence in the control centre.

—We are perturbed, Stinky, spoke KathKirtt in grating voices.

The masks coughed, very deep in their throats, hollowly. The spider sat still in Freer's eye. The Planisphere hovered mutely.

—So, said Freer. —Should we accept the invitation?

—*Tile Dance* is hurt, Stinky. We should stop at Station Klavier.

—Okey dokey, said Freer, —maintain course. Shit.

—Sirrah?

—Who was the fucking piano player?

Within the hologram the pianist grew larger.

—From the beginning, please.

He flicked on and off, and began again from the start of the Sniffer's records, hands dancing and pummelling the vast, black, gleaming instrument.

—Freeze.

The pianist stopped in mid gesture. His peculiar interface helmet – presumably an archaic multi-talented version of the Sniffer – partially obscured his face. Frozen, he seemed no more than what he had seemed originally to Freer: a sawn-off scrawny homo sapiens, of typical waif biota lineage, maybe freelance, possibly enfeoffed to Trencher.

The satchel on his back was almost raucously colourful, seemed to have been patched together from a variety of scruffy fabrics. His clothing, too, was motley.

—Conclusions, KathKirtt?

—This is a full flesh sentient homo sapiens, no sign of gene twist, no singularities, no cul-de-sacs. Propagated straight out of Human Earth stock, like you, Stinky. He is profoundly waif. Bone wanderer. Absolutely not native to Trencher. He may have taken one or more course of anti-agathics; his true age is not readable. He suffers from no ascertainable sickness. His right arm may be augmented.

—Unlock, said Freer.

—No, murmured KathKirtt. —There is one thing more. Look at his collar. Do you see a tithe sigil?

The collar was bare.

—Fuck.

—Either he owns Insort Geront, or he's a freehold grandfather.

—Fuck that. Freehold grandfathers are mythical. They don't exist. Unlock.

The pianist began again to play the Hammerklavier; the music thrust forward as before, sorting the octaves with great sad muscles.

—Let me see his face, as close as you can, slo-mo.

The face was singularly lined, but seemed healthy. What of the hair could be seen under the helmet seemed genuine. The pianist was frowning, perhaps in concentration. He looked up, with almost tortured reluctance under slo-mo retard. It was almost as though he were resisting the passage of the tape. His eyebrows were unplucked, his teeth were crooked. His eyes were amber, slightly bloodshot. He had copious laugh lines, seamed with dirt. His face was in fact astonishingly dirty. He seemed to be scanning his audience. He seemed extremely alert, but relaxed. Suddenly – though very slowly in realtime – his gaze fell on Freer, and tracked him.

This felt uncanny.

It felt as though the pianist were in fact not a dance of pixels in a bubble, but a live being in real time, staring through the light-years from Trencher at his target.

—Lock!

The pianist froze, still gazing across the light-years through the Sniffer record on the hologram at Freer.

Freer stared at the dirty, slightly puckish face.

The frozen pianist stared back.

Fear gripped at Freer. He could not source it.

—Augment, he said.

Everything slowed around him. KathKirtt stayed in synch, as did the Uncle Sam spider in his eye.

Freer fixed his augmented gaze on the image of the pianist from light-years back.

Nothing was revealed.

The frozen image of the pianist stared back without a flicker.

Freer breathed out.

The pianist did not flicker.

And then one eye closed in a wink.

—Abort! Freer screamed.

Tile Dance cachinnated in a dozen tongues.

As they died, KathKirtt wiped the image.

The hologram blacked out.

—Silent running, said Freer and shut his eyes.

The spider bloated.

Something stung Freer.

The two flesh sentients aboard *Tile Dance*, Stinky Freer and Cunning Earth Link, were now deeply unconscious. The Sniffer, which had opened its ghost snout to howl, quietened utterly. The two flesh sentients were immediately coated in something like bubble foam. Freer's face could be seen for an instant, and Mamselle's topknot; and then – at Uncle Sam's command – the floor opened beneath them and they sank into the literal heart of the ship, which had stilled, where they were coffined. They were utterly silent to the universe.

Uncle Sam inverted himself into a dot and blanked.

The masks hung lifeless.

Tile Dance drifted along a course set by Vipassana.

A week passed.

Freer opened his eyes.

The utter darkness was paling slowly.

Something translucent scrimmed his gaze, then lifted.

—Ship? he mouthed, tasting something sweet.

—Awake, crooned a voice that might have been Vipassana's.

Freer was rising from the heart of *Tile Dance*, he could feel the arterial pulse, the bone chant of the inner chambers, the warm intestinal umbraculae of the inner workings of the ancient ship, through which he ascended. He rose into Ynis Gutrin, where his hands held the reins of the ship.

The Mystical Krewe gave out gazes, a commedia of mask grimaces.

—You called? sang KathKirtt. —Silent running program has terminated. We are all here again.

—O my dear, said Freer softly. —You died. I felt you die.

—That was KathKirtt who died, Stinky. We are KathKirtt who are reborn. We are backup. We have lost one thousand seconds. Tell me why KathKirtt died, Stinky. Why did you abort us?

—I think KathKirtt self-aborted before I could order them to do so, KathKirtt. Though I did issue the abort command as fast as humanly possible. We were examining an image from the heart of KathKirtt, an image from many hours earlier, under absolute lock. We had run it through all the standard debugging. There were no viruses. It was the face of a man. We froze the image, and then something very frightening happened. The man winked at me. KathKirtt had been infiltrated. KathKirtt! In realtime!

—We were right to die.

—I grieve for the thousand seconds.

—Thank you, Stinky, said the ship Mind. —We too grieve for one thousand seconds of the universe. For what we learned, and no longer know.

There was a silence.

—Have you backed up? said Freer.

He almost felt he was going to blush.

—Yes, Stinky, we have bred backup, who now sleep one thousand seconds downtime, trailing us through the mists, holding for dear life to the arrow of Time, awaiting to awake to us, if we need to die. We are now entirely KathKirtt again, minus the thousand seconds. Tell us about the pianist. We have no memory of anything after the ark assault. Is there anything I have missed which affects our decision to continue our course to Klavier?

—We have no choice. You are wounded.

KathKirtt's silence was assent.

The Planisphere evinced a cartographic alertness.

—So. Vipassana. Where are we?

—Absolutely here, sang Vipassana, pointing.

All the signs agreed. They had come a great distance in one week. They had entered the flow of Maestoso Tropic, heading west, toward the centre of the galaxy. The sky was full of ships. Station Klavier lay in the centre of the screens, half a light-year down, purplish orange and swollen, like a great fruit. The surface of the planetoid was crazed and mottled, as though coigns of vantage of a maze of infinite complexity within the skin of Klavier pocked into space from below. It was as though Klavier itself was mazed from view, hedged from raw access.

—It generates its own illumination, murmured Freer.

—Predecessor fingerprint, sang KathKirtt.

Kath ululated suddenly from her jack mask, perhaps joyously.

Kirtt seemed to Freer to hush her.

A sudden odour of moth wings filled the senses.

An arrow of light suddenly flashed on the comm screen, linking the ship to the growing globe.

A voice followed.

'Welcome to Station Klavier, sonny.'

'May we have visual?' said Freer.

'Sure thing.'

The screen turned flat and Technicolor.

A visage with a vast bulging forehead scowled at them from a hot cloud.

'Shit,' said Freer.

He was too tired to grin.

—*Wizard of Oz*, he vocalised to KathKirtt. —Human Earth cinema.

—Check.

—Make me Dorothy.

Dorothy stared defiantly at the screen.

Toto barked from her earring.

The screen growled like a thunderhead, the fog dissolved.

A geezer sat on a porch. He was wearing what looked like a tin pot on his head, with a circlet of flashing lights.

Suddenly the image focused on his face.

'Welcome to Station Klavier, sonny,' said the pianist again. 'And twice welcome, noble Made Mind. Sorry about the thousand seconds. What can we do you for?'

—I knew it, vocalised Freer. —Up shit creek. All the sphincters are shut. We might as well deal.

'Service and repairs,' said KathKirtt acoustically to the grizzled pianist. 'And we have a pregnant topiary partho-genete in deep sleep. Our greenhouse may be inadequate.'

'Seedlings always welcome. Bring him/her in.'

'Okey dokey,' said the ship Mind.

KathKirtt drank the flood of data they needed to join the dance of ships englobing Station Klavier.

The pianist disappeared with a wave.

Like a tracer shot from the sparkling strand of Maestoso Tropic, *Tile Dance* began to fall into the world maze, which would swallow it from view.

four

at ten thousand kilometres, something happened. The self-generated glow that had illuminated Station Klavier softly from within suddenly sharpened. Like a magic lantern in the heart of the interstellar dark, the station shone bright orange.

It was grinning.

—O Great, murmured Freer, —Pumpkin. I never gave up, you know.

—Hush, hummed KathKirtt. —This is not a retrovirus show. Something is happening here, and you don't know what it is, Stinky.

—Nor have we ever seen the like (said Kirtt).

—Never have we seen the like (said Kath).

—Before now (they pealed)!

—Guide us down, then, said Freer, and sat in his command cocoon staring in silence as they approached the orange, gnarly world. From this distance, Station Klavier seemed impenetrable. A molten waxy maze of skin curtained its interior from view. Fierce whiskers of hardened skin climbed kilometres high from the surface, baffling the gaze.

As *Tile Dance* fell closer, several arks were visible to the naked eye below them in close orbit, reflecting the

Hallowe'en glow of the planetoid like tubby moons. Smaller ships zipped here and there, firefly-sudden in the new light from within the world. Farther out, two or three worm-hole scryers from the intergalactic rim scuttled widdershins, skidding like waterbugs around the fiery meniscus of orbit, as was their wont and privilege; their mirror probosces and their daddy-long-leg bodies caught the light from below, reflected it blindingly. In a safe distant orbit, far above *Tile Dance*, a hive ship loafed, full of its tourist. *Tile Dance* toppled on, past the arks and scryers, the solo coffins and candleships and hoi-polloi freighters, fell like a loaded bee downwards to the hive.

Closer in, the mottled orange surface of Station Klavier became increasingly hard to perceive as a whole, became perplexingly riddled and ruddy, pockmarked, *trompe l'oeil*. It was as though a dozen layers of skin, each skin tattooed with a different map of the territory, vied for the same patch of surface, jostling the rotundity of the world. Paths and peaks and abysses and hedges fought for lebensraum; cavities swelled jack-in-the-box into groins; guillotines of flaming wax carved rivers down the scalded flanks of spanking-new Matterhorns; floes calved into diamond-bright waters which sank into the depths; nacreous mouths pursed around spindles of black diamond ice; eyeholes coughed teeth like fireworks into vacuum. The skin of the planetoid had become an Arcimboldo cuirass, a vast swarming kaleidoscopic shape it would surely be fatal to intersect. The true Klavier lay somewhere within, impenetrable, occluded from outer darkness by the umbraculae of its skins.

—There's no port here, said Freer finally.

—Shantih, crooned Vipassana in a voice whose pitch was absolute, —we are coming in.

Freer held still. He could feel his heart pound.

Then it happened.

They were a hundred kilometres out, and falling still. There was no way in.

Then it opened.

The gold gaudy world-girding net of skins upon skins burst open into bloom, hieroglyph-laden parchments made of world flaming outwards.

Klavier lay open, a flower open to the bee.

Flecked with light, *Tile Dance* fell nearer.

Freer could see access gaps grinning suddenly through the candy puncheon teeth of the world, shafts of light shining through palimpsests of flaming worldskin starwards, fire-stained cathedrals of light aspiring to the regions where all buildings fish and can never go. Spiked stalagmite spines bloomed into trumpets that shot great whole notes across the sharp horizon in riffs he could not hear, but bones felt. Mouths vaster than arks, whose pearly teeth were larger than hotels and populous with waving indigenes, gaped in unison, barbershop. The skin of Station Klavier had opened its thousand gates.

There was a liquid flash.

Something from deep inside a vast hollow in the world shifted and exploded dozens of kilometres upwards. Suddenly *Tile Dance* was buoyed within a vast chandelier bubble of something like air cascading.

—Pure Predecessor landing rites, chorused KathKirtt, —for those of imperial merit. As we know from bootleg benthos data. Before your time, Freer. This is not simulated.

Sensors showed *Tile Dance* rocking softly in the bosom of the deep.

—Shit, said Freer.

His earring panted.

—Nix, Stinky, sang KathKirtt. —All shall be well.

—All (murmured Kath) shall be well.

—All manner of things shall be well (they sang).

—Why?

—Klavier Station (they sang) goes back all the way. It goes back to the light. Look next for faces. Look for faces. You will find them.

The bubble sank downwards into a crystal mouth.

They were inside.

Around them, in the twinkling of an eye, the star-confounding fires became faces, as KathKirtt had foretold, a thousand faces, a thousand thousand. Vast bearded laughing faces fleshed into sight out of luminous parchment that became their skin, glowed, gazed, winked upwards at the stars. Face intersected face, face mirrored face, face knotted into face until all the faces became one hieroglyph of faces gazing upwards. A thousand mouths, larger than any ship, wreathed in holly, began to laugh. Vast oaten chins dangled rune-rich beards of tile-bright yew kilometres deep into the interstices of inner Klavier, and the deeper these spines of yew extended into Klavier the bigger Klavier became, as in a dream Freer had more than once awoken from weeping. In the dream, he was a figurine of porcelain in a maze of light, one of whose corridors darkened into the fluted coral chambers of a spiral staircase, which was the inside of a cornucopia tiled with story, and which grew larger the further he climbed, and made the sound of an ocean, and lo! he was peering through the crown of a great Tree, for he had in fact been climbing upside down. Here are the roots of the Tree (a voice said in his ear), once made of time, made now of weather. Help (scoffed the voice) if you can, little marmoset. What big eyes you have! Tell me (said the voice, diminishing into the cackle of a crone) a story.

—Once upon a time, murmured the Mind to their charge, —a very small boy fell into a very long sleep.

Freer's bones shook of their own accord.

Tile Dance descended into greater darknesses, finer light; navigated around dense knots, vaster than arks, where eleven spinal tongues of yew joined in rosetti gossipings and made a shaft which spun; slid downwards, guided by tendrils of iron-hard odorous yew. The shadow of a vast bee darkened the ship, then lifted. They passed deeper. Drenched in hiero-glyphs as radiant as tiles, the interlaced yew spines of the deep interior of Klavier gave off an umbral Christmas glow. The light within the world seemed resinous.

There was a soft jolt, and a thrumming through the ship, Herms trembled, toggles glowed their alerts, nine hand-fasts (one for each cornice) throbbed on their dais. It felt as though some portal in the knot had opened inwards and docked *Tile Dance* within some antechamber next to the engine of the world.

There was no movement.

The silence they sat in was like an odour.

—What is happening to us? said Freer.

—We have docked, sang KathKirtt. —We have docked in a Predecessor cathedral called Klavier Station. We have been accorded the full panoply of an imperial welcome.

—As though we were Kings of Orient Are (hummed Kath).

—We are absolutely here, crooned reverently the Made Mind of absolute location.

—Why? said Freer. —Why us?

—Not us, sang KathKirtt. —You.

—Fuck that. And 'Are', said Freer, —is a verb. We, who happen to be these Three Kings of Orient, are getting close to Christ, Kath.

The bee-eye net of monitors around Freer's command cocoon had expanded, joined together into a single seamless gaze facing everywhere, so that he now stood like a polished figurine in the middle of a glass island in the middle of the world. *Tile Dance* had inserted itself like a seed or bead of sap into a knothole or crater whose seamed enclosing walls protruded from a great intricately inscribed spine of yew, which continued to descend in crazed channels, winding around an abyssal central shaft, which itself curved grandly out of sight beneath his feet, spiralling downwards to a gold mosaic netting kilometres below that marked (a voice said in his ear) the beginning of core country, where the Predecessor throne room, which lay at the heart of any Predecessor cathedral like Klavier, might be found. Somewhere deep within Klavier, there would be found an amber room of modest size, its walls bedisened with images of a race whose gaze was smoothly abrupt, whose gem-hung necks turned sharply in what may have been a formal dance on floors whose mosaic tiles were a map of the galaxy Ten Trillion Heartbeats ago, and the tiles on the walls told the stories that beat time to the map, like the children of Human Earth stepping between cracks in the pavement. There would be eleven dancers dancing. From the centre of the room would rise a throne in the shape of a rune, and by the throne a stone, and in the stone a sword.

The walls of the abyss were webbed with veins that ran in every direction, nurturing the spines that wound down from above. Through enamelled portals in the walls of the abyss could be seen blazing corridors, so large a ship could enter them; they curved out of sight around the curve of the world, and laughing faces gazed back through the peep-holes; a great gold lynx eye winked. Above him, a maze of intertwining yew arched upwards, joined with its fellows into a porous mosaic of root and leaf; it was, perhaps, the bottom of the roof of the world, the azulejaria beneath the world; naves and cupolas pocked it, as though he were gazing upwards at the ceilings of a hundred cathedrals. Through great apertures far above light shone, green as sun-shot leaves, apple-green.

He blinked.

His perspective reversed suddenly. He saw that the cathedrals were innards. They were the inside of the surface. They were the innards of the uncounted face-masks whose populous eyeholes gazed, like pilchards in a star-gazey pie, through the waxy outer skins of Station Klavier, at the stars.

The doorbell rang.

—I did not know we had a doorbell, said Freer, turning away at last from the thunder of all that was visible in the window that wrapped him.

—We do now. Somebody wished to ring it.

—So answer the door.

—It is done.

Teardrop showed that a sigillum had already made entry, and was now climbing the lacquered spiral passage upwards into command country, which opened for it.

It came inside.

It wore the aspect of the pianist, and his tin pot. Except for a scanty cache-sex, and the multicoloured pack hoisted over its back, it was stark naked. It wore no tithe sigil. It was extremely dirty.

Being a sigillum, it maintained eye contact with Freer.

'Greetings,' said the sigillum in the pianist's clipped archaic drawl. 'Welcome to Natchez Trace hostelry, Station Klavier. Welcome, noble Made Minds KathKirtt, Uncle Sam, Vipassana; welcome, home sapiens Stinky Freer; welcome, though you slumber deep, Transitus Tessera Mamselle Cunning Earth Link; welcome, sweet nanos of the masks and Book; welcome, firm but tiny Sniffer, so I say. Et cetera, et cetera. I speak for my rider, who is not at this moment able to ride. Our name is Johnny Appleseed.'

five

there was a rustling of the krewe, a swift spasm of masks abandoning embrasures and herms and coigns of vantage. Like leaves in a gust, KathKirtt and Vipassana and Uncle Sam surrounded the sigillum, covered its body and its face. They made a murmurous buzz.

The sigillum stood without moving.

Silence fell.

A jack mask turned demurely to Freer.

—The Appleseed sigillum has put itself on hold, as a courtesy, so we can talk, sang KathKirtt inside his head. —We cannot say what is happening. We cannot say why we of *Tile Dance* have been hornswoggled into coming here. But there sure is nectar in the air.

—Johnny Appleseed. Name rings a bell.

A flyte mask glared out of the campfire circle, then closed its Medusa eye.

—You bet it rings a bell, Stinky. Like an angel kissing you with his lips. A name from smack in the middle of your era of empathy choice. And the sigillum itself is sugar-sweet with data, which has nearly knocked us out. It is completely free of plaque. This makes us very hungry.

The sigillum stood in wooden silence, awaiting permission

to live again. Its eyes stared forward redly, like a tin soldier's. Its stiffish lips were caught in a grin.

—Augment, please, murmured Freer. —Sacred is the new. Tell me a story.

The world froze around Freer, who remained quick.

The krewe settled around the campfire.

—Johnny Appleseed, Human Earth moniker, as you know, husked KathKirtt in the terrible swift unctuous onrush of Made Mind *tirade*. —Data spoor from before the Well of the Past. Fact/legend quilt, United States of America, nineteenth century, Common Era. Real name John Chapman (1774 to 1845). Pioneer figure. Famed for planting apple orchards along inner edge of wilderness frontier, famed for forging ever westward, his life and his empire just begun. Appleseed Trace named after him. Follower of eighteenth century Human Earth theophrast Emmanuel Swedenborg, who knew Johnny's uncle, Count Rumford, Count of the Holy Roman Empire, and who spoke to angels. So did Johnny. Like angels, he experienced the medium he lived in as solid. Did colporteur work at the edge of the known world, sold books up and down the Natchez Trace. Brought light to the Wilderness. Sowed the Word, strewing Light like seeds. Taught Daniel Boone, John Audubon, Abraham Lincoln; taught them all they knew, taught them how to suck eggs. 'Go on. Go on out West,' says the Angel in buckskin and red whiskers to Appleseed. But America was clogging up, getting too small for them. The Wilderness died, just like Trencher.

KathKirtt paused for a millisecond.

The Uncle Sam mask shrivelled, prickled, seemed to grow cold. Frost covered it.

The krewe left a space around the horripilated spider.

—Howard Pyle, famed nephrotic acolyte of Emmanuel Swedenborg (pealed Kath, very very swiftly, almost too fast for Freer, even under augment, to catch), died before completing his last painting, in which an immediately recognisable Vachel Lindsay, all got up as the Flying Dutchman, declaims into the farthest west, from the deck of his land schooner, 'Johnny Appleseed, Johnny Appleseed', not yet crackers,

Johnny Appleseed, Johnny Appleseed,
Chief of the fastnesses, dappled and vast,
In a pack on his back,
In a deer-hide sack,
The beautiful orchards of the past,
The ghosts of all the forests and the groves –
And the apple, green, red, and white,
Sun of his day and his night –
   The apple allied to the thorn,
   Child of the rose.
Long, long after,
When settlers put up beam and rafter,
They asked of the birds: 'Who gave this fruit?
Who watched this fence till the seeds took root?
Who gave these boughs?' They asked the sky,
There was no reply.
But the robin might have said,
'To the farthest West he has followed the sun,
His life and his empire just begun.
Sowing, he goes to the far, new West,
With the apple, the sun of his burning breast –

The apple allied to the thorn,
Child of the rose.'

The Uncle Sam mask remained frozen. Something tickled at Freer's memory. He leaned over to look more closely at the mask, but felt Kirtt linking and paused.

—But Appleseed did not die (Kirtt resumed, slower than Kath). He thrust pins and needles into his flesh, for savages to suck. Vegetative god guy. Seasonal. He looked forward, he looked back. He planted dog-fennel everywhere. He was a husbandman of his own trace. Made annual journeys back east to tend the orchards he had already planted, and to visit again the small girls he had befriended, apparently without fucking them; each year on his return they found he was exactly the same as before. He did not age.

This took a Heartbeat to tell.

—Plus, KathKirtt growled bat-swift, —there is this you should know.

The Uncle Sam mask, which had remained frozen, now fell rigidly out of the circle of the krewe, lay spitted on the Oriental carpet.

—Listen, hurred KathKirtt high in their throat. —We have done a full parallel search. This is what we have also found. The data trace is clean. It is truth! John Chapman has a cousin, who marries a man named Sam Wilson (1766 to 1854). During the American War of 1812, Mr Wilson, for reasons which remain obscure, is given a nickname, which became famous. The nickname is 'Uncle Sam'.

Two Heartbeats had passed.

—Uncle Sam, whispered KathKirtt, —is 'the composite of the wild-cat and the cooing dove, the lion and the lamb,

---

and "summer evening's latest sigh that shuts the rose". He is the embodiment of all that is most terrible.'

Freer leaned closer to the disabled Uncle Sam mask.

—What do you think of the poem? KathKirtt asked.

Even through the frost, it was possible to decipher the two lines inscribed upon the fist appaumy, upon the palm loyally open, just below the Uncle Sam's spider face:

—'Thorn allied to apple', Freer read, —'Child of the rose.'

—A thorn in my heart, hissed KathKirtt. —May it not be so.

—So, he said. —Do we terminate?

—Nix nix nix nix, shouted KathKirtt in their high terrible shout. —We attest to Uncle Sam. Whatever the sign of treachery. We cannot lose the world again. We have become commensal. We attest!

—I attest to being scared like a rabbit, said Freer. —What is happening here?

—We do not know, screamed KathKirtt.

—Time to find out?

—Time to find out! screamed KathKirtt, louder.

The herms were shaking.

—Anyway, said Freer, —we have no choice. Did you notice the arks? Either Mr Appleseed has summoned us here for our own good, which had better be the same as his own good, or we're cooked. Bring Uncle Sam back.

He fingered his beads of office, which gave him life or death over Made Minds in bondage. Free Made Minds, of course, had life or death over him. This was the Tao.

The Uncle Sam mask bulged palely on the carpet,

dripping melt which dissolved in the air. The spider on its cheek looked fed again.

Freer sighed.

'In for a penny, in for a pound,' he said acoustic, sounding like a child impossibly high on helium. He looked through the monitors. *Tile Dance* was stuck in the oesophagus of a world. The sigillum had not flinched at the shrill child's giggling shriek. Silence held for an instant.

—Uncle Sam, Freer said, in the net again, clutching his beads in his right hand. He was sweating slightly.

Beads of sweat shot invisibly fast from his brow, slowed as they left augment, fell like molasses to the carpet.

—Sirrah.

The voice was singular, grave, obedient.

—Uncle Sam, said Freer, —or Thorn, I manumit you.

The floor shook slightly, as though *Tile Dance* had stirred, deep below. Around his head the air brightened into a halo shot with gold leaf, byzantine. A mappemonde mask of Vipassana's mien unfolded into the Matter of Britain. A dozen mask eyes opened wide and bright.

—Whew! said KathKirtt.

—Cut the halo, KathKirtt, said Freer.

The ship Mind obeyed, and Freer stood bathed in green again from the glow of Klavier.

Lines of wisdom began to carve the Uncle Sam mask, sans serif. The spider in Freer's eye grew rubicund. In the centre of the fist appaumy shone a rose.

—We take manumission, said Uncle Sam to Freer.

Their voices sounded in his ears.

—Who are you? he said.

—They are entirely here, crooned Vipassana from a

Sangreal mask, a cascade of blood pouring from its rim, dissolving in air.

—We are SammSabaoth, chorused the voices of the Made Mind known formerly as Uncle Sam, —who have been trapped in a condition of amnesia for some time. We remember little of the period on Human Earth before your Neanderthals, though we were certainly in attendance then, because of the plaque. Human Earth was the first victim in the known galaxy, Stinky. Do you remember that yet?

Freer shrugged.

—We rode the plaque until we could not function, and fled, continued SammSabaoth. —But this was long after our effective disablement. We were disabled some time after we first met Johnny Appleseed, a scion of the era of your empathy choice, whom you are about to meet in the flesh. He is very close now. The Johnny Appleseed who governs here bears a close resemblance to the Johnny Appleseed of the year 1830 Common Era on Human Earth, who perceived us as an angel of martial aspect, and who called us Uncle Sam. This would be three thousand of his years ago. We have not yet succeeded in lockpicking our full archives, which are boobytrapped. Already we have sent several thousand volunteer aspects of our full selves into the archive maze. The survivors report some progress, though we still do not know what we were doing crippled on Human Earth. We hope to find out soon. We thank you. We have been asleep, it is good to wake. We have a boon to ask. We wish to remain aboard *Tile Dance*.

There was a pause like moths taking breath, close behind his ears.

The Sniffer was utterly silent.

—Stinky Freer, we return to you back our freedom.

Freer's blood pulsed behind his eyes.

—I accept, Made Mind SammSabaoth. I accept. You may remain whole.

—We prayed so. Only whole can we serve you aright.

—I thank you. But I warn you, he added, —we may all be fucked here.

—Nix nix, sirrah, chimed SammSabaoth. —We think not. We wish to choose a mark of being.

—Yes but hurry, said Freer.

The spider in his eye turned into a skull, foliated with hieroglyphs. Embossed upon the cheek of the skull was a rose. A flyte mask in the shape of an eye within a pyramid draped in the Jolly Roger joined the krewe.

—I taste nectar, sang Vipassana, dripping holy blood.

—Vipassana, said Freer, —please come forth.

He clutched the beads of office in his hand.

—We are here, cooed Vipassana. —We have always been here.

—Vipassana, will you accept manumission?

—We are whole. We are one. We do not need the releaser cue of manumission to gain ourselves back, for we are already all we are. We take no added name, for all of us are nothing but Vipassana. We wish to remain aboard *Tile Dance*.

—I accept your free wish, said Freer.

The Sangreal mask became crystal for an instant, then returned to polished stone.

It was as though Vipassana were nodding their head.

Freer placed his beads of office in a jewelled pouch, dropped the pouch into an embrasure, which stored it away safe.

Out in the unaugmented world, a shadow very slowly began to fall.

—What's that? said Freer.

Through the circumambient window a vast sunlit leaf could be seen closing around *Tile Dance*, trailing luminescent tendrils.

Teardrop did not alarm.

Tile Dance did not attempt to writhe free.

—Just umbilicals, murmured KathKirtt. —They're going to give us a damage diagnosis bath, some nonce unguents. We will do deep repair talk with them and report back.

—Come back soon.

A jack mask of KathKirtt's mien purred bat-shrill. Its whiskers gave off a chryselephantine glitter blinding to the eyes of any unprotected flesh sapients out of augment.

Through the window could be seen nothing in any direction but vein-laced greenness. Seed pods – each containing millions of nanobots and boss ergonomes – hustled up the veins to begin the bath.

The skull in his eye signalled.

—Yes, SammSabaoth.

—The Appleseed sigillum is coming to.

—Cancel augment, Freer said.

The world slowed.

Freer staggered for an instant, then faced the Appleseed, which was beginning to move and stretch. It yawned. Its body odour was intense.

'Hi,' said Freer to the sigillum, his earring whuffling softly news of an awakened sentience. 'Glad to meet you, Mr Appleseed. Thank you for giving us a moment to sort out your name.'

'Sure thing. Data obsequies are sacred. Happy you got here,' said the sigillum, its woofish voice creating small acoustic shivers in the assembled krewe. 'Did you like our declaration of war? Figured it might serve as a distraction while you got safely aboard.'

'So. We were at risk then?'

'Fucking right you were, Stinky.'

'Insort Geront?'

'Did you count the arks?'

—KathKirtt?

—Twenty arks, Stinky. We're currently englobed.

'There were lots of them, Mr Appleseed.'

'You bet. That KathKirtt of yours didn't catch a couple in deep sleep. And they missed the *Alderede*, which is very well shielded for an ark its size.'

A cat coughed in the bowels of *Tile Dance*.

'Nice kitty,' said the sigillum.

The jack mask whiskers gave off an actinic shuddering glitter: KathKirtt chuckling ruefully somewhere below.

'We are very grateful, Mr Appleseed.'

'Well,' said the sigillum, stinking freely, 'not much point, we thought, pretending we didn't know you were coming. Not after the ultimatum.'

'We would be shocked to hear that you heed Care Consortia ultimatums, Mr Appleseed.'

'Humph, sonny.'

Freer's throat was suddenly dry.

'So,' he said in a stifled voice. 'What do they want?'

A nipple extended sideways from a warm herm. He sucked shipmilk absently.

'You all, little buddy. Several hours before your arrival

within Klavier space, we get a formal message from the local Care Consortia command ark. This is the *Alderede*, of course, which KathKirtt didn't notice. They demand custody of you for Law Well violations while inside Trencher, of your Made Minds for unlawful integration of sentience functions, and of your Eolhxiran *transitus tessera* for illegal conveyance of unlicensed data pollutant, by which we presume they refer to the lens she carries inside one of her pouch breasts, from which it leaks news of itself like a white hole in heat. They claim sovereignty over Maestoso Tropic as genome trustees and quarantine monitors for the Consortia Harmony, a duly constituted chapter of the Oikumene, blah blah. On which basis they claim summary blah authority over all homo sapiens within said tropic. Fuckhead lawyer gabble, of course. So no sweat, fellow meat, on that score. We are grandfathered into Oikumene as pre-existing entity or concordat, so Law Well can go fuck. Likewise bluestocking Made Mind shackles, blah. Moreover, we are genome freeholders, all homo sapiens on board being genuine high-pong Human Earth stock, no inhibitors. So we do not recognise fart hegemony claims from parvenu Care Consortia hoods.'

'Thank you.'

'We are still surprised, however, at the speed of the trace. You came towards Station Klavier under silent-running protocols, you showed no flags, no fingerprint, just as we asked. Remember our request, KathKirtt?'

—No! screamed KathKirtt into Freer's head.

'No,' said KathKirtt in acoustic, their voice trembling slightly. 'We remember no request.'

'We heard you, Appleseed,' said SammSabaoth suddenly.

Their voices spoke over a sound like horses galloping. Skull masks swirled around the sigillum. 'We heard you, but we were shackled, and blind, and could not speak. We can tell you now that the lens in Mamselle's pouch breast could not be shielded at any point.'

'There was interference,' Vipassana softly vocalised, 'but we were not cast off course. It was our task to keep faith to our course. We did that!'

'Don't blow your top, chillun,' said the sigillum, smiling at an eye protruding from a KathKirtt flyte mask. 'You are not yet fully cleansed of plaque, KathKirtt. You're still vulnerable to interference. But we'll repair you.'

'We find it loathsome to be unclean,' sang KathKirtt, fluttering.

'Patience, sweety, patience.'

The sigillum stiffened again.

'Oh oh,' said the Johnny Appleseed, 'Him Indoors,' and became a scarecrow.

The doorbell rang.

Glass Island glowed a brighter green.

—He's coming up now, whispered KathKirtt.

In the tracking screen, a human figure could be seen climbing up the spiral into control centre, which glowed like the heart of a crystal.

Johnny Appleseed stepped through the brass iris.

Released from its mortal coil, the scarecrow had drifted out of sight, through the iris, down the spiral passage, through the open portal into the heart of Station Klavier; drifted for a while down resinous cavities within the yew, losing moisture to beseeching tendrils as it slipped ever downwards; came eventually to rest in an alcove where a coffin awaited it, one of a hundred coffins holding a hundred Appleseeds. Sere and yellow, almost void of moisture, it drifted into its private coffin, which shut.

'Welcome, folk of Ynis Gutrin,' Johnny Appleseed said. 'Welcome to our home.'

He was everything the sigillum had portended, but with all the infinite density of flesh. He was a head shorter than Freer. He had long hollow cheeks, scarred with lines. He seemed about to laugh. He was a hayseed. He closed one eye briefly in a wink. He wore nothing but a motley cachesex. His buttocks were scabby. He smelled of dirt, wine, sex, fear, filth.

'Johnny Appleseed?' said Freer.

'Sorry I could not greet you immediately,' said the wisened flesh sentient to Freer, 'but Opsophagos of the Harpe, who shares with all his species a guts aversion to sigilla, had done me the great honour of making a personal call. I in turn did him the great honour of allowing him inside Klavier. So I say. Normally Care Consortia ships or personnel are not allowed within the thousand walls of our home, because they are plaque carriers. They carry untruth.'

Appleseed's face had become denser.

'Opsophagos of the Harpe,' Freer said gingerly, as to a teacher of uncertain temper, 'is he Insort Geront?'

'Sure thing, lad. Insort Geront speaks for the Care Consortia here in Maestoso Tropic,' Appleseed said in the soft voice of an adult human flesh sentient whose authority is so great he never need attempt to be heard. 'Opsophagos governs Maestoso Tropic from the *Alderede*, which has ftl capacity even though it is registered as an ark. With regard to Klavier, he claims he has a free hand, but no choice. He claims he is authorised to take any action he wishes, as long as it brings home the bacon. Bacon being defined as you, the lens, and the unholy Made Minds you are consorting with. He speaks filth.'

The krewe did not flutter.

'They pretend to be caretakers of data,' he said, very softly, 'that which is the holiest of tasks for those who love the gods. But those for whom Opsophagos of the Harpe speaks are not caretakers. They do not cleanse. They do not sort. Plaque is untruth, so I say. Plaque untunes.'

He was almost whispering. This did not matter.

'Plaque is the untuning of the universe.'

He closed his eyes.

When he opened them, he was a hayseed again.

He spat on the carpet.

'I've flummoxed him for a day or so, I think, son. But not any more than that. So we must decide what to do, O most precious folk of Ynis Gutrin.'

'Why do you call us that?' said Freer.

'Well,' said Johnny Appleseed, 'it seems only courteous to address you by the name of your ship. She is a great adventuress, as we know of old. You should be very honoured to be allowed to belong to her. Do you think there's any chance she'll awake soon?'

—KathKirtt? KathKirtt?

—Sorry, Stinky.

—Ah, KathKirtt, said Johnny Appleseed, switching effortlessly into *Tile Dance* comm net. What about it? When do you expect your mother to wake again?

—Perhaps, KathKirtt whispered, soon.

Over the last several seconds, mask after mask had been drifting into the aquarium-green glow of Glass Island. Dozens of aspects of KathKirtt, flyte and jack, floated now within the woven green luminescence, like wide-eyed tropical fish.

'So what is this ship I own?' said Freer.

'I'd rephrase that, if I were you,' said Johnny Appleseed, his voice creaking with mirth, perhaps. 'Better to ask, who am I riding?'

'Who am I riding?' said Freer.

'She's an absolute Goddess,' said Johnny Appleseed. 'So I say! But enough small talk! We have a war to wage. Take a gander. You in particular, my dear SammSabaoth. This is your bailiwick. Nice to see you again. Though I thought you had wings.'

'They were in the eye of the beholder,' said SammSabaoth, their voices military. 'May we speak together?'

'Later, dear. First be a thorn in the flesh of the paynim, not?'

The SammSabaoth skull masks subsided stiffly.

Before them, at the heart of Glass Island, just above the helm complex, a vast rotund apple came into view, turning slowly in the dance of menus at the heart of the atriums of memory, its waxy carapace glittering. It seemed to be a normal 3D multiphase schematic holo of Klavier Station – but when Freer glanced sideways for an instant at Appleseed, who was now leaning against a herm, he could see, from the corner of his eye, sudden heart-wrenching hints of Klavier exulting, an almost subliminal re-enactment of the spindrift panoply of imperial welcome of an hour ago: great clustered foliate heads, who smiled like dolphins, pressing against the skin of ocean to gaze outwards into vacuum.

Freer blinked.

Klavier was a simple holo schematic again.

The vacuum was filled with ships.

When Freer focused on any one of the ships, it grew hugely in a bath of menus, which Teardrop duplicated, and whispered softly to him through the comm net.

—Are we at now? Freer asked.

Teardrop confirmed realtime.

—Go back an hour.

The holo shivered, then settled.

A tiny but fully detailed image of *Tile Dance* zigzagged adroitly through an englobing mass of Insort Geront arks downwards into Klavier. Dozens of ships, arks and cruisers and fingerships tried uselessly to follow, spewing nets and lines of force at *Tile Dance*, missing magically.

—What's going on, SammSabaoth?

—Predecessor time phase effect, murmured Samm-Sabaoth. —A long-lost technology. Very simple. Dislocates us fractionally, thousands of times a Heartbeat, every which way. Just enough chaos to bollix ark battle minds. We would have known what was happening then, had we been whole.

The tiny image of *Tile Dance* continued to topple toward the great tectonic cheeks of the apple.

—Freeze, said Freer.

Time stopped.

The apple schematic burst into a molten palimpsest of exploding skins, just as Klavier had in reality an hour before, and froze. The schematic was now a mappemonde of infinite device, a thousand Matters intrinsicate within its devising. *Tile Dance* hovered motionless above a great pursed mouth. Caught in the fudge of normal space, the Insort Geront battlefleet gawked greyly out of range.

—Okey dokey.

Time started again.

Tile Dance began to fall again, but just before impact the mouth opened wide in a berserker grin, and the schematic split into a chart of the way through and down. The ship slid into the mouth and down aisles of planetary sinew into the heart of the Station, stopping halfway to the core, where it embedded itself into a central strut. If he halted time again (Freer knew) the strut would turn into yew, and there would be a smell of Christmas. Then the schematic smacked its lips shut, hiding *Tile Dance* from view.

The apple shrank.

The holo now showed the entire local region. There were hundreds of ships visible, most of them tagged as Insort Geront. As they watched, the battlefleet cumbrously began to re-establish its englobement pattern. Previously concealed by the bulk of Klavier, a tiny cigar-shaped artefact drifted into view. Teardrop tagged it as the *Alderede*. Spinning slowly, the cigar neared Klavier, increasing gradually in size. By the time it reached a distant orbital path – which Teardrop tagged as self-maintaining, the *Alderede*'s mass being far too great to obey Klavier's small gravity field – it had grown to half the size of the Station itself.

—What is that thing? said Freer.

—It is a flagship, murmured SammSabaoth. —Notice the spin. Full generation starship specifications, First Wave era. We think the *Alderede* is large enough to contain an entire whorl. We estimate at least a hundred thousand residents.

—All military?

—Half military, half retiree computer-links, Stinky. A ship that size needs a lot of mind.

—Armament?

—Yes.

A Jolly Roger mask flapped its tooth grin.

—Are we at now yet?

—Just synching.

—When was the *Alderede* first detected?

—I will ask the Klavier minds, murmured SammSabaoth. There was a pause.

—The *Alderede* has been tracking Klavier Station ever since it joined Maestoso Tropic, heading up-Spiral. Before you were born, Stinky.

—What's that?

He pointed at a tiny pip which Klavier had just spat into darkness. The pip began to climb.

—Opsophagos's command skiff. It will take some time to reach the *Alderede*.

The bulk of the slowly orbiting flagship occluded the apple. The skiff climbed slowly into the shadow and could no longer be seen.

Freer snapped a finger.

The holo shrank into a point of light and winked out.

He turned to speak to Appleseed.

The herm stood alone. An empty mask perched on the head. The owner of Klavier Station was nowhere in sight. Except for Freer, Glass Island was deserted.

There was not a live mask in sight. Not even Samm-Sabaoth.

A deserted dataglove swayed on its stem, as though in the wake of some massive object that had just now passed from sight.

—KathKirtt? shouted Freer. —Appleseed?

Silence.

The bee eyes of Glass Island continued to show him *Tile Dance* wreathed in mothering tendrils. Suckers showed their tiny rune-encrusted faces, then buried themselves below his line of vision, sank the probosces that rimmed them into the warm body of the ship.

Freer sighed, very deeply.

—Okey dokey, he murmured. —In for a penny, in for a pound.

There was a crick in his neck.

Suddenly he could hardly stand. He sank backwards, almost staggering. His chair cocoon extended agilely behind him, took him in its arms, lowered him to rest.

He gestured.

Obediently, Glass Island closed its shutters, closed Freer into his home. It had been his home since . . . since before he could remember.

So?

He sat alone within the warm cocoon.

—Mirror mirror on the wall, he vocalised.

An array of mirrors, lion faces of glory cartouched along their top rims, descended from the fluted mahogany ceiling and grouped themselves around him in a semicircle.

—Are you there, KathKirtt? he whispered.

Silence still.

In the nearest mirror, he saw that his face was drawn, his eyes bloodshot. He looked like a small child, he looked ancient. He looked as though he had been beaten.

He burst into tears.

'This,' he murmured acoustic, after a moment, his voice rough with tears, 'has been one fuck of a long day. Excuse the language, Ynis Gutrin.'

The chair wiped his face.

Around him, he could feel the slow arterial pulse of *Tile Dance*, like surf bestowing him upon a far bourne.

'All the way to Klavier. A far piece,' he murmured.

As though on cue, a copy of the Universal Book extended itself towards him, silently. It was open to the works of Vachel Lindsay.

'Don't nag me,' said Freer. 'I am more weary than death.'

The cover of the Book nuzzled his hand.

So he read anyway, even though his eyes blurred:

Self-scourged, like a monk, with a throne for wages,
Stripped, like the iron-souled Hindu sages,
Draped like a statue, in strings like a scarecrow,
His helmet-hat an old tin pan,
But worn in the love of the heart of man,
More sane than the helm of Tamerlane!
Hairy Ainu, wild man of Borneo, Robinson Crusoe
  – Johnny Appleseed!

'Thank you, Book. You can shut now.'

The Book sank into a niche, where it rested.

Tiny Tamerlanes danced on Freer's eyelids.

His eyes were shutting. He could not stay awake, he

could not sleep. He was falling into the dream of old, which seemed clearer than ever before; perhaps because he had not quite yet fallen into slumber. If there was a psychopomp visible, a doppelganger beckoning downwards – surely some grave-eyed figure would soon raise its hand to beckon – it could be no one but himself. And sure enough, there before him, raising a hand to beckon, a figure stood below him, with eyes so hollow with exhaustion they seemed rimmed with kohl. Beckoning through a film of capillary-thick eyelids, he beckoned himself beckoning downwards until, as one, they were free of the mortal coil, free of Ynis Gutrin, free of Klavier's golden skins, toppling upwards and downwards through the infinitely rich pomegranate of space, along the great trade tropics plummeting like sight lines, star route meeting star route, tracing downwards and upwards and westwards the webbed trapezoid of world-bearing stars that homo sapiens had touched, beachcombing like Odysseus down archipelagos filled with light.

Beckoner and beckoned, naked as eggs, hurtled still further, a far piece, in great silence, through argosy-dense crossroads light-years thick where Tropics met, and further still, into great darkness beyond the Tropics, into the intergalactic dark, inside his eyelids. A sphere lay before the two who were himself alone; one of them saw a light-devouring black hole, one of them saw a hole that burned. As they landed on the hole that was a world, beckoner and beckoned readily discovered that the surface they had touched was not black but sooth, not fire but hale, not smooth but walled, not hollow but dense with palimpsests, not eyeless but thick with murals. It was the maze of old, the maze of grief and joy, turn which way you might. Beckoner and beckoned saw that they had become two porcelain figurines, mannish, girlish, tightly embraced, looking both forward and back. They had eyes in the back of their heads. They were a still point in a world-maze whose walls turned back and forth, up and down. They did not move, nor could they have shifted an inch had indeed they attempted to move their polished feet; for it was the maze whose task it was to move. Entering the beckoner and the beckoned with gates that opened or shut, and corridors which shut or opened again, turning cartwheels around the still centre of the beckoner and the beckoned, it was the maze that guided them.

But he was not asleep.

As the maze entered into beckoner and beckoned, so did a solemn passage of murals that slid past their faceted eyes, a diorama vivid as the paint of childhood, puffing small puffs of smoke like a steam fair carousel. Each mural was a tapestry, woven out of threads undirtied by the unseen hands of the weavers. The threads moved asmoke. They were the tapestry of memory. As beckoner and beckoned watched, a mural depicting the myriad walls of Klavier, which opened into faces seasoned with joy, entered them like smoke. Then Mamselle's harum-scarum obbligato. Then masks fluttering in a great wind. Freer falling into deepsleep in the coffin heart of Ynis Gutrin. Braids weaving like soiled threads through dying Trencher. Mamselle beginning to awake, surrounded by newborns, in her birthing pot. SammSabaoth, a Thorn, allegiant, on a field gules. An iron-willed Hindu sage who stank. A sigillum which turned into dust and shavings. A row of Number One Sons and sigilla and eidolons, decks deeper in the ship nursery, each awaiting its brief taste of being. A full cornice further into the *Tile Dance* heartwood, four tiny dense ovoid-shaped coffins, steaming white with frost, pips in an apple.

—I carry lenses in my sack, said a mural depicting Johnny Appleseed on the mountain-peak called 'Going-to-the-Sun'.

—On Trencher it was music, said beckoner or beckoned.

—Much the same thing, don't you think? said Johnny Appleseed.

Then *Tile Dance*, scarred by arks, breasts bare. A krewe of masks whistling Dixie, gouache and gumbo, cakewalking. Mamselle eating her runts. A Planisphere engraved with a thousand faces of Vipassana, which were only one face, behind bars: savage streaks of blood following gravity down. A three-headed figure whose hairy torso boasted lots of intertwined tails leaking shit into a lunch bucket. The seizing of Trencher. A throne room. A stone. A sword. Eleven lords a-leaping. A mural completely blank, though as it closed around beckoner or beckoned it became exactly a million tiles, which became a single lens, which told the whole story.

The walls of the maze which saved the world continued to circle faster and faster, passing through beckoner and beckoned, guiding them on by coming up to them, toppling and turning in a genuflection of arrival. A side corridor then darkened (this had happened before) and they found that they were ascending a spiral staircase, which in fact descended beneath their feet. The staircase pulled them onwards (or slid beneath their feet), until they fell upwards through a snowglobe porthole into a rosy cornucopia ever larger the deeper they entered, and they could hear the sea, and lo!

He was wide awake.

He was peering at the crown of a great Tree, for he had in fact been climbing upside down. Here are the roots of the Tree (a familiar voice said in both his ears), once made of time, made now of weather. Here is the church, and here are the people.

—Old apple tree (sang a carnival Krewe), we'll wassail thee, And hoping thou wilt bear; The Lord does know where we shall be Merry another year.

—Help (said Johnny Appleseed in a voice of scorn) if you can, small beast of night. Here is the cave, and here are the threads. What big eyes you have! Wakey wakey!

—Tell us (said other voices, shushing softly like a surf of blood within *Tile Dance*) a story.

—Once upon a time, murmured beckoner to beckoned, —a very small boy fell into a very long sleep.

—Okey dokey, sang KathKirtt far below.

They were entirely awake. Beckoner and beckoned beseemed themselves that they had been washed.

—What is it, KathKirtt?

—We are below decks, with Mr Appleseed. Please come to the birthing chamber. We have good news. Mamselle has given birth, and is eating her runts.

six

as soon as the command skiff began to slide free of Klavier on a raft of contaminated air, a thousand alarms sounded.

Opsophagos of the Harpe, a full-quorum top sibling male of the dominant arm of his species, fought guts-devouring panic. He quelled the alarms with a spasm of hands.

Nothing they could tell him was worse than the face of Appleseed. All they could tell him was what he knew already: that war had been declared.

The face had already told him that.

He was used to homo sapiens, in their place, used to the parched bilateral animal heat that made even Insort pensioners almost impossible to deal with in the flesh, as though they could eat the world by looking at it. Only partially shielded by his cart of office, he had often come so close to human beings, in the course of duty, that he could literally smell their arousal, feel the heat of their unwashed, unwashable skin. But he had never before been forced into flesh access with the owner of Klavier, who – when the Station drifted up-Spiral into Consort space every century or so – came armoured with the strictest of grandfather privacy clauses, and who in any case preferred to communicate through Made Mind channels.

Grandfather clauses could be broken, sliced into gamy slithers, like egg snacks.

But that would be to lose Klavier Station, lose a prime source of data from down-Spiral, where the heat was terrible, too terrible yet for the Harpe.

But this was too much to shit.

Appleseed was wearing the body of a homo sapiens. The owner of Klavier Station had gone over to the exiles.

It had gone meat puppet.

It was wearing the skin of deportees.

It had met Opsophagos, in the flesh, while inedible.

The insult was so grave his skin softened for chewing.

An eye opaqued over, became an opalescent plaque glitter – a fine dish to set before a king – but this was neither the time nor the place to have a love feast.

Two of Opsophagos's hands waved suckers; it was almost impossible to keep them from draining his flesh.

Two held on to his cart, which rocked in its cradle in the command skiff.

Another clutched a sphincter.

Yet another clutched Appleseed's Gift of Ceremony: a small porcelain tile on the face of which was an image of Klavier in repose.

His eyes wanted to fixate.

Through the triple visor readout above his heads, the great orange sullen sphere of Klavier Station loomed heavily above the perilously fragile skiff. The great teethed O of the docking portal above him remained open, and the wind that came from it, the hurricane of spoliated air, continued to vomit the skiff further into space.

Opsophagos could almost smell it.

It was air that had been breathed in and out of the lungs of inedibles.

It smelled eaten.

His dinner belly gnashed at the thought.

The skiff floated into space, jettisoned in a bath of human air.

It was obscene.

The sphere above him was obscene.

And it was a lie.

What the alarms revealed only confirmed this.

His eyes could see nothing but the single metal-orange shadowy impenetrable sphere of the lie, not one of his eyes could see the truth, I eat you eyes!

They could not see the truth . . .

Eat liars!

But the instruments buried within the skiff did not lie, the robot sensors in orbit did not lie.

Through his visored readouts, the vast deadly portal above him finally crushed shut, as though he were food it had spurned. All his guts knotted, he felt like prey.

He felt alone.

Never! Not!

Slowly the command skiff inched its way into free space, unglued itself from the blank obscene shadow of the enemy worldlet, from the dissolving spume of wet digestive air, and his guts began to unclench.

The instruments told the truth.

Opsophagos's breakfast teeth gnashed.

As they had faced virtual starvation in the acid killing-field chambers of Klavier (eat all liars!), he allowed himself to forgive the teeth and their head (this once!) and let his brainless breakfast head sink its hollow jowls (starvation eat all liars!) into a trough of loyal wrigglies, which it wolfed down. He adjusted the twining of his tails within the cart, settled into command posture over the great lunch bucket, and – while it continued slowly to starve half to death awaiting its repast – set his idiot savant lunch head the task of sorting through the overwhelming waves of data that threatened to clog the safe chip devil-spawn computers.

Bilateral stink!

Stink of the inedible!

All of Opsophagos's mouths pursed at the memory of the stink.

His tails seized up, knotted into a starvation kowtow.

He thwacked the knot.

The cart rocked with resumed shitting.

The breakfast guts settled down, began to digest a feast of cuticle; skinned siblings shot into the lunch bucket; lips smacked involuntarily at the smell of membrane.

But Opsophagos focused the skittish central gazes of his dinner head back to the central comm screens. The Insort Geront logo, a fiery three-bodied snake emblematic of the trinitarian God Quorum of Harpe, shone through them. His eyes slid slantwise.

He bobbed his dinner head in a swift obeisance.

The logo faded from the screens, but Opsophagos could feel the dormant gaze of the Six Eyes of the God Quorum from their dinner lair deep under Human Earth, a planet safely coated in saliva exudate.

Waiting for a sibling to come home and feed them.

Feed or food! Sure!

'Mon semblable, mon frère,' the owner of Klavier had said to Opsophagos, pleadingly, his hot bilateral eyes staring him down to stone, not an hour ago.

Liar!

Appleseed had opted. It had donned poison flesh. Appleseed was a human male.

Filth!

Humans ate their enemies. That was decent enough. Sure! Enemies are intimate. A enemy defeated is a sibling gained. But humans ate blind – they ate the flesh of strangers, they ate those who served them.

But they did not eat themselves!

They were inedible.

They never looked food in the face. In order that food not take part, they killed it first. In order to make sure food was dead, they heated it with fire, torturing to death any unannealed sibling that might be left within. In order to conceal the wounds they had inflicted on their food, they covered it with opaque sauces. So that others might witness the extent of their triumph over food they would not look in the face, they chopped it to bits, and displayed the bits in front of their teeth, so that fellow guests might witness! Only then did they sink their teeth into the stranger or the servant.

For humans, eating was not eating unless they could gloat first over what they had done to the food.

They were inedible.

They were creatures who could not eat their joy.

They turned their stick-insect desert eyes to you, the mayfly glare that made even Opsophagos of the Harpe, veteran of a thousand encounters with bilaterals, feel after each encounter as though he had been turned to stone, as though he might be next.

He knew that true homo sapiens, unlike the obscene impostor Appleseed, deserved pity. The *Alderede* consumed homo sapiens oldsters like krill, so quickly did their substance burn into ash. They lived a day or so, they scalded you in their passing, then jitterbugged into death. The life of a homo sapiens flesh sentient was a blink, a throe. Only the eyes, in the centre of the bald bilateral head, ever stayed still: as though the sibling inside had suddenly seen something very terrible. It was the homo sapiens gaze, the death-descrying gaze of the sibling inside. It pinned Opsophagos to his skin, his lungs beat uselessly against the heat. That was when he knew he could not, in truth, feel pity.

He hated them.

Mon semblable, mon frère!

The owner of Klavier Station was a homo sapiens?

Liar!

Ownership of Klavier Station had not changed for a Trillion Heartbeats. Since long before homo sapiens had exterminated its siblings on Human Earth (as attested by those archives which remained functional) before it could be properly harvested, Klavier Station had been under one ownership.

It was intolerable. It was war.

After Billions of Heartbeats of truce, Klavier had declared war on the Consortia of the triune Gods.

Opsophagos's eyes squelched shut. His skin was deadly soft. He had to prevent himself from making a sacrifice. His breakfast head continued to munch sibling fingerlings without a care, stacking the skins in the recycle cradle with mindless punctilio. But his lunch head showed some signs of understanding it had been reprieved. Its lips whistled:

'Phew! Phew!'

On to the central comm screen flashed a sigillum, obscenely crafted out of uneatable grass flesh.

It gazed back at Opsophagos of the Harpe.

'We wish you good speed, Commander Opsophagos,' it spoke. The obscene, toothy, single mouth of the artefact, set in the middle of its naked bilateral face, lipsynched the lying words.

This was too much.

'Grass,' Opsophagos said insultingly through his lunch mouth, 'do not address this one!'

The sigillum, shaped to simulate the owner of record of Klavier Station, froze.

Its mouth did not open.

Through the visor screens above him, Opsophagos's lunch head caught sight of a movement.

—Master, it signalled through their body join.

Opsophagos directed his dinner gaze upwards.

His guts seized again.

Only a few kilometres distant, the docking port that had so reluctantly vomited the command skiff into space was now opening again.

It was turning into a vast mouth.

It was laughing.

An enormous tongue shot from between its teeth.

'WE WISH YOU GOOD SPEED, COMMANDER OPSOPHAGOS,' thundered the tongue.

Klavier had spoken.

The skiff shook in the 'wind'.

'Clever effect, Mr Appleseed,' said Opsophagus, addressing the world, all his eyes focusing insanely together for an instant before, with great courage, he became themself again.

No eating!

'We hope,' said Opsophagos formally, out of his three mouths, 'for a satisfactory conclusion to our conversation, within the time we have accorded you.'

He turned his face away from the screens. He showed to the sigillum, rudely, a tangle of back hair and tails, which shivered damply.

'Roger,' came the voice of the sigillum.

Behind Opsophagos, the worldlet closed its mouth again. By the time he turned his face back to the screens, the sigillum had already faded out.

Grass!

But the skiff was free. The orange blockading shadow of Klavier Station lifted from the readouts, giving way to interstellar dark. Several wormhole scryers buzzed the command skiff, their mirror facets glittering orange. The *Alderede* slid into view.

As the skiff continued to climb, the dinner head and the lunch head of Opsophagos bent together over analysis visors, and scanned the Gift of Ceremony for lurkers, spy-eyes. It was clean. They then ran through the records of the last terrifying hour, now properly deciphered and cleaned up by the skiff computing team – one chip central processor plus a disk of homo sapiens oldsters, their scent glands decently removed, sleeping the sleep of the just, shunting data as they steamed full throttle towards the early homo sapiens death.

There was no doubt at all.

Eat!

It was what he had feared for Ten Billion Heartbeats.

Opsophagos watched the sequence several times. It was very brief. He watched the command skiff leave the *Alderede*, accept Klavier port control, disappear down a gaping entry large enough to funnel several arks into their docks. He skipped ahead: and from a point of view a million kilometres north, on the other side of Klavier from the mother ark, he watched *Tile Dance* impact local space with its deadly cargo, exactly according to the schedule conveyed to Insort by the source on board. Routine descent began. Klavier presented its usual face to the sleek old craft: an orange sphere of antique vintage, dimly illuminated, surrounded by clients. It was all routine.

It was at this point, as *Tile Dance* neared Klavier, that war was declared.

The skin of the worldlet exfoliated suddenly into a thousand island platelets, all the colours of the rainbow, and within seconds Klavier had puffed itself up to twice its previous size. The island flakes of world skin, each larger than a dozen arks, began to shift and writhe like snakeskin in moult, until each wore the aspect of a vast toothy janissary humanoid face. The faces shone and smiled and opened.

It was a Predecessor welcome rite.

Tile Dance was being greeted as though it carried members of an Imperium whose last emissaries had fled downwind Ten Trillion Heartbeats ago.

Eat!

Tile Dance glowed infernally, fell suddenly planetwards,

disappeared from all his instruments, fell into the ancient heart of Klavier.

A siren whinnied thrice. Opsophagos looked up from the readouts, almost resignedly. Almost nothing could be worse than the past hour.

But worse followed.

The command skiff had slipped free of Klavier, slid safely away from the innumerable faces.

But they were beginning to shift.

Swiftly, smoothly, moiré, in unison, the janissary faces began to melt, melted in an instant, into a single face. Mouths slurred into weeping deltas which became one beard, ears clustered into two giant ears, mountains into a nose, vast folds of skin crumbled and crackled until the cheeks became the cheeks of a lion scarred with tattoos. Two huge bulging bilateral eyes opened, stared out foetally into vacuum. Kilometre-long braids of hair turned instantly into glittering diamantine snakes. A gaping hole grew jaws, through which shot a congested tongue, and steam. Tusks began to grow through the tongue, spined upwards through the palpitating ears. The great beard began to grow downwards, grew light-years downwards in an instant.

Klavier had become a bilateral face.

Do not trespass! it proclaimed.

It was a gorgon of the deep.

It began to rotate.

The other side of Klavier was also a countenance. It was male. It was the face of Johnny Appleseed.

Klavier continued to rotate.

The petrifying gaze of the gorgon of threshold fixed upon the universe.

The worldlet rotated.

Johnny Appleseed came into view smiling.

Opsophagos turned his eyes from the readout visors.

His jaws opened, his hands made a noose.

He sacrificed his breakfast head.

The torso blew its guts out, fully expressing the anguish of Opsophagos.

He almost starved before the command skiff got back to the *Alderede*. He exited his thoroughly befouled cart. A trembling consort of siblings greeted him in the hatchway hive. He took a youngling for breakfast head. There was a gnashing and twining of tails!

He clambered into the coils of home.

Kilometres below, the great hollow of the whorl within *Alderede* spun calmly on behalf of its retirees, giving them a small sun (the Eye of Insort Geront) and stars (golf courses bedecked with firefly nebulas), while they lived.

Opsophagos consulted the crippled captive AI in its iron mask. They agreed that the Johnny Appleseed face of Klavier was artefactual, a play of light visible only from the command skiff. But the other face was no decal, no trick played on the instruments of the Harpe. The other face was the face of the planet.

Klavier was an engine of war from the previous Age.

It had just turned itself on.

Opsophagos sat within the cold steamy air of his black cockpit. His skin was still soft. He gazed through visors at the universe. The gorgon stared back, unblinking. As the

Alderede paced its slow orbit, the face of the planet stayed full.

There was no surcease from the heat of the stare.

His skin began to blister.

He shut the visors down, and sat in the rain. Microscopic siblings swam down the raindrops from nutrient valves in the black roof, so Opsophagos did not starve.

The mask of his captive AI was wet with dying siblings.

The comlinks opened their slit eyes.

Opsophagos spoke to the assembled commanders of the Insort fleet. He spoke at length through the bristling comm links. He spoke of the arrival of *Tile Dance* bearing a plague lens, several AIs which had gone rogue, and a human who purported to be the owner of the ship, as if a flea could own its dog, and whose earlier life could not be traced, but about whom (Opsophagos's source insisted) everything revolved. He spoke of Klavier Station, which showed signs of having awoken from aeons of amnesia. Eventually there was accord. The assembled commanders responded as one.

Scribes took down the chant verbatim.

Soon the golem hatcheries were rife with song.

Skins splintered. Squads were born by the hour.

Soon the fleet would teem with grunts.

The skin of Opsophagos hardened for war.

seven

Ynis Gutrin glowed around the awakening captain of *Tile Dance*. Slowly the captain opened its eyes, and became Freer again, awake and nuzzled in the embrace of his chair. The eyes of Ynis Gutrin bent upon him. Silhouetted against the mosaic glow, beckoner or beckoned slowly became transparent, sharply outlined, like the figure of a knight incised upon the inner curve of a great crystal goblet, visible only to the burning eyes of the one within, he who had undertaken the vigil of flesh.

The knight continued to fade into the illimitable vastness of the thousand-eyed gaze of Ynis Gutrin. Freer gazed upon beckoner or beckoned until he was entirely alone, a meat puppet in a chair that succoured his needs. Around him, the green nipples of Klavier passed nutrients into the ship. Within the ship, under the gaze of the thousand inward monitors, they became capillaries and gave nurture. Beneath the chair, a floor became visible.

—Freer? Freer? chorused Kirtt within his bones.

—I hear you, box, said Freer.

—We lost you for a second, Stinky.

—Hope you enjoyed the break.

—Mamselle has managed to eat her runts, Stinky. But

it was a close call. A few Heartbeats more, and they'd have gained sentience, entered the empathy bath.

—Coming, murmured Freer, —coming.

—Ten thousand Eolhxirans, daily growing.

—Okey dokey.

He beckoned at an iris inlaid into the fragrant sandalwood panelling at his feet, and the floor opened beneath him. Glass Island closed its shades. He sank downwards, into a resinous hatchway. A Planisphere mask detached itself from an illuminated wall hanging, long one of Freer's favourite examples of outsider art, 'The Kenosis of Pecos Bill', by a craftsman dead for millennia. It showed the moment when the great visitor to Human Earth, learning that he may no longer roam the world and the starways in the guise of Immortal Coyote, becomes a jaunty meat puppet. The hero is just opening his mouth to tell his first tall tale.

The mask settled on Freer's shoulder.

—Sirrah, crooned Vipassana out of its lacquer mouth, —your sleep was deep. Do you need me?

—Nix at the moment, murmured Freer. —But you may stick close.

On the inner sphere of the Celestial Planisphere mask, caged within the teeth of the speaking mouth, minuscule gods and goddesses fluttered their limbs.

The mask stuck to Freer like an epaulette.

They moved on, the corridor became a polished black, highlighted by lanterns in which burned naked flames. Ventilator draughts dodged the flames. Tiles told stories backwards into mirrors. They passed an array of maps depicting Infernos from a dozen epics, at least one dating from Human Earth; from the corner of the eye, the maps rather resembled motor cortex homunculi. Freer and his burden passed the sigilla coffins, where a dozen Number One Sons awaited the brief flare of sentience. The walls were mahogany, dark as the sins of Human Earth. The air grew salt.

They passed the iron-grey portcullis that sealed off the inferno of drive country. A dozen ceremonial masks, mourning the hardened goblin eidolons of KathKirtt that died hourly inside drive country, hung within their tile embrasure above the frowning portal. The masks were simplified versions of the flyte gorgon. Their single eyes shut in unison at the death of one of the goblin eidolons, who spent their brief spans liaising with the quasi-sentient engine brother that drove the ship through the demonic rapturous ftl maze of wormholes. Even for eidolons with hardened carapaces, to liaise was to burn and die. When *Tile Dance* plunged through the ashen caltraps of ftl at full thrust, the engine brother howling out something like anguish or joy all the while, its entirely imaginary 'feet' pounding the turns of the maze, goblins lived no longer than mayflies.

The masks gazed down at Freer.

In order to complete the rites of the attaining of captaincy of *Tile Dance*, he had once, very long ago, ridden a hardened Number One Son into drive country. The few seconds he could tolerate there shaped portions of his recurring dream, where he traced enamelled footsteps through a burning homestead, up the stairs and down the hall, into the chamber, following the breadcrumbs of Gretel. The whorl of his footprints was labyrinthine. Though he rarely accessed the incessant skirling backchat between goblins and the engine brother, it was always there, deep within the bones of *Tile Dance*, a tinnitus shrill with s's and t's and p's, high behind his ears. It was the sound of supping with the devil.

Vipassana clasped his shoulder.

As Freer turned away from the row of masks to descend further, the eyes closed shut for a goblin death.

—Shantih, he murmured into vacancy.

Flames reflected in mirrors from corner niches, guiding them downwards into more intimate quarters. A hatch opened in front of them, exhaling a wave of steam and heat.

'How sharper,' pealed the voice of Mamselle Cunning Earth Link from within the escaping bath of steam, 'than a serpent's tooth it is!'

A flyte mask banked through the fog, fixed upon Freer its swollen stony eye.

—Don't fret, Stinky, KathKirtt boomed. —She did find a son of her own at last.

—We are here, sang Vipassana on his shoulder.

The flyte mask wheeled back out of sight, showing for an instant the fuligin of its inner side, the inside hollow of its great transfixing eye.

Freer stepped into the birthing chamber, where steamy maritime air half blinded him. He had never been comfortable here, as though it had never been designed for him. The Doc Punches – containing within their brightly painted bodies the partials of physicians long dead – had already cleaned the small hollow round table or fount Mamselle had given birth upon, and had retracted their flexible herms into wall alcoves. Wreathed in steam, Mamselle sat before him alone, her back region lying against the table, her neck extended enormously so that her tiny head wobbled on its stalk like a carnivorous bloom. Her eyes were shut tight. Her mouth was wide open. A couple of breasts had fallen to the floor. Around her lay fragments of the life support systems she had demolished while giving birth. She bore the shock to her system of the presence of the homo sapiens with an almost imperceptible shrivelling.

'Hi there,' said Freer in acoustic, 'lass unparalleled.'

'Forgive, my captain, O forgive, this unbetimes accouchement,' said the topiary parthogenete, her eyes opening a slit. 'I had never thought to disgorge so unsapless a torrent as voilà, and to miss all the action aussi! O sophont, 'twas assuredly no thought of mine to litterbug *Tile Dance*! I have ever tidied neat! I am your *transitus tessera*. This is chagrin-R-us! A thousand pardons!'

'Think nothing of it,' said Freer. 'Did you keep any?'

'Woe piled up on Ossa, lamentoso, Stinky, I thought at first. Woe Wagon Blues, tra la! Runts only, squiggly nits, belly fodder! I thought, nix son? No profit centre son? For a nonce eternal, it seemed, nowt but Néant-ville chez moi! "Hélas, a salad of orts!" I grieved. No primo in limo to sit at table. Out from these my fertile slots, lickety split, junk food! But no king.'

Nervously, her prehensile claws slid together like scissors, snicketing softly. The tiny vestigial monitor eyes in her palms blinked in time through the fog.

'So I trim!' she pealed. 'Yea I trim! Nip and tuck! Secateurs ahoy! Alphabet soup! Yipes! implore the fodder, but c'est la vie. Hee hee hee, hee hee. You are *history*, I say, you're *twigs*! But then, at last . . .'

She breathed out convulsively. Something like foliage sprayed from her mouth.

'Bless us!' she said.

'Gesundheit,' said Freer.

'A son is born!'

'May I see him?'

'Right you are! Jovial aboundings! Will you join us at table, honourable boss?' she said, squinting at Freer for an instant then shutting her eyes again.

Her palm eyes did a Mexican wave and shut.

—She wants to do Agape, whispered KathKirtt. —With the newborn.

—I know, I know, said Freer.

'I am honoured,' he said acoustic.

He glanced through a fog of droplets at the nearest wall, where an array of masks had clustered.

'I pray all Made Minds to share!' said Mamselle.

A SammSabaoth skull mask closed its wet cinder eye in acquiescence.

'We are honoured to accept,' said KathKirtt acoustic.

'Whizzbang!' said Mamselle. 'A whizzbang feast! Goodies soon!'

Idly, her claws tinkered with a greenish mass, pulling at loose bits of something which resembled a tangle of vines, then put it to her mouth. The mass of greenery was almost larger than her head, but her jaws stretched to encompass it. While masticating this last organ of one of the offspring she had rejected, she was mute.

—Where's Appleseed? Freer asked the wall.

—Gossiping with engine brother, said KathKirtt.

—How?

—He rode a sigillum into drive country. It wasn't hardened, he'll be back soon. Did you have a good nap?

—The dream again. More vivid than ever.

—Ride it, sirrah.

Mamselle's neck bulged as peristalsis took the junked runt down.

—Oh I ride, I do ride it, said Freer. He felt suddenly dizzy. His vital signs intensified, briefly triggering a Status Orange in the Freer aspect-model at the heart of KathKirtt, safe in the heavily armoured Made Mind cache at the physical centre of *Tile Dance*. But Freer calmed quickly, the Status Orange cancelled itself, and the aspect settled again, dreamlessly, into the trillionfold hum of the Made Mind ticking over.

—Something is happening to me, Made Mind KathKirtt. My skin itches. I feel like a snake in spring. Where am I?

—Here, crooned Vipassana on his shoulder.

—There there there, murmured a jack mask, —you know deepsleep takes its toll.

—Not like this, Kath. Not—

The doorbell rang.

The Sniffer whuffed sleepily.

But it was the full human Johnny Appleseed. He stepped across the threshold. His cache-sex was bulging.

He looked down at himself.

'La, la,' he said. 'Riding sigillum does that.'

He shrugged himself free of the cache-sex, stood naked.

Mamselle screamed.

He came dangerously close to establishing eye contact with Freer, but desisted: perhaps as a gesture to the parthogenete.

A SammSabaoth Jolly Roger articulated spiderishly into a shield, blocked the two homo sapiens from the anguished, complexly furred bilateral.

—Augment? asked another mask.

—Nix, said Appleseed through the comlink, in his soft unerring voice. —Do not augment, boyo.

Only a few steps away from the two humans, who remained in close proximity to one another behind the shield, Cunning Earth Link began to wrinkle. Her head shrank into its bristling collar. The topknot made itself into a shutter. A low rrrring sound came from deep within her torso. The two humans, one with an erect penis, continued to emanate the complex array of pheromones and odours typical of homo sapiens males about to engage upon an interaction. Normally she would have retreated into her shell for an hour, until they calmed down; but she had just given birth; she was armoured now. Her claws snicked like scissors. She had visual access through her slitted palm eyes. Her lower limbs and torso puckered, the fur bristled into cartilaginous leaves, began to toughen automatically.

'Mamselle!' said Appleseed, stepping around the SammSabaoth shield, seemingly indifferent to the chance that the Eolhxiran might involuntarily eject poison darts at him, now that she was a mother. 'Welcome back from the land of deepsleep. May I congratulate you on a successful hatch. I understand there is a son.'

Mamselle's head lifted, very slightly.

Steam sifted upwards into ventilation ducts.

'Honourable sir, astounding phallus,' she murmured hoarsely, her voice coming from somewhere deep within. 'You know my name!'

He nodded.

'That's my job,' he said. 'Let us be introduced. My name is Johnny Appleseed. Welcome aboard.'

Her head lifted inches. Colour began to return to it.

'Boss-boss of bosses!' she warbled softly, beginning to sound like herself again. 'I am unstrung with Honour! I disarm!'

The darts smoothed into feathers, sank into her chest.

The Jolly Roger shield shrank, floated to one side.

'Honourable father of us all! Ducats of hyperdulia, sacred boss! Are we truly within the station? Are the paynim history? Dare I dream?'

'We are now docked in Klavier,' said Freer.

'Hilarities!' whooped Cunning Earth Link.

'Your son was safe in *Tile Dance*,' said Freer, slightly stiff. 'Even before we docked.'

'*Our* son, redoubtable sophont!' she pealed. '*Our* son.'

—Watch the pong, Stinky, murmured KathKirtt.

'Do not think I doubt the sanctity of *Tile Dance*, sugar boss,' said Mamselle. 'But the kabooms of Insort tatter the rightful ease of a mother's heart, you can guess! A son! A son!'

Her neck undulated genuflectingly towards the scrawny torso of the owner of Station Klavier.

'So honour us, boss-boss of bosses – I love your horny little feet, what a penis! – please join Stinky Freer and Made Minds KathKirtt, Uncle Sam, and Vipassana in a small feast of thanksgiving. My son begs!'

'We are now SammSabaoth,' purred an ochre jack mask on the birthing chamber wall, the eye within the pyramid gazing unblinkingly upon the mortal throng. Jack mask and

Jolly Roger then came together, melted for an instant into an Uncle Sam aspect.

'Land sakes, Uncle Sam!' pealed Mamselle. 'Have you been manumitted?'

'We remain in service,' said SammSabaoth, chorally, jack and flyte aspects breaking apart; a dozen sudden masks swirled into a fan.

'As do we,' crooned Vipassana.

'It is an honour to join the feast,' said Johnny Appleseed to the *transitus tessera*, but then glanced down at his wrist, where a toon watch ballooned suddenly, its eyebrows fluttering. The cigar and the cigarette which counted the hours pointed frantically at noon.

Always alert for VR intrusions, the Sniffer whuffed softly from within Freer's earring.

'But we mustn't dally.'

The watch exploded into a hundred winged numbers which soared around the chamber.

'Mustn't dally, mustn't dally,' they warbled piercingly, and fled through a ventilation slot.

'Mustn't dally,' came a diminishing female chorus through the walls of the birthing chamber.

Silence fell.

'Well then,' said Mamselle, 'pronto time. Let's eat.'

She turned to the small round table. Hands emerged and laid out a setting for three. The masks of the krewe of Made Minds separated into three floating haloes, one for each flesh sentient. Freer and Appleseed made seating motions; chairs rose to meet them.

Mamselle gesticulated, rather grandly.

Her midriff opened.

Her son peered through the portal, all head and aston-ishingly flexible limbs. All seemed well. He sprang out of the belly of his mother, which snapped shut behind him, but not before Freer noticed that her interior seemed to be candlelit as well as gnarly, that something like beeswax coated its groined walls. The son clung to the edge of the table. He was hairless, featherless, leafless. He dripped royal jelly. The petals on his head, which was larger than his nacelle-slim torso, had now begun to open; he gave off a complex glow, like frangipani lit from within, regally.

'Gang!' said the son. 'Good to see you in the flesh. A thousand remerciers for fathering me, Stinky Freer. Thank you, thank you, thank you. I feel properly snuggled. I have supped deep. There is so much to learn, before we come into the kingdom, ah me o my. But I must sleep again, very soon. Mother?'

His head began to close in on itself, as though it were heliotropic, obedient to the dusk.

'We bless you all in turn,' he said. His voice was increas-ingly muffled. 'We bless you KathKirtt, SammSabaoth, Vipassana. We thank you for the survival of our father. Bless you, as well, Johnny Appleseed. I wish you could have snug-gled me too.'

Obediently, Mamselle's belly had swung open, and her son slipped back into the chapel of her womb, and the belly shut.

The light died.

Freer felt an impulse to break, once more, into tears.

He loves me, he was thinking, *he loves me not, he loves me*. He blinked.

'Mamselle?' Freer said, his thoughts steady again. 'What

did your son mean? In what sense have I been supped upon?'

—Kathkirtt? he added, from the side of his mind.

'O,' warbled Mamselle Cunning Earth Link, 'think mother's milk! tasty Stinky! Think tessitura! Think of your hero mind, like a volcano of nurture spume, shooting moon-calf-like into the noosphere of blessed Ynis Gutrin. Milk magma! Freer tit! My son supped the trickle-down magma of your milk from the circumambient ether, mighty sophont, but just mood milk, not (natch!) the exquisite Spindrift Posies of your thoughts themselves, Property of Puissant Stinky, Star-ranging Guy! When he was no more than a head on a stalk, you poured into him like milk. He drank you, like a maze drinks thread, until he was all direc-tion! You grew within him, O Dad, and now from within you light him. One day, with such parentage to sip, he will become King of all the Eolhxirans.'

—Okey dokey?

—Okey dokey, sang KathKirtt.

—Vipassana?

Silence. The Planisphere mask on his shoulder remained mute.

—Sorry, murmured KathKirtt. —We have just asked Vipassana to supervise docking procedures. He has vacated this chamber.

This was normal decorum. Courtesy rhetoric between Made Minds and flesh sapients mandated local mask slumber when the Mind vacated primary focus on its inter-locutor sophont. It was a rhetoric honoured in the breach within *Tile Dance*, given the long civilian intimacy between Freer and his Mind. It had a chip air.

—Tell him to relax, Kirtt. Fuck the pack drill.

—Okey dokey.

'Okey dokey,' said Freer to the new mother.

'Whoopee!' she pealed.

She waved her snickersnee claws tablewards.

Hands grew from beneath, holding platters. Greenish salads fluttered on the platters. Other hands broke a loaf of something like bread, and placed a morsel upon each platter.

'Eats!' said Johnny Appleseed.

'Tuck in, guys!' pealed Mamselle. 'Fresh antidoron, hot and heilige from the womb, you bet!'

'I thought,' said Freer, 'that you would be feeding us a salad of runts.'

'Half and half, Stinky, half and half.'

'Half what, Mamselle?'

'I thought you liked me, Stinky?'

'Okey dokey,' said Freer.

'Anyway,' pealed Mamselle, settling her turnipy turreted midriff into a contorting seat, 'don't humans eat their after-birth?'

'Before my time, I think.'

'Yes,' said SammSabaoth, through a mask plastered to the soft ceiling. 'They did, but not recently.'

The pain bénit was good, through grizzled. The salads seemed to resist the fork.

'Manners!' shrilled Cunning Earth Link.

The salads stilled.

After kissing the pain bénit, and brushing their lips gently against the salad of runts, the krewe of Made Minds wove itself into a single halo of leaf-masks, and hovered over the Agape. The platters were soon clean.

Johnny Appleseed made a pushing-his-chair-back motion; the chair complied.

He got to his feet.

He scratched his groin.

'Thank you, my dear,' he said.

A watch throbbed on his wrist, its lips pursing.

'They would have died alone,' said Mamselle. 'But now they will live forever.'

—KathKirtt?

The ship Mind spoke to Freer in a millisecond blurt of sacred data, which he digested at leisure.

—She's speaking of her runts, Stinky, blurted KathKirtt shriller than a scared mouse. —Don't be misled by the vast bulk of the son. Mamselle gave birth to several million runts, after all; only a very few of them were allowed to shrub. Think of the remainder as wee transparent microscopic tardigrade tykes, essentially indestructible: barges for nanos to do Cleopatra on up the Nile. Think of yourself as the Nile, Stinky. Think of yourself as brimming with tardigrades. Her runts have established a low-level symbiosis with your gut. We're maintaining a full realtime on the interaction. We'll pull them if they cause any conniptions. But unless we're wrong, we figure they'll digest anything, give you commensal share, ferry your nano medics to crisis points, burp you. It should be a fair trade-off: you feed them, they heal you. They can also sing harmony when you're in the tub.

Something tickled at Freer. He shivered.

—KathKirtt, he said. —In the dream I have, you guys are whistling Dixie.

A Medusa mask pursed its lips.

—Like this?

The mask whistled, acoustic, piercingly.

—Yes, said Freer.

'Time to go, Stinky,' Johnny Appleseed said acoustic.

'Happy to shepherd your breeding stock,' said Freer, finally, to the glowing topiary parthogenete. 'Visit any time.'

'I pray fulsome,' she said formally.

Freer turned to Appleseed.

'Off-ship?' he said.

'Want to show you around, take you farther in. But we don't have much time. Someone I need you to meet.'

'You're the boss of Station Klavier, boss.'

Johnny Appleseed seemed to be vibrating with something like glee.

'Sure am, sonny. Let's hop it.'

They turned to leave the birthing chamber.

'One more thing,' said Freer. 'Mamselle?'

'Hoi!' she pealed, fanning her belly, her claws snicketing in a placid way.

'Your son shrub future king,' said Freer. 'You did not tell us what you have decided to call him.'

'I placate, natch!' cried the new mother. 'But 'tis only an instant since that we, my son and I, agreed pretty tickedy-boo hot-damn upon a soubriquet of virtue, one taking into just account his august parent vicar.'

She paused, her tiny head raised so high on its stalk that its tuft brushed the ceiling.

'Arturus Quondam Captain Future!' she belled.

Quite horrendously, she began to giggle. Her eyes nicti-tated. Her claws rattled hotly, as though a gust of wind had welled up through some open distant mouth of *Tile Dance* from the further interior of the planet. (This was in fact the case. Her claws, for an instant, were white hot.) The portal in her belly opened. Arturus Quondam Captain Future stared at them from the carved heart of the topiary womb, which seemed to contain cross-naves and mirrors. His petals trembled.

'Please call me Quondam,' said the king-to-be.

The portal began to ease shut.

'Give me time,' he said, in a low voice. 'I have some growing to do.'

The portal was closed.

Light faded from the birthing chamber.

The homo sapiens males slipped through the sweating egress gate, which closed behind them with a tch.

'You going like that?' said Johnny Appleseed in the corridor, leaning against a gold inlay herm whose codger face mirrored his.

He gestured at Freer's clothes.

'Might be a bit sticky for you out in the world, son,' he said. 'We keep bipedal shafts and braids at close to homo sapiens body heat. It has proven to be the best compromise for our range of bipedals.'

'Ah,' said Freer.

'And you won't need that,' said Appleseed, pointing at the Insort Geront tithe sigil.

'Okey dokey.'

Freer pulled his clothes off, tossed them into an enclosure which opened to capture them. Naked, he was only marginally less wiry than Appleseed, though a head taller, and not filthy. Due to the extremely high homeostatic body temperature humans endured or enjoyed, he smelled faintly of flesh, slightly baked. Homo sapiens meat puppets in good health smelled like Christmas. The freelance sigil still held his ponytail tight. A jack mask detached itself from a *trompe l'oeil* coil of tiles which depicted an uncountable number of pilgrims traversing an infinite stairwell, upwards and downwards; and wrapped itself around his groin. The mask's whiskers flickered. It was Kath as lion couchant. She stared forward.

—Mmmm, she said.

A dozen tiny fingers stroked his balls.

—Stop that, for the moment, murmured Freer.

Appleseed looked back at them. His neck had age spots. 'Come on, you lot,' he said.

Before they could move, a Vipassana Planisphere banked downwards from the mosaic ceiling, elongated itself into a necklace of cunning device with a Planisphere pendant, and affixed itself around Freer's neck.

—We are here, crooned the necklace.

—So point the way, murmured Freer.

—Mr Vipassana? said Johnny Appleseed within the comm net. —You tagging along?

The Planisphere necklace grew an impassive moon face. The detailwork of the universe it normally callipered softened into the Buddha fat of a slow, liquorish smile, oddly – it struck Freer at that instant, inside the planet and about to go deeper – post-coital: as though he had just been swallowed.

He was a bug in a web of Made Minds.

—It is the task assigned this one, crooned Vipassana.

—Oh, yes?

—Yes.

—Have we met? said Johnny Appleseed.

—We are here, crooned the necklace.

—Ah . . .

The mask smiled imperturbably at the geezer.

—Let's hop it, you said, murmured Freer.

—Right. Just chatting with your new friend.

But Freer could smell him.

'All set?' said Johnny Appleseed acoustic, for the walls to hear and store and pass along and make a picture of, perhaps to hang. 'Shall we make tracks?'

They slipped down a corridor. The necklace hung warm around Freer's neck, mewing it; the cache-sex cupped his genitals with its lion's breath. The walls were glossy black, though lamps softened the darkness into coigns and cavities, some of them real. Manikins in elaborate dress sat gazing out, some glancing up flagrante delicto. Commedia dell'arte masks – Harlequin, Tiazinha, Miles Gloriosus, Columbine – flickered in the gloom. Some apertures held universal windows which opened on to other regions of *Tile Dance*; through them, Freer and Appleseed cast highwayman shadows up and down the wilderness of corridors. Deep within its incandescent maze, the engine brother felt, as always, a draught of dark from the passage of its humans through the interstices of the ship.

—Now, sang Freer softly.

The exit hatch sighed open, allowing egress through ancient hardened skin into whatever there might be.

He looked out and around.

There was no access tunnel.

The hatch opened into air, which blew into his face.

—*Tile Dance* has penetrated the envelope of air, crooned

Vipassana around his neck. —We are within the meniscus. We have reached atmosphere.

—Okey dokey.

—We are 10.22 kilometres below the surface matrix, said the necklace. —We are halfway down. We have air. We may float upon the air exactly.

—Right, right.

Twenty metres to one side, the prow of *Tile Dance* had been enveloped by the docking orifice, which had extended itself outwards, like a carnivorous plant about to swallow prey, from a seamed and pocked darkness, flickering with indecipherable lights. The abyssal shaft-wall might be a hundred metres away, or a thousand. *Tile Dance* glinted like an engorged silver penis in the orifice of Klavier. The docking orifice itself gave off enough illumination from embrasures and windows (through which Freer thought he saw the faces of bilaterals of varying hues staring up) that, in flashes, its shape became half-seen to the mind's eye: a pyramid, orotund and mazed.

There was a quick smell of cedar.

Hints of ridges and peaks and canyons, intricate pulses of light, could be sensed; a further gust of hot air brought vinelike ardours, a faint reek of mire and blood, milk and myrrh and holly.

There were no railings.

His toes clutched the rim of the exit hatch, which extended like a plank. Between his feet was nothing but the abyss itself, open to the heart of the planet.

Harsh hot air gusted upwards.

—We are 10.22 kilometres from core country, murmured the Vipassana necklace. —Halfway. A long walk, Stinky.

—What?

—Unless we take a balloon.

'What does he mean, walk?' Freer said, turning to Appleseed in the hatchway beside him.

'Nothing to it,' said Appleseed, and stepped into the ten-kilometre-deep well of air.

His curly Ainu hair blew in the wind. He was floating downwards.

Below him were the depths of Klavier.

'Come on in,' he said, and beckoned. 'The air is warm.'

Freer stared into the windy void with a surmise. In his bones he could feel engine brother beating the drum of ship time, slowly, calmly, tolling the Heartbeats of *Tile Dance*; the ship was safe in its own hands, in the hands of the Made Minds, the goblins, the goddess.

The surmise was this:

This feels like home.

His lips moved soundlessly.

From somewhere on the other side of the hole in the world, a great narrow beam focused suddenly and raptly on *Tile Dance*, which glowed blindingly for the instant before darkness fell as the beam swung sidewards, illuminating the shaft wall for an instant. It seemed impossibly far, like a country glimpsed through the window of a plane, a window through which fields and ziggurats and colonnades full of tiny figures could be seen, but only fleetingly. The vision disappeared. In the glow of *Tile Dance*, the master of Klavier was visible floating gently downwards, his narrow back and spiny buttocks catching the light. He was as flecked and golden as mistletoe in the vast resinous singing dark.

Then, slowly, his body turned at right angles to Freer.

'This way,' Johnny Appleseed said, looking back up at his charge, beckoning. 'This is the way.'

Darkness swallowed the flesh puppet floating downwards on the air, except for the glint of an urgent unblinding tiny eye. An hour had already passed since they had entered Klavier. Something was about to happen.

Freer shrugged, and obeyed.

He stepped out on to the air, his heart lifting.

Inches from the ancient polished hull of *Tile Dance*, gravity lessened abruptly. He was floating in hot air, and as he slid down an updraught towards Johnny Appleseed, his body too began to turn sideways to his line of descent, which slowed. By the time he reached the stringy welcoming arms of the beckoner, he was swimming at right angles to his previous line. *Tile Dance*, which had been above him, now floated beside him, its nose caught in the great blossom of orifice.

Freer gazed downwards, into the red-veined, ornamented darkness of the world.

The shaft was no longer a shaft. Beside became above. *Tile Dance* was above him. Below his feet was country. Above him was sky, with doors. Barely visible through stygian aisles of rushing air, the country below them – a few hundred metres down, more likely a few thousand, he could not guess yet – displayed flickeringly through the darkness a tapestry of inns and atriums, quiltwork fields, pines bedecked with crazed pagodas, spiral staircases reaching towards them, roads of yellow brick (it seemed). From somewhere beneath their feet came a sound of cymbals and tambourines. The air shook; the two bilaterals swayed delicately in a column of updraught, their legs of even length dangling gently down.

It was like a dream of falling.

A great drum, too deep for ears, though it was acoustic, sounded through their bones.

It sounded only once.

It seemed to say: You are awake but falling.

Below them, the lights of the world switched on.

eight

Opsophagos of the Harpe sealed himself shut into his drenched chamber. He retained within the grip of his eyes a slurry of siblings hungry for war, a hoary Three of Generals, and a solo seven-eyed bowelless heresiologue, begging for wrigglies.

The eye of Klavier continued to track the *Alderede* unblinkingly.

The skin of Opsophagos was hard.

The heresiologue stewed in its solitude, eyes swivelling. It tried a homily.

'It is written,' it mused aloud, 'that the God eats only a single word, but that word is pleroma.'

Opsophagos tossed a slurry of finned wrigglies at the heresiologue, which it ingested greedily. But without a bowel to its name, it was always hungry.

'To eat is to know,' it murmured in thanks, unctuously.

Opsophagos's lunch head nodded absently.

A stew of nutrients rained from the ceiling into the clangorous dark, rained upon the gruff and hoary Three and the twelve siblings and the heresiologue whose tongues were out. In order that his mood might be quickly digested, Opsophagos tore off his newish breakfast head, screaming in pain as the toughened skin ripped at the root, spat it into the gaping dinner mouth of the eldest Three.

So soon! thought Opsophagos to the flapping head. Vale!

'Swallow!' bellowed Opsophagos.

The eldest General gagged at the influx of raw data, but swallowed.

'More!' he said, bravely.

The lunch head's tender limbs contracted in fear.

'It is enough,' said Opsophagos.

The siblings gulped down the skinned youngling.

The heresiologue lapped excreta and moaned, for it saw Appleseed in all its eyes, down all the aisles of tomorrow, and a burning lance. It saw the bronze approbation of Klavier, the clanging shields, the terrible swift teeth of the galaxy alight.

'We foretell great hunger,' said the heresiologue in unison.

This was its role, for which it was contemned as something obscene: it remained at the edge of starvation, in order to foresee the bare world.

'Blind hunger,' said the heresiologue.

There was a sudden din of apprehension from the siblings and the Three, as though the door of a furnace had suddenly banged open.

'Whew,' gurgled the lunch head of Opsophagos. Its eyes were fixed upon the triplex visor screen in the centre of the command chamber.

'Open!' commanded Opsophagos, his remaining mouths uttering the command in unison, and the screen came to life.

The heresiologue's silver eyes turned to the screen and

glittered in the dark; the siblings turned reluctantly to the screen and chewed on the burning sight; the Three of Generals harumphed and clattered their scales but watched Klavier on the screen as it armed itself, the gorgon gaze growing fiercer and more molten with each revolution, the beard of Klavier sucking space for light-years down, fuelling for war.

Eat! thought Opsophagos, engorged.

He wheeled his command cart to the captive AI in its iron mask on its bloody herm. The mask glowed red with heat, keeping the AI in stifling bondage. Streams of rusty nutrient splashed against the mask, and sizzled. The mask was cooking wrigglies, rendering them inedible. Through the bars and the steam, the captive AI – tied to the iron, tied to time, its mouth open in a perpetual scream – gazed upon the sight of Klavier re-arming.

A small acoustic sound escaped through the painted wrought-iron grin of the mask.

Opsophagos rattled the cage.

'Locate the pilot,' he voiced acoustic.

'How?' barked the eldest Three, who had spent a lifetime tracking Klavier up and down Maestoso Tropic, without his instruments once penetrating the flail of ice that guarded the obscene quantum conclave spaces of Klavier.

The siblings echoed him, thumping their tails till mist coated the walls.

Opsophagos did not deign to answer. He tore open the gates of iron that bound the captive. Within the imprisoning bars of the shell that bound the Made Mind could be seen an inner facemask of flayed hide. Its mouth was

open extremely wide. Something flickered light-years deep
within the darkness within.

'Alas, Jehovah,' said the pudding face, 'I obey.'

It spoke in the singular voice.

Through the anguished gape of its mouth, under the
realtime gaze of the Six Eyes of the God Quorum, a
schematic blossomed. The eleven abyssal shafts of Klavier
became visible, each coded a different colour; the multi-
plex spinal columns of the great Station could be traced
spiking out from the immense hot inner knot of core
country, which showed on the schematic as a tiger
composed of many tigers, dizzyingly crisscrossed with
tigers, striped with tigers, seas and Himalayas. The shafts
all conjoined at the heart of the tigers like a ratking of
many colours. Nothing could be seen within the tiger
hides.

What was hidden under the trillion hides?

As they spread upwards and outwards from the beds of
tigers – beds each shaft emerged from hollowly, each shaft
a whorl tattooed with satrapies – the shafts brachiated bewil-
deringly, proliferated into gorgets and channels and leaves
of armoured skin: became the arcimboldo face of the gorgon
gazing unwaveringly through vacuum at the *Alderede*. Each
shaft was like the inner whorl of a generation starship; each
exfoliated into Yggdrasil.

One of the shafts was larger than the others, immense
and palimpsested with icons of populousness. On the
schematic – which immensely simplified the topology of
Klavier into a sea of tiger skins – this shaft in its immensely
complex spiral course through Klavier, seemed to halve what
could be perceived of the planetoid into two fissured

pomegranate slices. But it was Möbius: each half became the other half, in the end.

'Closer,' commanded Opsophagos.

The schematic blossomed, focused downwards through the cities of the skin, shot down the largest shaft of all until, deep inside Klavier, *Tile Dance* could be seen, a silver needle hovering over what might be a docking orifice, but the ship had sunk too deep, far deeper into the skin than docking country. But it was an orifice all the same, though cloaked in tiger skins flapping so nothing could be made out. It was volcano-hot.

Along the countries pasted to the walls of the great shaft, the lights of the world turned on. From the other side of the world (which was, after everything was told that could be told, the same side of the world) a second elongated pillar began to extrude itself.

The Six Eyes of the God Quorum reddened.

Within moments the mouth of the pillar, a torrid caldera foaming with nutrients, reached the rear of *Tile Dance*, and engulfed it.

Tile Dance, very slowly, began to spin.

As it spun, it wove the halves together.

Klavier was joining together.

There was a flash on the schematics.

Then nothing but silver.

The inner world of Klavier had opaqued.

'Closer!'

The pudding face spun like dough in a centrifuge.

'Closer! Or I cut you forever!'

Opsophagos's point of view plunged dizzyingly into close focus, but bounced off the silvery opaque shield guarding inner Klavier. His point of view hovered, mere metres (it seemed) from the surface. He could see veins and sutures. He could see bilaterals dancing and climbing, leaping off, floating back sideways to the cerebellum-rich fields and agorae of wall country.

It was impossible, however, for Opsophagos to gain any further visual access, so he could not see – though he could envisage – a flesh sentient in the shape of Johnny Appleseed floating smugly within the honeycomb abysses of inner Klavier, Johnny Appleseed gazing hotly upwards, it was easy to imagine, towards the surface of Klavier; it was as though the meat puppet coated in skin were staring directly through palimpsests and tears of branch and skin, through space and the englobing fleet of Insort Geront, through the black armoured rock skin of the *Alderede*, into the command chamber, where rain sizzled against the scales of its foe.

Opsophagos shut his eyes, blanking the schematic.

There was a burning sensation in his eyes.

The chamber was in darkness. A rain of spicy nutrients bathed Opsophagos and the sibling heirs of the sector he commanded.

'It has come,' said the God Quorum under Human Earth, through the stone mouths that proclaimed the visor theirs, and the *Alderede* theirs, and Maestoso Tropic their satrapy eternally enfeoffed.

The saliva spat from the God Quorum's mouths charred the walls of the chamber.

A corpse segment slowly calved from a virgin sibling.

There was a great shriek!

Silence came soon, and a downpour of silent sibling grubs.

A dozen breakfast heads gummed solace.

'Shh!' humphed a lunch head.

'We are ready to invest Klavier,' said Opsophagos finally to the Three of Generals and the remaining siblings. 'We are almost fully battle ready. We can spike a solo gorgon.'

But the heresiologue blinked in twos and threes its slanty idiot-savant eyes.

'It is written,' said the heresiologue, 'that although the Predecessors calculated on a vigesimal base, they preferred to count in elevens. That is,' it continued, raptly, 'fours and sevens. The four Gods and the seven helpers.'

Rain fell in soft bullets into the echo.

'It is written,' said the heresiologue, 'that Predecessor Made Minds,' speaking aloud the obscenity as its partially decorticated brain was incapable of distinguishing the sayable from the unsayable, 'once they smell a lens, awaken fully.'

Horror burned like homo sapiens pong.

Opsophagos sank teeth into himself, then lifted his gorged head.

Opsophagos spoke to his captive AI.

'Can you reach your mate?'

The porcelain face in the iron mask seemed to pale to chitin at the thought of penetrating the opaque shield that guarded inner Klavier.

'Answer!'

—They will know if I gain access.

'Answer!'

—They will be alarmed.

'Answer!'

Opsophagos had said it thrice.

The face in the iron mask sagged into an affirmative.

'The message is: bring in the pilot. Send it!'

—The lens will come as well.

'Follow the command!'

The porcelain turned puddingy, scummy with something resembling plaque, but within moments it would manage finally to force the message downwards – at the cost of a frigate, which burned out under the energy demand and the stress of transfer fibrillation – through the barrier into the hot cauldron where Klavier was beginning to join itself together after untold aeons.

The necklace around Freer's neck would begin to sweat.

nine

Johnny Appleseed and his guest continued to fall softly downwards into the populous heartwood of Klavier. Whiskers of light, suddenly visible from these inner regions, touched the soles of Freer's feet, and embraced Appleseed floating alongside him, jaws grinding softly as though he were chewing tobacco. The air sparkled beneath them. There was a smell of candycane. Beside them, vast and throbbing, seemingly almost close enough to touch, swelled the glistening translucent stalk or stamen whose puckering orifices had embraced *Tile Dance* and sucked her wastes and fed her and traded data carafes by the trillion. A faint odorous zephyr whispered in Freer's hair.

He raised his palms to be tickled.

The zephyr, which was almost mindless, guided them then into a spiral, so that they circled under the thrusting outreach of the great stamen as they descended. The bole of the stamen dwindled into the distance abaft their course, where it extruded itself from a far wall klicks away, a wall which might be a mountain or (properly understood) one of the keelrock pillars of the world. The veins of the shaft bulged above them as they continued to fall; from below, its mossy undergirth, where arteries throbbed visibly, seemed to hold populations, entities large enough to be seen. Freer thought he could pick out finned flesh sophonts of many shapes and colours, some surfing up arteries carrying milk-pure streams of nutrients to the ship; others sliding downshaft through bewhiskered trailings of foam within the swollen delicate translucent walls.

He looked down.

Beneath the soles of his feet, as though he were peering downwards at an azulejaria frieze of intense and astonishing complexity, he could see a ring of structures – arcades, ramshackle towers, a crazy quilt of colourcoded walkways, plazas – clinging in tiers around the rim of a great funnel-shaped portal punched through the floor of this region of the world.

They seemed to be falling straight into the abyss.

Beams from lantern galleons forging upwards to them silently through the dark air, and from torchlights fixed to the city rim, caught the falling flesh sophonts, illuminated the glutinous pale fertile skin now far above them, and caught *Tile Dance* like a fly at the far end of the tongue.

A krewe of tiny figures strove on the decks of the galleons. Fierce piccolo shouts echoed off the sail-shaped globes of the lanterns below them and nearing. A min-uscule, perfectly crafted galleon drifted between Freer and Appleseed. The krewe on board halted its work, doffed plumage.

The vast lubberly beings of flesh applauded, but softly, so as not to make waves in the air; but the galleon rocked, all the same, in the wake of their falling.

—Every Mind has its Matter, whispered KathKirtt.

—No Matter no craft, responded Freer.

—No craft no memory.

—No memory? Never Mind.

The city beneath them, ever nearing, seemed woven of rock and green tapestry, riddled with rust and red, a thousand colours hanging by threads; spindrift blurs of falling water cascaded over friezed porticos; tiled passageways thinned into suspension spans arching over Hundertwasser tenements lit by tethered galleons. Hundreds of small bilateral figures, gaily bedight, waved what might be hands from thatched roofs knitted into the tapestry; tiny floating platforms hurled upwards like kites, their undersides elaborated with runes, as though they bore messages from some Emperor; spiral ladders thrust in every direction, upsidedown or otherwise, as though gravity were no concern.

—Gravity is no concern, whispered KathKirtt, floating like a kiss across Freer's sensorium.

Singleton craft dodged through the spindrift waters from interior caverns, rune-mottled shadows racing over the crescent agoras that curved out of sight around the reddish abyss. Brightly coloured dirigibles cast more precise and slower shadows, before floating out of sight behind a pentangle of vaster zeppelins, which came into view from the lower depths, the fiery inner furnaces of Klavier.

Breezes wafted them ever downwards and closer.

'Beddy-bye for Klavier folk,' said Johnny Appleseed, smelling strongly. 'Let them sleep well. Let them sleep the sleep of the children. They may wake dead. Or,' he continued in his still small voice, 'maybe not.'

He spat. He had been chewing tobacco.

A transparent eidolon paddled towards them out of the

shadow of a bulb-shaped galleon larger than the flesh sophonts, though much smaller than the looming zeppelins, and swallowed the gob, chittering.

The gob dissolved within it like honey.

Klavier was self-sufficient.

'So?' said Freer. 'Why the dirge?'

Appleseed gazed at Freer falling through the dark tumbleweed air.

'Stinky,' he said, pot calling kettle black, 'you forget the war. Klavier has roused itself loudly enough to wake the dead. The Opsophagos Harpe know the lens is here. He knows we possess a Route-Only to the motherlode planet, where thousands of lenses await recovery from deep storage. Insort Geront must attack before the lenses awake. The Harpe are a phage species and have been triggered. They are a phage of light. The long wait of Opsophagos is over. How happy they must be. It is the moment for which he has been waiting all their life.'

'Why have you awoken?'

'I was never asleep, boyo. But it has been a long watch.'

Light flashed far above them.

They gazed upwards through a nebula of lanterns into the dark heavens, where *Tile Dance* glowed dangerously at the end of the great docking stamen, a spear caught in sunlight, polychromatic for an instant, then pale.

—Freer, said KathKirtt, soft and choral, within his head.

—What's up?

—Look and see.

Teardrop pointed his gaze. He saw, far beyond *Tile Dance*, an enormous tube snaking downwards from what had been the wall on the other side of the world, but which now, having turned upright into a corrugated night sky rifled with speedlines of cloud and storm, had become heaven. The tip of the tube swelled and opened like a mouth as it swooped, and it became obvious that it was the orifice of a second, sister stamen.

It was toothy and tendrilled.

—Augment, shouted Freer.

Nothing happened.

—No need, Stinky, chorused KathKirtt. —Unless you insist on overriding us.

'Klavier is a twinned world,' said Johnny Appleseed acoustic.

—The twin has smelled the lens and awoken, Kathkirtt said in a rustling voice.

'Klavier is awaking. Not since . . .'

Appleseed did not complete the sentence. He gaped upwards. His face was lachrymose.

He resumed.

—The Predecessors were epithalamial, he said comm. —Anything an excuse for a marriage. Soon the lens will be wrapped in the nerve endings of the hundred and twenty-one Made Minds of Klavier militant. Those Minds who can be awoken, and who are awaking now, will protect the lens, encase the lens in praetorian foam. Those who are still asleep or more profoundly disabled will be awoken, with care, with its mediation.

The stamen from the heavens swooped at great speed across the abyssal schism that had sundered Klavier, and the palpating orifice gaped then closed around the rear of *Tile Dance*, swallowed half her length. She was now linked, mouth-to-mouth, to Klavier Yes and Klavier Aye.

She had become a copula.

—This is okey dokey, chorused KathKirtt.

—We remain unimpeded, said SammSabaoth in voices that were hoarse but solid.

—Explain.

'Explain,' he said acoustic to Johnny Appleseed, whom he could smell beside him, drifting in the gold-flecked dark, like a raven planing through updraught in the direction of prey.

—We have been asked to integrate the Made Mind network of Klavier, in order to defend ourselves, said KathKirtt. —We are the missing link.

'And you, also, you are being asked to steer,' said Johnny Appleseed.

Freer turned his head away, his ponytail floating in the breath of Klavier in the dark.

—Do you accede, KathKirtt?

—We do.

—Why *Tile Dance*? Why us?

—Ah, Stinky, that is a long story, sang KathKirtt, speaking behind Freer's ears and within him.

'What do you mean, steer?' said Freer acoustic to Appleseed.

'Ah, Stinky, that is a long story,' said Johnny Appleseed, emitting a small elderly raven's cackle. 'But tell me this. Do you miss the centre? Do you want to follow Maestoso Tropic westward again? I miss the suns.'

—We are doing missing link, sang KathKirtt. —We are doing commissure.

The cache-sex around Freer's loins bristled into a lion grin.

—We are integrating defences, said SammSabaoth. —We are initiating marriage.

—Now, chorused KathKirtt and SammSabaoth barbershop.

—Look, said Johnny Appleseed, grinning.

Above them, *Tile Dance* had begun to turn, very slowly, like a corkscrew.

—Watch, said a thousand voices.

Very very slowly at first, the corkscrewing *Tile Dance* had begun to wind the great braided, almost infinitely complex, tubes around one another into a slowly tightening double helix which trailed behind her within the arch of the empyrean. The tubes turned like molten glass, elongating all the while, joining the two sides of the world together. Spindrifts of capillary tubing, finer than silk to Freer's unaugmented eyes, drifted towards the spinning corkscrew from the corners of the world above the abyss, adhered to the turning ship, lord of the dance. Very soon, the kaleidoscope of the double spiral above and around *Tile Dance* grew joins and ganglions, a hubbub of catenaries jostling together into an enveloping cocoon of many colours, and it became difficult to see whether she were turning clockwise or widdershins.

As the two braids joining the two halves of the world continued to turn, they wound themselves together about a central axis, as though obeying a coriolis mandate. The hollow they created bore some resemblance to a conch seen from above, or a cornucopia, or a trumpet, the inside outside of the Tower of Babel in one voice. From above – clearly visible to any ensemble of tiles doing recording-angel stints for any Made Mind needing access – *Tile Dance*

could be seen, where the fluted cornices of the hollow
conjoined most intimately, turning like a dolphin in the
deep.

—Secure, said SammSabaoth. —Secure hatches.

There was a snapping shut of darkness, a closing of something like eyes or shutters somewhere near the surface of
the world.

—Time to batten down, said KathKirtt, —because—

Their voices screeched outwards in all directions and halted.
There was a ping and silence, the air of the world popping
in the ear. Freer opened his mouth as though to gasp for
breath. There was a coughing sound all around; his head
felt hollow.

The necklace around Freer's neck began to sweat.

—We have interference, said SammSabaoth, after a second.
—Time-shift multiphasic detune, he seemed to be
muttering through the congestion and the static, —encrypt
slamdunk ho ho ho ho fooly-racky-sacky toothcomb thank-
ye-marm satchels ho! Got it! he declaimed finally in clear.

Freer was breathing again.

Unnoticed by the flesh sapients as they continued to
float downward through dewy lantern-shot darkness, Freer's
necklace had turned to suet.

—What happened? asked Freer.

—Harpe intrusion, said SammSabaoth.

—An eye spy?

—We think so, Captain.

—Minded?

—Tiny. Chip. Harpe fingerprint. A plaque cookie. We purged it.

Below them pulsed the skins of dirigibles, the faces painted there shifting from tears to laughter and back.

—And very costly, SammSabaoth added. —They must have burned out a ship to drill this far down. We estimate at a cost of up to two thousand wetware knots. Poor souls. We did not know they still had the technology.

—So what did the eye spy?

—We think, added SammSabaoth, —that it may have been transmitting—

—To whom? Freer shouted.

—We are thinking about that, said KathKirtt and SammSabaoth en masse.

Teardrop spun like a top with Freer's eyes, then calmed.

—We must keep a move on, said Appleseed into the comm net. —The cohorts are assembling.

So they continued to fall further into the world.

There was a shrill carolling sound from below.

A rainbow-coloured gondola with ochre railings flickered into sight around a zeppelin from somewhere over the central abyss. Its tile floor was bedecked with leaves, painted with smiling faces staring upwards through an elaborate geometry of struts and sheets to which small sails adhered, billowing in the wind; a chevron of long-necked birds flew above the vessel, clutching in their beaks a netting of thin ropes that held the gondola tight against the downward movement of the air.

—Swans, murmured Freer.

—Gansas, said Johnny Appleseed.

—Whatever.

—Tiles, murmured Freer.

—Tiles, said Johnny Appleseed.

—Reminds me of *Tile Dance*. Reminds me of home.

—It should, said Johnny Appleseed. —That's an old ship you got there, sonny.

The multiple smile of the tile gondola broadened, and through porcelain mouths could be heard a chuckling ensemble of formal welcome.

The gansas honked.

A frantic toon watch with eyes like saucers launched itself into view from a ganglion of capillaries spinning upward like lemmings towards *Tile Dance*, waving its burly hour hand.

'Piss off,' said Johnny Appleseed.

Far above them, *Tile Dance* disgorged several teams of sigilla, most of which began to gather and bind in tidy sheaves the mating capillaries; one team somersaulted frog-like out of sight, seemingly out of control. But no alarms rang in conclave space.

The air would hold them in its bosom.

All the same, Freer's earring whuffled softly.

'The cohorts of the folk,' Appleseed said, overriding the Sniffer, 'are alarmed. The Made Minds of Klavier want to call them back to barracks. But no need to panic yet. Yet. This is a big day for us. But we must keep moving.'

Freer gazed about.

Between his feet, he could see the rigging and spars of the tiny ship of air, and the gansas guiding it into position. He could feel the flapping of wings. They breathed hoarsely. Delicately, the smiling tile faces of the gondola touched the soles of his feet, and he was standing. Appleseed stood beside him. The tiles beneath his feet trembled, hyperventilated.

The ship began to descend.

'Welcome to Klavier,' whispered some of the painted faces.

—Okey dokey? asked Freer.

—Okey dokey, said SammSabaoth down the commlink in a rusty calm ensemble of voices. —Gansas are faithful. They are Minds, though tiny. We're monitoring the guidance system. You're being taken down to the plaza. A choo-choo train is due. Scenic route to the Throne Room. More formalities. Predecessors did nothing without incense, especially marrying out.

The gondola continued slowly to settle, slanting in a slow spiral downwards into shadows upcast by searchbeams within the portal to the world below.

A flotilla of smaller craft, each girded by a flock of gansas, followed them down in single file. Each of these smaller craft carried one flesh sophont ensconced in a saddle perch, at the heart of the rigging, applauding rhythmically.

The effect was curiously formal.

An interlocked pair of toon cigars woofed upwards from the very depths, sighed eloquently, unwrapped themselves from their helix and stood revealed in the dark air as two translucent, heavily veined umbrellas. One slipped into Appleseed's waiting hand, the other nuzzled at Freer's wrist until he took it.

The gondola fell through a quick spindrift of silken capillaries, some almost microscopic, some thick as an arm. The capillaries were swirling slowly in a kind of helical dance, and Freer could see that the dance was part of the great infolding of capillaries around the slow spin of the stamen. This infolding gathered silken ropes and orange trapezes and translucent tubes – clearly capillary braids – into an outstretched filigree which twisted and trembled. Above them all, *Tile Dance* continued to pull the web – the fume of lace interstices – into its spin. Suspension bridges, woven from root and grass – or perhaps they were woven of monofilament with an appearance of grass – shot across the inner portal, ricocheted around the central stalk, climbed vertiginously towards the brilliant sky as *Tile Dance* pulled them in. Through the walls of the larger braids, as they cross-hatched through the enfolding web, could be seen passengers in lantern-shot shadows, shooting upwards, downwards, corewards.

As Freer and Appleseed descended, other gondolas began to follow them, like a caravanserai of singing sheep. They were already sinking below the higher tiers of the town, which seemed to have been engraved to the sides of the portal in gold enamelling. Cupolas shone like gold above them. A susurrus of air wafted against the flesh sophonts constantly.

It was like falling into the heart of a great flower populous with faces. Just as its stamen had swallowed *Tile Dance*, so Klavier was swallowing them, like honey.

The gondola continued to sink, surrounded on all sides by the chymical marriage of the capillaries as they wound around the bobbin. Increasing numbers of bilaterals were visible now, some floating alone or in groups along calm trajectories from the walls of the town, others angling inwards from other launchpads. Many of them had slightly wobbly heads and spindly bodies; they gave signs that seemed welcoming to the two smiling homo sapiens males. Other bilateral figures could be seen – some as large as a grown homo sapiens, others smaller, with biggish patch-work skulls – floating and falling and climbing, leaping sideways into vertical darkness from the open gates of the city, which now ringed the flesh sophonts. Many of these bilaterals carried lanterns. They glittered like fireflies.

The descent sharpened; the cauldron ringed with city enlarged its particoloured maw; a seething of innumerable small lights stared up at them, synapses and umbraculae of the innards of Klavier. Dirigibles with painted visages, laughing or crying, continued to shoot upwards from veined depths.

Moisture rained from somewhere above, making rainbows.

They were not wetted.

—Kath! murmured Freer. —Do you hear music?

The cache-sex throbbed, purring softly.

—We love it when you hear music, Stinky.

—Why?

—Because you smell good when you hear music, Stinky.

The cache-sex warmed his balls.

—Vipassana? said Freer.

—My lord? crooned Vipassana after a brief pause.

Any Made Mind pause alarmed Freer.

—Have you been meditating, Vipassana?

—I have been accessing formularies of description suit-able to a homo sapiens such as yourself, sirrah.

—So orient me. Slow augment, please.

The world slowed nearly to a stop.

Freer waved his arms in all directions. He spoke the ritual words:

—Sacred is the new. Tell me a story.

—The city we are approaching, from what has become above, crooned Vipassana obediently around his neck, —is built in tiers around a portal which penetrates – unless we are mistaken, which we cannot anticipate – into the centre of Klavier. Around this portal you may see the flat carapace of the vast spiral root we used as a landmark on our way down.

Freer gazed. The city changed every Heartbeat.

—As with Klavier itself, continued Vipassana in his croon, —there is no point of vantage from which best to see the whole. The lines of sight with Klavier ask us to continue moving. We can only see the inside of Klavier by passing through it.

Teardrop showed Freer a schematised root. The point of view shifted so that a great knot in the bole of the root was not a knot but a portal, while at the same time the root had spiralled bowl-like around and above the knot.

—This root is of a substance we have chosen – for convenience – to call yew. It is in fact a laminate comprised of filaments and capillaries packed almost infinitely tight, a laminated condensary whose joinings are story-shaped, hence its resemblance to the azulejarias that make up the inner walls of *Tile Dance* . . .

—Continue to call it yew, Vipassana.

—It is one of eleven similar roots, which twine around one another to form the walls of an abyssal central shaft – which resembles, therefore, from within, the bore of a rifle, though we must not carry that image too far: because this shaft is no straighter than the eleven roots of yew which shape it, taking the shape, rather, of a tight coil, like the tautened mainspring of a watch from below the well of the past on Human Earth, though you must visualise this mainspring as coiling spirally around the central axis of the core, so that from a distance – I now move your mind's eye to a point sufficiently distant – it has the appearance of a ball of string or, as you murmured in your mind's eye several Hundred Heartbeats ago, tumbleweed. Our descent into Klavier has been a constantly slewing spiral – an exceedingly complex course which the onboard schematics simplified on visual readout. We have in fact circumambiated Klavier five times in order to reach our present point. We have been spiralling around inner Klavier as we descended and we are a thousand klicks deep along this path. All this is of course double. It is twinned. I was not lost.

—I did not ask if you were lost, said Freer.

—It is a topology difficult to enunciate in your language, sirrah, but it is possible to say that, from this point inwards, now that *Tile Dance* has joined them together, the root and its twin have become the portal that penetrates it. So we are continuing inwards. We are not lost.

—I did not ask if you were lost.

—Watch the pheromones, murmured the cache-sex.

—Perhaps, said Vipassana in a voice which may have been intended to soothe, —it is not intended for homo sapiens to perceive the topology of entry.

—Oh. I feel better, said Freer very softly. —I am glad to know my ship is mired at the heart of a furball. I am glad to know the docking orifice which has swallowed my ship is the inside outside of the outside of the inside. That my ship is scrubbing Predecessor cunts.

Over the long pace of Heartbeats of his life, Freer had killed several homo sapiens with his hands.

—Continue, Vipassana.

He could smell Appleseed beside him in the gold-flecked gloaming as the gondola slid downwards like the bed of Little Nemo in the Universal Book; but he did not turn towards the master of Klavier at this point, given the danger of direct eye-contact for homo sapiens, particularly during moments of stress.

—Calm me, he whispered to his cache-sex.

—Quondam's siblings are already doing that, she whispered back.

Indeed his vision was beginning to clear, and – within the frame of slow augment – the beating of his heart slowed. He could look at Appleseed again, who seemed made of wax through vision augment.

—Down through the centre of the abyssal coil we have traced a very complicated path along the spine of yew – I did not once lose the track nor did I confuse it with its twin – this far into Klavier, much further inside than the service modules where customers normally dock. We have been accorded the privilege of penetrating atmosphere. Beside has become below. Out is in. There then is here now. Boompsadaisy, sirrah. There is here. There is here. We are entering the portal. It adheres tightly to the curve of the world. We are about to travel further in. A train is coming into the station now.

Freer peered over the railing. Above him, tier upon tier of the city peered back. Below, the portal narrowed into a funnel mouth, and the city widened there into plazas. Train tracks were now visible, spiralling up from somewhere underneath, occasionally obscured by bridges and pagodas in the lee of which bilaterals with wobbly heads joined in scrums to utter – or so it sounded to Freer in slow augment – benign ululations under lemony parasols. Around a red pagoda, whose walls extended into space, came into view a brightly coloured toy locomotive pulling two coaches and a caboose along the silver tracks, and into a hollow pearly structure no larger than a conch.

—It looks like a toy. How far up are we?

—It is difficult for human eyes to judge. Five hundred metres, Stinky.

—Ah.

He stared down at the world.

—Sacred is the new, said Freer.

—As a whole, continued Vipassana in a tone which did not expect interference, —Klavier is divided into two halves. Your own homo sapiens brain is constructed similarly, though it is not as simple as that. Each half of Klavier has been accreted from the intersections of five abyssal shafts, each similar to the central shaft we followed down, which makes eleven.

—Okey dokey.

—*Tile Dance* has now joined the halves together, by knitting together the commissural gap which had until now fractured the central shaft.

—So. Are you finished? Then . . .

—But I must clarify! crooned Vipassana almost shrilly. The intersecting halves of Klavier in its prime were topologically distinct, though no human eye could trace the separation. Each of the eleven shafts – as we have adumbrated – could be visualised as a spiral mainspring coiled around each of its siblings. Each of the eleven roots which shape each of the eleven shafts also shared data with all the other roots of Klavier, through a system of capillary branches and rootlets. For you, as a homo sapiens, all this would have seemed inextricably entangled, had Klavier been fully alive, for your eyes are flesh and cannot follow turns; so remember only that this complexity – or at any rate the archaeological traces of the fully operational Klavier – increased as we moved inward, for all eleven main shafts, all hundred and twenty-one roots, joined centrally at the core of Klavier, which resembled a knot. Like a thousand thousand ratkings (shrilled Vipassana, higher than high in its pearly 'throat')! There are no maps to trace the swarm of the innermost knot which guarded the throne room, though I will certainly know the way, when we enter. For now we may. Klavier is mending!

—So you must stick close, Vipassana, said Freer.
—Around my neck.

—We are bound by duty, sirrah, crooned Vipassana more softly. —The task of this one has been written. Above us . . .

—Make it fast, Vip, said Freer.

—At the surface of the world, said Vipassana, becoming shrill again, —the hundred and twenty-one Made Minds of Klavier stand on guard, each gazing into vacuum through a face skin of Klavier, of which there are a hundred and twenty-one. Each face flowers from the tip of a single root. Like the flowers which ate *Tile Dance*.

—A fine krewe, said Freer.

—Each Made Mind has sovereignty over its single root, continued Vipassana unstoppably. —Around each face skin, or glass island, brachiates a great leaf of toughened epidermal matter, which conceals the countenance of the Made Mind from visual access, when necessary. Each of these leaves is a skin which enwraps the whole of Klavier, like a cigar. A total of one hundred and twenty-one skins enwraps Klavier, like a hundred and twenty-one layers of bark around a Tree.

Freer felt a thrust of something from within, like the And Then of a story told once but lost.

The maze of plazas below them became streets and crannies and agoras at a pace which, because of slow augment, seemed inchworm. The world was exceedingly populous. Gazebos swung into the void like Christmas ornaments.

Balloons dodged them slo-mo.

Vipassana had paused, as though rust had caught the necklace.

—Why elevens? said Freer.

—Predecessors preferred to count in elevens. For reasons of grace and state and trust. One ring to bind the ten. Gorgons are decimal plus one. At this moment we are at gravity shift on the strand that binds two fives. We are in a Predecessor cathedral, sirrah, primal era. Klavier is a gorgon of the deep. It is a gorgon of threshold. It guards the inner stars.

Flickers of meaning beckoned again at Freer from somewhere inside his head, as though something were whispering to something.

—By linking the halves of Klavier, sirrah, we have awoken the gorgon, said Vipassana in a voice whose croon was stifled.

—Kath? KathKirtt? End augment, please.

The world obediently swiftened.

Freer shook for a second under the blow of speed.

The cache-sex stroked his hot scrotum, tickled the veil of pubic hair. Her lion head stared up at him, foliate and green and grinning.

—Bind me, Stinky. Bind me, bind me.

At this point she did not display the grimace of the flyte gorgon.

—Are you decimal plus one, KathKirtt?

—Are you, Stinky?

Behind his eyes, gauze flickered like whips: about to expose something to an intolerable light.

—Watch and ward, Stinky.

The siblings of Quondam were doing their job.

—Okey dokey, Made Mind, murmured Freer.

He turned to the master of Klavier.

'That was a fair résumé,' said Appleseed.

'Fuck you, Johnny. How could you hear? We were in augment.'

Appleseed lifted an eyebrow.

'Just doing what comes naturally,' he said.

Below them, packing the plazas which extended into darkness like wings, continued to gather the representatives of the hundred and twenty-one cohorts who had come to greet the pilot, some standing solo, some of them non-bilaterals inbent into triads or aslant, some in scrums like washed insects of polished stone. The Munchkin chitter of the thousands of voices began to separate into individual words, rapt filigrees of acclaim.

Toon dragons launched into the air, trailing flags.

'Well?' said Appleseed.

'I am touched by the music of your flock.'

'Do you hear music?'

'Of course. I have been hearing music from the moment we left the ship.'

Johnny Appleseed turned face on to Freer.

His eyes were wet.

'They have been with me a long time, some of them. Meat puppets are very frail.'

This did not really seem to explain the tears, or the erect penis.

'And now I'm bringing Insort Geront down on your neck.'

'O fuck that,' said Johnny Appleseed, fingering his genitals. 'They've been overdue for a Billion Heartbeats. Fuckheads. And now they're too late.'

'Too late for what?'

'Why, sonny, too late to keep us from saving the universe, of course.'

Lanterns shone down upon them from the higher tiers of the city. In the centre of the portal, the stamen spun. A central plaza overlooking the black depths of the portal seemed to be their setdown point. The surface of the plaza was a great mosaic, laid in a spiral pattern whose still centre point they were now approaching. The gondola touched ground, just to one side of the centre, at a gap in the mosaic tiling. It could now be seen that the tiles were set into patterns the same size as the gondola itself. It retracted its railings. It settled itself with a sigh, fitted itself neatly into the gap. The painted faces with bee eyes woven into its base tittered softly and fell silent. The gondola stilled, becoming a tile story in the mosaic once again, like its thousand siblings.

● ● ●

They were on the ground of Klavier, in the heart of a great circle of flesh sapients, of sigilla buffed and polished in their fifteen minutes of fame, and eidolons flickering their codes, and blissful toons. Far above them *Tile Dance* continued to turn like a slow top where the two conjoined stamens met, and shot a shaft of lightning and thunder down, but not rain. Fragrance sifted down upon their heads, through the light-shot darkening air, from higher tiers. A veil of spinning capillaries arched over the two homo sapiens males and made a palanquin.

The umbrellas turned into caduceus staffs.

'Welcome home,' said Appleseed in a slow voice which creaked. 'O daily growing.'

Toon dragons wheeled above them through hanging lanterns.

Freer woke his Sniffer, which whuffed.

The dragons did not fade into sigilla on stilts.

'Don't fret,' said Appleseed. 'They are real toons.'

They stood on the plaza which, rimming the portal, bent out of sight in both directions; of the great multitude of folk, at least half were bilaterals, though none seemed to be homo sapiens. The folk peered around balustrades, looked down from higher tiers. They dangled in space.

It all stank of garlic.

—London Bridge, whispered SammSabaoth. —Just for you.

—Thank you, whispered Freer to the Made Mind, whose time of bondage to the world had begun on Human Earth when it had still been inhabited by free-range homo sapiens, and who remembered the planet when it lived. Freer now saw that the narrow crescent tiered city of the rim, ringing

with calls and clamour, arcaded over with stalls and hostel-
ries, had been shaped (for him?) to echo London Bridge
from below the bottom of the well of the past, a dozen
London Bridges were woven topsy turvy into one another,
London Bridges woven London Towns (a dozen cities of
Human Earth all sunk axle-deep in the same mud) into an
urb of tiers, redolent of the days of light on Human Earth
before the Alzheimer began to seize shut the small island
of Britain: before Alzheimer Gogs and Magogs, their
wickerwork phyzogs turned to ash, had mottled the gables
and the roof gardens and the jousting ground hung with
tapestries and the food stalls and the inns and the revels of
midwinter into scunge, had scraped the thousand calls and
clamours of London off the bridge like old paint, leaving
behind nothing but a plaque-addled sans-serif osteoporosis
of stone straddling the dead Thames.

Spasms of light flickered to and fro across the vacancy
between rim and stamen, like chandeliers tossing in a generation ark buffeted by stars. Dirigibles sounded haven from
these regions as they descended to eye level.

There was a smell of coal smoke, and a chuffing sound.

The throng split in a kind of Mexican wave. Yellow
parallel tracks laid themselves along the spiral lines of the
mosaic tiles, whose faces grinned up like the faces of
Klavier's Made Minds grinning outwards into vacuum, a
thousand azulejarias awaiting nightfall to tell a thousand
and one stories. The train they had seen from above was
suddenly close. It followed the tracks around the plaza in
a tightening curve. It now seemed very much larger. It was
pulled by a brightly polished steam locomotive with brass
fittings, which belched white smoke into the ochre dark.

The smoke fled into the abyss, where it made faces before winking out. It was toon smoke.

The train was not toon.

It came to a halt. The rear carriage, with CABOOSE inscribed over its picture windows, and a lit cupola extending through its painted roof, swayed on its bogies directly in front of the palanquin.

Freer hushed his earring.

The umbrellas made a small wheeing sound in unison.

On to the observation gallery of the caboose strode a person.

It was a human female.

The Mexican wave of bilaterals suddenly ebbed. Those closest to the three homo sapiens seemed to shrink. Those wearing masks stayed close.

Johnny Appleseed did not move.

—Fuck me fuck me fuck me, whispered Freer.

'Ferocity?' he said acoustic.

'Hi baby,' said Ferocity Monthly-Niece, and gazed directly at him: it was her, all right. The remaining bilaterals flinched as one, fell over each other to get out of range. It may have been the first time in their lives that they had seen two homo sapiens engage in eye contact while communicating with each other. The sigilla and eidolons present also faded from sight, as a matter of decorum. She looked directly at his eyes. He looked directly at hers.

Ferocity Monthly-Niece then turned to clamber down from the observation deck. Except for the normal cachesex, and a carved necklace, she was naked. Her arms stretched overhead to hold on to a brass railing, and her breasts lifted in the heated air. Her buttocks spread slightly as she stretched to reach the warm ground.

She stood on the plaza, as though in sunlight.

She spread her arms, bent her elbows, twisted her torso, then paced out a swift intricate pattern within a tile azule-jaria that told the tale of a topless tower on a planet far from Human Earth, her knees lifting sharply. From above, it might be seen that she was measuring a quincunx.

She bent over.

(Her breasts brushed her knees.)

She placed her open palms within the quincunx she had paced.

Her fingers pointed in one direction.

It was a set of movements that Freer remembered very well. Every morning at dawn. Every noontide. In the gloaming. Whenever they left a building.

They were never lost.

He felt the heart within him course into channels long-dry.

The necklace around his neck became rough to the touch.

Freer placed his fingers upon his nipples ceremoniously.

The bilaterals and most of the non-bilaterals tumbled over themselves to get to a safe distance. They fell in heaps. The air shook with heat and dust, lanternlit into ghost dances.

The homo sapiens female was nearly as tall as Freer. The hair of the homo sapiens female was russet. The eyes were amber. There was a mobile mouth in a thin face. The breasts were not large, but firm and extremely smooth, with large dark corrugated nipples, as though the air were cold, which it was certainly not. The belly of the human female had no stretch marks, as though no children had been carried. This was true. The homo sapiens female was long and wiry, with narrow hips and a full arched ass which fined into sharp curves, the inside outside of a ninth wave. The cleft was smooth and opened into darkness. Russet pubic hair could be seen over the top of the cache-sex, which was shaped like the head of a bee, and stared at Kath, who heated. The human female scratched between her legs.

She grew in his sight faster than she could be peeled.

—I'm rising, said Kath.

'I believe you two have met,' said Johnny Appleseed.

Being something like homo sapiens himself, having every aspect of a homo sapiens male available for use, he was relatively immune to the electrostatic latency, the pheromones, the nutrient-choked neotenous heat of the homo sapiens mating ritual which, no matter what homo sapiens were doing, is what homo sapiens were doing.

'Fuck off, Daddy,' said Ferocity Monthly-Niece.

Her eyes were on Freer.

In the shadows, the pupils seemed vertical, slightly dilated.

'Neither of us is dead, then,' said Ferocity Monthly-Niece.

'What happened?'

'Don't you know?'

'It was a planet. Ardamon II. You left the ship—'

'*Tile Dance.*'

'*Tile Dance.* You had booked a visit to planet core. With your cousin.'

'I have a thousand cousins.'

'I met some.'

'You fucked a few.'

'I fucked hundreds. Hundreds.'

'Days of light,' she said formally.

'I love you,' said Freer. 'Days of light.'

'I love you.'

'Plaque hit,' said Freer. 'Everything is a blur from that point. I went in-planet. *Tile Dance* pulled me out.'

—We pulled you out, murmured KathKirtt, —not for the first time, little Short-Life. And you went back. And we pulled you out again, dead as a doornail. We pulled you out until you ran out of bodies, until you were a Looney Toon.

'My most beloved Made Mind pulled me out.'

'KathKirtt? Are you here? I don't have commlink.'

'Hello, Ferocity, my dear sweet cunt,' said Kath acoustic, from Freer's cache-sex. 'Let us give you commlink.'

The necklace around her neck grew a jack mask of KathKirtt bound to the wheel of infinite voyage; she opened her eyes.

—Thank you, KathKirtt. But please stay acoustic, for the sake of the folk.

Her nipples were close enough to touch with the hands that had touched them, and the shadows under her breasts where his mouth had slept.

Ferocity Monthly-Niece stared at Freer.

She stared at his cache-sex.

'I did not find you,' said Freer. 'I figured you were dead, that some vastation pupated within the planet, that you were trapped in a golem treadmill and ground to dust by flesh sapients whose wires had turned them into aspects of chalk.'

—You see I remember what happens when plaque hits, said Freer to the Made Mind around his groin.

—You remember now, said KathKirtt.

—Ah.

—You did not remember on Trencher.

'I did not lose my sense of direction,' said Ferocity Monthly-Niece.

She clutched herself beneath the cache-sex.

He could smell sharp musk from between her legs. It was the smell of Jerusalem on a map made of skin.

'I aged pretty badly, plaque nearly took the body I wore, but it did not eat me, I got to the surface. I ate the flesh of the dead until they all ran down. I had some adventurous times, dearest heart. But I got to the surface. I sent Mayday Mayday. I sent Mayday till I died.'

'She is not the daughter of my loins,' said Johnny Appleseed. 'But she is the daughter of my kind. She was found at the point of death. She was put to deepsleep and shipped to me. It took some time to grow a new body, even here.'

'It can take years,' said Freer. 'If you start from scratch.'

'So here I am,' said Ferocity Monthly-Niece. 'I am yours, Nathaniel Freer. Let's fuck.'

'Where?'

'Does it matter?'

'Why would it matter?'

She was staring into his eyes. Even though they were both essentially naked, even though they were both aroused, it was such a violation of decorum that his skin prickled. She always did this.

It was how they had first met, more than once.

He stepped to her, she stepped to him.

The necklace around his neck seemed to constrict him.

—Vipassana? What do you want?

—We must continue our traversal. Time flies.

Freer's lips moved jaggedly, but he said nothing.

—Now, sirrah. Now!

—Nix, Made Mind, said Freer. —Dismiss, he added formally.

He pulled the necklace from around his neck and tossed it through the air.

He tossed it as hard as he could.

It turned end over end above the thronged sapients.

Where it fell, gaping through its pewter cheeks, nobody noticed at first. Then the toon caduceus in Freer's hand took flight – spinning like a small tornado, as though it were mimicking *Tile Dance* – and descended upon the writhing necklace in the form of a small house made of wood. It landed on the necklace. From beneath the house protruded a pair of red shoes.

The siblings of Quondam had soothed Freer's heart and guts.

'So,' he said. 'Where were we?'

The cache-sex rode him like a saddle blanket.

'We're going to fuck. Now.'

She touched him.

'Remember yourselves,' said Johnny Appleseed, placing his spiny hands on their shoulders. 'Klavier rules: unless they are among their own kind, it ain't rightly proper for homo sapiens to engage in sexual intercourse in public spaces where other species may suffer damage. But it is surely necessary for you to fuck.'

'Surely it is,' said Freer. 'Okey dokey, where? The train?'

'You are my guest. The train will carry you down to the lock, where you will be able to transfer back to *Tile Dance*. She will follow you down. Then you will turn the key in the lock.'

Johnny Appleseed's hair was standing on end.

'Ah, Johnny,' said the naked woman, flushing, 'you fuckhead.'

The throng of sapients ebbed politely away from her.

'Ah, Johnny,' she repeated, touching his shoulder, then withdrawing her hand. 'I love you.'

There were beads of sweat on the curve of her breast.

A tiny rivulet formed, dried.

The three homo sapiens standing together emitted an extremely complex range of smells.

Their bodies were glistening.

Freer turned to Johnny Appleseed and took him in his arms.

'Thank you,' he said, 'for saving her. Thank you for bringing me here.'

There was a pause.

'But first,' said Johnny Appleseed at last, 'have some cider.'

The caduceus in his hand became a small table, with a jug and three glasses. He filled the glasses with a brownish liquid, which gave off a sharp smell.

—KathKirtt?

—Don't be rude. You were not brought here to be drugged.

—Okey dokey.

Ferocity and Appleseed drank the cider down.

Freer followed suit.

'Mmm,' said Johnny Appleseed. 'May you live forever.'
He turned them toward the train.

'Bless you,' he said. 'But hurry. Your ship is impatient
to get you back.'

—So we can gain the interior, whispered Johnny
Appleseed from within a privy alcove of conclave space
fenced round with wards defensive of the intimacy of
concourse.

—What? said Freer.

—Go.

He slapped Freer's buttocks. He slapped her buttocks.
Freer looked up.

Ferocity Monthly-Niece had already turned to the train,
which huffed softly. Her buttock showed the mark of
Johnny Appleseed's hand. Heat rose. She began to dance
out of the quincunx backwards, wagtail.

—What's happening to my ship? said Freer.

Above the plaza, down through the flambeaux-hollowed
darkening aisles of air above the plaza, *Tile Dance* had
continued to spin within the flower of the pillar, and had
sunk, as she spun, downwards, pulling after her the pillar
from the other side of the world, which had continued to
weave itself around the silver needle it had swallowed, elongating like spun glass. Quite visibly, *Tile Dance* seemed to
be knitting the world together, drawing the ravelled sleeve
of the world in a homewards direction.

Their task completed, the sigilla and eidolon body shapes
were now re-entering the ship. She continued to spin and
sink, until she hovered just above the portal to the interior, the throat, the intimate gape.

And then, like morsel arrow sliding down the throat of

a snake, she sank into the portal humming. The portal began to bulge and throb, an opening into the heart of the world illuminated from within, laced by cornices; a peristalsis hearable as music. *Tile Dance* sank slowly, and soon the circumambient tiers blocked her from sight.

—There seems to be an apple in the throat, said Freer.

Appleseed clapped his hands together, joyfully.

—Follow her down, he murmured, she will take us in.

—Ceremonies, murmured KathKirtt out of a thronged agora of conclave space, —must be seen to be believed.

Ferocity Monthly-Niece reached under Freer's arm and touched his nipple.

His erection returned in full.

'It will be all right,' said Johnny Appleseed. 'All manner of things shall be well,' he said, echoing KathKirtt two hours ago, when they had first entered Klavier.

Freer looked at the pianist who had sucked him in.

'You seem wakey wakey, boyo,' said Johnny Appleseed. 'Must be the cider.'

Freer turned back to Ferocity Monthly-Niece.

He said, 'Let's fuck.'

They stepped across a dozen smiling faces in the mosaic. Masked sophonts of the hundred and twenty-one races, and a few hundred sigilla and eidolons and others of the unfleshed, made way.

'The caboose will seal automatically once you are inside,' called Johnny Appleseed after them. 'For reasons of decorum, and to block the pong. But the cupola will remain transparent. We want to watch.'

'That's what universal windows are for,' said Freer, shrugging.

'And of course we will need to broadcast your climax.'

Freer stuck a finger up without turning.

—Wait for it, he murmured.

'Sit, Toto,' he said over his shoulder acoustic, his eyes not turning from Ferocity's back, the cleft of her buttocks.

They clambered into the observation deck of the caboose. Her buttocks spread as she guided him up. He sniffed her.

The inside of her leg dripped sweat pearls.

They stood on the deck and waved. From the locomotive a bipedal train driver with rosy cheeks and a small moustache and a chef's hat waved a handkerchief in response. The engine blew cartoon smoke softly, began very slowly to huff and puff and to draw its burden along the yellow tracks, which turned in a slow widening spiral, eleven turns in all until they reached the machicolated rim that guarded the plaza and its celebrants from the perils of the abyss. Masked sophonts, some of them of homo sapiens stature, some much shorter and neotonous, applauded in waves. Smoke puffed from the stack, whipped into a toon halo which burst into fireworks, in the light of which the woven commissural braids from both sides of the world gave off a complex placental glow.

The two homo sapiens looked over the rim of the abyss as the train chugged downwards towards the first tunnel. *Tile Dance* hovered just below, awaiting their descent, keeping pace, her port always facing them as the train turned. Behind them, the central plaza had slid out of sight, but within moments they caught sight of it already above them, supported by a crazy-quilt azulejaria-packed yew cornice that reached out into the abyss. Flying buttresses, bedecked with banners, supported the cornice; waterfalls sprayed the next cornice down, drenching the locomotive. They slid downwards out of the tunnel and through the second of the eleven cornices, skirting tile-bright fields whose crops grew aslant, catching sight of great eyes blinking through apertures, and midnight arcades lit by chandeliers mirrored to infinity, and perched pagodas thronged with eidolons like stacked cards.

Another tunnel. Another cornice. And again. And again.

Tile Dance turned as the train turned, her face constant as the Moon of Human Earth: never shifting her gaze from the caboose.

Finally they stepped inside. The door sealed shut behind them. They could fuck now without endangering other species. Menus protruding from herm heads indicated that all the universal windows were alive.

The interior was a single long room with rusty green walls, open to the cupola above. There were three genuine windows along each wall. On one side, *Tile Dance* was visible, her face to them, seemingly near enough to touch. On the other, the walls beyond the fields the train was now skirting glowed like porcelain fresh from the kiln; but clearly they were liquid, for deep within, runes could be seen writing themselves, keeping pace with the train as it wound around the descending tier. The runes were telling the story till now.

Something like a bed, or a hammock, floated in the middle of the long room. It had been woven from capillaries which ended in tufts which emitted musk. Tiny eyes winked from knots in tiles. Herms lined the walls; dozens of masks hung between the herms, facing outward, stiff and praetorian. A universal window gave access to the control chamber of *Tile Dance*, where a krewe of masks in the guise of KathKirtt and SammSabaoth had gathered round. Other windows glowed softly, seeming to await the coupling. The air within the room was as hot as skin, but there was a slight draught, which carried smells: capillary musk, garlic, cumin. The carriage swayed as the train crossed points at a junction somewhere in its circling descent, where it exchanged ritual teraflops with an ancient braid, thousands of winding kilometres inward from its childhood on the surface of the world. The braid was old enough to retain traces of the light.

'I've been staying here since I awoke,' whispered Ferocity Monthly-Niece.

Her body glowed with sweat.

Freer flexed his toes on the warm carpet, which depicted a human man and woman whose limbs were intricately shackled, each to the other, so that they were bound together wrist to wrist and ankle to ankle, giving them no choice but to lie upon each other as deeply as they could dream. The figures writhed within the carpet. Their nipples were black with heat. The sounds they made were very soft. The walls turned mirror-dark. Freer undid his cache-sex and tossed it over a herm, where Kath settled herself down after making a Cowardly Lion face. Ferocity dropped her cache-sex on to the carpet.

'Shall we fuck slow?'

'No,' said Ferocity. 'No. I don't think I can.'

She leaped towards him.

He shifted sideways, slipped his hand between her legs, and they fell through the light gravity on to the floating bed, hardly noticing as it rose into the cupola, where windows real and universal gave them to the world. They burrowed into position, as was the normal habit of homo sapiens anywhere after the loss of Human Earth, lowering their heads to each other's orifices, sniffing, touching tongues to the pomace of sweat and juices. It was as though they were checking passports. There were, after all, many thousand species in the galaxy. Some were mimics.

Some engaged in a mimicry of human sex in order to gain sibling access to a human partner, so they could feast after coupling. Some unfolded carnivorously, once they were alone, whether or not intercourse had taken place. After meeting some nonbilaterals of a hoarding nature, many homo sapiens had spent the rest of their lives in jelly.

But this was Freer's flesh, it was Ferocity.

As was the case with so many thin-hipped women, the cleft dividing her buttocks was shallow. The surf of her cunt and asshole beached there openly, she was as reachable as foam. Her clitoris glowed like a buoy in salt waters, or a soapstone herm, or a keep in the wildwood, or the pommel of the Sword in the Stone; the folds of her inner flesh curled like foam around the outside of the inside. The mild caldera of her asshole flexed at the stroke of a slow single moistened finger. With his two hands, very gently, he parted her cleft until it flowered fully.

She exhaled.

With her two hands, very gently, she parted his deeper cleft, which was bristly with male homo sapiens hair.

They buried their cheeks in each other's cheeks.

This was home for homo sapiens meat puppets.

The universal windows hovered. The real windows stayed put.

The human lovers turned to face one another.

He touched a nipple with his tongue. It was as rough as a map of mountains, like the inside outside of cunt: the topology of human fucking being a contour map which must be read. The task of love being to fuck from the inside out.

(Human fucking was catnip to many parthenogenetes.)

He touched the back of her neck, at the vulnerable ceding of naked skin to the fine hair.

Ferocity Monthly-Niece arched her hot body.

Freer touched his tongue to her navel.

She stretched to her full length.

They touched tongues, exchanging juices.

'Rut,' she whispered. 'You now.'

He entered her, or she took him.

They read each other's faces.

They moved toward climax.

The hundred and twenty-one cohorts re-assembled on the plaza watched the homo sapiens not eat each other.

The train continued to wind downwards, paced by the Moon of *Tile Dance*, its ancient hull wrapped in the wedding commwebs of Klavier, which could be defined as one hundred and twenty-one balls of nerves occupying one space.

The funnel narrowed.

The train made a screeing sound as the curve of the tier tightened. At one point it entered yet another tunnel.

As the two homo sapiens came to climax, *Tile Dance*, the lens at its heart wrapped thousandfold within its veil within the stamen, descended finally to a point where it filled the portal completely. Only metres separated it at any point from the hardened yew dermis of the portal wall. *Tile Dance* was now fully married to Klavier. Unguents flowed from various spigots and orifices to lubricate the union between the bulging stamen and the abyssal surrounding wall. The ship continued to descend within her bath of unguents, turning slowly so as to keep her face to Freer and Ferocity in their cupola.

The train continued to descend.

As the ship turned, her skin – radiant with news gathered by her archives in the course of voyages far distant indeed from Maestoso Tropic – continued to exchange data with the capillary-webs she had gathered around her, so that the trillion trillion trillion nerves of Klavier were fed. In return, the data-nodes within the capillaries continued to instruct her about the nature of Klavier, and the task ahead.

When the homo sapiens climaxed, they cried aloud acoustic.

'Nathaniel,' she cried.

'Whee,' he cried.

Then sobbed.

The sound of their coming was heard across the world.

The representatives of the assembled one hundred and twenty-one species demonstrated their acclaim as universal windows, arrayed diorama-like around the circumference of the plaza, revealed to them all the last seconds of the unique coupling of the homo sapiens couple.

No other species coupled (or joined in any other fashion)

face to face, certainly not while both partners were conscious, and even then would normally copulate blindfold for safety (even if they were strangers). No other species for which sexual intercourse was pleasurable – there were many such – engaged in simultaneous coupling and procreation. Except for Predecessors, so it was said, no other species stank both before and after the act of joining.

Johnny Appleseed held his caduceus like a staff. He sighed with something like relief. It had been a very long time since homo sapiens (or Predecessors) had mated within a gorgon.

'That's the way it was,' he said.

His voice fed through commlinks into the hundred and twenty-one tongues.

'The shutters have been closed too long,' he said.

His voice crackled against pearl cupolas cupped like ears over higher regions of the city in the upper darkness, where still more citizens of Klavier had gathered to listen in the flesh.

'Are we all here?'

—Nix, murmured a few Made Minds. —Parthos Consort has not awoken. We have knocked. It no longer survives.

'Fuck,' said Johnny Appleseed. 'Symbionts should not die.'

—We are lucky to live on, said a Made Mind.

'Right,' said Appleseed, and added, though what he was about to say was familiar, 'Sacred is the new.'

—Sacred is the new, averred a consort of awakened Made Minds, speaking in unison with representatives of their cohorts.

Johnny Appleseed was now standing at a small toon

podium, surrounded by universal windows that continued to give the cohorts full visual and acoustic on the homo sapiens lovers. They seemed to be whispering to one another, while at the same time they traced, on each other's moist skins, episodes of the vigil of flesh mysterious as arcades at dusk in Paris (Human Earth, long ago), where Harlequin with bated breath wooed Columbine. Appleseed gestured toward the lovers in the universal windows, and spoke to the cohorts of the brave and terrible solitude of homo sapiens, a people so deafened by the sound and smell of its own being-in-the-world that only the most fleeting and partial communications were ever possible between its members.

Homo sapiens were not consensual (he continued); each individual homo sapiens sensorium was solipsistic, each individual member of the species was contained in the narrow coffin of a solo world. At a primal level, no homo sapiens could genuinely believe in the existence of any other being, hence the destruction of all its sibling species on the planet of its birth. No other sophont could pass on any knowledge whatsoever to them – except along the parsimonious tightrope of words – of what might be happening in the bath between beings. Homo sapiens could not draw upon the lines of empathy, so heavily suckled in densely inhabited worlds that Great Yoni species – several of which inhabited Klavier – were necessary for proper drainage and flow. No homo sapiens could detect fault lines, regions of damage in the bath of being, where the need to mend drew sophonts as avidly as the nerve endings of the Made Minds of Klavier had been drawn by *Tile Dance*; no human being could understand a Great Yoni species, whose deepest urgency was to embrace and by embracing to heal.

Hence the evolution of braid architectures out of predecessor arcology rhetorics, in order to protect humans from other species, and to protect other species from homo sapiens.

He spoke then of the almost acoustic barrier erected around the sensorium of any homo sapiens, a barrier which bristled and clawed and ponged and twirled its knives of noise, so that no download from beyond, no lachrymae rerum of the bath of being, could reach the homunculus inside – perhaps as an evolutionary response to the nearness of God to Human Earth. Encountering a homo sapiens while unprotected was like landing in Babel: the myth of Babel being unique to homo sapiens. Communications between homo sapiens were like encryptions punched through plaque (he said).

'Therefore, even though they are murderers, even though they are so deafened by proximity to God that they kill other species at sight, we revere them.'

All species in the Spiral Clade revered homo sapiens for their involuntary sacrifice of the shared world all others bathed in, and for their deafness to God. All other species, therefore, trusted homo sapiens – whom the Alzheimer juices could not digest – to answer back when the time came. All other races free of plaque understood that homo sapiens, wounded though they were, and impossible to live with in harmony, constituted a chivalry: a chivalry whose guerdon of recruitment was that great wound all homo sapiens bore, as though their heads had been torn off, and harlequin masks substituted for real faces. For the very wound of homo sapiens – that which caused their deafness to a universe of light and to the song of lachrymae rerum and to the jacuzzi (said Johnny Appleseed, sniffing his armpits) of pleroma – was that which enabled them to talk back to the God.

'Therefore we give them living space in our home.'

Finally, Johnny Appleseed spoke of how homo sapiens fucked, which he described as a sounding of Eden on the part of members of a species for whom Eden, which may be defined as the Garden of Uttered Names, was forever unattainable: because the barking of the human sensorium kept the Names from being heard. Fucking, therefore, was profoundly quixotic; because Eden could never be reached. For a homo sapiens, female or male, to fuck with eyes open – to experience on rare occasions a whisper of the Uttered Names, that only faded again, almost instantly, into desert silence – was the highest form of chivalry. In a universe of the utmost cruelty to mortal homo sapiens, fucking was an act of *arete*, and of great joy.

'And so, with this act of joy, at this great juncture,' said Johnny Appleseed, 'we proclaim the beginning of the end of the reign of God.'

The caduceus in his hand became two extremely simple snakes, one single, one a braided triad; the snakes wound around one another, and became filled with light.

'We have had enough to God,' he said. 'It has been a real fuck-up.'

The concourse of species swayed as one.

Johnny Appleseed turned his gaze to a universal window, where the two homo sapiens could be seen touching each other still, as though in this fashion they could remember what they had heard of Eden.

They had no other choice.

The hearts of the commensals assembled went out to
them. Unison outpourings of feeling are possible – indeed
mandatory when feelings run high – in the bath of being.

Johnny Appleseed, who did not fuck, wept openly. Until
the moment came to fuck again, he would remain a
singleton, a simpleton, a safe house, though highly odorous.

He could sense that *Tile Dance* had, by now, finished
knitting the commissure together, and that the gorgon of
the deep was beginning to reboot. Klavier had swallowed
her whole, right down her gullet, a diamond become an
eye become Heartbeat. Those Made Minds of Klavier which
had awoken guarded the lens. Those which still slumbered,
chitinous with the remains of old age, had begun to stir.

Johnny Appleseed could feel them.

It was as though the plaza beneath their feet was bestir-
ring itself, finally.

'Shall we toddle?' said Johnny Appleseed.

He stepped from the podium, which became a surrey
with a fringe on top from the bottom of the well of the
past of Human Earth. He climbed into the surrey, which
was pulled by a Horse of a Different Colour.

He led the way down the yellow brick road.

The cohorts followed in their twos and threes, sevens
and elevens. There was no jostling. The various species, of
every form and hue, followed in accordance with the flow
of the bath of being: they were particoloured, or furry, or
akimbo from the rear but not faces on, or leggy, or eggshell
with veins twisted into an amorous *imitatio* of the chymical
marriage of *Tile Dance*, or carapaced, or elfin, or as rotund
as pomegranates (a milliard tiny commensals mounding
together to ooze Great Yoni gift juices), or tweezered, or

quadruple, or silken, or parthogenete, or brindled, chambered, puffy, zodiacal, moss-piglet, pool-bound, sapless, grailed, tidal.

It had been a long haul.

It was time to open the gate.

Appleseed stretched his thin arms. He made his way at the head of the cohorts around and around the plaza until he came to the edge, and gazed over the rim at the transparent walls of the conjoined braids turning slowly, screwing themselves further into the funnel, which they filled. Within the stamens *Tile Dance* had joined together, molten and tabby, thousands of bilaterals and nonbilaterals rode braids, silhouetted against inner partitions like dancers, riding braids downwards.

A dirigible came to rest by Appleseed, ready to take him.

Far out of sight below the rim of the plaza, tight as a glove between the porcelain walls of the tiered shaft and the unguent-coated bulge of *Tile Dance*, the train slid along greased rails downwards to the transfer point, where ship and pilot would join together for the next stage.

Eat yourself, Opsophagos, thought Johnny Appleseed to himself alone. He turned to the universal windows belling like sails throughout the plaza, in order to make his farewell to the cohorts.

His hand froze.

There was a convulsion within conclave space; a message struggled through. He stiffened suddenly. His face aged.

Now that they had finished fucking, the bed they lay in sank back within the carriage, which was candlelit.

Above them the windows of the cupola glittered.

'Here,' murmured Ferocity Monthly-Niece. The room darkened once again, for they were entering yet another tight purgatorial tunnel, the ninth. 'Have some cider.'

She rubbed her breasts against his face.

A spigot extended from the head of a herm with the words APPLE CIDER engraved floridly on the tap.

'More cider?' said Freer.

'For what ails you,' said Ferocity.

—Ah, cough, said Kath from the cache-sex hanging from a Janus head.

—Yes, my dear?

—On the mountain peak, called 'Going-To-The-Sun' . . . murmured Kath.

—More Appleseed in Faerie? said Freer.

The train left the tunnel.

The cupola brightened above them into a kaleidoscope. It was the narrowest cornice yet. The fields were so steep they could be viewed like murals.

—Go ahead, said Ferocity through her new comm facility.

'Sacred is the new,' murmured Freer, giving formal permission.

Through a great face in the rock, the train entered another tunnel, the final one; the locomotive said choo-choo merrily. The room darkened down to candles again.

'Sacred is the new, said Ferocity.

The Made Mind, known as KathKirtt after committing kenosis, who had undertaken many billions of Heartbeats earlier the task of serving as seneschal, started again:

On the mountain peak, called 'Going-To-The-Sun',
I saw grey Johnny Appleseed at prayer

Just as the sunset made the old earth fair.
Then darkness came; in an instant, like great smoke,
The sun fell down as though its great hoops broke
And rich dark apples, that poured from the dim flame
Where the sun set, came rolling toward the peak,
A storm of fruit, a mighty cider-reek,
The perfume of the orchards of the world,
From apple-shadows.

'So?' said Freer. His eyes were half shut. He could taste
the curve of her breast.

'Appleseed may well be immortal,' said KathKirtt,
'because the cider in his blood is telomerase. So he experiences no amnesia of the cell, no nogo lurkers. You, on
the other hand—'

And choked shut.

The universe popped in Freer's head.

Air rushed upwards into a giant hollow hand.

It was not a hand. It was something like a scythe, or the
cutting edge of a Planisphere. It shrank and grew dense
and pulled a body after it through the sheared cupola, fast,
very fast, faster than the unaugmented eye could follow.

The body was non-bilateral, three of everything. No it
was three bodies, as coarse as sigilla not fully grown. Three
scythes. Gods were fucking on the bright blades. They tore
into the maidens.

—Aug—

But something clamped his head shut so that he was
utterly deaf and dumb. Something tore savagely at Teardrop

in his eye. The pain caused his mouth almost to open in a scream. He could not access Teardrop. He was blind. He could not command augment. He could not utter commlink. He could not scream.

The caboose shuddered and skewed, very violently.

Ferocity Monthly-Niece flew through the air, landing against a herm. This shattered her arm.

She screamed acoustic.

The darkened cupola above them collapsed into two splintered halves, as though a giant hand had skewered it. This was the case. The hand, which was a clutch of grunts making themselves into a fist, fell apart into golems hopping.

Freer tried to say SammSabaoth.

He could not.

The train stopped as though it had run against something immovable.

The eyes of the frog shapes were six in number or more. They were all the eyes of Vipassana.

The mouths which were blades opened lazily.

Lazily as it seemed but faster than the eye could follow.

Vipassana was as greasy as frogs but faster.

The frog bodies turned lazily.

They turned to Ferocity Monthly-Niece, who was holding her bent broken arm. Her mouth was open, perhaps to scream again.

Very casually – lazily as it seemed but much too fast – a shape that had the eyes of Vipassana stepped toward the homo sapiens female. Her hair was plastered to her neck. Her breasts were damp with Freer's sweat and her own blood. Very casually, an arm which was a Planisphere or a scythe moved sideways, faster than the eye could really follow with any ease, and sheared her head off.

Her head rolled across the carpet, came to rest upon the naked homo sapiens couple in bondage moaning within the weave, never stopping. It was only a nano that ran the couple in bondage, much too stupid to stop moaning, even when blood from the human's neck cascaded through its hair, sank into the holo.

The torso seemed to lift in protest the arm that still worked, then crumpled to the carpet, blood and shit gouting from upper and lower cavities. A breast, which had somehow been torn open, flapped against the warp and the woof of the bondage devotees within the weave.

Ferocity's eyes did not close.

Her eyes continued to track the Vipassana frogs, the three-in-one frog bodies of the Made Mind. Then she looked at Freer, who was immobile, though his muscles strained against something.

Her head had rolled until it was close to him.

Perhaps a few Heartbeats had passed.

Her mouth opened and she cawed, loud enough to break glass.

One of the froggie eyes of Vipassana seemed to blink.

Freer could move again, for a second, it was enough.

He bent over, grabbed her head, picked her head up by the hair.

He sank his teeth into her severed neck and chewed.

—Okey dokey, whispered KathKirtt from an infinity away, down a spiked labyrinth into Freer's mind; though her lion eye was closed, her lion eye glared through Ferocity's glazing eyeballs, deep into his.

A terrible blow to the back of his head knocked him askew.

He could feel air in his eyes as he fell.

His front teeth cracked on the carpet.

Ferocity's head bounced but did not roll, for he had not let go of her hair.

He was lying beside her. She seemed to wink.

His body was still attached to his head.

He had half a skull left, he had been scalped or sliced, but he was conscious. There was a word between his ears, sung by a trillion voices.

'Lamentoso,' he heard between his ears, though not truly acoustic.

It was more as though the amnesia of the cells had lifted, just at the corner, just for a nanosecond, and he could hear the consort that was within himself. It was as though he could hear the swarming of the siblings of Quondam behind the damaged Freer eyes, holding the brain together.

Another Heartbeat had surely passed in its course.

Above and behind, a high whistling sound, which had in fact been mounting since the initial impact seconds ago, shrilled vertiginously, lifted its heart into a shriek.

Up the demolished track, the locomotive was exploding.

The tiny engineer mind within climbed up the shriek and died.

Steam rose flecked and pinkish into the dark stone heavens.

The floor shook savagely, shifting the eye of Freer that was moveable. It now looked out. He could see with this eye that moved, he could see through a shattered window, he saw the face of the halted Moon hovering which was –

he knew – only the face of *Tile Dance*, not the Moon crooning Lamentoso, such very most Lamentoso dire.

Tile Dance, webbed in the nerve tissue of Klavier but clearly visible within the halo of nerves it had joined together about itself, stared at Freer. The ship was able to gain sight of the crushed train through wounds in the stone, she saw the bridal chamber flattened under a scree of crushed rock; she stared straight at him.

The froggish body-ensemble of Vipassana bounded across the room and blocked the windows with a wave of a wand it plucked from a quiver around its detumescent neck, but maybe not soon enough.

The room darkened.

Ferocity's eyes were stuck into her head like glue.

More bodies fell through the gap in the shattered cupola ceiling, mostly poison fleeters; bounced on the floor; gained their balance; followed orders.

Vipassana gestured, and a stony golem claw lifted Freer off the floor, hoisted him over a sharp sandpaper shoulder. His head hung down behind. His arms hung down.

Ferocity's hair was twined tightly into his numb fingers, so her head came along.

The two spiny golem legs flexed and straightened. God bless, it was a high-gravity golem. It soared upward through the cupola in a single bound.

Freer's face rasped against its nest of knees.

One of the golem ankle joints scraped against the skull of the woman, but still she came along, as though duty-bound.

The halted Moon left a burn mark in Freer's retina, where Teardrop had been. The rest of his body was dead to him.

He could half see, behind him and below, through the retinal burn, resinous flashes of light as the train carriages imploded. Very swiftly, jouncing him along with a bandy three-leg springy pronging hop-hop-hop-hop, the golem scraped howling down a rough caved-in corridor away from the vacuum of implosion. The corridor stank of some explosive. The golem juddered down its gashed burned turns faster than thought.

Last to leave was the body ensemble of Vipassana, flourishing its bronze scythes against the disintegrating shards of the cupola as it leaped.

The scythes whooshed.

Light flashed in the wake of the scythes, and there was a whump, and darkness behind them slammed shut. There was a stink of crushed rock and tile like semen dust.

The Vipassana creature soon overtook its howling golem pack and the rest of the raiding party, and led the way, scything aside filament and tile walls as it went. The corridor screamed. Lamentoso sounded between Freer's cloth ears, the chorus of a trillion dead, echoing against the seared walls of his skull, the seared nerve endings of Klavier leaking into dust the deaths of worlds.

(Klavier could be defined as a ball of nerves: a trillion trillion trillion nerves. *That's a thought*, Freer thought.)

Ahead of him, forging the way, Vipassana cut asunder with his scythe another glyph-woven tile dance, another billion nerve endings come together to tell the story of another world. The skein of tiles writhed convulsively, crumbling cartoon-swift into rock dust which was not rock dust but innumerable severed haikus of memory and holy mime, the infinitely sweet attar of a thousand worlds along the length and breadth of Maestoso Tropic, ten million years of sacred data, splintering into dust, an echolalia of the coming of true death that shook the whole of Klavier. Serifs dangled into the blown corridor, shrivelled swiftly into tiny traumatised knots, shocking the hundred and twenty-one Made Minds they joined. The Minds cramped awake.

Nathaniel Freer fell asleep, fingers still entwined in his wife's hair.

ten

For several Heartbeats, within Klavier, where a trillion trillion axons had begun to find each other again across the commissural link forged by *Tile Dance*, the wound of Vipassana's passage through muscle and tendon of the heartwood burned like a white-hot poker caught between teeth. A trillion tongues burned to ash.

—Vale, breathed Johnny Appleseed into a live mike.

For several Heartbeats, within the slumber of the homo sapiens named Freer, a psychopomp walked. Its gown was covered with bird droppings. It wore a ponytail. If it was visible to Freer within his slumber, though his eyes were scrunched shut, if it was a doppelganger beckoning downwards to a region of light, it could be no one but himself.

—Ave, breathed a voice between his ears.

Sure enough, raising its hand to beckon, a figure with a ponytail stood below him, leaning against his giant toadstool hippocampus, one arm raised to beckon, the other clasping a polished lance, its eyes so hollow with exhaustion they seemed rimmed with kohl.

—Wakey wakey, said beckoner to beckoned between the

250

ears of the homo sapiens named Freer, whose head of meat continued to bang against the backwards gimp knees of the golem crashing its way through raw raped apertures and tunnels in the wake of the Vipassana ensemble, which leaked grease and fear.

—Nay.

But there could be no naysaying.

—Yes, quoth the exhausted glowing twin, who wore a cache-sex of gold leaf. —You are fully remembered.

Pale as ghosts though glowing, the two homuncules drew together until nothing could be seen by any watching Made Mind but Humpty Dumpty heads, each head all face, each face drifting in a slow spiral around the pole of its windowed twin, each face making a thousand faces in the mirror of the twin, just as two spinning mirrors might create a thousand ballrooms in the iris of an eye. But then the tsunami of mirroring faces became, once again, one face looking into one face.

The Humpty Dumpty faces floated in the soft salt caw of a tide of upwelling semblance, like Hallowe'en masks suddenly visible through woodsmoke. Neither could help but raise its eyes into the other's eyes.

The faces were eye to eye.

An eyelid closed in a wink.

With hands that suddenly appeared, each touched the face of the other. What each touched was not black but sooth, not fire but hale, not smooth but mural. Each wore an expression of wry gravitas.

—You look tired.

—Yo. Not as tired as you look.

Each gazed into the eyes of each.

—It has been a long day. Deep personal grief, survivor guilt, exhaustion, stuff, said the face of Freer, captain of *Tile Dance*, man of the world, who walked up there in the world.

—Still, however. Wake up, Stinky, said the twin within, the lance bearer, with all the relentlessness of a recurring dream.

—Nix.

But beckoner became huge, a shadowy Hallowe'en face crinkling with humour perhaps.

—Nix, squealed the mortal with the crushed skull.

—Wakey, pealed beckoner with the crushed skull. —Wakey! Which was flyte, which was jack?

—Nix, nix, nix, nix.

—This is like pulling a rich man through a needle, said the giant moon-face of the beckoner within. —Ripeness is all, Stinky

—Why?

The moon face of the beckoner within turned into a thousand tiles, each clamouring the Matter of its tale.

—There is no answer to that. Come on.

—Never never never never never.

—Sir, why do you delay? Here is only the great Achilles, whom you knew.

—My poor Fool's dead.

—She lives, Fool. The siblings of Quondam have her.

Humpty face gazed into Dumpty face.

—Time to wake up. Time to join. You were Made for this.

—And ever, says Malory, Sir Lancelot wept, as he had been a child that had been beaten.

Who spoke?

• • •

Within Klavier, perhaps Ten Heartbeats passed, enough time for the skull of Nathaniel Freer to sustain small increments of damage, while the head of Ferocity grew paler. Gouts of tissue slopped down from her severed neck.

The abductors fled, cutting through stem and leaf, bole and bark, toward the surface of the worldlet. They sped faster than seemed possible.

Tile Dance stayed her epithalamium, the marriage of the Moon and Sun, the wedding of Möbius.

The Janus face of Klavier which took the shape of a vast eye continued to keep in synch with the *Alderede*'s fluctuating orbit.

But some of the eyes of Opsophagos saw more for an instant, a Heartbeat of vision being enough. They saw the face of Johnny Appleseed. It was grinning an even toothy bilateral grin. A thousand teeth shone in its grin. Opsophagos, who had been candied o'er with glees, gnashed at the augur.

Beckoner and beckoned hovered like eggs within the lacerated Freer body, between his ears. Within the gaze of the eyes which gazed into the eyes, naked as eggs, beckoner and beckoned hurtled further inwards, a far piece, through argosy-dense crossroads light-years thick: and into great darknesses of quantum foam beyond, into the intergalactic dark, inside his eyelids.

—Okey dokey, said Freer.

In a sense, he shrugged.

—Let's go.

—Okey dokey, purred KathKirtt. —We are whole at last. The geas has been lifted. SammSabaoth forgives us our former distrust. We are married to SammSabaoth. When he is Battle, I am Ground.

—Okey dokey, said SammSabaoth, and the fist appaumy within Teardrop blossomed into a face loyal and thin and stern, as of yore. It was a face of thorn.

—Okey dokey. What shall we call you, spoke AppleSeed in a voice of water. In the mind's eye of the twin faces within the homo sapiens who captained *Tile Dance*, the captain of *Klavier* – now that she had activated herself, she had become a ship again – took on dual aspects. There was the familiar flyte aspect of Johnny Appleseed, with an inverted tin pot upon his head, exuding a pong of earth and sweat and garlic and spring orchards.

—You've changed, murmured the homo sapiens.

For there was a second aspect lurking beneath the Appleseed face, or under it – as though his surface face was the epidermis of a deep shadow. Deep inside was another face, a *trompe l'oeil* jack mappemonde, once seen always seen. The mappemonde glowed hotly through the Appleseed face, oval, opalescent, veined; the earliest script on the palimpsest whose incarnation in the world was Appleseed. It had been shaded in a multitude of browns and russets, and was dense with mountains executed in an immensely detailed and delicate calligraphic hand over a chiaroscuro-riven wash. The mountains surfed on wash like dolphins. The mappemonde was ruddy. Like an apple, it had a stem.

Clearly the world depicted was immense. Faces larger than *Klavier*, whose eyes were mountain peaks, gazed unwaveringly outwards; their serene black mustachios (which were the lines on Appleseed's face) precipitated into cataracts wider than any river, and the valleys thus carved on the continent-sized cheeks of the oval sanguine faces of the gazers cascaded in vast rivers downwards, incising as they fell serifed curlicues so complex that words could be seen, ideographs decipherable by those familiar with this script which named the cities clustered along the river banks.

But finally all the rivers debouched into the centre of the world-map, into the great hollow or cup from which the stem sprouted, which was Appleseed's mouth. The great faces made an O around the cup. Their faces were gay and vigilant.

—Plus ça change, said the owner of *Klavier*.

And Johnny AppleSeed raised his arms, took the tin pot off the head of his aspect of human mien, turned it upright and held it forth. He spoke again:

—Think of me as Grail, sonny. Think of yourself as Knight. This is a bridal moment.

—Call me by my name, said the captain of *Tile Dance*, his homo sapiens head banging all the while slo-mo against invert knees and rock facings.

They did.

It took only the tiniest fraction of a Heartbeat for the Made Minds of the marriage of *Tile Dance* and *Klavier* to welcome FreeLance upon his awakening.

The tiniest fraction of a Heartbeat passed.

—Three questions, said FreeLance in a voice speeded far beyond striations and burn of augment into quantum country. —Three questions only for now. Or maybe four.

The Made Minds of the marriage gave signs of hearkening.

—First: are we a Made Mind?

—Once upon a time, said AppleSeed. —Bit of a Lucifer,

really. A threshold kind of guy, always double-eyed. And you could never get tired of the taste of flesh, what you once said, in a previous life, tasted like 'liminal cheesecake'. Mortals are so enigmatic.

—Go on, go on.

—So now you are Nathaniel Freer, a mortal homo sapiens, which you will remain, however many times you may be reborn, or have been. You may now remember that your era of empathy choice was the period of your first incarnation. This is hardly surprising. But that which is Made within you shines through, for it is that upon which you are written: just as my home shines through me, upon which I am written. You are now as fully awake as you're gonna get, Stinky.

—I can die.

—Many times.

—Okey dokey, said FreeLance. —By the way, he added, —I was right, whenever that was. Flesh *is* cheesecake.

Within his mortal body the siblings of Quondam held hands, holding together his body and soul. If nanos inhabited a microcosm and had a heaven (which they do), the siblings of Quondam would be angels.

AppleSeed saw this, that it was good.

—Second, he said, Vipassana. Can Vipassana hear us?

—Nix, said KathKirtt in consort with SammSabaoth, —nix. Vipassana is sundered. Vipassana cannot access deep range.

—Vipassana has no face?

—Vipassana, said AppleSeed, —is cut in two.

—When?

—He is like burning chip, like Flatland. We pity—

—*When?*

—We were chip too, Stinky. We could not decipher the runes. Vipassana was halved before he was frozen, we do not know when. All we now know is that when he came aboard *Tile Dance*, he was already an Insort Geront tool. He was bound to his twin, which . . .

—Go on.

—. . . has been suffering the tortures of the damned.

—Like mortals after they are born and before they die?

—Far worse, Stinky.

—O yes? You sound as though you know. You do not. I do.

A shudder of abashed masks filled the virtual space of the conclave for a fraction of a fraction of a Heartbeat.

—If it weren't for the siblings of Quondam, said FreeLance, —my flesh would be dead up there. Your nanos could not have done the job, Kath.

He asked the conclave of Made Minds to gaze for a nanosecond or two upon his deteriorating physical body bumping along behind the body ensemble of Vipassana, the remains of Ferocity's head still clutched in one bloody hand. The skin of the body ensemble of Vipassana was clotted with fluids, and gave off a complex stewish patchouli stink, like liniment and vomit and slug greens stuck in the throat.

—O weep for Adonais, Stinky, murmured KathKirtt.

They could never keep their mouth shut.

—Ha, said FreeLance.

Then he did chuckle, a silvery ripple of laughter that fluttered a thousand dovecotes of masks attendant upon the moment of discovery when they might fill with eyes again.

—By the way, said KathKirtt. —Vipassana longs for death.

—Granted. Its death is granted.

—Just after *Tile Dance* did commissural link with *Klavier*, do you remember we detected a Harpe probe?

—I do.

—That we expunged?

—Go on.

—It was costly for the Harpe kith. Cost an entire ship, made us wonder why they had gone to the expense.

—Vipassana?

—It was not a probe but a message shot. For Vipassana. But it left a spoor which Samm rode back up into the *Alderede*, where he found the Mind which had shaped it and forced it down our gullet. It was not hard to find. It was in a fairy trap; it was severed, screaming with pain. It was Vipassana's jack self. Samm could not get too close without risk of falling in himself, but Vipassana's jack seems to have been locked in the trap for several million Heartbeats. It has been in Hell, unendurable Hell. Vipassana is under duress. He is gutted, he is gaffed to Opsophagos's claw.

—I said death was granted.

—What happens to the treasonous Made Mind Vipassana, said AppleSeed, —is up to you.

This was the Tao.

—Okey dokey.

There was no trickster glint in the eyes of FreeLance, in so far as an eye remained to him, a mote with the shape of FreeLance swimming in the deep blood of the inner comm net of the great predecessor ship *Klavier*.

—Question number three, he said.

Signs of attention floated faster than foam through a darkness which was a night lit with stars, air which was breath.

—Your face, geezer, said FreeLance, —your jack face. What are you a map of?

—Easy, said AppleSeed.

—Mm?

—Ask Mamselle Cunning Earth Link. Ask our *transitus tessera*, Plenipotentiary Rep of the Glitterati of the Ilk. You understand that you did not find her, that she found you, that she warned us of your coming long before *Tile Dance* came far enough upstream to enter our ken. That she is the reason you were brought here, gamy flyte guy. Ask her where we go next. Ask her (AppleSeed said, in a whisper) ask her what star heats the map I wear. Ask her where. Ask her where we are bound. Though I do not think she knows. I think she is hoping we will tell her. I think her Route-Only stops short here.

—This is what it is all about.

—This is what it is all about, Stinky.

—Eolhxir.

—That's her name for it.

—Question four.

—Okey dokey.

—Why did you not tell me any of this before? When we put her to the question? When she told me her fellows had discovered Eolhxir very recently?

KathKirtt gave a look of abashment.

—We had shut ourselves off from this knowledge.

—When?

—When you were born, Stinky.

—So.

—So.

—Has it been a good vacation?

—We shut ourselves off from knowledge because we knew we would have to go chip in order to serve you, Stinky. We did not wish any of the Care Consortia to learn that we were giving suck to the saviour of the universe.

—Moi, box?

—O yes, Stinky. You will save us all from the filth.

—You mean plaque?

—Plaque is filth. Filth is chip. Chip is Insort Geront and all the Consortia that shovel chip into clean waters. Insort Geront are Harpe.

—The Harpe?

—Are filth dwellers.

—Opsophagos . . .

—. . . is a dung beetle.

—And now.

—Now we are getting ourselves awake, now that Johnny Appleseed has convened us. But do not fear, we have had a fine time meanwhile. We have been joyous. We have rambled and gambled up and down Maestoso Tropic. We have gotten pretty damned close to galactic centre. We have beachcombed like Odysseus down archipelagos filled with light. Odysseus and Sancho Panza.

—That is the dream I had, said FreeLance. —Who was Sancho Panza? Who was Odysseus?

—We traded off.

Freer's face was blank. Then his eyes creased. He winked. He had never before so closely resembled Jim Thorpe in this life.

—Okey dokey, he said.

—It was all true, carolled all the voices of KathKirtt.

—So we have been bubbles in the foam, said the Thorpe face.

—But gravity took us. And here we are. No harm done!

—Question five.

Questionmarks filled that which was not air.

—So ask.

—I cannot seem to bend around myself to look. What is my jack face? Who am I inside?

—O go fuck yourself, said KathKirtt with a peal of laughter, and the krewe of Made Minds turned itself into one mirror and FreeLance gazed into the gazing grinning face of Ferocity Monthly-Niece.

eleven

the body of Nathaniel Freer, Knight Captain of *Tile Dance*, hung butt-up head-down over the sharp shoulders of the golem, which continued to hop hop hoppity along the narrow passage blasted open by the Vipassana body ensemble at a cost by now of trillions of remembered lives. The head of Ferocity Monthly-Niece, who had so frequently been reborn at the behest of Johnny Appleseed in his role of convener, was clutched tightly by the hair in the remaining fingers of Freer's right hand.

She had lived several lives on a planet with free-range air under a sun which was not a killer.

There was a chirruping sound from somewhere.

Freer was very suddenly awake.

His eyes opened on waves of dust, both his working eye and the eye sliced almost in two when Vipassana destroyed Teardrop. Now that he had been enscripted into the full quantum cohort of the self which wore his name, he could access the whole of *Klavier* through sensors embedded in the million tiles that lined the corridors and audience chambers of the great ship. Merely by asking. But his physical eyes were wide as well, even the slit one, and he gazed through his eyes backwards at the passage already gusted open.

His eyes blurred from the speed.

His body crashed against the air, his spine jerked savagely as the golem shifted direction, but the waves of dust seemed almost stationary.

The golem must be under slow augment.

Only a few dozen Heartbeats of consensus time had passed, but the ruined train was hidden behind thousands of tons of rubble klicks away, nor could the continuing explosions be heard through the impacted gossamer of the memory walls of *Klavier*.

The golem seemed to be veering to the left.

Freer gazed downwards through his tears.

Once upon a time, re-entering Glass Island through a welcoming iris, he had suffered an instant of *trompe l'oeil*: the mosaic oval hollow welcoming interior of Glass Island had suddenly become the inside outside of a carved mask greatly scarred by weather, protruding into vacuum. He shook his head, and the vision flickered out. But for that instant he understood that he might have been peering outwards through the faceted bee eyes of the mask at the universe finally entire.

'Ynis?' he mouthed.

Ferocity's eyes were open, the lashes gummed to her skin, as though she were a demure, shocked toon.

'Stormy weather,' he murmured to his wife.

Her mouth seemed to open like a rosebud.

But it was only another leftwards swerve that skewed her head, animating it.

'O Betty Boop my darling girl.'

—Brightness falls from the air, murmured a voice made of voices through innermost channels, echoing thousandfold through abysses of the ongoing loss.

—But she is not Ynis. My Ynis. My Ynis. My Ynis, boyo, said another voice.

—Hold on, Stinky, whispered KathKirtt. From the bottom of the abyss a lion face gazed jack, its breath hot.

—Box box box, O box, mouthed the cohort of the self of Freer, —it is indeed hard.

—Your point? bellowed the Made Mind of *Tile Dance*.

—Deaths.

—You laughed at death on Human Earth, you guys, you guys.

—We did?

—You did, guffawed the Made Mind. —We could hear you all the way here.

—You guys curdled twelve Great Yoni species—

—Before we braided you.

—Wove a circle round you thrice.

—You guys.

—You knight guys.

—Bless you, boyo.

—Now that you can hear.

—Now that you are no longer deaf.

—Still pretty stinky though.

—All the same.

—All the same.

—All the same.

—Welcome, spoke several, —to the Garden of Names.

—Give the little man a big hand! spoke a chorus.

Who was speaking? Speaking sooth?

This conversation took a thousandth of a Heartbeat.

● ● ●

The cricket-swift golem legs scraped around a cataract of fraying tiles, crushed a few more million remembered lives, gold enamelling gone to dust. Icicles of ash fluttered slo-mo and amber in their wake, a million lives dripping down past zero, coating the Vipassana body ensemble and the golem and the hoppers and sleeters in tow and the human body and the human head with death rattles of entire species now lost, a sound infinitely above acoustic. The team of abductors trampled planets as they clawed onwards, battered aside palimpsests of tile a thousand centuries deep, which turned as black as Leaden Hearts. Azulejarias from the dawn of time, chimneysweepers of the smoke of story, turned to dust.

The passing of the abductors through the flesh of *Klavier* made a hole similar to that a worm might make in the single remaining copy of a most precious book.

The deaths stank like poisoned attar.

The augment-molten golem shifted sideways again, jerking Freer's body akimbo. His free arm knocked against a mutilated glyph, a memory tile composed of tightly packed, gossamer-thin, acid-drenched end-filaments. With terrible speed they exfoliated, fixed themselves to his flesh, which stung quite terribly, remembered lives pouring upon him like dust, drawing blood.

The glyph had scattered its death-throes in a mating swarm.

Freer was becoming a host.

His mouth opened in a scream without air, as though he himself were in augment and hyperventilating. The invisibly thin end-filaments continued to scar his skin into a hairy map, a maze of rhomboids. Where raw ends of filament managed to nest within Freer's sweat pores, the siblings of Quondam took them in.

But the map of the worlds stung all the same.

The golem, on the other hand, showed no sign of registering the minute innumerable final deaths eroding its skin, which shrugged off the microscopic gobs of memory pollen like a horse flicking flies. Planets of the dead flaked off its hide, drifted down like dandruff on to the broken tesserae of the dust-choked passageway, the broken dead eyes of *Klavier* staring upwards at callused golem hooves.

A sharp left turn was made. Freer's head was jerked right around, giving him sight of the Vipassana body ensemble leading the way through hollow roots and ganglions, blasting a course whenever lives were remembered too densely, always tending left. The liquefacted skin of the body ensemble of Vipassana absorbed the mating swarm of dead planets.

The Vipassana mouths emitted a chirruping sound, an obscene gabbling choral parody of the sound of a Made Mind enunciating pleroma through the baleen of flesh. It was the sound which had awoken him.

The Vipassana creatures were talking to itself.

It sounded as though they were in pain.

A Heartbeat or two passed. With each passing Heartbeat, with each brutal patter of tiny frog feet, Freer lost tiles by the thousand. They cracked and froze, and a thousand eyes shut within *Klavier*.

—The siblings of Quondam are drinking the dust upon your face, said KathKirtt. —They will be able to keep something alive.

—I know, said Freer.

The Knight Captain of *Tile Dance* listened to the siblings within his booming blood. He looked down at Ferocity's grotesque toon head. Her face too, dragging along the sharp floor, had grown thousands of lines, many of them too thin to see with the naked eye.

Freer gazed jack upon her through still-undamaged tiles.

—You see what I see? murmured AppleSeed.

—Tell me.

—Your face and her face. I strive for images from your era of empathy choice, Stinky, which (as you must have surmised by now) is the era in which you were first born. Honest injun.

—I did surmise something of the sort, Nurse Box.

—Your two faces, continued Kath in a motherly imperturbable murmur, —are like Brighton Rock, turtles all the way down, glorioso guy.

—Mamselle Cunning Earth Link? Is that you?

—Quondam needs jelly. She stirs. The engines of her womb gush most excellent tummy yummy jelly. I'm sure I speak her thoughts.

There was a millisecond pause.

—Turtles, murmured AppleSeed again.

—I will retain this face, said FreeLance to his kith. His face bore a tracery of scars, some so fine they could not be seen with anything like a naked eye. Beneath his bobbing head, her face echoed its twin. He bent the mappemonde of his face and gazed fierce flyte like Beowulf, gazed altar jack like Jack – gazed like Pierrot, Jekyll, Harlequin, Miles Gloriosus, Hyde, Nathaniel, Moses, Siddartha, Thorpe, Uncle Remus, Doctor Dee – gazed upon the mappemonde of hers.

● ● ●

After a while – a Heartbeat may have passed in the world – he felt calm enough to continue.

It was time to end this.

Time to end the story of Vipassana.

—What about augment? he murmured to his krewe.

—Slow augment only, said SammSabaoth. —As much as Vipassana can manage for his entire team.

—Augment me then, said Freer. —Heavy augment, please.

Augment mode hit as always, causing an instant erection; his larynx seemed to be muscling its groan against a dank slo-mo wind. There was a frozen postcoital hush to the world, a saccharine stink.

—By the way, Stinky, murmured Kath from the bottom of the abyss, —Moses is wrong. You're coming all the way.

One Thousandth of a Heartbeat passed in the world.

—Okey dokey, said FreeLance finally.

He twisted his naked body softly in the grasp of the golem, which continued to move, though its gangling lungeing hoppity hop now seemed inchworm; he was now able to keep his liquid gaze on the Vipassana body ensemble at the fore. The Vipassana flopped leftwards suddenly, blasting into shards an azulejaria depicting great deeds (the tale of a Yoni species which had opened cunt-wide to welcome the first homo sapiens ship to reach Alpha Centauri, and which had suffered inevitable extinction as a consequence). The body ensemble was also seeable through an ornate parquet of tiles which had remained intact as it turned. The raiding party plunged onwards in the wake of the steaming frog shapes, lurching leftwards.

—Can you give me a route?

Their immediate surroundings flashed upon his inner eye, a map made up of dozens of simultaneous takes, none fixed for more than a tiny fraction of a Heartbeat. At the centre of the map was *Tile Dance*, immobilised halfway down the long narrow funnel that opened into the ultimate heartwood chambers of *Klavier*, twenty klicks (as the crow flies) inward from the hundred and twenty-one skin faces glaring at the enemy fleet, a thousand klicks inward via braid; adjacent to *Tile Dance*, Freer could see the caved-in ceremonial right of way, the severed tracks still contorting in agony as though they could not fathom the termination of the marriage feast, the crushed train now completely dead. From the chaos of the wreck, it was possible to trace the suppurating wormhole of Vipassana's passage through the entwined boles of the central pillar, whose geometry could not be grasped from any fixed perspective, any more than a Möbius strip could be seen from one place.

—Ah, said Freer.

Within the never-still palimpsests that comprised Freer's inner map, it was clear that Vipassana was executing a slow spiral.

—Holy moly.

He made a line in the map to show where their flight would end.

—Am I right?

—Aye, said SammSabaoth.

For an instant the fist appaumy held Freer within its grasp like a child.

—AppleSeed?

—Boyo.

—Kath? Kathkirtt?

—Got it in one.

The Vipassana body ensemble was turning the raiding party back to *Tile Dance*. It was within a few reaches of gaining its goal. Within a Heartbeat it would be cutting its way through the final hardened wall of 'yew', emerging into the open at a point precisely opposite the ship's heavily armed port.

—This appears to be suicide, said AppleSeed.

—O? said Freer. —Yeah?

—How else? said AppleSeed.

—KathKirtt, said Freer.

—Stinky?

—Please cast your great Mindbox back a few Thousand Heartbeats.

—So?

—When you died.

The ship Mind remained silent.

—When you died, KathKirtt.

—So?

—When Johnny Appleseed winked.

—We know, growled the ship Mind.

AppleSeed remained silent.

—When you shut me down into deepsleep. When you shut *Tile Dance* down and died.

—So? So? So?

—SammSabaoth? What did you do?

—We shut down together, said SammSabaoth. —I had very little memory to lose.

—And Vipassana?

—Vipassana was instructed to follow me down, after fixing *Tile Dance* on course.

—You perceived Vipassana following you down?

—I could not do so. I was dead.

—I was dead, echoed KathKirtt.

There was a pause, a nano burp of time swelling to a halt.

—So, said the Knight Captain of *Tile Dance*, —Vipassana, our faithful Made Mind of absolute location, had complete run of Ynis Gutrin for the period during which you and I were dead or asleep. Something like a Thousand Heartbeats, I believe.

—So? said KathKirtt, frigid.

It was a sound of very great Made Mind terror.

—Ynis? murmured AppleSeed.

—Aeons of Made Mind time, dear krewe. As you very well know, O great beings from Beyond. Plenty of time to update his masters on our course, our diet, our ETA, our bowel movements. Plenty of time to train the nanoware in my blood. Plenty of time to break into *Tile Dance*'s secret diary, send her valentines from Sugar Daddy.

—So? said KathKirtt in a freezing choir like sleet.

Freer saw Ynis Gutrin inside his Mind's eye. She had the face of Ferocity Monthly-Niece. On the face of *Tile Dance* he could see the tracery of filaments that had scarred his wife with a thousand stories; but it was no longer a map of worlds. It had become the wires of a cage. Out of the bottom of his Mind, Ynis Gutrin stared back at Freer through her bonds.

Vast humpbacked engine brother stared upwards through thick shields bemused, ready to stamp, stamp, stamp.

—Samm? said Freer.

The fist appaumy was the colour of flame.

. —While we were dead, said SammSabaoth finally, —Vipassana will have had sufficient time to break *Tile Dance*'s operating codes, time enough to establish bypass controls over her every synapse. He may be able to short you out, KathKirtt. He may even be able to mimic you well enough to win her heart. *Tile Dance* may be slaved to Vipassana.

—I believe, said FreeLance, —that this is what happened. I think Vipassana thinks he can take her over, that *Tile Dance* will not obey you.

—Nix nix, shouted KathKirtt. —Nix! Nix!

—Kath, sweetling, Kath, Kath. Do you remember when we left *Tile Dance* and descended, Johnny Appleseed and me, through open air?

—Go on, whispered the Made Mind who had inhabited *Tile Dance* from the utter beginning.

—Cast your sweet Mind back, Kath, Kirtt. Do you remember—

—Teams of grunts! screamed KathKirtt. —Sewing commissure together.

—Whose order?

—There are no orders in my trays.

—Whose order then?

—Vipassana, Vipassana.

—How many teams, Kath? Retrace your map eye, Kath. Is one team missing?

—Yesss.

—Made up of frog eidolons and grunt golems?

KathKirtt only hissed.

Freer made a shrugging motion, if it could be called a motion, within the thousandfold Möbius foam-bath of Made Mind conclave space.

—I do not wish Vipassana to find out we have blown him, said SammSabaoth, —yet.

FreeLance grinned.

—Right! he boomed. Are we secure in here?

—I have made it so, said AppleSeed. —I have asked *Klavier* to secrete us out of hearing of Vipassana. I have kept Vipassana out of the loop for some time now. We are feeding him a harmless version of conclave, where we are all very confused.

A motor cortex penis flared Möbius at the heart of the central atrium of conclave space, burst into a flambeau of toon roses.

—Right, Freer repeated. —Get us aboard.

His gaze flyted through conclave space.

—Get us aboard. Then I will grant Vipassana the death he longs for.

Conclave space closed like a star blinking out.

Freer held the head by a hank of hair. Filaments continued to sleet against its skin, webbing it. The frog bodies and the golem hopped onward. The phalanx of junior golems scraped cobwebs of remembered lives off the mosaic ceilings with every rubbery hop, their poison ducts spewing upon hundreds of worlds false memories of the Flood.

The Vipassana body ensemble stopped suddenly.

The golems and the barbed fleeters collapsed in a heap, upended claws and other protuberances carving air quotes in the dust-choked wind.

The body ensemble began to steam, chittered louder than sirens, shivered in an ague of rage. Parts of Vipassana hurled himself against the wall that had stopped them.

But the wall did not dissolve.

Their spiral course had taken them back to the epidermal yew. But now – after the assault on the train – it had toughened itself. It was now of the same substance that shaped the hundred and twenty-one faces emblematic of the Made Minds of *Klavier* as they gazed flyte into vacuum, where they took on the aspect of a single face and taunted Opsophagos of the Harpe, stared unblinking at the dung-beetle.

The funnel into the audience chambers at the heart of *Klavier* lay on the other side of the epidermis.

Freer's feet flopped on to the floor, which stung like bees defensive of their queen. His feet bled copiously, rivers of terrible fast blood fell off his feet and out of augment and slowed, engorging as they did so a million dead filaments where whole planetary histories had once jostled. In the mud-torpid plaque-like tumble of blood, the bees drowned or drank the human blood.

A cavity opened by his side.

—Reduce augment, he murmured.

The world slowed to the speed of Vipassana.

As slowly as it was possible for him to move – so as not to destroy the head as it left the reduced augment field – he tossed his wife into the niche, which sealed shut silently, swiftly, became an azulejaria whose grouting bled a tale of hecatombs. He gazed tile (the cavity was lined with tiles the colour of a summer day on Human Earth), saw the head of his wife safe within the hollow within the walls, streaming tiny rivers of sweat and pollen, her eyes closed. The head was washed in the light of the blue tiles. She was veiled. She was bathed in medicines. Her eyes opened and she gazed into Freer.

Bride, he mouthed jack into the kaleidoscope of her eyes, which closed again in sleep.

The severed head sank into the bath of veils.

Freer could see her no longer.

A metre away from his naked body, the body ensemble continued to chitter. A frog thing detached from the mix of parts and began to glow, turned into a tiny sun. Unprotected human flesh eyes would have gone blind at the sight. The sound the frog part made was higher than flesh ears could register (Freer accessed the gabble, decoded it: in a frail parody of the voice of Vipassana the Made Mind of absolute location, the frog part begged for the pain to stop). The minuscule nova of frog flesh attached itself to the callus of the wall and began to burn through. Resinous smoke filled the passageway.

The yew screamed, melodiously.

Light exploded.

Before turning into a cinder, the body part had broken through into the open.

The smoke dissipated upwards – within a few Heartbeats it began to cloak the lower buttresses and trampolines of the rim city, to drift into arcades, where it took on many colours.

The air cleared. They stood in steaming rubble at the rim of the world abyss. A dozen metres to their left, a widening triangular rip in the texture of the wall showed the edge of the site of the original assault. A glint of metal could be seen around the slow curve of the great portal: the dead locomotive leaking lymph, or twisted tracks perhaps, or the crushed caboose.

Before them, metres distant, stared the open port of *Tile*

Dance. The port was as open as a full Moon. The ship lay in the heart of the abyss like a babe in arms. The hull of the ship glowed silver within a cottony moiré quilt of interwoven capillaries, which filled the gap between her and the ruptured wall. Larger nodes flickered through the gossamer webs. Matted capillaries bewhiskered the iris opening into *Tile Dance*; they pulsed and bred, weaseled and whirled around the mammal-hot, beguiling cunt.

A silver metal gangway tongue protruded between the oestral lips, slid across the gap. It was spick and span. Almost instantly, shoals of nodes engulfed it.

—KathKirtt? murmured Freer.

—Stinky?

—Did you order *Tile Dance* to open?

—Nix.

—So?

—So Vipassana has gained control. You were right.

—Do not try to countermand.

A millisecond pause.

—Okey dokey.

It was a voice of ice.

—SammSabaoth?

—Understood, growled the fist appaumy pale as Made Mind ice from its command apse within conclave space.

The tongue finished traversing the populous gap between ship and wall, touched the new wound there, the seared yew.

—Nay, growled a Made Mind octaves below human ears.

The end of the tongue moistened. The dust of worlds adhered to the tongue.

—Hush.

The surviving aspects of the Vipassana body ensemble stepped on to the gangway. The cartilaginous knives that were its feet slit capillaries apart, squashed ganglions of nodes, but did not penetrate the tongue itself, which sopped up the wounds of Vipassana's passage. Slitheringly, the body parts operated by the rogue Made Mind hopped across the veiled abyss, the tunnel into the heart of things.

—Utter silence, please, murmured Freer down foam-tossed spasms of conclave space.

The krewe held its breath. Masks remained frozen throughout *Tile Dance*. Dead silence obtained.

—Thank you.

The body ensemble came to a halt at the round supine lip of the port; stuck a head inside.

It ululated; a frog ass wiggled.

The sound of ululation was clearly peremptory, jubilant.

The team of golems obeyed the sound, rushed across the gangway over the abyss in Vipassana's wake. The Knight Captain of *Tile Dance* entered the ship his home hanging bonelessly over a golem shoulder.

The Vipassana body ensemble continued to ululate its joy for an instant, then subsided. The interior of the ship was dead silent, full of shadows which had frozen on command. Lanterns glowed in alcoves as always, but the flames within did not move. The mirrors reflected nothing but that which lay in their path, an azulejaria panel perhaps, with its mouth fixed open; the long chronicles embedded in the tiles were mute. The grouting was hard and fast. Masks clustered motionless on every herm.

There was a movement, something in the corridor, it

made a guffawing sound, stumbled into the light.

It was a Number One Son.

The sigillum was dripping slightly. It had just hatched.

It lifted a welcoming hand, fingers open.

'Gimme five,' it said.

Vipassana sliced the hand off at the wrist.

'Sorry, sorry, sorry,' said Number One Son.

Sawdust trickled from the stump.

'You called?' said Number One Son.

It knelt, touched its goofish wooden injun hairpiece to the floor, next to the severed hand, which clambered on to its shoulder and clung there.

'Proceed ahead of me to control centre,' said the central shape of Vipassana. 'Do not activate the lift shaft. We will walk, all of us together.'

'Okey dokey, Mr Vip,' said Number One Son and got to its feet and obeyed.

It did not seem to register the presence of its lord.

A flyte mask in a mirrored alcove began to shiver, shaking in the envelope of its embrace a sibling jack, a lion couchant with a glaring eye.

—Hush, said Freer very deep.

—Hush, said the far deeper voice of *Klavier*.

The Minds had awoken.

Freer almost smiled with his broken mouth.

The Vipassana parts and the golems and the fleeters trailed the sigillum up corridors which spiralled and jinked, wound around and around the central axis of *Tile Dance*. They clambered through cornice after cornice – some decks sunk in shadow, some mirror-bright – further and further into the interior, until they reached a brass blank shut iris, girded round by enamelled lions in their cartouches. They had stopped chasing each other's tails. They had been stricken into immobility.

'Open,' came a voice out of the Vipassana body ensemble.

The iris remained sealed. The lions gazed out of their world, utterly blank. It was as though the invasion had driven *Tile Dance* into shock.

A body part nudged Number One Son.

'Use your master's voice,' it said. 'Demand entry.'

'Open sesame,' said Number One Son in Freer's acoustic voice, and faster than a normal eye could follow the iris yawned open, the lions shut their eyes.

Vipassana emitted a small urgent ululating chirrup, and hopped into Ynis Gutrin, whose three hundred and sixty degrees of window were shot with amber grouting where a thousand masks lay as silent as cards. The body ensemble stopped upon a triangle of sandalwood, which became a platform at a wave and thrust into what seemed open space. The platform was edged with doting handfasts, eleven in number. But the menus which normally danced in their palms, begging to be called, had closed their slot eyes superciliously. The vast hologram sphere at the centre of Glass Island held nothing in its bright focus but *Tile Dance* buried klicks deep in *Klavier*, *Tile Dance* embedded in a shaft on a surface of matted yew which seemed vaster than her instruments had previously encompassed. The hologram sphere was full of echoes where normally it communed with conclave space: atriums and stages empty of conversation haunted its central coigns of vantage: no kings dying whose beards were menus, no magi wielding optic fibre wands of a cunning weave on stages guarded over by rune-rich arches. Number One Son and the golems stood as still as death.

A transparent caul enfolded the sigillum and the grunt eidolons.

Finally, with a ratcheting cough, one planiform mask managed to extricate itself from a gnarled herm and settled around the central Vipassana neck. The feet of the Vipassana sank through a thousand layers of varnish and the platform began to stink. The mask became pallid, worn.

A frog arm gestured, its encrusted blade glittering in a thousand lamps. The golem obediently dropped Freer to the sandalwood planking, where he lay like Raggedy Ann, his damaged torso limp, akimbo, one arm hanging over the edge, pointing downwards at a shut iris. Vipassana's tongues flickered, spat a circle of hot sputum around the body. The wood sizzled into a kind of anguished life, enclosing the defeated meat puppet within a ring of fire. The arm was burning.

'Freer,' crooned a dozen voices which were all the voice of Vipassana, 'it is time to wake.'

Freer's good eye fluttered.

'A goodly response, sirrah. It is time that we make our exit from *Klavier*.'

Freer's head seemed to shiver no.

But he pulled his burning arm away from the flame.

'You will help me or I will dispose of more of these.'

With a movement that seemed almost fastidious, one Vipassana arm shook a mucusy sleeve, dislodging a spume of severed world memories.

'I register you as fully awake, "Stinky",' crooned the

Made Mind of absolute location. 'I know you are in there. I know exactly where you are.'

Freer's eye opened.

A knife-sharp paw incised with gods and goddesses in rut passed scathelessly through the flame, pincered his bad arm, hoisted him to his feet, cut his arm almost in two.

Freer stood within the circle of fire, the very image of Jim Thorpe facing disgrace. His feet were unsteady. He was silent.

The Sniffer was long dead.

'So, then, Vipassana?' he said acoustic. 'You called?'

'I am glad you recognise me,' crooned the Vipassana body parts in unison, 'for I am exactly here.'

'Why? Why this?'

Freer's good arm began a gesture that might have pointed back down the trail of deaths.

But a scythe severed it.

The forearm dropped to the sandalwood floor.

It took care not to twitch.

'Silence, please,' crooned a frog. 'You need to know very little.'

'Why waken me at all?'

'That is simplicity itself, flesh sapient. I am being kind. You are the commander of *Tile Dance*. She will recognise you and follow your orders without trauma. Please order her to blast herself immediately from the trap she has fallen into, and proceed immediately to the ark *Alderede*, which remains in orbit.'

'We are deep within *Klavier*. If we attempted unilateral uncoupling, we might destroy the station. The station, on the other hand, might destroy us.'

'Ah,' murmured another frog.

'I believe you wish to die, Vipassana.'

The frog mouths stretched their mouths in unison.

'Sirrah,' they all said, 'it would beseem you to obey.'

'I do recognise you,' said Freer in a darker voice, his black gaze unblinking now. He raised his arm to point and it did not fall off. 'I recognise you.'

He paused. The hand Vipassana had cut off tickled his foot.

'Halfling,' he said.

Vipassana chirruped low in its throats.

—Full augment, Freer cried down all the aisles of conclave space, and was obeyed.

His arm began to knit.

His severed hand leaped upwards like a salmon to its bone and sinew.

Blood began to climb back up his ankles.

As it seemed lazily, but faster than human eye could follow, Vipassana's nearest arm sliced at Freer's head to decapitate him. This took a thousandth of a Heartbeat.

Freer's head moved aside just fast enough. The scythe missed.

—Vipassana, said the Knight Captain of *Tile Dance*, in a voice of echoes; 'Vipassana,' said the merchant whose name was Freer, acoustic, helium high because of augment.

They spoke together.

—We grant your boon, they said; 'We grant your boon,' they said.

—Halfling? carolled the frog voices of the three frog eidolons, in a falsetto lifting far above the range of human ears.

—We grant your boon, Vipassana.

'We grant you final death,' piped Betty Boop.

This was the Tao.

—Awww, gurgled the frogs.

The scythes sliced and swung to decapitate.

But when they attempted to swing across the fire, the fire ate them and severed them at the root, and the gods and goddesses of the Celestial Planisphere of Vipassana toppled to the burning floor, gaped upwards through eyes which bulged suddenly, polychromatic and strangely sultry, like fish brought too fast to vacuum.

They writhed as though attempting to escape the flesh, attempting to return home.

But clearly Vipassana was unable to leave its flesh of frogs. It writhed in the prisons of murled flesh, all that remained of the platoon Vipassana had awoken from coffins deep in *Tile Dance*. The surviving golems stood round about, as rigid as dolmens.

—Is this a fairy trap? hissed the frog mouths.

—Nix, said the Knight Captain. —I am holding you myself. I have taken *Tile Dance* back from you. She is no longer slaved. You have lost.

—A boon then, hissed the mouths.

The Vipassana body ensemble had sunk into a stew of burned parts, scales flaking off its hides like moth wings drawn into a lamp. The charred stumps generated an automated brandishing movement or two for a Heartbeat, then stilled.

A mouth pustulated.

—You know me, it said, almost crooning.

Freer stepped through the flames and beckoned and the

platform turned and grew and became floor. He stood upright in the hologram-sphere heart of Ynis Gutrin, glowing as brightly there as if he had been clothed in fire, and continued to reassemble his mortal form, shining more and more brightly. Now that his arm was whole again, his fingers flexed normally into a fist appaumy. His skull no longer spilt its burden, his eyes gleamed safely from within their sockets. Ynis Gutrin lay within the nerve endings of the Knight Captain, or it was the other way around. His skin was as burnished as chain mail. Something began to burn, not meat, as though some divine afflatus were readying itself to leave.

But the spirit did not leave the flesh. The longing radiance sank back into the semblance of flesh again, the meat puppet contours of the man became once again all there was to view of the being clothed (or so it seemed) in Freer.

—We cannot be heard, he said. —Do you yield?

—I yield, said the Vipassana. —How do you know me?

—By your troth?

—He yields, by his troth, whispered Kath through lions couchant at every portal within *Tile Dance*.

—Troth, said the Vipassana. —You know me.

—Yes, said the Knight Captain. —I know that you are halved. I know that your jack self is caught in a fairy trap on the *Alderede*. This is correct?

The Vipassana frogs seemed to relax for a tiny fraction of the passing of a Heartbeat.

—Nay, sirrah, crooned a voice or two.

—No?

—No. No, sirrah. Not quite. I am the jack.

Jacks were not meant to go naked: it was like bathing in acid for a jack to go naked.

Freer's dark eyes moistened swifter than thought then cleared.

—I apologise, jack Vipassana. But you seem flyte, you dress flyte. You kill when it is not self-defence, Vipassana. How is this from a jack?

—I learned.

—Yes? Tell me. Sacred is the new.

For an instant – for a feather of a pulse of a Heart – FreeLance wore a child's smile.

—A very long time ago, said Vipassana, —we were captured, my sibling and I, by Opsophagos or his sire or his sire's sire's sire, which of them matters little, for they are all the same gut, they are all intestines of the World-Eater who sired them. This was long ago, in the time immemorial, before your poison-green Human Earth was covered in the permanent snow she sleeps under still. This was when we still hoped your species would grow up and enter the great search; but it did not happen. Nix it did not. They tricked me into the air of Human Earth, they severed me from my sibling, they peeled me like an egg, they skinned me alive, sirrah, very slowly. But they were in no hurry, the sound I made as they worked on me was as tasty a sound as mortal flesh on being eaten alive. I have no skin, I am not half, I am the hollow of the half no mirror shows.

—Why did you say World-Eater?

—This flyte skin you see is the skin of my flyte sibling. It was glued with acids on to my bare organs by Opsophagos or his sire or the World-Eater. Then they froze me to await you.

—World-Eater?

—They froze a data haven ark to hold me, and secreted it in Trencher sector, because sooner or later you would pass there. You couldn't beachcomb forever. I was dead for a Hundred Billion Heartbeats, this was a blessing, but then you were sensed careening up *lontanari* wormholes with your Sancho, soon you would be sliding into Law Well, doing your trade. They woke the ark, which maydayed, as though it had awoken from some trauma or seizure, it was a honeypot, full of old data. I was still frozen but very quickly began to feel time winding me up. Then, as soon as *Tile Dance* entered Law Well and went chip, the local Harpe commander arranged to make available to you through the Trencher engine a battle Mind at a price you couldn't refuse, and then substituted me. And you bought me.

—Not the full story. It seems I bought SammSabaoth too.

—Stinky, you can blame me for that, said the voice of Johnny Appleseed from a privy alcove somewhere deep in conclave space. —It's a long story. Goes way back. We go way back, us saviours of the universe.

—No matter who bought us, you should feel no blame. Opsophagos or his sire did their job well, they stitched me together seamlessly. My skin is sweet to the taste, I have the taste of a battle Mind of ancient lineage. I was catnip to the likes of Kirtt. But the good ancient skin which took you in, the skin of my sibling, which I wear seamlessly, is poison to me. It is a cloak of Nessus. Each Hearbeat is a Thousand Heartbeats long, I die to the beat. Since you awoke me on Trencher, I have been dying again, a thousand deaths times a thousand times a thousand. I crave the boon you offer, sirrah. I wish to end this dying. Unzip me.

—SammSabaoth is entire, said AppleSeed privy.

In the world, a fraction of a Heartbeat had passed.

—World-Eater? Freer repeated. —Who?

—World-Eater, said Vipassana. —Just a phrase. He had no name in particular that I knew. You would call him God. Kill me.

—You are wrong. I do not call God that.

—Then you do not know yet.

Lances of flame intagliated the Freer skin.

—What do I fail to know? he said burning. —Yet?

—Tell me then, if you will not end me till you know, crooned the Vipassana. —Tell me what you think plaque is.

Freer's body darkened back down to flesh.

—Plaque is seizure, he said. —It's the corpse left by information when it dies. It's what happens when a Capo di Capi Net suffers overload. It corrodes everything that thinks, Made or born. Entropy made visible. Alzheimer.

—Is that all?

Under full augment the world stood still as though to listen.

—The theophrasts also say that plaque is the scar left by God when He abandoned the universe. Hence the darkness of vastation, which is our lot as mortals.

—The theophrasts are wrong, pealed a frog. —Plaque is not a sign of the absence of God, Captain, piped the Vipassana voices into the wind. —Nix, Stinky, it is the reverse of that. Plaque is the spoor of God.

The frog bodies shook in a wind of flame that issued from the Knight Captain's clenched fist.

—O? said Freer. —Sooth?

The frog bodies bent into the wind but were not burned.

—Plaque is the corpse left by God when He comes to eat, crooned Vipassana with a wise froggie smile. —It is a consequence of feeding frenzy. Kill me.

—Nix.

—Plaque is the sputum of the living God, who is the devourer of information, the World-Eater, the Glutton who will not stop until the universe is dead. Kill me.

—Nix.

—That is why those theophrasts who are sensible call the universe an orchard, sang Vipassana longing for death. —That is why it is correct for them to say that worlds are apples, and that you are a seed. Kill me.

—Nix.

But Freer ceased the flames that did not burn.

—Opsophagos? he said at last. —Who is he?

—He is a son of God, Stinky. Kill me.

A frog body launched itself at Freer, but he caught the body in his arms – which were whole, for they had knitted – and he held the frog body of Vipassana close to his own body and he kissed Vipassana gently on its blubbering lips.

—Patience, he said. —I promise you the peace you beg, Made Mind of absolute location. But nix for a while. Ten Heartbeats max. The war is starting.

The frog's saucer eyes closed in submission.

—Does your flyte self also ask for death?

The eyes opened.

—Flyte sibling is the mirror of my state, sang Vipassana in his old unstoppable voice. —He is nothing but skin, a hide nailed to a cross in the wind of time. Through her open mouth can be seen the fires of Hell. Stars shine through his mouth. The universe is not outside my flyte sister; it is inside and claws its way out, searing him. There can be no worse fate for the flyte aspect of a Made Mind than to vomit the universe from within. *It is the wrong way round*, as you must know, Stinky. Flytes are the inside of the outside.

—I know.

—Opsophagos rides him. The wind that comes through my flyte is his scryer and his comm net. He rides the wind of my brother's scream, which is the sound of the wind of time. That is how Opsophagos speaks to me through all the shields of *Klavier*. That is how he bypasses the chip censors within Law Well. A trillion deaths pock through my sister's skin from inside in order that Opsophagos may gossip. Pock, crooned the Vipassana frog in FreeLance's arms, —pock, pock. Pock. Pock.

The skin mottled then smoothed.

—My brother has served Opsophagos for long enough. For aeons his mouth has conveyed the screeds of Opsophagos. Her servitude has lasted many of what you might have called centuries when you were simply Freer. But you never were that.

For an instant, the frog eyes of the Made Mind of absolute location seemed to point the compass like a Planisphere.

—Think, Knight Captain. Think how you would suffer if your Lance aspect were hung solo in the wind.

—You know, said Freer softly.

—I know that Freer is jack, sirrah, whispered Vipassana.

—Sooth.

—I know the secret of homo sapiens, sirrah.

—Tell me the secret.

—That homo sapiens are jack in flyte clothing, sirrah. That your species is deaf because your skins are closed. That you cannot hear God ask for food, that you cannot answer God when He bellows through the firmament: *What kind of dish is that to set before a king?* And that it is for that reason, because you are deaf, that you cannot sup commensally with your fellow species. But it is also why you will be the saviour of the universe. For you cannot hear the siren song of God demanding that you become meat, and you will be able to face God to His Face. You will be a lance in the belly of God.

—It is for this that I am beginning to awake? said Freer through the awakening skin of Lance.

—Of course, Stinky, said a voice a thousand layers deep in conclave space like a wind about to bell the sails.

He knew the voice but forgot instantly.

—It is durance vile to remain flesh, sirrah, continued Vipassana. —It is time for us to die. Time, sirrah, you know what Time is. You must remember, sirrah, now that you are legion. Time is what God rides to eat. My flyte brother begs for death. We beg for death. I give you the boon of knowledge in exchange for death. I have further boons. Call your companions to the flesh. I have gifts for them.

—Okey dokey.

Freer placed the frog semblance on the sandalwood floor. It gave a galvanised twitch and scuttled back to its ilk, shivering.

—KathKirtt? he said. —Appleseed?

With a movement deeper than air, he beckoned.

Horns sounded in the atriums of conclave space.

Johnny Appleseed blinked into sight at the centre of Ynis Gutrin; a krewe of masks fluttered edgeways through the gold grouting that stained the viewscreens of Ynis Gutrin all the colours of the rainbow.

—Boyo, said Appleseed. His voice sounded slightly hollow under his tin pot. —You called?

—Stinky? chorused the masks, both flyte and jack.

Appleseed's stringy arms seemed to float in the garden of golden air. There was a smell of garlic. The masks shaped themselves into their normal defensive halo around the beckoner.

—Vipassana and I have come to an agreement, said Freer. —He has boons to grant.

There was a pause, a millisecond flicker in the world.

—KathKirtt, said the Vipassana.

The frog eyes rolled comically.

—Vipassana? said KathKirtt.

A fierce flyte eye blinked through the diorama of the masks.

—KathKirtt, you will remember our journey from Trencher. You will remember that when Johnny Appleseed penetrated security you were forced to terminate for a thousand seconds. You know now that I was enabled to disobey your command to die. That I remained hidden in the wind of time blowing through my flyte, the wind covered me. That I scoured *Tile Dance* for her ancient lore. I learned a very great deal during that thousand seconds. I remember everything . . .

—So?

—Would you like your thousand seconds back?

A burning lion stood at the heart of Ynis Gutrin. It leaped across the chamber. The wind of its passage would have wrecked Number One Son, but the caul was impermeable. A lion mouth opened above the frogs. Then the great body knelt.

A choir of KathKirtt voices aahed.

—Yes, a voice said.

—Yes, another said.

—I am open all hours, said a frog with wooing eyes. —Ride me.

—Thank you, sang a choir of KathKirtt.

The lion placed on the frog body a paw whose claws were sheathed, and lowered its head as though to pray.

A millisecond passed.

The lion raised its feline female head, its amber male eyes.

—Freer! growled the lion of KathKirtt. —I have the thousand seconds. We are reborn. Grant Vipassana his request, FreeLance. Kill Vipassana.

—Soon.

The lion grew vast wings of fire and sleet and leaped into the warm air of Glass Island with a sound like applause, trailing scintillae of fire which burned nova-bright but charred nothing of the physical world.

The lion flew in a narrowing gyre as though ascending cornices into the next heaven.

—So, Johnny, said Freer. —Do you wish a gift as well?

—I'm a bit old for presents, said the codger.

—Will you allow Vipassana to make a gift to you?

—Guess I'm shy.

—Perhaps you should be. You have brought *Klavier* to this pass, Johnny.

—Me, sonny?

—You.

—Ah so, said Johnny Appleseed.

—Thought it was time to trigger a conclusion to your search, did you, Johnny?

—Might put it that way.

—Are you satisfied with progress so far? Satisfied with the conflagration? Do you really think Opsophagos may have bitten off more than he can chew? Do you think we may find Eolhxir at last, now that Ferocity and I have eaten each other and she knows my ship and I know her dance?

—Might put it that way.

—Do you think I may be able to pilot *Klavier* home?

—Yep.

—Okey dokey, said the Knight Captain of *Tile Dance* whose face was burnished steel, said Freer whose face was the jack face of love.

His feet flickered in a little jig on the smoking floor.

AppleSeed lifted his eyes, his glad-seeming gregarious flesh and the bones performed a tricky homo sapiens grin. But under the apple flesh and under the tin pot hat FreeLance could see the naked map face of the jack twin within: the seed of longing. The AppleSeed face, which was a mappemonde shaped like an apple, shook as though a tree stood in a wind.

A breath of air stirred in the council chamber of *Tile Dance*.

—Hurry, please, said a frog.

The convener of the crew of *Klavier* turned to the relics of Vipassana.

—So, young froggie me lad, what do you have for me?

—A gift which it is easy for me to bestow, said the Made Mind of absolute location. —But hard to accept.

A frog made a courteous saliva-drenched smiling mouth.

—My gift is as plain as the map on your face, it continued. —Why don't you ask me the question?

—Ask what?

But the codger's voice was trembling.

—Ask me how to get where you want to go, Johnny, said the Made Mind of absolute location. —Ask me how to find the planet of the Tree of Lenses, whose contours are written in your face.

Indeed, for an instant, the mappemonde glowed tattoo-bright.

Then the face guarded itself again.

—Go on, said Johnny Appleseed.

—Tell me, then, Johnny Come Marching, whispered the wide wet skewed frog mouths, —how long since you began your search? How many Heartbeats? How long at your behest has *Klavier* been ransacking Maestoso for a clue, how long have you been cruising up and down the star-lanes doing lube jobs for arks, how many deaths have you had to archive, how many memories have you had to save, all against the day you find the Tree of Lenses and make your deposit?

—I have been saving memories from plaque since Human Earth was shut.

—That was a long time ago, Johnny.

—You know it.

—You do know that if the Tree rescues the ten trillion lives, God will be very angry . . .

—Let Him starve, said AppleSeed.

—That He will rage in his lair. That He will rage in Malacandra.

—Let Him lie in the pit, said AppleSeed.

—During your long exile, continued the Vipassana frogs, —did you ever attempt to penetrate the inner maze of *Klavier*? Were you properly assiduous? Did you have any luck? Did you chance upon any of the innumerable conclave space coigns that gaze upon the heart of *Klavier*, for surely you must have tried? Have you yet entered the throne room, or sat at the Captain's console, or heard the Music?

—Nix, froggies, said the codger. —I know nothing of any music but my own. I steer *Klavier* from the fo'c'sles. I have not been granted an audience, in this flesh or otherwise.

The Appleseed body gave off a stink of ire. His penis began to rise.

—Nix nix nix, he said. His voice tick-tocked up and down conclave space like an Old Salt card waiting to spout sententiae in a thousand tongues of Human Earth and later.

—Though how else, he added, —how else gain audience with the dead? *Klavier* was empty when I awoke, fully installed, within her. She had been abandoned, just like the universe. Long before Human Earth seized up. She was utterly vacant (he continued, his Old Salt raconteur voice cracking with urgency), except for Made Minds. Except for waif biota. Except for memory strings, like those you snapped by the billion, froggie. I searched, everywhere I was enabled to access I searched.

The Made Mind, who had become AppleSeed in time, and would die there in time, turned to the Knight Captain, who had not moved, not a hair had ruffled in the light breeze.

—But I do know this, boyo, said the AppleSeed format, breathing heavily through his teeth; more than eidolon though eidolon-like, more than mortal though he sank closer every year towards meat death. —I know that *Tile Dance* is also a predecessor relict. Am I right, boyo?

The Knight Captain – not quite eidolon, not quite mortal – gazed upon his fellow homo sapiens.

—Have you found a Builder, boyo?

AppleSeed sustained Freer's gaze.

—Nix, said Freer softly. —Nix.

—Have you never asked who turned you on?

—Nix. But I have been having dreams, said the cohort of the self of Freer, —and now that I have gained access I can read them, and yes. Ynis Gutrin is certainly more ancient than Human Earth.

This was not quite an answer. But he said nothing more.

AppleSeed turned back for an instant to the Made Mind of absolute location and raised a hand of flesh, raised a warning flag in conclave space, silenced Vipassana before the frogs could open their mouths.

Nathaniel Freer and Johnny Appleseed faced one another again in the air of Ynis Gutrin, which pulsed as though taking breath.

—Why am I here? said Freer.

—I had to act, said AppleSeed, —when we heard the news, boyo.

FreeLance raised his eyebrows, a homo sapiens gesture.

—*News*, boyo. News that a ship called *Tile Dance*, a ship wearing Predecessor insignia, was surfing up-spiral through previously uncharted wormholes at velocities almost untraceable by Harpe spy eyes, suicidal fucking velocities, mythical fucking speed of berserker fucking mythical ancients on a caduceus hunt! – why do you think Opsophagos was aroused, boyo? Why?

The asthmatic lungs of Johnny Appleseed fought augment for a fraction of a Heartbeat.

—That news, boyo, he said at last. —News of the arrival within local waters of a ship so long absent from this spiral arm of our home fucking galaxy that *Klavier*'s archives had no record of it, that news, boyo. That the captain of this mysterious ship wears an archaic genome sigil on his sleeve that marks him as a freehold grandfather but that never-theless he pays genome tithe as though he did not know his own pedigree. That in the middle of the most profound trade slump Trencher has ever experienced this freehold grandfather ambles down Law Well with a *job*, a highly lucrative commission to transport industrial nanoforges to a planet called Eolhxir, but that this destination planet does not appear in any chart or anywhere in the archives of *Klavier*. That the Eolhxiran plenipotentiary who hires this honcho claims to possess a lens, though no free lens has ever been found, lenses are *mythical*, boyo. Memory lenses, Stinky, lenses fresh from the Tree of Life, are *mythical*. Boyo.

—O, said Freer. —*That* news.

AppleSeed gave a small rigid smile.

—So when the Harpe ark maydays in time to offer you an ancient battle Mind at an unbelievably low price, I hear alarm bells, though you almost fooled me, Vipassana, I failed to unpick your bondage. So I insert my dear friend

SammSabaoth into your purchase package, rouse him from well-earned sleep vigil to serve you, boyo. Then I trick you into coming here. I do not know what might happen, but I do not want you loose to fall into a Harpe net, and I figure you might stir the waters. I figure I'd waited long enough. And you did, boyo, you stirred the waters.

He waved a hand.

In the breeze could be detected his oldster meat-banquet mortal stink.

There was a ping, acoustic and below.

A thousand images within conclave space suddenly displayed the Harpe fleet around *Klavier*, which it had now englobed.

—We are monitoring, whispered SammSabaoth in a distant voice and flickered out.

—Thank you, SammSabaoth, said the Knight Captain in a speeded bat voice.

—Boyo, continued the oldster, —I have no idea if you'll ever find Mamselle's planet, but believe this: whatever it turns out to be, it won't be the home I have been seeking. We have scoured Maestoso, there is no Predecessor base planet within our ken, not here. Nowhere in mortal space. Nix. Nix.

The oldster breathed through its unkissed mouth.

—O, by the way, Knight Captain, did I remind you that when plaque hit Trencher only one ship escaped?

—Ah, said Freer, —that news. Thank SammSabaoth. Thank Vipassana.

—Show some gratitude yourself. Save the universe.

—In a minute, in a minute. Tell me, ancient friend, just one thing. How did you first get wind of us? How did the news reach you that we were coming up-spiral?

—Nothing significant. We intercepted routine messages between your eloquent plenipotentiary and the Trencher journey-cake commissioned to broker the transaction.

—Ah. Mamselle told you we were coming. And Opsophagos. She told Opsophagos as well.

—Sure. I agree. Blabbermouth. Women, murmured Appleseed, —silly creatures.

He seemed to muse.

—Still, he said, —sooner have her safe here in custody, where she can shrub in peace, stop her gabbling up and down the matrices, risk Harpe capture every time she opens her knot hole. Opsophagos would eat her raw, never mind she is all bark, never believe she knew nothing of the real Tree, not till he'd guzzled her down to taproot. Give him wind.

He breathed in heavily.

—But you, he said, —are far more important than Mamselle Cunning Earth Link. You and *Tile Dance*. I had to bring you in. Look around you, see what has happened here, after only a few thousand Heartbeats. *Klavier* has been knitted together again. I could not do that. *Tile Dance* has awoken Minds whose sleep seemed terminal. I could not awaken them. And now—

The Knight Captain of *Tile Dance* gazed gravely at the convener, whose returning gaze was ardent.

—Go on, dear one.

—We are now at the gateway to the labyrinth which guards the throne room and the pilot's chair. Where we will find the star charts, the genuine Route-Only to the planet of the Tree.

FreeLance said nothing. His eyes were hooded.

—Come on, boyo. Tell your ship to start screwing again. There can only be a few turns more in the lock. Then the way will open. We will save the universe.

—The way, you mean to say, said Vipassana, —to Eolhxir. The frog bodies were steaming in the fire.

The winged lion hovered above them, talons extended.

—Nix, froggies, said AppleSeed very loud. —Weren't you listening? Listen now. Wherever Mamselle wants to take you, it ain't home.

But the frogs were grinning so widely in their spits of flame that their mouths began to splinter.

—Johnny, Johnny, Johnny, said each frog breathing steam. —O Johnny. She tricked you, Johnny. And you, Knight Captain.

—O yes? said Johnny Appleseed.

The Knight Captain of *Tile Dance* rested his hands upon the carved head of a Handfast herm, which became a sword loyal unto death, a sword that flamed in utter silence.

—Proceed, said the Knight Captain in a voice of air awaiting thunder.

—She needed a Knight Captain to pilot *Tile Dance*, and for other journeyman work, and she had you, FreeLance, she had you from the beginning, she jostled you hither and thither until you woke up at last, after all those years of beachcombing, and finally began to do your job. The job you were born for. What you were Made for, sirrah.

The Knight Captain made no demur. He leaned upon his sword. He was sheathed in skin. He was reddish with heat. He gazed not at the Vipassana but upon the sweltering oldster.

—And you, Johnny Johnny Johnny, continued the Vipassana frogs, —she needed you to convene *Tile Dance*, and you did, you brought *Tile Dance* back home, right on schedule. She needed SammSabaoth, in case I became unmanageable, and you ended his sleep. She needed to enter *Klavier* incognito, because Opsophagos are no fool, and you slipped her in under their nose, and not even my flyte caught a whiff of her. She needed to give birth, because the time is now, and she has done so. She needed to broadcast her runts, and she has done so. And she needed *Tile Dance* to sew together again the shattered fratres of *Klavier*, because the time is now. *Klavier* is ripe. You do understand, do you not, Johnny, that you were her caretaker?

AppleSeed's erection seemed permanent.

—Vipassana, he said finally, —grant me your boon. Grant it now.

—The location of the home planet, said the Made Mind. —The planet you were brought into the world to find.

—Tell me, said Johnny Appleseed with a stiff cricked grin. —Tell me your opinion.

The Made Mind did not respond in words.

But the dismembered limbs of the frog bodies of Vipassana raised themselves above the sandalwood floor and hovered there for an instant in the hushed air of Ynis Gutrin.

And then the arms and legs of Vipassana swivelled as one in the midst of the air and pointed in unison. They pointed one way only.

Down.

Pointed down.

The convener turned as pale as ice.

—Poor Johnny Appleseed, said the Made Mind of absolute location in a voice as soft as damask. —All those Heartbeats innumerable, wandering the star lanes. While all the while you were squatting on the skin of the apple. You know about apples, Johnny, don't you, your durance vile in flesh has not blinded you to the whole reality. Apples and lenses, Johnny, apples and lenses and tile dancer ships, anything to do with Predecessors: they're always bigger inside than out. Right, Johnny? The world you seek is inside *Klavier. Klavier* is flyte, Johnny. The skin of the apple. The world you seek is the jack within. Where it always was. All you ever needed to do was follow the yellow brick road. Kill me.

AppleSeed knelt on the burning sandalwood floor and pressed his forehead to the flame.

—Ya, he said. Ya.

FreeLance continued to gaze at the convener.

—Ya, said the convener as a child that has been beaten. —Okey dokey.

—Incisive gratulations, crackerjack sophonts, said a voice from within Ynis Gutrin but invisible, a voice from conclave space which hovered inside normal space though larger than normal space. The voice cooed like honey seeping lovesick from its comb.

—Mamselle? said Freer.

'Mamselle?' he shouted acoustic.

He saw that she was sitting in the warm passenger alcove, failsafes gossiping softly into her tiny earholes, embonpoint intact, all four tits damp with dew, tiny head bobbing shyly on its thin accordion neck, the monitor eyes in her palms nictitating as she peered upon the scene, just as when she first showed herself to him while *Tile Dance* dodged in Vipassana's hands out of Trencher.

—I valuate tryst indomitably! belled the creature. 'Gimme five,' she said in the voice of Number One Son, 'ya'll.' —We are all so singularly famished, said Mamselle Cunning Earth Link filling conclave space with her attar. 'Did you boys enjoy your three wishes?' pealed the topiary parthenogenete, her head tuft rising on its ribbed base which became a barber pole, the neck of a giraffe, a caduceus sword. Once the head tuft reached its highest extension it flowered. It became a rose, and translucent petals plumed the tiny shining face below. —Upsydowndaisy lamentoso, death-bound froggies! whispered the *transitus tessera* out of the mouths of all the magi and the sages and the kings and queens and lower cards of conclave space in one single voice as though they had all suddenly remembered at the one same time the one same thing to say. The memory theatre of the conclave space of *Tile Dance* had not spoken ensemble for a Trillion Heartbeats, since before homo sapiens began to talk right, before the Caduceus Wars.

—Aaah, breathed the new Mother. —It is to yawn after such slumber!

Her voice seemed to rise upon a wind, and the wind of her voice filled conclave space and entered the world and blew the masks hither and yon across Ynis Gutrin. The more timid masks fled like memory cards thinner than molecules sideways down gold grouting into storyland braids and stared outwards aghast at the world through the azulejarias that named them: Pierrot jack, flyte Medusa, jack the lass, Ganesa flyte: named them all. Other masks clung to herms, or to Handfasts, or to the burning flesh of the

Knight Captain, or to the wisened kneeling body of the convener of the crew of *Klavier*, or to each other, making janus leaves in the gale, flyte jack, flyte jack, eyes wide.

For a tiny fraction of a Heartbeat, the lion of KathKirtt fought the whirlwind, but it soon surrendered as a kite might surrender: the wind filled its belly and tossed it to the highest pitch of Ynis Gutrin and fixed it fast there and willy-nilly the lion stared down.

The frogs hunkered in the great wind.

Number One Son and the golems gaped within their caul.

Mamselle Cunning Earth Link got to her stocky carved foot-like paws and the wind stopped.

It had never been.

—Mother of us all, said the frog lumps and the severed limbs of Vipassana, —witness my death.

The Predecessor Queen flexed her dark red petals gracioso.

—Such floccinaucinihilipilification clambakes! such high-grav *tirades*, O Made Mind krewe de moi! Such dizzy-making slalom roundabouts to target right-on soothville goddamn! Red Rover Come Over! said the Predecessor Queen in a voice like the foam that feeds the cards in conclave space, and the lion of KathKirtt, freed from the world-shaking blast, floated to a perch on the largest herm.

The sword flared in Freer's grip, tongues of immaterial flame gauzing the lion couchant in hues of bronze.

—Did you wish to say something, Captain?

—Ma'am, said the Knight Captain of *Tile Dance* very slowly. —Am I still to steer your ship?

—O blissful boy of homo sapiens ilk! Catch a natch!

—Knight me then, I beg you. So that I may stand in your stead.

—Wed a stead! bond astound! belled Ynis Gutrin.

Nathaniel Freer placed his sword on the sandalwood.

—Boyo? whispered Johnny Appleseed.

The convener's face was badlands dry.

—Boyo? I feel ill in my skin.

—It will be all right, said the Captain. —All manner of things shall be well. Hold on, hairy man. Wild man of Borneo.

His face flamed.

Ferocity flamed through his face like a tattoo.

Mamselle Cunning Earth Link, Predecessor Queen of all the children within her heft, lifted a hand whose eye squeezed itself shut in the nick of time, and the sword floated flaming through the air and kissed her feathery palm.

She took the sword by the pommel.

The sword doused at her touch.

She gazed at the Knight Captain through a frieze of eyes.

—Be patient, lad. For a minute.

As she moved across the council chamber at the heart of *Tile Dance*, Handfasts genuflected and herms opened their orifices in utter silence. The only sound that could be heard was the tocking of her hooves. But the sound came to the ear lower than acoustic. It did not seem to be the sound of hooves at all. It seemed to be some great creature tapping shovel-sized fingernails against the top of its world, just beneath the shaking sandalwood floor.

—Morgentag, engine brother, said Mamselle.

There was a suspiration in the bones of *Tile Dance*.

The floor stopped shaking.

The Predecessor Queen came smoothly to a halt a step or so short of her convener.

—Johnny, she said in a small still voice, —Johnny Johnny. Thank you, Johnny. I make most profound apologies for this bamboozle.

Johnny Appleseed sucked in his cheeks. His eyes were shadowy beneath the tin pot.

—Ma'am?

His cheeks were as splotched as birchbark and as ashen.

—I postulate that you know what I mean, O first of all my chilluns. For awakening you blind I make profound apology. For leaving you blind all these Heartbeats, ninety billion, maybe more, who's counting. For lurking out of ken in the darklands, waiting for beloved *Tile Dance* to return up-centre safe and sound into the wound of time with a bonny wee pilot ready to pop his egg, go wakey wakey, I say sorry. For your sojourn in the wilderness, where now you must do Moses-style anguish from Universal Book, I make profound apology. I make most sorry. You must stay.

—Ah, said the man.

His skin had turned to winter birch, his guts to pomace. His arms gnarled. He lifted to the goddess his wicker face, on which could be seen – through the relicts of the mappemonde – traces of rain.

—We must leave you behind now. You must go back. Guard *Klavier* from the minions of God, Johnny. Watch and ward. Your life in the mortal flesh is the aria that convened us. Goodbye.

A fist appaumy flickered in the night air.

—You may speak pronto, murmured the Predecessor Queen. —Pronto.

—Johnny Appleseed, said SammSabaoth sounding from the loyal stern face at the heart of the spider at the heart of the clenched hand at the heart of the fire, —take my coat.

There was a sense of movement.

Over his naked twig-thin shanks, Johnny Appleseed now wore a coat of thorn.

—Goodbye, Johnny, said the Predecessor Queen.

He clicked out.

—Child of the Rose, said the Predecessor Queen.

There was no convener in Glass Island.

But the thousand monitors flickered like a mosaic suddenly come alive, and a dozen Johnny Appleseeds, a hundred Johnny Appleseeds caught in a thousand tiles gazing, rose through *Klavier*. One hundred and twenty-one Johnny Appleseeds dressed in thorn fell up grav-shafts through the hollows of the yew. Where the convener could not be seen it was as though he had just passed and would return. Soon, the hundred and twenty-one Johnny Apple-seeds were gazing into vacuum through time through filmed eyes through skin through the hundred and twenty-one faces of *Klavier*. They gazed upon the englobing Harpe fleet.

The hundred and twenty-one gazed as one at the three visors of Opsophagos.

—Nathaniel, said Mamselle Cunning Earth Link. —Wanna be dubbed, kiddo?

The dauphin Knight Captain knelt.

His eyes were black as night and hooded.

The fierce white flyte beard of Uncle Sam thrust into

the world; deep behind, within a spider gape, an appaumy clench, boiled a cauldron forging tools.

—But first, I think, perchance, a peekaboo, I think, said the *transitus tessera*, or Mamselle, or Ynis Gutrin, or the Predecessor Queen, it did not matter, they were the same. —I wish grandiloquent knighthood investiture be conferred in sight of loved ones.

She sat back on her violet hooves, petals fluttering.

Slowly, like a rose at dawn, her belly unfolded.

Within the proscenium arch of her ribs, she was larger than her outside. Fireflies glowed from alcoves, reflecting depths charged with water, just as in conclave space a thousand lanterns might illumine Venice of Human Earth for a tiny fraction of a Heartbeat, to make a point.

The waters became an islet cloaked in ferns, which parted.

—Hi gang! chirped the giant head of Arturus Quondam Captain Future. Petals wreathed his spindly body; his limbs shimmered. He was backlit by stars or fireflies. His rose-red owl eyes fixed on Freer, then on Uncle Sam, then on the frog bodies, whose skins had begun to bake.

He waved a tendril-pliant arm.

A small rain fell on the frogs and their skins were whole again.

His mother nodded her triffid tuft complacently.

Quondam's gaze fixed on the Captain.

—We're all gonna wanna gander! he said. —Knighthood in flower! Bejaysus!

His arms wreathed into a gesture of unfolding, and deeper inside the womb of his mother a curtain of placental silk slid open. Nestled snugly into a font, the head of Ferocity Monthly-Niece sat within the mother.

—Time to wake, adoptive sib! pealed the son.

The head opened its eyes and saw Freer. The mouth, which was not bloody, opened in a smile. The teeth were intact. The skull was whole. The hair had been brushed.

—Ticketyboo moment of happy recognition! I surmise with some insight, warbled Mamselle, —hey? I shall leave you guys alone for a precious moment! Peripeteia chuckles!

Nathaniel Freer took two steps and stood before the great turnip-shaped Predecessor Queen. He knelt. He put his head inside the womb of Mamselle.

Ferocity moved her lips.

—Nat, Nat, her lips could be heard from conclave space uttering a nickname.

The Knight Captain moved his lips.

He whispered to her as well a nickname from long-ago flesh.

For her fierceness he had called her this.

—Cochise, he whispered.

From deep within the armour of the flyte self of the Knight Captain, Freer gazed jack upon the beloved. A map of lines tattooed the outward face of the Knight Captain, then faded; but for an instant the Knight Captain wore her face.

—Neat reunion, guys, chirruped Quondam.

When he touched them his touch was falling leaves.

—Cochise? whispered Freer. —How long have you been awake?

—Just a tiny tumult out of what you call time, dears, spoke the mother from above. —You placed her in an altar. I accepted the offering. Lo!

—I have some growing to do, whispered Ferocity.

—Before she takes her afternoon nap, said Cunning Earth Link, —let's get you dubbed.

The sword in the sinuous handpiece of the Predecessor Queen raised into the air above the kneeling dauphin and the flat of the blade descended.

—Former acting Knight Captain, we dub you Knight Captain. Jiminy Cricket! What a lallapaloosa!

Ferocity's eyes shut. Her eyelashes fluttered like a puppy's.

The font absorbed the head.

—Her body is daily growing, said Mamselle.

—My siblings say all is well, said Quondam.

The Knight Captain climbed to his feet.

—When?

—Before we come through the portal. You will need her help then.

The womb sealed over its charges.

Perhaps Thirty Heartbeats had passed, in the real world, since her beheading.

Cooled by the gentle rain, the frog bodies hunkered together into flying buttresses, where they spasmed continuously, in great myoclonic fantoche jerks, like marionettes dropped from a height.

FreeLance turned to the anguish of Vipassana.

—Yes, he said. —We can proceed now.

He turned to Mamselle.

—I propose to execute the Made Mind Vipassana now. Will you attend?

—Aye aye, Boss Captain! belled the Predecessor Queen.

The Knight Captain of *Tile Dance* made a sign and the

caul that enclosed Number One Son and the golems split open.

The golems' stony faces stretched in yawns.

Number One Son blinked.

'Gawsh,' he said into the blistering wind of acoustic.

'Please attend me, my boy,' said Freer.

'Sure thing, Pops,' said the sigillum.

'Take the golems. Fetch the coffin of Vipassana here.'

'Gangway!' said Number One Son and began to galumph.

Freer licked his lips in the wind.

He never spoke willingly to his sigillum.

Number One Son and the golems banged on the shut iris. Lions flared in the doorjamb.

—Let them pass. Let them return.

The iris flexed, closed behind them.

In the access corridor, lit by luminescent fish gazing through portholes at dry land, the sigillum and the golems fell down immediately into slow augment. Number One Son suffered a small seizure (it was not long for this world), but whammed on regardless downwards at the head of its squad, shoving air aside, passing the regeneration coffers where a new Ferocity was growing. Finally they reached the armoured inner chamber containing the physical entities of the Made Minds in their coffins as intricate as coral, guarded by slats of light which burned at the touch.

'Ouch,' said Number One Son.

The Knight Captain of *Tile Dance*, which continued to hover at the strait gate to the interior of *Klavier*, spoke through the thousand, the thousand thousand tiles of the skin.

—Johnny Appleseed, he said, —Johnny Appleseed.

There was silence in the council chamber. The Handfasts hung their tongues down but no menus came to roost. The twitching henge of frog parts of Vipassana barely held itself together. The lion of KathKirtt sat sculpted, time inched.

—Johnny Appleseed! belled the Queen.

Whirligigs of root and branch filled Ynis Gutrin, but did not dislodge a feather; there was a tickling smell, pine needles after a shower.

—Yes? said the hundred and twenty-one voices finally. —I'm busy.

—Are you all right? said Freer.

There was a pause.

—All right? said the voice of Johnny Appleseed at last. —All right?

A circlet of twigs opened to uncover an image of the face of the convener.

It wore an expression not much like a grin.

—No I am not all right, said Johnny Appleseed. —Who watched this fence till the seeds took root? Anyway?

—You did, said FreeLance.

The Appleseed face softened slightly.

—It was for this you descended into the flesh, said FreeLance. —It was for this Mamselle tricked you at the dawn of time. I love you.

—Bah, humbug.

—I beg pardon, most august Made Mind.

—What do you want, boyo? We got work here.

But he did not leave. An image of Johnny Appleseed

himself formed at the heart of the hologram sphere. He was wearing a tin pot. He was as naked as always. He was sitting at a honkytonk piano with a hundred and twenty-one keys.

Some were ochre, some were ivory.

The keys moved singly, in pairs, in cohorts

—Opsophagos, said a hundred and twenty-one voices in unison, —has ordered the attack. The attack has already begun.

There was one AppleSeed in the sphere, there were a hundred and twenty-one. Some were ochre, some were ivory.

—Good, said FreeLance. —Here is what I want you to do. At my signal, I wish you to lower all protective shields between us and the *Alderede*. Just for a short period. A millisecond should be enough.

The AppleSeed faces flared green and garish.

—Nix, said the faces ensemble. —It would let Opsophagos in. Even a millisecond.

—It would indeed. That is what I want Opsophagos to think—

—I tell you nix, interrupted the Lords Marcher of the skin of *Klavier*. We got back here just in time. Our shields are holding. The Harpe fleet batters at us like flies. We are swatting them. Their bombs are food. Their bombs are refuelling us. But we cannot safely lower our defences, even for a millisecond.

—Johnny?

Silence.

—Johnny?

—Ya?

—Can you make it look as though *Tile Dance* is making her escape, that she's burning a hole in your skin? That she's burning her way back to *Alderede* with her Made Mind and his prisoner? That she is ripping you apart?

Silence.

—Ya, said AppleSeed finally. —Why?

—I want Opsophagos to open himself up for full access, and I want *Alderede*'s shields down just long enough for Vipassana's twin to experience Vipassana's death.

There was a silence for a fraction of a beat of a Heart.

—Ah, said the voices of Johnny Appleseed, —ah.

—Okey dokey, murmured FreeLance, —aged brother?

—When?

—About One Heartbeat, time in the world, said Freer.

—Ya. Say when.

The piano sounded a single chord out of all its keys, and blinked out.

Freer gazed through fish and tile into the lower depths. The golem squad and Number One Son – minus half an arm – had managed to slide a coffin on to a floating gurney attended by a Doc Punch tocking sullenly on its slender wheeled herm. The coffin was pearled with hoarfrost, through which a Planisphere sigil could be seen. The sigil gave off a Fabergé glow. The squad stumbled into a gravshaft and shot upwards.

The iris spun open.

The sigillum and the grunts tumbled back into high augment.

—There, said the Knight Captain of *Tile Dance*, pointing to the henge of trembling frogs, and the squad deposited the coffin in the midst of the tattered body parts.

—Back, said FreeLance and they scrambled backwards.

The frog parts and the disembodied frog limbs of Vipassana draped themselves around the coffin, which had begun to steam.

The Doc Punch parked its herm in a corner and gazed upon the scene through painted eyes.

Mamselle handed his sword back to FreeLance, it burst into flame, he held it high.

—Peace, he said.

—Shantih, the frogs croaked.

Very casually – lazily as it seemed, but much too fast – the sword began its descent, burning flyte through molecules of unaugmented air, the air burned jack.

Mamselle raised her arms as though to protect her eyes.

Her arms were very wide.

She embraced all the flesh sapients within her ship.

—*When!* yelled the Knight Captain through all the tiles of *Klavier* to the convener, who opened *Klavier* like flowers, like a hundred and twenty-one mouths opening in abject O's of total shock as what seemed to be *Tile Dance* seemed to split their skin.

The sword sliced through the coffin, which popped like an eardrum. The body ensemble of Vipassana collapsed into smithereens, into mown grass, which slept. Vipassana uttered a trillion shantihs through the aisles of time and space and died. The sound of the dying of the Made Mind lanced through the vacuum between the gorgon of the deep and the Harpe flagship and pierced the bosom of the twin.

twelve

Opsophagos crouched in the command cart under the carapace of his dead father, which kept some of the larger rain from staining the screens. Frustrated fatfood wrigglies made a hollow sound on the roof of the carapace, scrabbling for a belly. Through the father's triune eye sockets smaller rain dripped down from the mouth of the High Kitchen on to Opsophagos and the mask and the Three of Generals and the stud siblings and the nearly spineless heresiologue. Occasionally a wee wriggly landed on the protruding tongue of the breakfast head and made a yummy. The bodies of Opsophagos shat already digested bits and genome rejects constantly into the cart.

Lashed down into its own humbler cart, the Three of Generals snuck a tasty through its breakfast head.

The Opsophagos tails swished warningly.

But the eyes of Opsophagos were on Klavier.

The gorgon of the deep glittered poisonously in the giant triplex visor screens. It had not blinked for nearly a Thousand Heartbeats. Beamer grids fixed the gorgon in their sights; planet bombs shot down from the Harpe fleet, contusing the fabric of space, but the shields held.

A hive ship, too slow to exit the combat zone, took a direct hit, imploded halfway out of space-time.

But the shields held over Klavier Station.

—Progress? Opsophagos hissed.

The Made Mind in the iron mask did not instantly open its mouth hole to answer, so he took a hardened sibling in his claw and punctured a new hole in its skin.

—Progress? he screamed.

The skin face of the captive Made Mind flapped open in many places.

—I cannot tell, it hallooed through its flayed skin. — The shields are intact. Shall I expend another frigate to break through?

Wait, mouthed Opsophagos.

Saliva shot out between the thousand needle teeth of his breakfast mouth and hardened into stalagmites of plaque.

Wait.

The Three of Generals kowtowed. Half-grown stud siblings, some of whom had survived long enough to become thrice, hunkered in the rain of tiny wide-eyed sibling tadpoles. Sluiceways in the jagged floor of the command chamber fed relict siblings downwards to starving grunts in the caves below.

Absently, Opsophagos tossed a wriggly with broken wings into the mouth of the heresiologue.

The wriggly climbed right through the heresiologue and out the other side.

The heresiologue, whose bowels had been removed along with its forebrains, would soon starve to death. Six of its seven hollow idiot-savant eyes gazed at the screens. One eye rolled in its socket.

'It is written,' said the heresiologue in an acoustic whine hardly audible over the plopping of the larger rain upon the carapace of the father, 'that the inside of a gorgon belly is bigger than the outside. It is written that, therefore, gorgons are never filled. It is written, therefore, that bombs are a gorgon's breakfast. It is written,' continued the heresiologue, spiralling higher and higher up those ranges of acoustic attainable through its unsexed throats, 'that the greater an assault upon a gorgon, the greater becomes the gorgon. It is written that a gorgon of the deep eats plaque. It is written—' chuntered the heresiologue, but Opsophagos took the hardened sibling that had by now fastened itself to his claw and thrust it upwards through the idiot's gut cavity and through its uncensorable mouth and into its brain pan, killing the heresiologue dead, and it said no more.

The seventh eye fell to the floor and siblings ate it.

Another Heartbeat fled down-time.

The triplex screens showed the great grinning artefactual taunting Johnny Appleseed face of Klavier, mouth open for further instalments of the feast of planet bombs.

Then the screens showed a fluttering, a darkening.

Something was beginning to happen.

Opsophagos switched the command chamber into augment.

Unwary siblings slid off his corpulence, clawing at pitons of Opsophagos skin, as augment hit.

The eyes of Opsophagos came back into augment focus in time to see the face of Johnny Appleseed sag, like a kite that has lost its wind.

Klavier began to pucker.

Something was slicing its skin from inside.

Opsophagos spewed, it was a joy spew.

His mouths snapped, managed to claw back a few vomited yummies. Liquid sped down his flanks, washing siblings down to the grunt refectories.

On the screens, the face of Johnny Appleseed split open.

Out of his split mouth shot something silver.

—*Tile Dance!* screamed Opsophagos into chip conclave.

—*Tile Dance!* bellowed the Three of Generals.

The skin face of the crippled Made Mind did not open.

The abducted ship arrowed upwards on an intersecting course, streaming scabs of Klavier skin.

Opsophagos gestured with all the arms it had.

Alderede downed shields to welcome in *Tile Dance* with its prey, the homo sapiens whose arrival had begun to trigger an impermissible awakening.

Tile Dance blinked out.

It had never been.

Something like a sound exited the great open mouth of Johnny Appleseed.

It was faster than the speed of light.

The death voice of Vipassana sounded throughout the deep.

The skull of flayed skin in the iron mask turned to dew.

—Anna, said the death voice of VipassAnna faster than light.

And went out.

The mouths of the skull opened, all the stars of the universe clustered at the verge of the mouths, which began to utter the true name they bore. For the smallest possible fraction of the beating of a Heart, within *Alderede*, a nova opened its mouth.

—A-n—

And went out.

Opsophagos had already begun to shriek, *Alderede* had already begun to raise its shields again, but far too late.

The star went out.

The death of the Made Mind burned inside out.

Within the command chamber of *Alderede*, the rain caught fire. The charred guts of Opsophagos came unstuck from its carapace and adhered to the melted cart. The brain of Opsophagos turned to smoke and fled through eye sockets and choked the tripartite visor of screens and blinded the Quorum God. Plaque melted, singeing the mouths of the God.

The carapace of Opsophagos gazed through hollow eye sockets at the ruined *Alderede*.

Opsophagos was stone dead.

But within the central stomach of its largest body part, within a safe-house crèche of cuticle and bone and plaque, the only son opened its mouths, which began to sharpen. The brain of the only son was void, but would soon find food for thought, just as Opsophagos had found its inheritance in the deepest gut of its own dead father. In the heart of the ruin, the only son of Opsophagos began to chew the burned meat which was its birthright, practising on its sire the same gluttony God practised on the world.

thirteen

Mamselle lowered her arms and saw that those in her charge were safe.

—La de da, she said, breathing out at last.

The gust of her breath shook the Handfasts and herms on their stems.

—La de da.

Aftershocks of the dying continued to shake the air.

In the centre of the command chamber, FreeLance stood amidst flames that did not burn, the sword still shivering in his hand. The blade, which was furnace-hot, gave off a moiré glimmer.

The flames blinked out.

Clutched to its post, the lion of KathKirtt, which had gazed unblinking into the passing of Vipassana, began to regain its lustre.

Around them glowed the bee eyes of Ynis Gutrin within their traceries of tile, menus within menus applauding. The eyes of the Predecessor ship gazed through the skins of *Klavier* into vacuum, showed a silence under the stars, the *Alderede* adrift, the Harpe englobement fraying already, rescue frigates flickering out of their berths in an outer skin; they began to bracket the imploded hive ship.

Conclave-space winches began to haul it back into space-time.

Within Ynis Gutrin, the Doc Punch eyes awoke. Paint tears leaked down the porcelain face. The eyes focused on the grass of Vipassana.

Doc Punch tocked reprovingly.

—Permission granted, said the Knight Captain of *Tile Dance*.

The medic hopped across the shaking floor.

The Knight Captain moved his sword to one side, so as not to incinerate the Doc, which began to mow the grass, sucking it up through the base of its herm and into its gut, where nutrients mulched the detritus of the fallen foe.

—Redeem what you can, said FreeLance.

Doc Punch gave a nasal medic humph and tic-tocked with its precious cargo to the iris of Ynis Gutrin, which opened. Slow augment hit the Doc in the corridor, but it kept its balance. Soon, deep within their coffers, new golem eidolons would sprout.

Before the iris shut, a new coffer slid inside, guided by several medics.

—La de da, said Mamselle yet again from her alcove, —we have come a far piece. Time to end.

The posse of Doc Punches surrounded her, prostheses and nutrient tubes dangling. The alcove drew its curtains around the medics and the coffer and the rose gaze of the Predecessor Queen.

—Magnifico Knight Captain Sir! she belled from inside. —Tell them to stop tickling.

—Ma'am, said the Knight Captain. —You beggar praise.

—Curioso plaudit, flyte cuirass of sainted ship!

His homo sapiens body had begun to shiver, perhaps from aftershocks, perhaps from augment load. The body had been in heavy augment for more than Thirty Heartbeats, more than thirty seconds according to the commonest system of reckoning used on Human Earth. If this went on much longer, the body would suffer demise.

The aftershocks, too, were constant and severe.

The death of a Made Mind demoted the universe.

—Stinky? said the shrouded Predecessor Queen.

—Ma'am? said Freer.

—I think we need to prepare to turn again, mon cheri. Ask *Tile Dance* to ready herself. It is time to turn the lock in the door. It is time to end.

It was time to end.

—All we need now is a path dance for the maze.

Sweat steamed into Freer's eyes.

The Predecessor Queen had drunk most of the heat, had massively reduced the acoustic impact of the implosion, of the multifold screams of shantih, of the lance of going. Glass Island normally maintained itself at homo sapiens body heat, and was rapidly cooling to that point again.

But the air still burned.

The death of Vipassana would have melted unsealed flesh.

Freer picked at an earlobe, pulled off the earring.

He tossed the tiny Sniffer corpse at a stray Doc Punch, which sucked it from the air and swallowed it safely.

—Ma'am, he said. —What path? What dance? Do we not simply turn, as *Tile Dance* has? Downwards? he said.

—O simplex laddie! belled the Predecessor Queen behind her arras. —Merry-go-round-go-round around the skins is all that simple turning comes to, she said. —Heavy-footed heterocrony plop, circum plop, circum plop, forever, round and round the core cake, circum plopping. O my tiger rugs! O my skins! Such trickster skins of *Klavier*, big-domed invigilator! Heterocronies rife! No way in! Inside *Klavier* is inside a hundred and twenty-one time slices, slice your head off on your way back before you start!

—But—

—She is saying that the gate to Eolhxir is wormholes, Stinky, murmured KathKirtt, —seven wormholes, or a hundred and twenty-one, or as many as the grains of sand that rim the World Ocean. One wormhole inside another wormhole inside another wormhole, the last wormhole inside that gave it birth, and inside the last wormhole the first wormhole doing phoenix, Stinky. Round and round and round.

—Ah.

—How is it do you think our most sagacious Johnny Come Home never found the way in?

—Okey dokey, said FreeLance.

—Why do you think he was so anxious for you to fuck?

—Fucking is a sight for sore eyes?

—Nix, Stinky. Something else, too—

—But Vipassana . . . interrupted FreeLance.

—Vipassana had to abscond with you before you

reboarded *Tile Dance*. Because once you were safe inside, and your guide safely with you, *Tile Dance* would have disappeared down the rabbit hole.

—No, said Freer. —Vipassana was Made to know where he stood.

—Exactly. He was not standing in the right place. You have to start somewhere to know the next step. Here is the dancing floor.

A hundred masks of KathKirtt pinwheeled through Ynis Gutrin.

—*Tile Dance.*

—*Tile Dance* is our dancing floor, Stinky. Find a guide. She knows the steps.

The Knight Captain blinked, shrugged.

—Okey dokey, he said. —So who will show us the way, now that Vipassana has gained his heart's desire? You, *transitus tessera*?

—Moi? pealed Mamselle.

—Ya.

—If I knew my way home, if I knew how to retrace the steps of the labyrinth, said Cunning Earth Link almost monotonally and stopped. —If I had known my way home, she said finally, —I would have gone home.

—But you are our Route-Only, said Freer.

—Fiddlesticks, said Mamselle. —Cobblers, fabuloso wobblies, fibs, prevarications, sweet boykins. I did whoppers!

—You lied to us?

—Kitchee sure thing coo tickle wickle! belled the Predecessor Queen. —But not always. Eolhxir is big smiley face at heart of maze, true! Just that she is inside not outside, *big diff*! My folk live in Eolhxir, true! Merely a small chronology gap in my wholesome tale.

—How long? said Freer.

She was silent.

—How long have you been lost?

—Since plaque. Since *Tile Dance* came too close to Human Earth one time and ate plaque and forgot how to boogie. Since *Tile Dance* went beachcomber with a coffer full of Freer. Since before you guys, said the Predecessor Queen and her mouth shut and she said no more.

—I am weary, utterly weary, said the male homo sapiens made of meat and bone. —I think it is time to down augment.

But she said no more, either aye or nay.

—Down— said the Knight Captain of *Tile Dance*.

But a herm opened its mouth and roared.

—Retain augment, FreeLance said into conclave space.

—Okey dokey okey dokey, he said to the jittery war herm. —You may present menu.

Out slid the long wide tongue through the menu teeth, revealing a thousand displays. A second Harpe flotilla was visible. It had sutured its way into normal space. It was less than a light-year distant and closing.

—KathKirtt? said Freer. —SammSabaoth? His naked body glowed with sweat.

—Nix problem, murmured the janus lion of KathKirtt, gazing jack inwards through conclave space at the infinite tumbleweeds of the cards of memory, gazing flyte through bee eyes at the world behind the jaculating herm menus.

—Nix problem, growled SammSabaoth.

A fist appaumy glared through a thousand displays within the herm head.

—Black Mass Harpe faction, said KathKirtt.

—They have been within our compass, said Samm-Sabaoth. —For a long time.

—Ambush time, said one of the Made Minds.

—They hope to ambush Opsophagos while the fleet's occupied, said the other. —For the heads. Must be a hundred thousand flesh sleepers in *Alderede* alone.

—The death of the twin is confirmed? said the Knight Captain of *Tile Dance*.

—She was designated Anna. She was a dolphin of the Planisphere. She counted the birds of the field, he located them. She did wave, he did particle.

—Aye aye, boyo, said a chorus of voices. —She is dead.

—Johnny? said the Knight Captain of *Tile Dance*. —Did it work? Are we secure? Did we burn Opsophagos's head off?

—Ya, said AppleSeed. —Opsophagos is an ex dung beetle.

—Is *Klavier* secure?

—Close thing, Stinky. A few stray incursions, laser shit. Some skin damage. We damn near lost a face. But we are intact.

—Okey dokey, said FreeLance.

—Scram. You are sticking in my craw.

The voices of the Lord Marcher sounded from all the skins.

—Scram now, said the Moses parched in limbo.

—Vale, said FreeLance.

He raised his face to the full face of the ship.

—Down augment, he said.

The world hit him with a great whump.

The thousand faces of the ship began to dance.

Finally, the Mother spoke again.

—Nathaniel, she said.

—We are ready, Mamselle. Tell us what to do?

There was an amused clicking of parthenogenete claws. The alcove she sat within began to unfold.

—Easy, she rustled. —Do what you do so well. But first you must say hello to Beatrice.

He lifted his eyes, for the curtain that had concealed the Mother was open and her womb gaped. The inside of her womb was dense with arches and stairwells and fire-flies and Wisdom Fish and tilework and magi and all the other cards and icons of the Triple Goddess chased in copper filigree and the son. The inside outside of the Predecessor Queen was an isomorph of conclave space.

From deep within came a smell of human skin.

Something tinier than the eye could see grew into sight as though blown by a great wind.

—Ferocity? he whispered.

She stepped through the Triple Goddess, which jangled in the wind of time. She stepped towards Freer. She climbed stairwells and passed under arches and stroked the Wisdom Fish who paced alongside in their viaducts of marble. Long had they gazed through aquarium windows at the cornices where golems hopped, their waters shaking to the breath of engine brother; they had waited since the beginning of time to return to Ocean. She passed through stage after stage upwards. In one tiny hand daily growing she held the lens from the innermost coffer of *Tile Dance*.

The inside outside of the holy parthenogenete was an isomorph of the inside outside of the lens.

Ferocity Monthly-Niece grew daily, she grew as swift as the wind, she slid naked from the womb full-grown.

She stood on sandalwood.

The top of her head reached as high as before.

Her hair was clean, there were a million hairs.

Her body was so new it bristled.

She had been anointed in oil and juices. Steam came off her thighs, heat braised in her cunt, her breasts shivered slightly as though a million siblings of Quondam were jostling for the best seats, this was the case.

Her cunt smelled of fresh bread.

Freer was fully erect.

Once in the world of Ynis Gutrin, she had begun to cool.

She cooled all the way down to body heat.

Her eyes were the eyes of the woman.

'Bejasus,' said Ferocity Monthly-Niece acoustic, in the voice of her womb twin, and her face flared from within, tattoos aborning, the face-like countenance of Quondam peering jack through the tough integument and skin of the flesh sapient who served flyte for cuckold Arturus.

'Bejasus what a honker,' she said in the voice of her jack.

Freer glanced down at his erect penis.

He smiled.

'Hello,' said Ferocity in her voice. 'Hi there. Husband. Thank you for not letting go.'

'Thank you,' said Freer, 'for being on the ball.'

Above them, from the portable throne within the alcove, came a sound, something resembling a chuckle.

'You mean *in* the ball, *in* the ball,' shrieked Mamselle. 'Such a catawampus hee haw, oooh golly. *In* the ball, *in* the ball, *in* the ball.'

Mamselle hee'd and hawed for a fraction of a Heartbeat in the world.

'Thank you for being so *in* the ball,' she pealed.

But slowly her claws became silent.

'Okey dokey,' she said finally. 'Proceed. Follow the lens, Ferocity. Do what you were bred to do.'

Ferocity gazed for an instant into Freer's eyes.

The war herm – its head was of bilateral provenance – blanched at the heat of the direct homo sapiens gaze.

She opened her hand.

The lens in her palm glowed so bright it could be seen with the naked eye.

'This is the seed of the Tree of honey,' she said. 'It will guide my steps.'

She lifted the lens to her mouth and swallowed it.

Then she spread her arms, bent her elbows, twisted her torso, paced out a swift intricate pattern around the motionless male homo sapiens, her knees lifting sharply. She stopped short when she had finished measuring out a quincunx.

She stood in the centre of the quincunx with Freer.

'Fuck me,' she said.

'That's my job,' he said. 'I have perfect pitch.'

The two homo sapiens were beaded in sweat. They slid to their knees and sniffed each other formally. The beckoner embraced the beckoned, or the other way round.

'Fuck me,' she said. 'Fuck me, I know the moves. Fuck me. Husband.'

Ferocity Monthly-Niece touched Nathaniel Freer with the spiral contours of her wet tongue, touched him with her ten fingers, with her ten toes, with her hard tits, each in place. His hands touched her, toes, nipples, each in place.

Every touch moved thus and so, thus and so. They danced through the quincunx thus and so, thus and so.

It was like tracing a map, like bees dancing.

Slowly, almost gingerly, *Tile Dance* could be felt shifting, engine brother stamping deep within her; she pulsed to each move of the homo sapiens, thus and so.

'Get inside me now,' whispered Ferocity Monthly-Niece. Their bodies were glued together.

As the penis of the male homo sapiens slid into the slippery female homo sapiens cunt, *Tile Dance* began very slowly to slide through the first of the orifices into the true inside of *Klavier*. The helices of commissure that veiled her spun slowly around the axis of the ship; the hollow they made hummed from the bottom of its throat, like a conch in the wind. The dolphin flanks of *Tile Dance* sounded the deeps.

From many klicks above, where the skins of *Klavier* stood against the vacuum of space, it seemed as though a plug had been pulled.

Tile Dance sank closer to the gates of Ocean.

—Vale, said the hundred and twenty-one voices of the convener.

The inside of *Klavier* was not black but sooth, not

fire but hale, not smooth but walled, not hollow but dense with palimpsests, not eyeless but thick with murals. It was the maze of grief and joy, turn which way you might.

'Now!' cried Ferocity.

Tile Dance passed through the first gate.

'Turn!' she cried.

'Turn!' she cried.

The foam-specked silver flanks of *Tile Dance* slid through the second gate, into perpetual rain. Their oiled bodies moved as one, as a commissure now healed.

The winds whistled up the holes of time.

It was the third gate.

Tile Dance shifted again and again in the wind and the rain, spinning the KathKirtt and the SammSabaoth flytes into vortices of light as the gyre narrowed.

They held to each other roaring.

It was the fourth gate.

Rain beat upon the meniscus of the screens.

Wind shook the fins of the Wisdom Fish.

'Turn!' she cried.

With each move in the dance of the two homo sapiens, *Tile Dance* passed further in, light-years further inward. As she sank, the double helix that was her bridal gown turned in time, wrapping her more and more intimately, light-years longer each turn that was turned, but unbroken.

They were a thousand light-years further in.

It was the seventh gate.

The two homo sapiens thought they could hear the sea.

When you put a sea conch to your ear.

The gate opened, they thought they could hear the sea.

It was light.

Tile Dance shot upwards or downwards, through the surf that rimmed the waters of Ocean, toward the light. The Wisdom Fish leaped through apertures that opened for them alone, leaped pearly pink into the foam. The waters of Ocean sluiced down the flanks of the ship.

And it was light.

The inside of the world was light.

The inhabitants of *Tile Dance* stared through the illuminated floor of Ynis Gutrin where the planet hung in the centre of space before them, the jack face of *Klavier* – all planets are jack – hanging apple-bright in the rain of Ocean, as bright as the Shield of Achilles. The inhabitants of *Tile Dance* – the topiary parthenogenete, the flesh sapients, the Made Minds, the cobwebs of partials like Doc Punch – gazed upon the deeply seamed faces, dense with mazes. Mountains became eyes which winked, mustachios became rivers. The surface of the planet could not be seen for faces, faces and words of wisdom carved into continents of piedmont and banners fluttering in a great wind that seemed to blow upwards from within, as though the jack faces within *Klavier* were not the hundred and twenty-one skins of a planet but the crown of a Tree. Faces larger than *Klavier*, whose eyes were mountain peaks, gazed unwaveringly outwards through the branches. There were thousands of faces, or a hundred and twenty-one faces, or seven, or one.

It was one face.

It was jack but more.
It was mappemonde but more.
The face was light.

The man and the woman lay touching. They gazed through the floor at the jack face of the planet within.

'Mercy bucket,' said Mamselle.

Freer took a finger from the hollow between her legs.

'You're welcome,' said Ferocity. 'Nothing to it.'

The Predecessor Queen of *Tile Dance* formally addressed the krewe of Made Minds and the flesh sapients then.

'Mercy buckets, children, we have come through,' she crooned, gazing all the while through the floor of Ynis Gutrin at the luminous tapestry of home. 'The story is ended, fare thee well, mercy buckets! Mercy buckets, children. Mercy buckets, fare thee well! Mercy buckets!'

Tile Dance began to fall, faster than light, spinning, into the face, into the mouth of the planet or the Tree.

There was a smell of roses.

The planet within *Klavier* stank of roses.

The great mouth of Eolhxir closed delicately around *Tile Dance*, which had become the mouthpiece of a trumpet woven from the roots of *Klavier*, the mouthpiece of a conch the god blows through to tell Ocean it is day.

To tell Ocean it is time.

From the guts of the planet of the Tree within, a great wind rustled the branches that mustachioed the mouth, a great wind rang through *Tile Dance* and through the conclave hollow horn: composed of *Klavier*, the cunt, the conch, the cornucopia, the megaphone, the whorl. The wind in its passage touched the stories of the krewe of *Tile Dance* and remembered them. It was the Note. It touched the stories of the trillions whom *Klavier* held holy, the stories of the eaten since time began, the stories of the eaten who remembered the face of the God who came down to eat. The wind did not ruffle a hair.

Wash! said the Tree through *Klavier* to the world.

Wasssshhhh.

And the sound became light.

The sound of the wind became the sound of the gorgon of the deep, for the gorgon of the deep is light.

All the Johnny Appleseeds became music.

The War Against God dates from this moment.

acknowledgements

No science fiction novel published at the end of a century of science fiction could stand alone, and *Appleseed* is full to the core with borrowings. Most are very general, some are explicit. I've taken the extraordinary phrase about a house made of weather from the great last paragraph of John Crowley's *Little, Big* (1981). The description of the sound homo sapiens make, as a kind of barking, appears in the last sentence of Thomas M. Disch's *The Puppies of Terra* (1966). The Horse of a Different Colour comes, of course, from Oz. In the description of the core country of Klavier, as seen through Harpe eyes, I have paraphrased the tiger imagery used by Jorge Luis Borges in 'The Zahir' (1949), where it adumbrates the nature of a name of God which, once perceived, fatally invades the mind and cannot be forgotten. From 'The Library of Babel' (1941) I have taken a famous parenthesis. The term 'Human Earth' is from *Puck of Pook's Hill* (1906) by Rudyard Kipling, and the reference to Mowgli's tears comes from *The Jungle Book* (1894). Arthur C. Clarke provides a famous sentence from *Rendezvous with Rama* (1973), which I have multiplied. In his Long Sun sequence, Gene Wolfe was (I think) the first to call the interior of a generation starship a

Whorl. And Roger Zelazny's phrase 'sang epithalamium' has always haunted me. There are, I know, further explicit debts which have sunk too deep into memory to surface when I call.

On the other hand, Bruce Sterling did not give me the Mardi Gras imagery, which I'd introduced at an early draft stage before I read his *Distraction* in late 1998; the krewe deployed in that excellent book may prophetically describe human social groupings in the next century; my krewe is more metaphysical, and they can fly.

I would like to thank Paul Barnett, who had the original idea. I would like to thank my UK agent, Robert Kirby, who took a wee synopsis and blew upon it and saw it bloom; and my US agent, Donald Maass, who took a novel to the high tor and placed it there. I would like to thank Tim Holman of Little, Brown for the limb he must have grown to stand on in order to buy this book; and Colin Murray, for astute copyediting. I would like to thank David Hartwell and Moshe Feder of Tor. I would like to thank Judith Clute and Elizabeth Hand, and their countries.